TARGET SWITZERLAND

A PAUL MULLER NOVEL OF POLITICAL INTRIGUE

WILLIAM N. WALKER

DEDICATION

For

My wife

Janet Smith Walker

with deep thanks for her love and support

and for my children,

Gilbert, Helen and Joanna,

who mean the world to me.

.

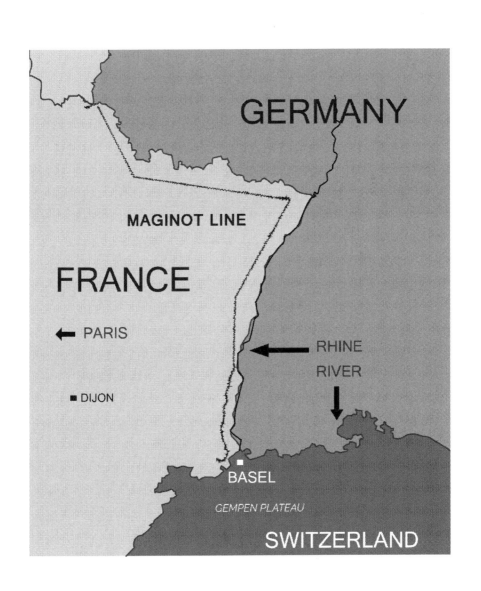

TABLE OF CONTENTS

TABLE OF CONTENTS – CONTINUED

THE INCIDENT AT LA CHARITÉ-SUR-LOIRE
JUNE 1940

The column of tanks clanked along the dirt road that ran southeast alongside the Loire River. Grassy banks sloped unevenly along the river's edge and shoals and sand bars sprouted in its path. It conveyed the impression of a placid, lazy, waterway, a sense magnified by the soft blue sky and puffy summer clouds overhead.

But the Loire was a wide and powerful river and the current flowed strongly toward the Atlantic Ocean far to the West. It was a formidable barrier and the orders from Division were to find a way across.

Lieutenant Karl Albrecht sat easily on the turret frame of his *Panzerkampfwagen II* tank, his legs dangling into the open turret. Dust was everywhere as the tank tracks ground into the sandy soil; his goggles were useless, scarred and leaky from overuse. Albrecht tied a handkerchief around his nose and mouth hoping to find relief. He wore no helmet, only his small, visored cap. He'd broken his sunglasses long ago and hadn't been able to replace them, so he kept putting a hand up in the direction of the sun to try and reduce the glare. It didn't help very much.

Christ, it was hot! Mid-June and no relief for days from the burning sunshine. The hot, dry breeze sent the dust swirling, seemingly able to find its way into every nook and cranny.

i

He unscrewed his canteen took a short swig. He could see another of the small villages that dotted the riverbank off in the distance. It would surely have the usual fountain in the center of the village square where they could halt briefly, splash in the basin to wash off some of the grime and refill their canteens. He didn't anticipate any resistance. They'd seen almost no evidence of the French Army since the breakout across the Aisne, what was it, five no, six days earlier. Somehow, Division had been able to keep sending enough fuel trucks to keep them moving with only minimal delays and they'd been able to supplement their rations with food and wine seized from the French along the way.

Today was June 14, his mother's birthday. He'd hoped he might be able to find some way to send her a postal card. But there was no chance of that. Even if he'd found a card to put in one of those large brass mail boxes he'd seen in every village they'd passed through, the chances of it finding its way to his home in Wiesbaden were nil.

But the thought led him to muse, as he nodded in the heat. How would he ever be able to describe to his mother–to anyone, really; even to remember for himself–the events that had led him to this somnolent afternoon? It was only five weeks since his unit, part of the 2nd Panzer Division of Army Group A, had plunged into the Ardennes forest and begun the long-awaited invasion of France, fighting their way to–and finally across–the Meuse River.

There had been fierce battles at the start and the French tanks, the SOMUA S35, the Renault R35–and especially the fearsome

Char B1 with its 47mm turret gun and 75mm howitzer in the hull–
were formidable adversaries. But their tactics proved no match for
the combined arms striking power of the German forces. Albrecht
smiled, recollecting how time and again, close radio contact within
the Division's other units had led them around dug-in and
immobile French positions and allowed them to exploit
uncoordinated French tactical initiatives. His highly mobile Panzer
unit took full advantage, pouncing on French formations to inflict
damage, then glancing away, around and behind, sowing confusion
and panic.

After the breakthrough, the Division commander had ordered
their Panzers into a *flaschenmarch*, a formation they'd had
rehearsed many times for just this kind of warfare. It comprised a
roughly 1,500 meter frontline and a mile in depth, moving as a
single, powerful block–a juggernaut that swept aside everything in
its path. The advance went straight across country, over unplowed
fields and through scattered villages, felling hedges and fences,
crossing irrigation ditches, uphill and downhill–it didn't matter;
they just kept moving. They encountered almost no enemy troops,
except stragglers who put up no resistance and whom they came
largely to ignore.

Crossing roadways, they would find themselves advancing
through throngs of refugees–old men, women and children all
fleeing, on foot, or with wagons, some pulled by livestock, all
burdened by the belongings they were carrying. They were
terrified of course, shrinking into ditches or huddling together to

avoid the machines. His men had yelled at them to go home and threw some of them bits of food as they roared along, waving happily at the occasional pretty girls, who seemed to slide still deeper into their terror.

They had crossed the Seine somewhere southeast of Paris; the bridges very conveniently still standing, and they'd cheered lustily as they left that famous waterway behind. Division finally called a halt while they re-grouped and re-organized for the lunge south toward the Loire Valley and east into the Cotentin Peninsula and Cherbourg.

The only real constraints on the advance had been wear and tear on the vehicles, but mobile workshops provided support, manned by mechanics who had become skilled at finding ways to repair treads, fix balky engines and lubricate moving parts. Few of the Panzers could any longer reach their 30mph factory-rated speeds, but they could keep moving over long distances and eat up territory.

After the pause to re-fit, Division had ordered them to change tactics and align themselves into multiple columns aimed at different destinations along the Loire River. They were to search for bridges that remained intact which could be secured and used to cross over to the south bank of the river. They'd learned by radio that a column off to the west, on their right flank, had entered Orléans, found it abandoned and had captured a railroad bridge that French sappers had waited too long to blow. More troubling was word of heavy fighting still further west at Saumur, where French forces had made a determined stand.

But, Albrecht continued to muse, his column's journey had been uneventful. They'd reached the banks of the Loire and, as ordered, turned east, following the river's topography. They passed through small towns and villages along the riverbank. Most had bridges and all of those had been blown by retreating French forces. But, he shrugged, he was confident that German engineers could rapidly rig repairs that would put the bridges back to work soon.

One thing that did concern him was the seemingly never-ending stream of French civilian refugees that flooded the roadway and impeded their progress. They were a sorry, shambling lot, mainly walking–or limping–slowly, often barely inching along, as people fell, belongings spilled, carts collapsed, or some other hardship interfered with their progress.

The road, like seemingly every roadway in France, was bordered on both sides by tall sycamore trees planted just inches from the edge of the road itself. Their unit commander had told them the legend that Napoleon had ordered the trees planted on every roadway in France so his soldiers could march wherever they needed to go in the shade. Albrecht didn't know if that were true or not and didn't really care. But the sheltering trees hemmed in the refugees, making it more difficult for his tanks to get through. He was thoroughly annoyed by having to slow down as the civilians tried to scatter at the approach of his column.

He knew he should be sympathetic to their plight; they were obviously suffering. He could see in the faces he passed the fear and hopelessness of disoriented and desperate people. But Goddammit they were in the way!

Often, he directed Ulrich, his driver, to swerve the tank off the roadway itself and take a parallel path along one side or the other of the tree line, allowing the column to by-pass the road itself. Usually, the tank tracks could easily crunch through the low underbrush or tall grass and make better time, swinging back onto the roadway when they encountered an obstacle–a wide irrigation ditch or a stone wall–revving their engines loudly in a threatening manner to hasten the desperate efforts of the refuges to get out of the way.

The road into the town Albrecht had seen in the distance was narrow, flanked by low, two-story red-tiled buildings, and led down to what seemed to be a central market. The French had removed the signs, but approaching the village square, Albrecht could see the familiar monument to the fallen of Pouilly-Sur-Loire in the Great War. The column pulled into in the square, which was empty and eerily quiet; no one to be seen. But the fountain they'd hoped for was only a disappointing pump and there was no basin to wash in, so they didn't linger. They followed the road as it narrowed along the river's edge with a railroad track running alongside as they exited.

Thirty minutes later Albrecht signaled the column to halt and allowed personnel to dismount, stretch and relieve themselves.

There was a grassy meadow alongside the roadway on the other side of the tree line. Albrecht pissed in a ditch then seated himself facing the river, his back propped against one of the Sycamores, and tried to snooze.

"Sir."

Albrecht sat up blinking; Ulrich, his driver, was squatting beside him.

"Lieutenant Runzer is looking for you."

Albrecht stood up and brushed himself off, then turned and saw Runzer, head of the unit's radio transmission detachment, standing by his vehicle, pulled up alongside Albrecht's tank. Its tall antenna swayed above them in the hot breeze.

Albrecht walked over and clapped Runzer on the shoulder before shaking his hand as they exchanged grins.

"How's the magician of the ether on this fine hot day?" he asked, referring to their running joke over Runzer's uncanny ability to tease radio transmissions out of the hissing spectrum.

"As sweaty and smelly as you are, Albrecht," he replied engagingly. "But look what I have for us." He laid a narrow booklet on the hood of his vehicle. "The local Guide Michelin," flourishing the small red-covered volume.

"One of our boys spied it behind the counter of the bakery where he was helping himself to some snacks. It's in French, of course, but it's got maps of the central Loire valley where we are now." He flipped the book open to a page that had a map and pointed to a spot on what seemed to be the Loire River. "In fact, I'd say this is exactly where we are at the moment."

Albrecht took the book in his hand. Sure enough, there was Pouilly-Sur-Loire, the town they'd passed through, and several turns of the riverbed as they moved east toward what seemed to be a much larger town ahead on the same road.

"Look," said Runzer, taking back the book and flipping a few pages. "This seems to show that in a couple of miles we'll be in some town called La Charité-Sur-Mer. It looks larger than the little crossroads we've been passing through. I hope it's big enough to have a truck service station with the right grade of diesel for this beauty," he said, slapping his hand fondly on the hood of his radio truck."

Albrecht took the booklet again and studied it.

"I don't read any French at all," he said, "but it does seem larger; look, that certainly seems to show a railroad yard," he pointed. "See how the illustration shows the single rail line is joined by other short tracks? There's clearly a bridge there too, probably a substantial one too, since it seems to cross a big island in the river. See that?" he asked, pointing. "It's labeled 'Faubourg', whatever that means. It also looks like there is some big church or cathedral there," he pointed to the photos of a tall, domed structure.

"Let's hope this doesn't turn out to be a place where the French have decided to make a stand. I'm ready to fight if we have to, but close quarters in an old town with narrow streets–especially in this heat? Not my preference.

"Still, we better get prepared."

Albrecht blew his whistle signaling the tank crews to remount. He reached down into the turret and recovered his helmet, hot to the touch even out of the sun just from the heat in the cab, and he put it on, fastening his chin strap.

The tank columns formed up three-abreast and Albrecht set a fast pace as the strike force moved toward La Charité-Sur-Mer.

They had been traveling not even ten minutes when the church Albrecht had spotted in the book came into view, crowning a hill and directly ahead. Tank crews still perched outside on the tank hulls began pointing to it and gesturing to one another. It was a huge structure and the closer they got the higher it seemed to loom above them.

Soon the red-tiled roofs of the town below came into view and Albrecht dispatched the six-vehicle motorcycle unit ahead to scout an approach. The machines roared down the dusty road toward the town, kicking up dirty plumes that blew in the hot breeze.

Nothing; no shots. Not a sound except the whine of the tank engines as they ground toward the town.

After only a few minutes, the motorcyclists returned grinning and showing thumbs up. The leader pulled his machine up beside Albrecht, slowing to keep pace with the lumbering tank.

"No sign of any trouble, sir," he shouted to be heard. "We rode all though town and the few people we saw took one look at us and ran for cover. They seemed shocked to see us and couldn't get out of sight fast enough. But we saw a few restaurants and bars that we might want to open up when we get there." He laughed.

"All right, corporal," Albrecht replied, "escort us into this charity town or whatever it's called."

Albrecht slipped down int his turret so he could stand with his arms still on the frame; if there were trouble, he could simply slide inside and fasten the turret, but he had better visibility this way–and it was much too hot to button things up. He waved the tanks alongside of him to peel off to the left and he gunned his machine along the main highway to the point where it became just a narrow entry, flanked by the now seemingly obligatory red tile-topped two-story stone structures. The noise of the engine echoed off the walls–which at least offered some shade–and he found himself entering the city center, an open square, featuring just the kind of fountain and basin they were looking forward to. Swinging around in the turret to look, Albrecht saw window shades being drawn and a few running figures at the edge of the square apparently scurrying for safety, ducking into doorways and slipping around corners. He didn't pause and revved the tank through the square toward the entrance to the wide bridge over the river. But as he pulled up to it, he could see that two of the arches closest to the town were destroyed. He looked around the edges of the parapets visible from the road but saw nothing suspicious. Probably done a day or two ago, he surmised, annoyed but not surprised.

Pivoting the tank, he led his short column to the left where the main road exited the square and continued heading east alongside the riverbank. Like the entryway at the other side of the square, the road was narrow, and he slowed, peering down side streets, many of which had laundry hanging from ropes strung between the buildings. Nothing, except a few furtive glances from behind curtained windows and a gaggle of boys who took one look at them, shrieked in fright and scattered.

After a couple of short blocks he exited the town and turned his column left, keeping to the perimeter, and moments later met up with the other columns that had reconnoitered the parts of the town that lay to the north. They'd checked everywhere except for the steep hill on which the massive church sat towering above them, silent and brooding. Its Gothic walls and tall, narrow windows conveyed a sense of isolation and seemed–literally–to be above the fray.

"Reports?" he said.

"Lieutenant, the only thing out of the ordinary is a train that seems to be abandoned, just sitting on a siding alongside the railroad station. It's on the edge of town," he said pointing the direction.

"Let's have a look," Albrecht replied motioning the corporal to lead the way.

Albrecht remembered what seemed to be a railyard depicted in the Michelin book and he told Ulrich to hand it up to him. Sure enough, the map showed how the railroad turned away from the river just outside the town and headed north, where it displayed a station and small yard alongside the town perimeter.

Moments later, Albrecht's tank and the rest of his column found themselves face-to-face with a train, composed of about a dozen dark red-painted box cars and a single locomotive sitting idle and seemingly abandoned on one of the auxiliary tracks alongside the main line. The box cars were securely locked, with large padlocks.

Albrecht jumped to the ground and mounted the cab of the locomotive, peering into the boiler and running his hand over its side.

"Nothing hot there," he said. "This thing's been here awhile." Walking along the train, Albrecht peered into the first boxcar between the slats and shook his head.

"I can't see a thing," he said. "My guess is that they pulled in here either because of our air raids–but more likely because they couldn't find a way across the river, the same as us.

"They got stuck, had nowhere to go and decided to run for it, figuring that we'd be right on their tail–which turned out to be correct." He grinned.

"Corporal, park a couple of our tanks at the back of the tracks to block any attempt to move this thing and assign the crews to keep an eye on it. We'll relieve them later." He glanced at his watch. "Nearly 8:30, men, time for dinner. We've got enough daylight left to organize quarters for ourselves and get properly fed."

Albrecht gunned his tank and led the way back toward the central square of La Charité-Sur-Loire where he found Lieutenant

Runzer's radio transmission car parked near the fountain. Runzer and his driver, shirts off, were soaking their heads and torsos in the fountain's wide basin, both wearing wide smiles.

"Come on in, Albrecht," Runzer said, soaking his hands in the fountain. "The water's fine."

Albrecht and his crew joined them, splashing water on themselves and one another.

Afterwards, wiping his hands on his dirty trousers and hand-combing his wet hair, Albrecht walked over to where Runzer was donning his shirt; it clung to his wet torso and he couldn't tuck it in, so he gave up trying.

"Runzer," he said," there's a train that's stuck in the railyard we saw on that map of yours; right over there," he gestured, "just outside the town; not a kilometer away. I just checked it out. Send your driver over because I saw what seems to be a refueling station there. You can probably get the refill you need."

"Kranzer! Over here, now," Runzer shouted across the fountain where a dozen men were now cavorting.

"Yes sir," said the driver, trotting over, trying to smooth his wet clothing and rubbing his hair.

"Lieutenant Albrecht may have found the diesel fuel we need. He'll tell you where to go get it."

Albrecht put his hand up, then shouted over to his motorcycle unit. "Corporal Brenner, I need you over here." Brenner joined them, removing his heavy gloves and took off the helmet and goggles he was wearing.

"Brenner, accompany Corporal Kranzer back to that train we just left. Off to the right of it there's what looks like a station and across the street I'm pretty sure I saw a refueling depot. See if the two of you can get Lieutenant Runzer the diesel he needs for the radio vehicle."

"Yes sir," Brenner replied. He hopped into the passenger seat as Kranzer went around to the driver's side and they quickly drove off.

***

"What a lark, eh?" said Kranzer as they drove into the street where Brenner pointed. "No fucking Frogs to speak of, perfect summer weather, great scenery; a real French holiday. If only we had some girls! Ha."

Brenner laughed. "Well, the night is young, Kranzer. Who knows, maybe we'll get lucky and find a couple of blondes who love the idea of German soldiers coming to visit them.

"Left here, then go straight.

"Right; there's the train," he said.

"And there's the refueling depot, where the Lieutenant said it would be," Kranzer said excitedly, pulling his vehicle next to one of the vertical pumps. "And here's exactly what I'm looking for," he said reading the label.

"Okay, Brenner, I'm going to fill this baby up, then I've got four big refill cans in the back; this'll take a few minutes. You go find the girls."

Brenner lit a cigarette–he'd found a French brand called Gauloise that he'd taken a liking to–and strolled across the street. The building did appear to be a station. It had a sign on it reading 'La Gare', whatever that meant. But it was empty, so he decided to walk a little farther along and have a look at the train they'd found. There was still some light–long summer nights in France were all they'd been cracked up to be–but he couldn't see anything peering into the first boxcar he came to. He tried opening the door, but it was secured by a heavy padlock

"What the Hell?"

He walked back to where two tanks had been stationed on the tracks to block the train from moving.

Tank crew members were lounging around, smoking and playing cards.

Brenner hoisted himself up on the hull of one of the tanks and unhitched one of the heavy wrenches from the built-in frame that secured them.

"I'm going to borrow this for a moment," he said, jumping nimbly to the ground.

The crew members shrugged. "Bring it back," one said, before resuming his card game.

Brenner walked back to the train. The boxcar he'd looked at was the last one and he figured it was as good a candidate as any of the others to look into.

By this time, Kranzer had gotten the fuel he needed and had driven the radio cab alongside the train. Brenner had begun trying to pry off the padlock, using the big wrench as a lever.

"Good idea," said Kranzer striding up next to Brenner. "Let's see what the Frogs were trying so hard to take somewhere."

But Brenner couldn't get the padlock to bend, and he dropped the wrench as he lost purchase.

Kranzer picked it up.

"Let me try," he said swinging the wrench like an axe and shattering the boxcar slats.

Three more times and the locking mechanism fell out of the battered door frame and landed harmlessly on the railroad ties beneath the car.

"So," Kranzer exclaimed, "let's have a look inside."

He slid the boxcar door open with shove, then pulled the steel ladder out of its slot and quickly mounted it, followed by Brenner right behind him.

Standing just inside the doorway, it was hard to see in the gathering dusk, but it was immediately obvious that things had been thrown into the boxcar randomly and without a plan. It was only about half full, and everything was heaped in a big jumble–pieces of furniture, clothing, big bags of what seemed to bedclothes or linens. Kranz saw telephones, typewriters–even a big teletype machine and what seemed to be office tables and desks–as if someone had tried to cram the contents of some unknown office suite into the boxcar.

Pushing things aside as they waded toward one end of the boxcar, they saw what seemed to be cardboard file cartons stacked atop one another. One was broken, with documents and file folders sticking out and piled atop one another on the floorboards. Even food; Brenner picked up glass containers of jam and jelly that had spilled from a cardboard box, and there were smears of mustard along with broken glass jars from containers that had evidently been dropped.

"What a mess," Kranzer exclaimed in frustration. "It would take hours to go through all this crap."

Brenner took a step in the other direction.

"Ah, but look at this," he said, pointing to a wooden wine crate nestled among the files.

"What have we here?" he said as he lifted it toward the door where there was more light. He pulled out one of the bottles and squinted at it.

"Something called Vosne Romanée," he said, shrugging. "Never heard of it." Then looking at it more closely he said "Doesn't that say 1926? Do you suppose this is some old pretty good wine?"

"Let's take it back with us," said Kranzer. "We'll keep a couple of bottles and give the rest to the Lieutenants; a little ass-kissing won't hurt."

He opened the radio car door and shoved the case on the floor in the back, along with the assorted documents that were stuck to the outside of the case and had slid between the bottles. They drove back to the square and found Albrecht and Runzer seated at a table on the terrace of a large, three-story building with a sign on its ornate facade identifying it as the 'Grand Hotel et Restaurant.' They were enjoying cigars that they had evidently filched from somewhere.

Runzer waved them forward as they drove up and Kranzer dug the wine case out of the back seat, carefully removing three bottles which he put back on the floor to keep, then hauled the case up to the table where the two officers sat.

"Success on the re-fueling, sir," Kranzer reported. "Enough even for our extra cans."

"Excellent," said Runzer. "So where did you find this?" he added, eying the wine case.

"The train, sir," said Brenner.

"We decided to take a look around inside one of the cars," Kranzer added.

"But they were padlocked," said Albrecht, extracting one of the bottles together with several file pages that were next to it.

"The padlocks weren't so strong sir," Kranzer said. "It didn't take much persuasion for them to fall off." The two men grinned.

"Look at this," Albrecht said handing the bottle to Runzer. "Vosne Romanée 1926. Whoo!

"That's some find, boys! I think that'll go very nicely with the meal we've persuaded the proprietor of this fine establishment to prepare for his new German guests." He and Runzer guffawed.

Albrecht pointed across the square to where a bistro was busy serving beer and food to the enlisted men.

"Go join your friends."

After they'd turned to leave, Albrecht yelled "Patron" at the doorway to the restaurant. A small, obviously frightened balding man in his 50's wearing a white apron shuffled toward them.

"Open this for us," said Albrecht, making hand motions to show what he meant–and bring candles now that it's getting dark," he mimicked lighting a candle and the patron nodded.

While they waited, Runzer pulled the wine case over next to his boots and began pulling the file pages out of it, stacking them on the next table.

"I wish I could read this crap," he said. "They certainly look like official papers of some kind, with all those stamps–here's one that's even got a seal." He waved it around as if it were a proclamation.

"Who knows? Let's put this with the other stuff Admin will be sending back to Division."

The Patron returned with the open bottle and two glasses. He gestured for them to allow him to pour a small sip into each and he gestured for them to smell the aroma, which they did–and found it very appealing. The patron then poured them full glasses and chattered at them, gesturing. Seeing they didn't understand, he abruptly put the wine bottle down on the table and muttered under his breath as he returned inside.

"We can do this ourselves, so fuck'em." Albrecht drained his glass and poured another.

At that moment, a staff car and escort pulled up in front the terrace. A corporal jumped out of the passenger side, came to attention and saluted.

"Heil Hitler," he said.

Runzer and Albrecht rose from their table, came to attention and returned the salutation.

"Captain Forster's compliments sir," said the corporal, obviously trying to sound important.

"Anything to add to the pouch I'm about to deliver to Division? They're now at Clamecy," he added. "Only about 60 kilometers. We've included information about capturing the train."

Runzer handed the corporal the dozen or so sheets of paper they'd found in the wine case.

"You might as well take these along corporal," he said. "They apparently came from the train, and they look official, but we can't read them, and we've got better things to do anyway."

The men pulled up their chairs as the patron delivered two plates of food–they had no idea what it was–and a side bowl with a green salad. The corporal saluted again before getting back in the staff car, but they waved him off as they dug into what they decided was a very tasty dinner–whatever it was.

***

Division headquarters at Clamecy was set up in a large ornate villa situated behind an ornamental ironwork and stone barrier with rhododendron blooms still visible on the bushes that screened it. A circular gravel drive led to a wide stairway with a tall doorway. The drive was crowded with vehicles and everything was brightly lit as Division, disdaining blackout rules, had mounted spotlights at the entry, where a detachment of military police manned a barrier, and over the doorway, where uniformed soldiers stood guard.

Arriving shortly before midnight, the corporal showed his pass and was granted access up the stairway. He was ordered to line up behind two other couriers who were waiting to deposit pouches on a large table, behind which a harried lieutenant took each pouch, labeled it, then signed a receipt which he handed to the couriers.

"Christ, I hope you're the last one, corporal," the lieutenant said wearily taking his pouch. "Too many of you and too much crap," he added, stamping the receipt and handing it to the corporal. "Off you go," he said.

Standing and stretching, the lieutenant piled the pouches into a black metal crate with two handles and carried it back toward the rear of the villa. Ornate furniture had been stacked against one wall and two long tables had been set up in the center of the room under a blazing chandelier. Pouches were stacked on one of the tables and at the other table, three men sat, reviewing the contents.

"I think this is the last of it," said the officer, placing the crate on the table and removing the pouches he'd brought in.

"They'd better be," said one of the men, not even looking up.

They'd removed their uniform jackets and sat in their undershirts. The windows were open, but the room remained hot and stuffy.

It was an hour later and the corporal's pouch from La Charité-Sur-Loire was among the last on the long table when Colonel Erwin Kaffke untied the bundle and spread out the contents on the table in front of him. Kaffke was a bespectacled, balding and heavyset man, too old for this crap, he told himself. He noted the progress report and strode to the map on the wall, taking a pen to mark the day's advance and the occupation of La Charité-Sur-Loire. He made a note of the abandoned train that had been captured, then he sat back wearily and began glancing at the papers, tossing them onto the now very large reject heap.

Then, suddenly, he stopped, and sat up straight in his chair. He held one sheet in his hand, then began carefully examining the few sheets just beneath it. He looked at them carefully, then put them down in front of him and stared.

"Holy shit," he breathed, nudging the two men next to him, both fluent in French as he was. The men were attached to the Intelligence Service of the OKH, the German High Command. The OKH was led by Major General Ulrich Liss, who reported directly to General Franz Halder, the German Commander-in-Chief. Kaffke's reverence for intelligence had been instilled in him by Liss who devoured information and seemed at times to be able to read the mind of the French High Command.

"Hans, Joachim," Kaffke said to the two staff officers seated with him at the table, "have a look at these. They're all labelled 'Top Secret' and look, this one is signed by General Gamelin himself."

"This one has the official seal of the French Defense Ministry," said the man called Hans. "It dated June 1st, only two weeks or so ago. What the Hell?"

Excitedly, the three men examined each of the documents that the pouch had delivered.

"These are fucking original documents," said Kaffke. "They're right out of the file cabinet of the French General Staff. Look, this one's addressed to Daladier and signed by Reynaud.

"I can't believe we're seeing this stuff; where did it come from?"

Kaffke quickly shuffled through the files spread out on the table, then pulled out what he was looking for, brandishing the file, then examining it closely.

"It was delivered tonight," he said, excitedly, "in the pouch from the unit that occupied La Charitè-Sur-Loire."

Kaffke continued reading. "They reported capturing a French train there. Do you suppose this material is from the train? And why do some of the sheets have dirt and–what's that, jam or jelly of some kind–stuck to them?"

"Christ, we've got to get our hands on this material." Kaffke gathered the pouch materials and hastily put them in a folder.

"Hans, wake up Major Irkins and tell him to get ready to move fast."

Kaffke rose and threw on his uniform shirt, not bothering to tuck it in.

"Where's the duty officer?" he yelled as he raced toward the front of the villa.

"Here, sir," a Lieutenant appeared in an adjacent doorway.

"Arrange immediate transport to a town on the Loire about two hours away. I'll need a motorcycle squad, a staff car for me and three of my men and a lorry to haul back some documents. Assign six armed men to the lorry as our escort."

"Yes sir," replied the Lieutenant, "I'll get everything organized right away."

"Advise Transportation that we'll need a map that can get us to La Charité-Sur-Loire; that's the name of the town," Kaffke said over his shoulder as he returned to the document room.

He tore a sheet of a pad of paper and quickly penciled a terse message to General Liss advising he was leaving headquarters on an intelligence collection mission and would report further.

Fifteen minutes later, the detachment assembled in the gravel drive in front of the villa. It was a beehive of activity even at this pre-dawn hour. As promised, a half-dozen motorcyclists and the car and lorry appeared. The driver of the staff car alighted and saluted.

With a bright moon to light their way, the small detachment made good time along the tree-lined roadways leading from

Clamecy toward the Loire. They encountered only one roadblock and the French guards quickly scattered into the night as the detachment plunged ahead, the lorry splintering the hastily constructed wooden rail fencing that had been erected.

The dawn sun first caught the tall rounded Romanesque tower of the cathedral high above the town, then early morning sunlight arrived.

"There's the train over there," shouted one of the soldiers standing up in the bed of the lorry to get a look at what lay ahead.

The detachment immediately veered in the direction he was pointing and pulled up sharply in a cloud of dust. As he stepped out of the staff car, Kaffke noted with approval that two tanks had been parked athwart the tracks to seal off the siding where the train was sitting. The handful of soldiers assigned to guard the train stood uncertainly, then came to attention and saluted as they recognized Kaffke's rank.

"Where is your commanding officer?" Kaffke inquired, motioning them to stand at ease.

"In town, sir," volunteered one of the men.

Kaffke pointed to one of the motorcyclists.

"Take this soldier into town and bring out his commander," he ordered.

Turning to another solder, he said, "Has there been an inventory taken of the contents of this train, private?"

"No sir," the soldier replied. "A couple of the cars have been broken into, but we've just been ordered to stay here and make sure it's not moved."

"We were delivered classified documents overnight that we believe came from this train," Kaffke said. "Anybody know about that or where the documents can be found?"

The soldiers looked at one another and shrugged, shaking their heads.

"Don't know, sir," came a ragged response.

Kaffke nodded, and began pacing alongside the train, peering through the slats.

Moments later, the motorcyclist returned with a sleepy-looking Lieutenant Karl Albrecht perched uncertainly on the back of the machine, clutching the driver's torso in front of him. He struggled clumsily off the bike and saluted.

Kaffke returned the salute.

"Lieutenant, your unit sent documents to Division overnight that appear to contain significant intelligence," he said. "What do you know about them and where did they come from?"

Albrecht looked confused.

"I'm afraid I don't have any idea, sir," he said and shook his head, trying to clear his mind and get his brain working.

Then he remembered. The case of wine that Runzer's driver had given them–and which they'd mostly consumed that night–and the documents stuck to the bottles that they'd sent off with the dispatch clerk.

Damn; if they find out we took the wine they'll charge us with looting the train and we'll get in trouble.

"Sorry, Colonel," he said. "We just took the town around dusk last night. I saw the train sitting there and assigned these men to stand guard, so the French didn't try to get it back. But I don't know anything about any documents."

Kaffke looked at Albrecht suspiciously, then nodded.

"All right, lieutenant; you can order your men to stand down. I'm authorized to search the contents of the train and impound anything I deem important. You can return to your billet in town while I conduct the search, but I'm ordering you not to move out until I tell you. I want your unit available to resist any French attempt to recover this train. Understood?"

"Yes, sir," Albrecht saluted. He could actually go back to bed, he thought to himself, but didn't crack a smile.

Kaffke walked the length of the train on one side, then back on the other side. Ten cars and only two of them appeared to have been broken into.

Kaffke turned to Irkins, "Major, you and Joachim take that one," he gestured toward a car that had been opened, with debris piled on the ground next to the track.

"Hans, you and I will tackle this one."

Kaffke swung himself up the steel ladder and pushed the door as wide open as it would go. The interior was still in shadows, but there was enough light to see the jumbled contents which seemed to have been loaded haphazardly. With Hans at his side, Kaffke, pushed pieces of furniture out the doorway onto the ground alongside the tracks to make room. There was a large mound of what seemed to be window drapes and several rolled-up carpets. They got rid of those too and shoved a coat rack of uniforms out of the way, along with a dozen large white laundry bags full of bedding which they spilled out the door.

Kaffke stood in the space they'd made for themselves, then stiffened.

"There they are," he said softly, and stepped over more debris toward the front wall of the railcar where four large carboard file cartons had been piled, one atop the other. They were surrounded by a hodgepodge of wine cases, food containers, office equipment– including what seemed to be a large teletype machine and what Kaffke took to be a field telephone switchboard. One of the file cartons had slipped onto its side, spilling some of its contents, which lay on the floor among the sticky remains of a carton of jelly jars that had also fallen and broken open.

Kraffke and Hans cleared a path, carefully gathering the loose documents off the floor. Finally reaching the cartons, Kraffke stooped to read the labels that had been affixed.

ARMY GENERAL HEADQUARTERS

HIGHLY CLASSIFIED

TOP SECRET

"Holy shit," he breathed. "What have we here?"

The two men carefully maneuvered the cartons to the doorway, taking care not to damage the broken one.

"Irkins," Kaffke shouted. "Over here; I need you both."

"Corporal," he yelled to the driver, "back that lorry up to the doorway so we can transfer these file cartons."

The cartons were light enough for Hans and Joachim to lift out of the railcar and slide onto the bed of the lorry. The four men then stood gazing at the cartons a little uncertainly. One of them had a large military seal glued to the cardboard, and Irkins, peering at it read, "Commander-in-Chief."

He turned and looked at the others with an expression of disbelief.

"Major," he said, "get that lieutenant back here with two dozen soldiers. I want you to supervise them and search every inch of this train. And I want his tank unit deployed right here, right now. We need to see if there are any more file cartons on this train and I want those tanks to protect us against any French attack."

Two hours later, the contents of the train had been thoroughly searched, most of the contents piled in stacks on the ground along the siding. They had found nothing more of value–intelligence value–Kaffke corrected himself; two of the cars had been stacked with paintings; others contained furniture and objets d'arts.

Valuable things, Kaffke reflected; but what he'd found was priceless.

While Major Irkins oversaw the search, Kaffke had clambered up into the lorry, seated himself on one of the troop carrier benches along the side of the truck bed and begun to examine the documents in the cartons. What a find! The cartons contained the files of the French Army Command–the originals–bearing signatures of Daladier, the Prime Minister; Reynaud, the Defense minister; General Gamelin, the Commander-in-Chief–even British Prime Minister Chamberlain and more recent documents signed by Winston Churchill.

One file caused Kaffke to stand up in excitement as he read it.

"The fucking Swiss," he said to himself. "Those fucking sanctimonious bastards." He was holding a file setting out a secret plan for the French Army to combine forces with the Swiss and attack any German advance across the Rhine into Switzerland.

Kaffke had been on the planning staff of the German Second Army that had prepared a detailed campaign that could be launched against the Swiss, flanking the French Maginot Line and surging across the Gempen Plateau, south of Basel, enveloping Geneva to the south, then pivoting to the west and driving toward Paris.

It was a brilliant plan. But it had faced internal resistance among senior ranks of the Army. The Swiss were neutral; they'd always been neutral. It was one thing to invade Belgium that claimed to be neutral, but everyone knew was aligned with France and the British.

But the Swiss; they were different. They were *genuinely* neutral and attacking them would create issues.

Kaffke sat down again and began paging through the thick file, reading with growing anger the details of troop movements by the French 8th Army, across the frontier into Switzerland. There was deployment into bunkers and redoubts prepared by both the Swiss and French for just that purpose, aimed squarely at creating a wall of resistance against advancing German forces.

Neutral my ass, Kaffke said to himself. This is the record of a secret military alliance between Switzerland and France. Ha! This'll blow to bits that neutrality cover story the Swiss keep telling.

Kaffke sat back against the truck bed, lit a cigarette and began to plan.

First, he wrote out a message to General Liss.

"Captured very high, repeat very high, value intelligence. Returning Division ETA 3PM. Suggest Meet."

Kaffke went looking for Lieutenant Albrecht

"I need this sent highest priority to Army Command attention Major General Liss," he said, handing Albrecht the single sheet, which he'd signed with a flourish.

"You're coming with me to Division."

The trip took an hour longer than planned because they had to slow down repeatedly in order to clear the roads of fleeing refugees that were headed in the opposite direction. Frustrated by the delays, Kaffke instructed Lieutenant Albrecht to order a Stuka attack on the road ahead to clear the way, but the debris and casualties left in the wake of the attack and the sheer terror that it caused among the refugees made things even worse.

So it was late afternoon before the detachment pulled up outside the villa that served as Division headquarters. A corporal ran to Kaffke's staff car.

"Sir," he said saluting. "General Liss requests that you report to him upon arrival."

Kaffke returned the salute.

"Major Irkins," he said, "arrange for those file cabinets to be transferred inside to our offices. Quickly and carefully," he added, turning to mount the front steps of the villa.

Major General Ulrich Liss was tall and slender with an athletic bearing, as befit a prize-winning equestrian. When Kaffke entered the large high-ceilinged room Liss was standing before a large map of the Loire Valley.

"You have something good for me, Kaffke?" he said. "There's a lot going on at General Headquarters, but your message caught my fancy, so I got the Luftwaffe to fly me down here to see what you found."

Liss didn't stand on ceremony, worked even longer hours than his staff, and didn't hesitate to engage in digging for facts and issues to find answers. He inspired fierce loyalty and Kaffke knew he would immediately grasp the significance of the intelligence that had fallen into their hands.

"Sir," he said leading Liss toward the office where Major Irkins was arranging the file cartons from the train, "would you like to read the files of the French High Command?"

He pointed to the labels and the French High Command seal, then pulled up two chairs for them at the table. The top file read 'Top Secret. Commander Only'. Liss opened it and began reading. Kaffke heard a swift intake of breath.

"This is Gamelin's file," Liss spoke quietly, almost reverently. "The French Commander-in-Chief. My God! How did we come to get hold of this?"

He continued paging through the documents.

"Here's a message from Churchill less than a week ago, for God's sake, with his signature right there."

Liss picked up the document and held it before him, blinking his eyes and shaking his head, then turned inquiringly to Kaffke.

"We discovered the files in an abandoned train in a little town called La Charité-Sur-Loire earlier today sir," Kaffke said. "Apparently, it got left behind during the retreat when the French government fled Paris," he continued. "Very early this morning we received a handful of secret documents from the train, so I took a unit there to check it out–and here's what we discovered."

Kaffke gave a big grin and spread his hands wide to encompass the four cartons.

"You conducted a search of the train?" Liss asked.

"Yes sir," Kaffke replied. "There was almost everything imaginable piled up in those railcars–they must have been trying to empty some government ministry, and in a big hurry, too, from the look of it. We left the rest of it under guard, so you can send men down to go through it if you want. But I'm confident that we've got all the file cartons."

Liss began shuffling through the files on the table in front of him, stopping now and then to read something more closely, occasionally shaking his head in apparent disbelief.

Kaffke hesitated, not wanting to interrupt; but after about ten minutes, he pulled out the Swiss file that he had examined in the back of the lorry.

"Sir, I think you'll find this material especially interesting," he said, handing Liss the thick dossier. "It's the record of a military alliance between the French and the Swiss armies against Germany."

Liss began reading.

"Christ", he said. "Nine divisions of the French 8th Army? All ordered across the Swiss border to the Gempen Plateau?"

"Why those, bastards," he said, slapping the file on his knee.

"That's what I said too," Kaffke replied grimly. "All the while protesting their 'strict neutrality'."

Liss returned to the file, reading carefully, but making a fist with his right hand.

After ten minutes, he sat back in his chair, absently pulled a pack of cigarettes from his breast pocket, swiftly lit up and after a deep drag, exhaled a plume of smoke. He raised his head, taking his eyes off the file and gazed into the middle distance, lost in thought.

Finally, he sat up, dropped his cigarette butt on the rug, grinding it with his boot, then turned to Kaffke.

"I don't have to tell you what a coup this is," he said quietly. He shook his head again and took a deep breath. Then he stood and began to pace.

"We need to get this to the *Abwehr* right away," he said. "Kaffke, you're going to escort this material to Berlin and deliver it to the Willhelmstrasse where Canaris and his counter-intelligence agents can take over.

"We'll skewer the Swiss over this," he said.

"Neutrality," he shook his head and fairly spat the word.

Less than two hours later, after a shave and an attempt to polish his boots and brush clean his uniform, Erwin Kaffke found himself climbing the short stairway into a small Focke-Wulf-10 cargo plane that had landed, then taxied to where Kaffke and his party were standing on a flat grassy meadow. The pilot wheeled the plane to a stop and turned off the left engine while the four cartons were handed up and stored, then, once Kaffke was aboard, he restarted the engine and wheeled the aircraft back toward the far end of the meadow. Kaffke was scarcely seated when the plane accelerated, engines roaring and, after a few bumps, soared into the air.

Looking about him, Kaffke discovered he was the only passenger. Then, as he settled back in the narrow uncomfortable seat, stomach churning–he'd never flown before–Kaffke began gazing out the aircraft's small window at the rapidly disappearing ground below as the plane swiftly moved into the clouds. Suddenly, he saw another aircraft flying alongside which he immediately recognized as a Messerschmidt M-109, with its gray camouflage and distinctive large black cross insignia.

Kaffke swiveled his head and, looking out the window on the opposite side, saw another Messerschmidt aligned off the aircraft's other wing.

Well, he said to himself, fighter escorts too. And feeling slightly self-important, he fell sound asleep.

When they landed, there was still a faint hint of twilight remaining in the summer night sky. Kaffke had no idea where they were, but he could see the outline of other aircraft and the shadow of nearby buildings. He decided they must be at a military aerodrome somewhere near Berlin.

As the plane taxied to a stop and the pilot killed the engines, Kaffke saw the hooded headlights of two automobiles approach the aircraft. The steps were lowered and Kaffke clambered off the plane, steadying himself on a concrete runway.

Two men in civilian dress, wearing double-breasted suits and fedoras, came up and shook his hand. Kaffke's ears were blocked from the descent, so he couldn't catch their names. They piled him into the back seat of a dark car–Kaffke couldn't make out the model in the darkness–loaded the file cartons in the second car and immediately the small caravan drove off. Soon they were entering a city–Kaffke assumed Berlin–and he could make out large buildings and streets with traffic and pedestrians on broad sidewalks. Blackout rules were in effect, so everything was dim and shadowy as Kaffke peered out of the rear window. He'd never been to Berlin before and he wished he could actually see it, instead of the quick snatches that were occasionally visible in the dim headlights.

Abruptly, the car turned a corner and paused at a gate where a guard with a flashlight checked the driver's credentials. Then the gate opened, and the car drove into a small entryway. Kaffke's car door was opened and he was directed up a short stairway toward a heavy door that opened into a brightly lit reception room.

Kaffke blinked, adjusting his eyes to the light from two large chandeliers that hung from a high, arched ceiling. He was immediately led into an ornate conference room where a polished table occupied the center of the room, surrounded by high-backed armchairs.

By this time, Kaffke's ears had popped and he could at least hear the six men who stepped forward to greet him and introduce themselves, but no titles were offered, and the names meant nothing to him. The file cartons were brought into the room and placed at one end of the long table. Kaffke was offered a coffee and an assortment of cakes, which he wolfed down, as the men gathered around the cartons and began a cursory, but excited, examination. They had obviously been told what to expect.

Finally, a tall, balding man, who wore large wire-rimmed glasses and seemed to be in charge, asked the men to take their seats on either side of him and motioned Kaffke to a chair across the table. Kaffke refilled his coffee cup and took another couple of cakes as he sat down. He realized he was ravenous, and he decided to take advantage of the opportunity to eat something.

"Colonel Kaffke," the leader said, a bit formally, "welcome to the offices of the *Abwehr*. As you know, we are the Military Intelligence Service of the Reich. General Liss,, who is our esteemed counterpart in the German Army OKH, has provided us a brief description of the intelligence coup that you achieved. We offer our congratulations and thank you for excellent work, which we are certain will be recognized and duly rewarded.

"You appear to have captured the original files of the French High Command. Extraordinary. Would you kindly explain to us how this came about?"

Kaffke swallowed the last of a cake, washed it down with a sip of coffee and proceeded to tell the story.

When he was finished, the leader–Kaffke heard one of the other men refer to him as 'Herr Frederich'–began questioning him closely.

"Why do you think those first few pages that you examined were sent to you at Division headquarters?"

Kaffke responded with a shake of his head.

"No idea, sir."

"They were in the pouch from the unit at La Charitè-Sur-Loire?"

"Yes sir,"

"But when you visited the unit, the commander didn't know about them?"

"That's what he told us, sir"

"And you didn't investigate further, Colonel?"

"No sir," Kaffke replied. "Frankly, I was more interested in trying to find any other similar documents and when we entered the first railcar of the train, there they were. I ordered a search of the rest of the train, and there were no other document cartons. When I discovered what we'd captured, my focus was on getting the materials safely into our hands and avoid any attempt by the French to recover them."

"So we are to believe that the files of the French High Command simply dropped into our hands by a stroke of pure chance?" Frederich's eyes bore into Kaffke's across the table. Kaffke was tired and still hungry. He felt his temper flare, but he remained calm. He felt his temper flare, but he remained calm and returned Frederich's gaze.

"I have reported to you the events that occurred," he said in a level tone, his hands folded in front of him on the table.

The room fell silent.

Finally, Frederich broke into a broad smile and slapped the table.

"Pure chance it is, then, Colonel," he said. "If I were you, I'd try to find a gaming table; you might make a fortune! Ha!" He looked around the table and his colleagues chuckled in agreement.

Three days later, Georg Frederich, Director General of *Abwehr's* Section IX–the Special Matters Section, as it was called– sat before Admiral Wilhelm Canaris, the *Abwehr* commander, in his large, high-ceilinged office in the *Wilhemstrasse* building that housed the key ministries of the German Reich, adjacent to the vast new *Reichskanzlei* that had been built for the Führer. The windows were open to the summer breeze and white lacey curtains blew to-and-fro.

"Admiral, the captured documents are in fact the original files of the French High Command," Frederich said. "Not everything, of course, in just four cartons, but a lot."

Frederich handed Canaris a document.

"This is a summary organized by subject matter. You can glance at it and we'll provide any of the raw files that you want to read."

Frederich smiled thinly, "Parts of it are, frankly, entertaining. Gamelin got so much wrong and he was such a pig-headed commander; no wonder we beat him so easily. Still, there's something unsettling about getting such intimate behind-the-scenes glimpses of the man; almost like peering into his bedroom."

Canaris glanced at the document before looking up.

"Yes. We'd better hope our documents are never subject to the same sort of scrutiny one day, hadn't we?" Canaris did not smile.

"I didn't include the most sensitive material in the summary," Frederich continued. "We found passwords, lists of foreign agents, descriptions of intelligence operations and some other items that I've passed to operations sections to pursue on a priority basis.

"I've also separated the Swiss dossier for special treatment," he added.

Canaris nodded. "I've read most of it; thank you for providing it before your translators got to it. The Führer will need the translation; probably von Ribbentrop too. But I wanted to read the raw documents myself.

"They very clearly lay out the terms of a Franco-Swiss military alliance and put the lie to the Swiss claim of strict neutrality.

"I'm briefing the Führer tomorrow. I'll get his permission to share most of this with Goebbels and get him to release a public broadside that will humiliate the French. We'll tell the world that we captured the train with the French High Command files and we'll quote some nice juicy parts. They won't know what we have and what we don't, so it will sow still more confusion and generate serious internal finger-pointing.

"Ha!" Canaris chortled at the prospect of the consternation that would ensue among French leaders in the wake of the news. "Heads will certainly roll.

"We'll get him to release the photo of the train too," he added. "Can't you just see it on the front page of newspapers around the world?

"But the Swiss material we'll hold very tightly. The Führer will instantly grasp the advantage the file presents him to blackmail and bully the Swiss–the kinds of things he's particularly good at," Canaris said dryly. "Together he and I can bring von Ribbentrop into the picture but exercise full control over him.

"The Führer will want to play the Swiss card himself."

Canaris stood.

"Frederich, I suggest you arrange to buy a few extra papers on July 3, 1940. They'll make good souvenirs."

Der «Berliner Lokal-Anzeiger» meldet am 3. Juli 1940 den Aktenfund von La Charité-sur-Loire. (Privatbesitz)

XIX

CHAPTER 1

Paul Muller swung himself aboard the tram as it glided along the Rue Gustave Ador between the lake and the steep hill leading up to the Cathedral of St. Peter that towered above the Old Town of Geneva. He felt a little self-conscious carrying his tennis racquet and kit, so he shoved them under the seat and behind his legs where they would be less conspicuous.

It was early May and the Geneva lake steamers were back in service, so the quai on his right was a hubbub of activity as workmen tugged on thick lines around the mooring bollards and passengers boarded and disembarked the freshly repainted white vessels. The tram crossed the Mont Blanc Bridge, took the right fork along the lakefront and headed toward the incline leading up to the Palais des Nations, the headquarters of the League of Nations. Even though it was a cloudy afternoon and the high alps weren't visible, Muller had a clear view of the Jet d'Eau fountain in the lake and the steep, rocky facade of Mont Salève rearing up behind it; a familiar sight, but always satisfying, and as he gazed out the window his face lightened in quiet applause.

The invitation from Stevenson to renew their tennis rivalry had come as a surprise. They hadn't played in years, and Muller assumed it was simply a ruse to introduce another agenda. That would be typically British. He didn't know what their intent was, but war was in the air, and plans and alignments–for nations and individuals alike–were in flux. That was certainly true for him–and for the Swiss intelligence service that was scrambling to protect a nation resolved to remain neutral but beset by challenges on multiple fronts–not least by its vulnerability to British economic power. So as he gazed at the familiar landscape passing outside the tram's windows, Muller felt a sense of anticipation at what new insights this rendezvous might reveal.

He alighted at the stop for the Hotel d'Angleterre, a handsome four-story structure topped by an angular slate roof with six glazed dormers and sweeping views across Lac Leman toward the distant Alps. The British had commandeered the hotel when the League was launched in 1920 and had occupied it ever since. They had transformed the interior into a little corner of England, with a reception resembling a London gentlemen's club, a pub featuring dart boards, Guinness on draft, and virtually every kind of British whisky, in addition to elevators manned by attendants costumed as Beefeaters.

Muller had spent considerable time there earlier, in the mid-30's, dealing with the British delegation during League debates over the fate of the Free City of Danzig. The lobby had always been loud and crowded, officials, clerks and hangers-on hurrying to and fro and demanding service at the bar. So he was startled when he entered, maneuvering his tennis gear through the revolving door, and found himself in a space that was practically deserted. A single reception clerk was standing behind the formal check-in desk, idly shuffling through some papers; the pub seemed empty, except for one lone customer sitting at the end of the bar and a barkeeper polishing glasses; there were no Beefeaters in sight. And it was quiet; not a sound to be heard.

It's like a tomb, he thought to himself looking around in disbelief; everyone's died.

Moments later, RCS Stevenson strode out of an elevator and advanced to shake Muller's hand. Seeing Muller's glance, he smiled and gestured grandly at the empty space, brandishing his tennis racquet like a baton.

"Rather like a movie set where they've completed the film, wouldn't you say? The cast is gone, the cameras stowed, but the props are still in place. Voila!

"Actually, it is a little eerie," Stevenson added, pumping Muller's hand and clapping him on the shoulder in a friendly manner. "But this is what brings me to town," he went on, steering them both back toward the entry. "The Foreign Office has decided to shut the place down and they selected yours truly to do the honors."

"The undertaker," said Muller in a soft tone, grinning.

"I prefer the movie set analogy," Stevenson replied. "More glamour."

3

Muller paused before entering the revolving door.

"Except in this case, the movie hasn't been shot yet; all we've seen so far are the previews."

They emerged from the revolving doors, both clutching their tennis gear.

"Touché, Muller," said Stevenson. "And we don't know how it'll turn out, do we? The script hasn't even been written yet."

"Enough black humor," Stevenson said with a laugh, turning as a black Peugeot sedan pulled up next to them. "Pile in," he said opening the rear door. "We've got some tennis to play–and for high stakes too."

"Tennis Club de Genève," Stevenson told the driver.

"Muller, they've just opened the first two courts this week; still preparing the others. But I was able to book us one of them. I hope you've been working on your backhand; I took a lesson earlier this year and I've perfected my cross-court smash."

Muller grinned. "My recollection from the last time I beat you is that you needed a lesson or two."

They traded jibes as the car passed through Bellevue, about a mile before the Collex-Bossy entrance to the Tennis Club, when the heavens suddenly opened, and they found themselves driving in a pelting downpour.

"Merde alors," Stevenson exclaimed loudly. "So much for tennis. What shitty luck; I was going to kick your backside. I guess this means that we'll have to go somewhere and start drinking now, instead of waiting till after I wiped you off the court. Suggestion? It would be too depressing back at the Hotel."

"La Perle du Lac just reopened too–and unlike the tennis courts it has a roof over it," Muller replied with a grin. "It's just back off the Route Suisse on the lakefront. Driver, do you know it?"

"Certainly, sir," the driver said, making a smart U-turn.

They had their choice of seats at this early hour and took a table by the window, where they could see occasional flashes of lightning across the lake as the storm moved past.

The waiter delivered two large glasses of Dewars scotch and retreated. They clinked glasses.

"May the film have a happy ending," Stevenson said, smiling and lifting his glass to Muller.

"A consummation devoutly to be wish'd," responded Muller softly, nodding his head. Then he looked at Stevenson.

"You're really shutting down the delegation here? And why someone as senior as you to supervise?"

"We're shutting down because the League has essentially gone out of business. You'll remember that last ministerial meeting back in March?"

Muller nodded. He was no longer involved in League affairs, but in the small confines of Geneva, events at the Palais were always scrutinized.

"It really was a sorry affair; a symbol of the League's impotence," Stevenson said. "The Spanish Foreign Minister flew to

5

Geneva to ask the League for help in resisting Franco's Fascist uprising–precisely the kind of mission the League was intended to address. And nothing happened; not even a toothless resolution.

"Actually, it was even worse than that," he added. "Most nations didn't send ministers; many delegations sent junior representatives to sit in at the session. And when the Spaniard was finished–what I gather was a very stirring plea for international support–the hall fell silent. Not a word of encouragement or declaration of solidarity; just silence, as the delegations filed out."

Again, Muller nodded. "I had drinks that night with a journalist who'd been there. He said there was an eerie feel to it; almost as if you could feel the League's relevance slinking out along with the delegations; the buck being passed unerringly into the void. Not unexpected by this time, with all that's happened. But still sad.

"And then to top it off, a week or so later, the government surrendered, and Franco took full control. It was as if the League didn't even exist." Muller said resignedly, taking a large draught of his whiskey.

"And that, my friend, is precisely why Whitehall is shutting down our League operations," said Stevenson.

"Point taken," said Muller. "But why you? Aren't you a little senior for a job like that?"

"Security. Over the years, we've collected quite a lot of sensitive documents, Muller," Stevenson replied. "The basement vault is fairly bursting. I'm to make sure they all get back to

England safely; they're even sending me an RAF plane to fetch them."

He peered over his glass as he took a healthy swig.

"We wouldn't want the Germans to suddenly invade Switzerland, capture Geneva and read all of our secrets, would we?" His dark eyes held Muller's gaze before glancing away.

"It is a bit of a risk, you know," Stevenson added, once more peering at Muller.

Muller sat up in his chair and put his drink on the table. "I think you're getting ahead of yourself, Stevenson. Switzerland is strictly neutral, and we've made it abundantly clear to both the Germans and the French–and the Italians too–that we will resist any violation of our territorial integrity. We're neutrals, not taking side. Any talk of a German invasion is off the table. Poland? Now that's a different story. I would be very worried if I were back in Danzig. But Switzerland? No."

Stevenson smiled. "But I got your attention, didn't I? Ha!"

He tipped his glass toward Muller again and smiled. "You're right of course. Switzerland doesn't seem to be a target for Herr Hitler–at least not at the moment. But to continue our movie analogy, who knows how this script will play out?"

Stevenson turned in his seat and signaled the waiter for a refill before continuing.

"Let's say Hitler attacks Poland–which, I agree, looks rather likely–and Britain and France declare war against Germany, as they've now said they would do. Where will they fight it out? On the same bloody fields in Flanders and northern France as the last time? Or will Hitler decide to invade Switzerland to flank the Maginot and attack France from the east? Think about it."

"We have," Muller said with a touch of annoyance. "Have no doubt on that score, Stevenson." He was not about to get into a discussion about the Swiss strategy to safeguard its borders.

Muller offered Stevenson a Gitane from his cigarette case, took one for himself, lit them both and changed the subject.

"You just said–ever so matter-of-factly–that Britain and France would declare war on Germany if Hitler invaded Poland. Is that really the premise that we ought to be operating on now? It seems rather novel."

He fixed Stevenson with an innocent smile and waggled his glass absently. Two could play at being provocative.

"Oh, come off it, Muller," Stevenson retorted impatiently. "You know perfectly well that Chamberlain made a declaration to that effect in Parliament a month ago."

"Yes, I do," Muller interjected quickly. "But I also remember that less than six months earlier, the same Mr. Chamberlain dismissed Hitler's threats to seize the Sudetenland from Czechoslovakia as–I think I'm quoting this correctly–'a quarrel in a far-away country between people of whom we know nothing,' At the time, I thought it was an odd way of putting it–rather conceited, in fact. But that's what he said."

Muller glanced out the window at the lake, then he turned back to Stevenson. "Now, you know as well as I do that Poland's even farther away from London than Czechoslovakia is, and the British don't know any more about the Poles now than they did about the Czechs then. But Chamberlain sacrificed Czechoslovakia and simply handed the Sudetenland over to Hitler at Munich. Now, in the case of even more distant Poland, he tells Hitler to keep his hands off, or Britain and France will go to war. A reverse somersault, all in the space of only five months. Very acrobatic. But it's a little hard to know what to really believe," he added quietly.

Stevenson seemed angry. He hunched his shoulders and leaned toward Muller, then he paused, ground out his cigarette in the ashtray and sighed heavily. He sat back in his chair as the waiter delivered their drinks and fussed with sweeping away the cigarette ashes that had fallen on the white tablecloth, finally depositing a fresh ashtray and turning away.

While they waited, Muller looked at Stevenson, who was running a hand through his hair. Were there flecks of grey that hadn't been there before? Muller couldn't tell for sure. Maybe the lines around his mouth were a little more pronounced and his eyes set a little deeper. Getting close to forty, Muller thought. But he still looked fit and energetic.

Stevenson had been the Foreign Office official in charge of the British delegation to the League when Muller had first been employed there in 1933 and he had been the one to arrange Muller's appointment as secretary to the League's High Commissioner for the Free City of Danzig. Anthony Eden, the

British Minister for League Affairs in those days, was Stevenson's boss. Eden had become the League's Rapporteur for the Danzig file during the ensuing bitter struggle between the League and the Danzig Nazi Party which was trying to seize control of the city. Muller and Stevenson had interacted closely during those two years, often disagreeing sharply, but also determined to manage the conflict. They had forged a professional–and a personal– relationship during those fraught times. Muller had also called on Stevenson for advice during his tenure a year earlier in Vienna where he represented the League in a futile effort to stave off Hitler's seizure of Austria.

In his Foreign Office role, Stevenson was privy to details of British policy, a trusted insider in that opaque Old Boys network. Muller felt his sense of anticipation stirring. Stevenson's allusion a moment earlier to a possible German invasion of Switzerland fed Muller's suspicion. That was no off-the-cuff comment, he was certain; it was provocation for a purpose.

Stevenson raised his fresh drink, tipped his glass toward Muller and took a deep draught. Then he set the glass down, folded his arms, looked at Muller and nodded, smiling thinly.

"It's reassuring to learn that you haven't lost your keen powers of observation in this new position I understand you now occupy here," he said blandly. "What is it? Managing Director of the Institute for International Relations? My, that sounds terribly interesting." His smile broadened. "Seems to me like it could cover a lot of ground...maybe some time you'll share your agenda with me."

Stevenson held up both palms as Muller's expression turned stormy.

"Of course, I don't expect that you'll do that tonight, old boy." Stevenson was grinning broadly now, enjoying the role he was playing. "But I just wanted you to know that we're pleased that you're occupying a responsible position here in Geneva, which probably enables you to pass along interesting information that comes to your attention in the field of–what is it? Ah yes, International Relations."

Stevenson laughed and took another swig of scotch.

Muller tried not to react this time, keeping his face expressionless. Of course they knew; British intelligence had been operating in Geneva for twenty years. It wouldn't have been very difficult to discover his Institute cover. But how much did they know beyond that, he wondered. Maybe more than he'd like. And who was the 'we' who were pleased at his new role? Well; his instincts had been correct. Game on, for sure.

He smiled back at Stevenson and proffered another Gitane which he accepted.

"I'm certain that nothing I'm doing here is anywhere near as interesting as Chamberlain's threat to go to war," Muller said. "I'm dying to learn what you can tell me about that. We can talk about my dull existence some other time."

"Fair enough," Stevenson replied breezily.

Muller nodded. "But it's a bit of a long story, though. We'd better order dinner."

CHAPTER 2

De-boning the truite meunière required their attention.

"One thing I'll certainly miss is the cuisine here in Geneva," said Stevenson, as he carefully removed the skeleton and placed it on a side dish. "We English have many strong attributes, but gastronomic skills are not among them. It's almost a point of national pride," he said, shaking his head and mopping up the sweet meunière with his bread, then pouring them both more wine from the chilled bottle of Aigle Les Murailles from the Valais.

After the waiter removed their plates, Stevenson wiped his lips with his white napkin, sat back and eyed Muller.

"Muller, I think Britain will honor the Prime Minister's declaration and will declare war if Germany invades Poland. Moreover, that declaration, if it is issued, will have a profound effect upon Switzerland, as I think you very well understand. I have invited some colleagues to join us later this evening and introduce that subject. I think you'll find it to be a revealing discussion.

"I understand the skepticism you've expressed about British resolve. You're not alone; the legacy of the Munich Conference is very ambivalent. But you have to understand what was happening in Britain when the event took place and its aftermath. Indulge me a few minutes to offer a perspective that I think you'll find edifying."

Stevenson accepted Muller's Gitane and exhaled a long smoky breath.

"There we were in September 1938," he said. "The government had been championing the policy of Appeasement for years, telling themselves and the public that this was the path to peace. People looked at Europe and watched Hitler strutting around and making threats. But no one took him very seriously; there was no sense of alarm–most Englishmen simply relied upon repeated assurances by Mr. Chamberlain and his ministers that Appeasement was working, so there was nothing to worry about.

"Then–seemingly out of the blue–Hitler issued an ultimatum to Czechoslovakia demanding that they surrender the Sudetenland to him, or Germany would declare war and invade. The Czechs responded by declaring martial law, mobilizing a million-man army and readied their very well-prepared fortifications to confront the Germans."

Stevenson paused to pour them the last of the wine.

"The British people suddenly awoke to find themselves facing the very real threat of a war in Europe that they hadn't expected and certainly weren't prepared for. And this time it wouldn't just be fought in France; German bombers would surely attack England and rain destruction from the air.

"The result was something close to panic. Sandbags were filled and piled up around public buildings, banks, stores and even the posh clubs in London. Slit trenches were dug in public parks and cellars and basements were readied as air raid shelters. The government began handing out gas masks and clearing hospital wards to make room for casualties. It seemed the nation faced attack at almost any moment.

"This is when Chamberlain uttered those mournful words that you cited earlier, Muller."

"But surely the Foreign Office knew what was happening," Muller interrupted. "Whitehall may be stuffy, but it's not stupid; Hitler's threats against the Czechs hardly came as a surprise to anyone seriously paying attention."

They paused as the waiter opened another bottle of wine, then retreated.

"You'd have thought so," Stevenson responded, "but the reality is that Chamberlain exercised such tight control over the process that hardly anyone outside his close knit orbit of Party whips knew what was afoot–and even they were often in the dark."

Stevenson paused and glanced over his shoulder to make certain no one was within earshot. It was a gesture Muller had often seen in his previous assignments in Danzig and Vienna, where uncertainty lurked around corners and conversations often had to be furtive.

This is not reassuring, he thought.

"Chamberlain concluded that he–and he alone–could tame Hitler." Stevenson said quietly. "He had no experience in diplomacy or international affairs; he'd never met Hitler–or even Mussolini. But no matter; he convinced himself that he was the leader who could satisfy Hitler and achieve lasting peace in Europe.

"So, he proceeded to concentrate British diplomatic power in his own hands. You'll remember, for example, how he forced Anthony Eden out as Foreign Minister in early 1938."

"Of course, I remember," said Muller in a testy voice. "That was when he didn't lift a finger to prevent Hitler from swallowing Austria. He just shrugged, saying they all spoke German anyway, so it didn't much matter."

Stevenson, nodded. "And later he circulated pictures of adoring crowds welcoming Hitler's arrival in Vienna–all to show up those who'd questioned his policy.

"It was all part of his plan," Stevenson continued. "He was confident that his acquiescence in the Austrian takeover had bought him leverage with Hitler and showed the success of his Appeasement policy."

"Some success," Muller muttered darkly. "I was there to witness the violence that the takeover unleashed; it was a vicious, sadistic orgy, Stevenson. Yes, the local Nazis welcomed him. But everyone else was deemed an enemy and treated that way–especially the Jews. I got out by the skin of my teeth."

Stevenson raised his hands as if in mock surrender. "Chamberlain didn't much trouble himself about those sorts of details," he said. "He was looking at the big picture, and he persuaded himself that consolidating German-speaking Europeans under Hitler's rule offered the best prospect for a peaceful outcome."

"So then came Czechoslovakia's turn," said Muller, his exasperation evident.

Stevenson nodded again. "The Sudetenland: that western-most province of Czechoslovakia–home to a very large Germanic population and surrounded by Germany. The border had been drawn–pretty arbitrarily–less than twenty years earlier when the Treaty of Versailles carved Czechoslovakia out of what had been the Austro-Hungarian Empire.

"It was a natural target for Hitler," he added.

"Goddammit, Stevenson, the border was drawn there for a reason," Muller spluttered in annoyance. "It contained the industrial heartland that Czechoslovakia needed to exist as a nation: steel, chemicals, coal, glass and more. Take that away and there's virtually nothing left to support the nation's economy. And they had a thriving democracy there, too," he added angrily, "despite Hitler's efforts to undermine it by arming the Sudeten Nazis and provoking unrest. Wasn't that something worth protecting? Plus, the Czechs had converted the Sudeten forests and mountains into a nearly impregnable fortress." Muller grew animated, his voice louder. "Concrete blockhouses and pillboxes, anti-tank barriers, heavy artillery and antitank weapons, all protected from attack and sited to destroy invaders. It was a mini Maginot Line; formidable stuff."

Stevenson put his finger to his lips, signaling Muller to lower his voice.

Muller took the hint, but continued quietly speaking intensely, his eyes locked with Stevenson's.

"The Czechs could have withstood any German assault–for at least long enough to give the French time to attack Germany in the West. We know from our intelligence–and you should from yours too–that the German High Command was categorically opposed to invading Czechoslovakia for just that reason. They stood a good chance of being defeated."

"That's the whole point, Muller," Stevenson said quietly but with equal intensity. "Chamberlain wasn't looking for a way to *defeat* Hitler; he was trying to find ways to *satisfy* him. Why? To keep the peace."

They both fell silent, glaring at one another.

Finally, Stevenson leaned closer to Muller.

"I've been encouraged–no, directed," he corrected himself, "to tell you candidly what really happened, so you will have the facts, which it is assumed you will share with Swiss officials."

Muller didn't react; he continued staring at Stevenson.

"I'm uncomfortable continuing this conversation here," Stevenson said looking around as the restaurant began to fill up.

"It's stopped raining. We can stroll outside where we won't be overheard."

He abruptly stood and signaled for the bill.

CHAPTER 3

Muller's mind raced as they made their way to the restaurant entrance. Stevenson was delivering him information under instructions–from whom, Muller wondered–obviously confident that he–Muller–was a secure channel to senior Swiss officials, whom Whitehall, or whomever it was that had put Stevenson up to this, didn't want to approach directly. And who were the newcomers he was inviting later, whom he said would have a message?

Well, the game certainly was on, as he had earlier assumed. Nothing for it but to listen closely to what he was being told.

The Peugeot was still standing outside the restaurant; Stevenson told the driver to continue waiting as they'd be back shortly, and they began striding along the lakefront quai in the direction of the Jet d'Eau, now lighted up in the deepening twilight.

"Let me continue with my description of what happened," he said. "The sequence of events is important to understanding how we got to where we are today.

They walked a minute or two in silence while Stevenson gathered his thoughts.

"It's not well understood that what became known as the Munich Conference was the last of three–well, really four–separate meetings between Chamberlain and Hitler. Each one had important consequences.

"Let's also get the dates right," Stevenson added.

"I mentioned a moment ago that the Czechs reacted to Hitler's threat to invade by declaring martial law and mobilizing their troops. That occurred on September 13, 1938, and galvanized Chamberlain into action, convinced as he was that he was the only statesman who could resolve the crisis. Consulting only a small handful of Cabinet Ministers–and not even seeking approval from the King–Chamberlain wired Hitler saying that he was ready to fly to Germany for face-to-face discussions 'to find a peaceful solution'."

Muller shot him a disdainful look.

'That's the way he put it." Stevenson shrugged. "Anyway, Hitler agreed. So the very next day, September 14, Chamberlain flew to Munich to pay a visit to Kehlsteinhaus–Hitler's Alpine castle located in Berchtesgaden.

"Quite an extraordinary moment, Muller," Stevenson paused for effect before going on. "Hitler was threatening to invade, the Sudetenland had exploded in violence, Czech leaders were mobilizing to fight, and the French and Russians were looking for ways to wiggle out of their mutual defense pacts with the Czechs. It was a First-Class diplomatic crisis.

"And there, tranquilly flying above it all, was Neville Chamberlain, making the first airplane trip of his life–think of it, Muller, it was his *maiden flight*–accompanied only by his secretary and a lone British Foreign Office representative, headed directly to Hitler's Eagle's Nest. He tuned out all the noise, supremely confident that he could do a deal directly with Hitler, avoid war and keep the peace."

They paused and lit Gitanes from Muller's cigarette case before resuming their pace.

"He landed at Munich Airport and was immediately whisked to Hitler's aerie. The two of them met alone, with only a German interpreter. Hitler was polite, but unbending. The Sudetenland must be separated from Czechoslovakia and conveyed to Germany without further delay. Chamberlain replied that he agreed 'in principle' but that he could not proceed without the assent of his ministers, which, he implied, would be a formality; he'd do what needed to be done and be back in a week for another meeting. In return, Hitler agreed to postpone his invasion until they next met. Chamberlain returned to London, convinced that he had taken Hitler's measure and found a man whom he could trust."

"Come on, Stevenson," said Muller, rolling his eyes in mimicry.

"I'm not exaggerating, Muller; this is what was going on. You need to hear this." Stevenson then continued, speaking rapidly and looking straight ahead as they walked.

"When he was back in London, Chamberlain was as good as his word. He arm-twisted the Czechs into surrendering the Sudetenland and aided the French in sidestepping their defense pact–even avoiding a guarantee for the rest of Czechoslovakia that the French proposed. Since the Parliament was in recess, he was able to avoid facing any domestic critics, and he secured Cabinet approval to return to Germany and complete the deal with Hitler, save only an instruction that he should ensure that the transfer of Sudeten territory and people was done in an orderly way and conducted under international supervision. On September 22, Chamberlain flew back to Germany, this time to meet with Hitler in Bad Godesberg–at the Hotel Dreesen, overlooking the Rhine. A nice place, I'm told; ever been there?"

Muller shook his head, somewhat bemused, but intent on learning what Stevenson had to say.

"When they met, Hitler immediately upped the ante. He told Chamberlain that their agreement in principle a week ago was no longer acceptable. Violence had spiked in the Sudetenland to such an extent that he must seize control of the territory immediately. 'Agree to hand it over by October 1 or I'll invade,' he said–and he even set a timetable. The invasion would kick off at 2 PM on September 28–less than a week away. He waved off Chamberlain's proposals for orderly transfer and international supervision. You must agree, he said, or the invasion will begin. So that was the message Chamberlain brought back to London. He wasn't rattled by it," Stevenson continued. "He remained persuaded that he could do a deal with Hitler. But the country certainly was rattled; news of a sudden and unexpected threat of war profoundly shocked the nation and that's when the panic set in.

"High drama, Muller," Stevenson's right hand traced an arc, as if to emphasize his point. "War fever was sweeping the country, including frequent news bulletins on the wireless that fanned fears of German bombers appearing in the sky to rain death on unprotected British cities. Tensions peaked as the nation ticked down the hours to the scheduled launching of Germany's attack.

"Just twenty-four hours before Hitler's deadline, Chamberlain addressed the House of Commons, called into Emergency Session. The atmosphere was electric, members crowding one another in the cramped space and a packed gallery buzzing with anticipation. Chamberlain made his entrance to subdued applause in recognition of the gravity of the moment. He appeared calm and spoke in a low voice, recounting the highlights of his pursuit of peace through Appeasement, as if reminding his audience of how much invested he was in his policy."

Stevenson stopped, then turned to face Muller.

"Suddenly," he said, almost in a stage whisper, "a messenger entered the gallery and a note was handed forward which finally reached Sir John Simon, the Chancellor of the Exchequer, who was seated directly behind the Prime Minister. He scanned the paper and passed it up to Chamberlain, who pushed it aside, only to have Simon shove it back in his hand. Finally, Chamberlain paused to read the contents.

"Then, seemingly reinvigorated, he straightened himself and announced that Hitler had invited him to meet again in Germany and that the invasion had been postponed. He then told the House he would accept Hitler's invitation and go to Munich. Pandemonium ensued, and the House exploded in huzzahs and whoops of support."

Stevenson turned and resumed his pace along the quai, Muller scrambling to catch up.

Their stroll had taken them as far as the Beau Rivage Hotel. Muller took Stevenson by the arm and led him across the Route Suisse to the tables and chairs under the hotel's awning, outside the street-level bar.

"Sit here," he directed Stevenson. "I'm ordering us cognac."

Muller ducked inside the doorway to the bar and returned, trailed by a white vested waiter carrying a tray with two large snifters.

"This conversation has gone on long enough that we need lubrication," Muller said good naturedly as they clinked glasses and lit up Gitanes. "All very interesting, Stevenson," he continued. "I assume that message you just described led to what we all know as the Munich Conference, a few days later, when Hitler, Chamberlain, Daladier and Mussolini did the deal and sold out the Czechs?"

Stevenson nodded. "September 30, 1938. Not a date to be
celebrated, I'm afraid. But humor me a moment longer, Muller,
because the most interesting incident took place the next morning.
The other leaders had left for home, but Chamberlain delayed his
departure and secured another meeting with Hitler. He brought
with him a brief memorandum that he had drafted overnight, by
himself; no coordination with other ministers or Cabinet. It was his
own idea and he was sure that he could get Hitler to agree to what
he was proposing. With peace secured, Chamberlain was in a
jubilant mood as they met–again alone except for Hitler's
translator–and he proceeded to offer ideas on how Great Britain
and Germany could expand relations and increase trade."

Muller sipped his drink. He knew the gist of the story but let
Stevenson continue.

"In the same upbeat mood, he presented the document that
he'd prepared, a declaration stating that the Munich accord was
symbolic of 'the desires of our two people never to go to war with
one another'. He told Hitler it was a bilateral statement of goodwill,
intended to preserve the success of the Conference they had just
concluded. Chamberlain proceeded to sign his copy with a
flourish, and he urged Hitler to do the same–which Hitler
proceeded to do, not even bothering with a formal written
translation, simply accepting the verbal statement by his translator.
Chamberlain was overjoyed," Stevenson went on. "For him, this
declaration was the pièce de résistance, and the crowning
achievement of his Appeasement policy –a joint commitment with

Hitler to keep the Peace. When he flew back to Britain that afternoon and landed in the rain at Heston Airfield that was the paper he waved to the adoring crowd that had come to greet him. That was what persuaded him to famously proclaim 'Peace in Our Time'."

They ground out their cigarettes and sipped their cognac.

Muller turned to Stevenson. "What you've just told me doesn't sound like much of a predicate for the declaration the Prime Minister issued a month ago, saying Britain would go to war if Germany invaded Poland."

Stevenson stood and walked to the door, signaling the waiter to refill their snifters.

"You're right, of course," he said, nodding in Muller's direction. "Chamberlain remained in thrall to his Appeasement policy and he continued to pursue it in the months following Munich–even after Kristallnacht, that vicious Nazi attack against Jews all over Germany in November–which, by the way, provoked a serious popular backlash in Britain. By then, there was serious dissent among some members of parliament, and even in parts of the British press; but Chamberlain ignored it–and in fact did his best to suppress any opposition. He actively pursued increased trade with Germany, and he squelched proposals to expand the British military because he was persuaded it would never be needed."

Stevenson sighed as he gazed through the glass's amber liquid. "I offer two examples of his mindset," he said, swirling his cognac.

"In late February, just a few months ago, he stated in a parliamentary debate that he believed Germany had no more interest in aggression that we did."

Muller began to protest, but Stevenson held up his palm to stop him.

"I know, you didn't see anything about that in the press, did you? That's because it was suppressed–that's the way things happen, these days.

"Then in early March, he told a group of journalists that since the threat of war had receded, he hoped to convene a new international disarmament conference by the end of the year."

Muller sat up in his chair and slapped the table.

"Christ, Stevenson, by then, even the press was reporting that Hitler was mobilizing to take over the rest of Czechoslovakia," he said sharply. "Surely British intelligence knew what was happening."

Stevenson nodded. "But Chamberlain and his cabinet simply didn't believe them. They were persuaded that Britain was entering a new golden age of peace and prosperity based upon the Munich conference and the declaration he and Hitler had signed.

"So, the news that Hitler had occupied of the rest of Czechoslovakia on March 15, landed in Downing Street like a bombshell right out of the blue." Stevenson shook his head, as if still in disbelief himself.

"It blew up right in their faces."

"I can only imagine," Muller replied softly. He hadn't before realized the extent to which the British leaders had been fooling themselves.

"What happened then? How did they react?"

"At first, paralysis and denial," Stevenson replied. "Chamberlain claimed that the German seizure was only 'symbolic' and the government's policy toward Germany shouldn't change. But by then the country had had enough; public opinion shifted almost overnight and political opposition–even within Chamberlain's Tory Party–finally boiled over. Chamberlain suddenly realized he had to shift gears, or he'd be ousted. So, two days later he made a speech condemning the invasion."

Here, Stevenson paused and smiled tightly–once more, to Muller's amusement, looking around to ensure they were alone.

"In truth, Chamberlain seemed most annoyed at Hitler's failure to discuss the matter with him before invading; he took it almost as a personal affront. Surely, he said in his speech, as a co-signatory of both the Munich Agreement and the joint declaration, he was entitled to be consulted.

"A suddenly disillusioned Prime Minister," Stevenson added, spinning his snifter absently. But also, an experienced and canny politician," he went on. "Recognizing that to retain power he needed to act boldly, Chamberlain proceeded to issue his Declaration that if Hitler invaded Poland, England would go to war."

"But Stevenson," said Muller softly, "he never uttered the word 'war'. He only said England would 'feel themselves bound to lend the Polish Government all the support in their power.' I'm pretty sure I've got the language right," he said, leaning forward and gazing directly at Stevenson, knowing full well that he had in fact quoted the language accurately.

"If Chamberlain really intended to threaten to declare war on Germany, wouldn't you think he'd have said so?" Muller had been waiting all evening to make the point. When he'd read the text of Chamberlain's statement in the newspaper back in March, he'd been sitting in a café and muttered audibly, 'War, for Christ's sake; say it!' And he'd smacked the table so loudly as to cause heads to turn in his direction.

But Stevenson waved Muller's point aside.

"Any diplomat knows what Chamberlain meant," he replied blandly. "If Hitler invades, England will go to war with Germany."

The two men sat facing one another, ignoring the raucous sound of loud dance band music coming from somewhere behind the Hotel.

Finally, Muller spoke. "I think we both know that Chamberlain's given himself room for maneuver," he said, smiling tightly. Then he broadened his smile. "Unless, of course, you're going to tell me that the Imperial Military Staff presented Chamberlain with a plan for how the British Army is going to go to Poland's rescue when Hitler invades that 'far off' country."

Muller drained his cognac, his gaze still fixed on Stevenson.

Stevenson drained his glass too and smiled back at Muller. "I'm afraid I'm not authorized to do that," he said softly. Then he leaned forward and fixed Muller with a steely gaze.

"Forget Poland," Stevenson said. "That's a sideshow."

Stevenson balled his fists on the table, his voice low and intense.

"Muller, you need to pay attention to the main issue and not get diverted. What's important is the strategy we are now embarked upon that will bring Hitler down and do so without having to launch the kind of new world war people are predicting. Together with the French and our other European allies–and with growing help from America–we have the power to crush the Nazi Reich and we will do so. We are encircling Germany diplomatically so it's totally isolated, our military is deployed to withstand any German effort to break our grip, and we will proceed to strangle the German economy, depriving it of the means to wage war."

Muller watched Stevenson straighten in his seat, his gaze direct.

"That, my friend, is the struggle that is now underway. Muller, we have moved beyond Appeasement and we're at work with our allies to mobilize our vastly superior power and defeat Hitler.

"Do not for a moment doubt our resolve or our capability. We will win."

Then Stevenson stood.

"Muller, I think we'd better find out where that music's coming from, he said, tossing a few francs on the table.

Muller rose from his seat and stood a moment, watching Stevenson stride to the corner and turn right, disappearing around the corner.

Well, he thought to himself. That was certainly direct; the British Lion was back and, in concert with allies, was ready to pounce on Germany. A decidedly different tone and certainly a different message.

Stevenson was no fool; this was certainly part of a plan. Muller began following Stevenson's footsteps, wondering what was going to happen next.

CHAPTER 4

The narrow street led away from the lakefront past the side entrance to the Hotel. Muller caught up to Stevenson as they reached the next intersection and there before them was the source of the loud music they'd heard earlier. A large red neon sign identified it as the club 'Rouge' and flashing strobe lights added to its glitzy appearance. The door and windows were open and spilled the sounds of music and crowd noise out onto the sidewalk. Several sporty cars were double parked in front. The doorway was crowded with well-dressed customers, with a tall, turbaned black man in a white uniform who appeared to be directing traffic.

Muller chuckled to himself, remembering when Rouge had been a dark haunt for prostitutes that he's used as cover years ago to meet secretly with a reporter and leak a sensitive story, confident that they'd never be spotted. Times have obviously changed, he said to himself as he and Stevenson strode to the entrance. Stevenson slipped some coins into the large white-gloved hand proffered by the turbaned man; up close Muller could see the uniform was stretched tight over a large torso and thick arms. The man's face was bearded, but bore scars; traffic director but also bouncer, and not someone to be to be trifled with, Muller decided.

The interior of the Club was garishly bright, lit by large brass chandeliers suspended from a dark ceiling. Silent pornographic movies (very pornographic, Muller could see at glance) were projected on two bare walls, surrounded by heavy red drapes elsewhere. There was a small dance band playing energetically from a stage on one side of the room with a dance floor in front, flanked on three sides by tables and cane chairs. A long bar took up the length of the room on the left.

"Christ, this looks like a cabaret they've resurrected from the Weimar Republic," Stevenson said as they approached the bar.

Muller laughed. "Geneva is *very* international."

The club was busy and there were a lot of very pretty women among the dark-suited men; professionals? Muller wondered. Probably some, but Geneva had more than its share of job opportunities for women and some of them were probably clerks and stenographers here for fun and adventure. Some weren't even bothering to button their blouses, Muller noted appreciatively.

When they finally got the attention of the bartender, Muller noted with a start that it was a woman. Really! He'd never seen that before anywhere. But there was no mistaking the gender when she leaned down to reach for the Johnny Walker bottle and two very female breasts with pink nipples presented themselves for inspection. The woman had short dark hair plastered back, glistening with oil. She plunked down their glasses, poured two shots into each–"doubles," she said, smiling–and pushed them nonchalantly across the polished bar, as if she'd been doing it all her life. Muller picked up his glass, offered a mock toast to the woman, who'd already turned away to serve another customer, and took an appreciative gulp.

Stevenson nudged Muller's elbow.

"Those two fellows I told you I wanted you to meet? They're over there," he gestured with his glass toward a table across the dance floor where two men were seated, each with a woman at his side, laughing and gesticulating–evidently very much caught up in the bawdy atmosphere. Hardly the place for a serious discussion, Muller thought, but Stevenson strode around the edge of the dance floor toward the two men, clearly expecting Muller to follow him.

Seeing Stevenson approach, they both stood with wide smiles.

"There you are, old boy," said the taller of the two, "and about time, too."

Turning to the two women, he gestured grandly in obvious dismissal.

"Sorry our little get-together had to be so brief," he said, "But we told you we need to save the world tonight and here are the friends we were expecting to help us do it. So, toodle-oo".

"Take your drinks," said the other man as the ladies rose to leave the table; "maybe we'll see you later." He smiled and blew a kiss, as they waved back and walked toward the bar.

Stevenson shook hands with the men and turned to introduce Muller.

"Paul Muller, meet two faces of the implacable British resolve that I spoke about a few moments ago. This is Air Commodore West…"

"Jimmy," said the man, interrupting Stevenson and vigorously pumping Muller's hand,

"And Consul General Hansen," the taller man, who also shook Muller's hand.

West motioned for Muller to take the seat between them. He proffered his flute–they were drinking champagne–and they toasted.

"God Save the King," said West, rather too loudly, then laughed and tossed off the drink, turning to the ice cooler and refilling his flute and Hansen's from the champagne bottle nesting there.

"So," he said merrily, smiling broadly, "we now get to meet the famous–at least famous to us–Mr. Muller, the intrepid diplomat and master of intrigue of whom Stevenson here has spoken so highly and whom he assures us will be our indispensable Swiss point of contact as we launch our campaign–and here cupped his hands and whispered, barely audibly–to bring down the Reich!"

"Ha!" West said, clapping his hands in mock applause.

Muller eyed West uncertainly. He was compactly built, stocky and broad-shouldered; probably fifty years old, Muller suspected from the steaks of grey in a full head of dark hair, but a young fifty. His eyes were dark and intense, radiating energy, but they were set in a plain oval face without strong features that Muller thought could provide a cloak of anonymity when needed. Maybe a useful appearance if one were in the intelligence business, Muller thought to himself. He was put off by West's cavalier behavior in this unlikeliest of sites for discreet discussion, but beneath the act he was putting on, the man conveyed an air of authority and competence. He seemed very much in control of the role he was playing.

Hansen by contrast was not just tall, but very thin, almost gaunt; his face was narrow and cadaverous, with prominent cheekbones, a thin mouth seemed pinched between a thick grey mustache and a lantern jaw and thinning hair was plastered over his skull. He seemed tense; coiled, almost, thought Muller.

Hansen leaned in with a smile that seemed forced and spoke in a tone so low Muller had to turn toward him to hear.

"Mr. Muller," Hansen said, "Britain is preparing to launch a blockade and conduct a campaign of economic warfare against Nazi Germany that will starve the German people and destroy German industry."

Hansen paused for effect.

"This is not some idle threat, sir. It is a program that has been approved by His Majesty's Government at the very highest levels. We have not yet formally announced it to the world, but there's no need to do so. Any knowledgeable observer of the German economy understands its vulnerabilities–certainly the Germans do– which is why they are trying so desperately–and failing–to insulate themselves from the overwhelming weapons that we possess and will deploy to destroy them.

"I'm told I should confide in you tonight the likelihood that the launch of this campaign may have the unintentional, but very likely collateral effect of also starving the Swiss and destroying Switzerland's economy too."

Muller stared at Hansen. The dance band behind them had begun belting out a loud boogie-woogie melody which seemed to envelop his head. What was this man saying to him? And here?

As Muller straightened up and took a deep breath, trying to clear his head, Jimmy West tapped his shoulder from the other side and leaned his head in close to Muller ear.

"And I'm told to confide in you, sir, that provided the Swiss cooperate with our campaign, we will strive to mitigate these unintended negative consequences.

"What do I mean by cooperation, you'll want to know?"

West smiled broadly at Muller and proceeded to answer his own question.

"Fairly simple, actually," he said. "Switzerland will cease trading with Germany and keep trading with us."

West cocked his head and gestured with his hands to show how easy it was.

"Now, of course, there will be a few exceptions that we'll need to address," he added. "But you get the idea."

Muller stared at him, dumbfounded.

Stevenson, who had been sitting across the table, had downed another double Johnny Walker and was clearly drunk, began slapping the table with an open palm, muttering "To the King, To the King."

Suddenly he leaped to his feet and began to sing in a loud voice.

"Rule Britannia, Britannia rules the waves…"

Muller heard loud French oaths and the crash of tables and chairs as nearby Frenchmen, seemingly infuriated at Stevenson's behavior, hurled themselves at him shouting and punching, causing the table to collapse and knocking Muller to the floor as the two sides collapsed into brawl.

"Fucking English whores,

"Always want us to fight your wars.

"No good Anglo-Saxon shits"

French insults filled the air as Muller covered his head to avoid being kicked and tried to slide away from the fight.

Someone fell on top of him and took a swing, but Muller ducked his head, used his shoulder to shove the man aside and begin crawling, finally getting up on all fours. He could see the big, turbaned bouncer race into the melee, knocking people down and separating others.

Then out of the corner of his eye, he spied Jimmy West wrestling with a Frenchman about his own size, the two of them locked in an embrace. Then he saw West loosen his grip, raise an arm and begin to sing.

"Allons enfants de la patrie!

Le jour du gloire et arrivé,

Contre nous de la tyrannie

L'étendard sanglant est levé !"

The brawling suddenly stopped, and the antagonists joined in singing *La Marseillaise.*

When they finished, with a rousing *Égorger vos fils, nos compagnes!,* there was a sudden silence, then loud laughter as the men began untangling themselves, clapping one another on the shoulders, smiling, hugging and resetting the tables and chairs amiably. The hostility had simply evaporated.

There were a few cuts and split lips that needed tending and waiters brought out napkins. The bouncer stood, hand on hips, surveying the extent of the damage, then strode back to the doorway, satisfied that the disturbance was over.

Stevenson was being tended to by West who dabbed at a cut on his chin. Muller saw that he also seemed to have a blackeye. Well, he deserved it, the damned fool.

Stevenson glanced over at Muller, who was still close to the far wall where he'd finally been able to regain his feet.

"You didn't do much to support your British hosts," he said.

Muller walked over to the three men. He made no effort to conceal his deep anger. "I remind all three of you and the government for which you purported to speak tonight, that Switzerland is a sovereign nation and has a policy of strict neutrality which we will aggressively defend and which I advise you to honor."

"Good night." Muller strode to the door and walked out.

CHAPTER 5

"It was all very weird," Muller said. He was seated in a small conference room across the table from Hans Hausamann, Director of Büro Ha, the private intelligence organization organized and run by Hausamann as an informal–but integral–arm of the Swiss Ministry of Military Affairs.

He had come to Bern to deliver a detailed verbal report to Hausamann on what he had been told by the British officials and the bizarre events that had occurred.

"As I walked back across the Mont Blanc Bridge that evening, I was seething," he continued. "The stupidity of provoking a fight in that night club–in fact, even setting up a meeting in a place like that"; Muller shook his head. "But more than anything I was infuriated at the arrogance of these two guys issuing outright threats to Switzerland on behalf of Great Britain–and doing so right in the heart of Geneva. Who the Hell did they think they were?

"And Stevenson, spinning that long story of how the blinkers of Appeasement were suddenly removed for Chamberlain after Hitler marched in Prague. Christ."

Muller removed his pack of Gitanes from a pocket, offered one to Hausamann, who declined, then lit it and exhaled a large plume of smoke.

"When I finally got back to my apartment, I was wide awake, so I pulled up my armchair, put some Beethoven on the phonograph, tried to calm myself and think through what had happened."

"And?" said Hausamann, smiling across the table; "did you have a sudden revelation?"

"I wouldn't call it that," Muller replied. "But I came up with a plausible explanation, at least.

"Maybe the snifter of cognac helped," he added, with a small smile, "but I recalled how many times the High Commissioner and I had disputes with Stevenson and his boss, Anthony Eden, back in '35 and '36 over trying to protect Danzig from the Nazis. We offered solutions, but they repeatedly rebuffed us and arrogantly– sound familiar?–asserted British policy positions that, in their view, took priority. 'Thank you for your proposals' they would say, 'but we've got bigger fish to fry–a grander strategy to pursue–so, do as you're told; go back to Danzig and let us–the big boys, WE BRITISH–run things.'"

Muller paused glancing at Hausamann.

"Do you remember sending me to London when I was the League's Commissioner in Austria–only a year ago–to seek British help in preventing Hitler from swallowing Austria?"

"Of course," Hausamann nodded. "We thought that Eden would stand up to Chamberlain and oppose Hitler's bullying behavior."

Muller nodded his head and leaned forward, hunching his shoulders.

"But they dismissed the idea out of hand with the very same arrogance. 'Run along, young fellow; we've got a policy and we don't need anyone's advice. Just fall into line'."

Muller ran his hands through his hair, taking another long drag on his cigarette before stubbing it out.

"The more I thought about it, the more I became convinced that what I had just experienced was simply another exercise in that same British mindset. 'We've decided on a course of action, and lesser mortals–like the Swiss–need to snap to attention and follow instructions'."

Hausamann leaned back in his chair. "And something happened that confirmed your suspicions?"

Muller dipped his head and smiled to himself in recollection. "After a very short night, I got up and walked to the café around the corner where I take coffee and croissants every morning. I was sitting there, feeling really crappy, munching my second croissant and having a look at the *Journal de Genève*, when all of a sudden, Jimmy West plops himself down at an adjoining table and hands over my tennis racket and the kit bag that I'd left in Stevenson's car. 'Wouldn't want these to get left behind, would we old boy,' he said cheerily, though, truth be told, he didn't look like he felt any better than I did. I beckoned Marcel, the waiter, and told him to bring coffee and another croissant for my guest. West thanked me and took a long swallow of coffee. 'Sorry about that cock-up last night,' he said. 'We certainly didn't plan to make it an evening for singing patriotic music'."

"I laughed in spite of myself, sir," said Muller. "Here he was, as hungover as I, and having to eat crow as well. But I waited, looking at him expectantly, and he finally added, 'It was also in rather bad taste to issue what probably sounded like threats to Switzerland'. '*Sounded like?*' I countered. 'No, not *sounded like;* those were deliberately delivered threats. Britain's going to starve us and destroy our economy unless we do what you tell us to do'.

"West put up hands in mock surrender, mumbled something about being apologetic, then said he wanted at least to offer an explanation; I decided to listen. He told me that Whitehall has set up an organization that hasn't been publicly announced yet, called the Ministry of Economic Warfare. It has full cabinet status and in fact has a mandate to operate across agency lines to do whatever seems necessary to undermine–and eventually destroy–the German economy. They've conducted a detailed sturdy and concluded that the German economy is in a desperate condition and facing the real prospect of collapse. Their plan is to push it over the edge a soon as they can, believing that when Germans can't get paid or get enough to eat–when the economy disintegrates, in other words–the whole Nazi edifice will crumble, taking Hitler down with it, and the threat of war in Europe will disappear. That's their vision, and they're apparently determined to pursue it.

"Sound familiar?" Muller added. "We're British, we've made a decision; get on board or else. They're a menace," he concluded shaking his head.

"I take it that Jimmy West, and the other guy you mentioned, Hansen, the Consul General in Geneva, are part of this new Ministry?" asked Hausamann.

"That's right," Muller replied. "They're the Ministry presence in Switzerland and seem to be operating outside regular diplomatic channels.

"I'll bet that goes down well with the Foreign Affairs people," said Hausamann sourly. "They've appointed a new British minister, here, a man named David Kelly, who's scheduled to arrive in a few days. I don't know him, but he has the reputation of being very old school and influential with Whitehall. I'm told our side was pleased at the appointment because it would seem to ensure that we could get London's attention when we needed it. I wonder what he'll think about this new ministry freelancing here?

"And what's the plan they're implementing that would lead them to threaten to starve Switzerland and destroy our economy too?" Hausamann frowned; it was obvious that he was annoyed.

"An economic blockade like the one they imposed in the Great War," Muller responded, "only more so."

He went on with his retelling of the conversation. "West painted a picture of the British Empire sitting astride most of the world's raw materials which it would deny to Germany. The Royal Navy controls the world's sea lanes and it would be used to cut Germany off from any supplies that the Empire couldn't block. He said that France was fully on board and would close its borders to German trade and that America was cooperating with them to a much greater extent than was publicly acknowledged."

"He made it plain that Britain expects Switzerland to play a vital supporting role in their plan by shutting down our trade with Germany and cutting off their access to financing. He said that he understood that this would impose hardships on Switzerland and that they were willing to discuss possible steps to minimize the pain. But he said the plan was decided upon and measures were being readied to put it into effect."

"It's the same old story, sir; the British have decided what's going to happen and our job is to fall into line. I was obviously just their messenger boy."

"Did you inquire why they selected you?" asked Hausamann.

Muller nodded. "When I asked West that question, he pulled his chair up even closer to mine and said very quietly, 'Anthony Eden chose you'."

"You can imagine my shock, sir," Muller said, looking at Hausamann with a bemused half-smile.

"Eden? Deciding to use *me* as his conduit? I was dumbfounded–in fact, I still am–but West held up a hand and went on.

"'Eden said he never like the messages that you were delivering to him, but he'd concluded that you were competent in your work–high praise from Eden, mind you," West added, saying that Eden didn't often bestow compliments.

"'So, your name was not drawn out of hat, Mr. Muller, West said to me, a little louder this time. 'You were fingered from the top.' Then he said he and Hansen had enlisted Stevenson to bring me to that abortive meeting at the Club Rouge. He added that Whitehall was confident that I would find the right way to deliver their message to the proper Swiss authorities."

Muller took a deep breath and spread his hands out in front of him toward Hausamann. "And that's the story, sir. West then stood up, handed me a card with just his name and a local Geneva telephone number on it, thanked me for the coffee and walked away."

Hausamann sat still for a long time, obviously deep in thought, his features immobile. He remained silent, his arms crossed and his head bowed, seeming to gaze at the table top. Finally, with a deep sigh, he sat up straight again.

"Well, Muller, we did dangle you out there to see if anyone would bite, didn't we?" he said with a small grin. "We thought that Institute for International Relations cover would be pretty good bait."

Muller nodded. "That was the plan, sir; there are a lot of people out there with agendas fishing for angles."

"But I don't think either one of us expected that you'd land Anthony Eden and the British Government, did we?" Hausamann's grin broadened; "I think you'd better stay over Muller; I'm meeting with the Minister later and you need to tell him your story."

CHAPTER 6

Rudolf Minger was unquestionably the most popular political figure in Switzerland. He had been a member of parliament for a decade and Minister of Military Affairs since 1931. He had overseen a series of programs to modernize the Swiss military, championing large bond issues that Swiss citizen-soldiers enthusiastically supported and which raised millions of Swiss francs to buy badly-needed arms and equipment. He still looked every inch the simple Vaudoise farmer that he had been, with a disarming manner that endeared him to the public. But Muller had learned from his father, who had worked closely with him for years, that Minger's outward appearance cloaked a shrewd and calculating mind that keenly grasped the challenges Switzerland confronted in the gathering European crisis.

As they were ushered into Minger's office, Muller was struck by how small and plain it was. He had visited ministerial offices in Berlin and London–even Warsaw–and they were all grand and ornate, as if announcing their importance to the world; but not here. A desk with two chairs, a conference table with seats for maybe a dozen people and no military flags or insignias on the walls. There was, he noticed, a view down to the Aare River, flowing swiftly below the steep embankments on either side, but even the window offering the view was smaller than he would have expected. This was clearly a space for business and not for show.

Hausamann introduced Muller and Minger shook his hand; his rugged features, weathered by years as a farmer, were encircled by a short white beard. He had bright blue eyes above pink cheeks and they were smiling in welcome.

"Mr. Muller, I'm pleased to meet you. I've learned of your exploits in Danzig and Vienna from Mr. Hausamann and of course, I've known your father for years; I was so sorry to hear of his stroke," his face bore a look of concern. "I hope he's recovering."

"Thank you, sir," Muller replied. "It's an honor to make your acquaintance. Father is better; he's recovered most of his ability to speak, and that's a big improvement, but his left side remains paralyzed, and he's confined to a wheelchair."

Minger shook his head. "That must be hugely frustrating for such an energetic man; it's the kind of affliction we all of dread as we get older. Please convey my best wishes to him."

He then turned to Hausamann.

"It's just the four of us, then?"

Hausamann nodded as they took seats at the conference table, introducing Muller to Roger Masson, the Ministry's Director of Planning, who had entered the room through another doorway.

At Hausamann's direction, Muller proceeded to deliver a detailed report on his meetings with the British. Minger paid close attention, jotting a few notes in pencil in a small notebook that he placed on the table before him. When Muller was finished, Minger thanked him, then paused, tapping his pencil quietly on the tabletop, apparently gathering his thoughts.

"I suppose we shouldn't be surprised," he began. "The British imposed their blockade and trade embargo during the Great War to devastating effect. If another war should come now, it's certainly to be expected that they would turn to the same weapons again.

"What I found most revealing about your report, Mr. Muller, is the apparent conviction of the British leadership—at least as it was conveyed to you—that the German economy is so weak that British economic weapons can bring it down—even without a war perhaps."

Here Minger paused and looked around the table quizzically. "And thereby rid us all of Herr Hitler and his Nazi regime?

"That sounds a little like wishful thinking to me, but we need to look at it. So, let's begin with some of the other points. Mr. Muller, you said Stevenson referred explicitly to concerns about Germany invading Switzerland by crossing the Rhine on our northern border, then sweeping east into France, entirely flanking the Maginot Line?"

"Yes, Mr. Minger," Muller replied. "He said that seemed more likely than fighting the same battles all over again in Flanders and northern France, and he clearly implied they assumed the Germans would capture Geneva too, which was why he said they were evacuating their files."

"That's of course our worst nightmare," Roger Masson said, puffing on a straight pipe. He was a slender, dark haired man with small horn-rimmed glasses and a bearing that seemed to radiate intensity.

"Geography has dealt us a very bad hand in that region, with the Gempen Plateau offering an avenue for an advancing German army to attack eastern France. They could simply bypass Basel and the southern end of the Maginot Line and head directly to Paris. Or keep going south, skirting the Jura Mountains, take Geneva and hit eastern France from there. Or they could do both. We are very much aware of the danger, Mr. Muller," he added, clenching his pipe firmly.

"I said as much, Mr. Masson," Muller replied. "I also told him in no uncertain terms that Switzerland is a neutral nation, but that we would defend ourselves against any nation that attacked us."

Minger nodded, clearly wanting to move on. "The border situation is what it is. As Mr. Masson said, we're aware of it and have a military strategy to address it.

"But it's interesting that Stevenson raised it with you so directly. I'd like you to try to find out–discreetly, of course–what

British intelligence knows about German intentions that may have led him to make that observation."

"Certainly, Mr. Minger," Muller replied.

Minger cleared his throat. "You also said that Stevenson told you their plan was to encircle Germany diplomatically and isolate it. That seems to imply that they're planning on making a deal with Stalin and enlisting the Soviet Union to help them too. How likely do we think that is to happen?"

"Stalin just replaced his Foreign Minister," said Masson. "Litvinov was an insider, one of the earliest Bolsheviks; but he's a Jew. That's a problem these days. The new Minister, Vyacheslav Molotov, was the architect of last year's purges that killed off God only knows how many Soviet leaders. We don't know all the details, but remember the show trials they put on before killing them? It all seemed pretty grisly. So if Stalin appointed him Foreign Minister, we have to assume that he'll do whatever he's told."

Minger began tapping his pencil again, his expression pensive. "There's every reason to believe Stalin should be open to doing a deal with the British and the French," he said. "He and Hitler are deadly enemies, and they're his natural allies. But I'm not persuaded that Bolsheviks can *have* allies," he added. "Their whole system is predicated on the downfall of the capitalist West.

"Countries like France and Britain," Masson said, nodding.

"Right," Minger continued. "Hardly a recipe for building alliances. If it comes to war, they'll surely choose the West over

Hitler. But I doubt we're at the point yet where they think they have to choose. They're more likely to stay on the sidelines pursuing their own goals until something happens that forces them to change."

"That doesn't mean that they might not be willing to help the British squeeze the German economy," he added. "I'm sure they'd be delighted to help. But how much could they really contribute? The Soviets don't trade much with anyone; they're hardly the lynchpin of a British embargo campaign no matter what Stevenson told you."

"And what about the Americans?" Minger asked, changing the subject. "Stevenson told you they were helping them a lot more than anyone knows."

"Right," said Masson briskly. "The British always speak bravely about their American cousins and the help they're providing. And they made a deal together last November."

"Yes, but what was announced publicly was pretty thin gruel," said Hausamann.

Masson then grinned and opened his hands together as if in supplication. "So, since they didn't really get much out of it, the Brits put out the word that there were secret protocols: military assistance, new arms deals, massive financial credit, you name it. All very hush-hush. American largesse dedicated to preserving the British Empire."

Then Masson brought his hands together and shook his head. "I think it's all bullshit. Roosevelt can't do anything without

Congressional approval, and he hasn't gotten it. I think Stevenson was blowing smoke on that one." Masson punctuated his conclusion by loudly tapping the bowl of his pipe on the ashtray to empty the ashes before refilling it.

"So, it appears the message that was delivered to Mr. Muller had some window dressing that we find unpersuasive," Minger said. "Not very surprising, I suppose, so let's take those pieces with a grain of salt. But the heart of the message–the part about Britain unleashing an economic campaign against Germany that will have a damaging impact on us; that's serious and warrants our urgent attention. And since that plan is apparently being driven by a British conviction that the German economy is on the verge of collapse, we need to understand that too."

Yes sir," said Masson. "But I'm not sure how we go about doing that; we don't have the kind of manpower and expertise that Whitehall can call on."

Minger nodded. "The only serious resource we have available on economic questions is the Swiss National Bank," he said, "and like central bankers everywhere, ours tend to be notoriously standoffish. But let me have a serious word with Frederich Fischer and see if I can't get us some help."

Muller knew that Fischer was the Chairman of the Swiss National Bank–the Swiss Central banker; he was another old friend of his father.

Minger rose to depart. He shook hands around the table, then turned as he was leaving.

"Mr. Muller, I'd like you to become our Ministry's economic expert," he said with an innocent smile. "Let's see if Anthony Eden was right about you."

CHAPTER 7

The christening ceremony had been just for the family. Muller's new nephew, Klaus, slept soundly through the whole event, not even awakening when the minister had blessed him with the holy water. Muller's brother Thomas and his wife Charlotte had proudly carried the infant, wrapped in a lacey white christening gown, to the baptismal font which was situated in a small chapel adjacent to the nave of the church. They had carefully handed him to the minister, a tall man, resplendent in his white robe and gold vestment, who performed the ceremony with quiet dignity. St. Peter's was the oldest of Zurich's four principal churches, and it awakened fond memories for Muller. It was here that he had first been exposed to the wonders of choral music and the joys of performing great works by the masters. That afternoon, as he'd entered the sanctuary, he'd conjured up those boyhood memories, glancing up at the massive pipe organ that had so often accompanied the choir, and he'd felt a warm sense of kinship.

His father, Karl, filled the wheelchair with his massive frame, even though his left side hung awkwardly, and he seemed to slump in that direction. He'd insisted on attending the baptism of his first grandson and he looked on with evident pride, despite his infirmity. Muller's mother stood beside her husband, one hand resting fondly on his right shoulder, a handkerchief tightly clasped in the other, which she used to dab at glistening eyes. Ann Muller remained slender and lively, but Muller had noticed new tightness in her features that reflected the strain of Karl's condition. Oskar and Greta, who had served the family since before Muller's birth were both there, beaming proudly.

Mathilda, Muller's younger sister, lived in Chicago and had not traveled for the occasion. She balanced a busy life as wife and mother of a young daughter and a full-time position doing research in advanced quantum physics. Like Muller, she was not close to her brother, but she had written an emotional letter to Muller lamenting her inability to attend the ceremony, primarily to support their parents–especially her father–and promised to book an overseas telephone call during the afternoon reception.

The only other person in attendance was Charlotte's older brother Christophe Francin, a Captain in the French Army, resplendent in his sharply pressed tan uniform, with bright red collar brevets and a line of medals on his left breast. Muller liked Francin; he had a good sense of humor and an appetite for informed discussion of events unfolding around them in the world.

Muller found him observant and valued his perspective as a knowledgeable French military officer.

Muller thought it typical of his older brother to excuse himself as quickly as possible after the ceremony concluded, saying that he wanted to return to the residence to welcome any guests arriving early for the reception. Thomas had overseen preparations for the event, ensuring that the guest list included the cream of Zurich society and leading Swiss government officials. Muller found it distasteful; it was as if his brother were using the christening of his son–which in Muller's view should be more of a private celebration–as an occasion to flaunt his appointment as Chairman of Muller & Company, the family-owned private bank. It was the bank that his father had run–successfully, but cautiously and modestly for thirty years–until the stroke had obliged him to step aside and yield power to his eldest son.

Muller did not stay in close contact with his brother; he'd never found any appeal in a banking career. Thomas had embraced it and never done anything else, occasionally making deprecating remarks about Muller's diplomatic assignments. Even growing up together, there had been distance between them. Thomas was big and burly like his father, quiet and withdrawn; competent in his studies, but more pedestrian than adventurous. By contrast, Muller was lithe and energetic like his mother, intellectually curious with an outgoing personality. He had become a competitive tennis player in contrast to Thomas's preference for tests of physical strength.

In recent years, Muller had returned to Zurich only rarely and he and Thomas had not seen much of one another. But when they had been together, Muller had sensed Thomas's dismissal of his outspoken opposition to Hitler and the Nazi regime. Thomas hadn't spoken up in favor of Hitler; he'd simply reacted with disinterest, apparently viewing what Muller perceived as a growing European menace to be little more than a shift in regional commercial stakes which affected only the financial scales that he was accustomed to weighing. He'd seemed oblivious to the violence of Nazi rule and the ferocious threats that Hitler regularly uttered to adoring German crowds.

Now, back at the residence, where the reception had begun, Muller was observing the dynamics that were in play. His father, in his wheelchair, was situated in the living room near the doorway to the terrace and garden where the guests were gravitating, drawn by the sparkling spring weather. He was attended by Oskar and offered his still strong right hand to greet the guests, most of whom he'd known for many years, smiling–as best he could–and engaging in banter and conversation, seemingly not affected by his occasional slurred word or two.

It was as if he were a one-man receiving line, thought Muller. Everyone stopped to shake hands and greet him, speak briefly, then–as if relieved of the obligation–strode onto the sunlight terrace and down the steps to the garden, leaving him behind.

The garden reception had been carefully choreographed; high-topped tables with white linen table clothes were strategically placed, with a full bar at one end and a flower-bedecked buffet table at the other, piled high with meats, fish, breads and fruit. Seating areas with chairs and small tables were tucked near the flower beds.

The guests were mingling, chatting and balancing buffet plates and drinks or wine glasses. Muller was hungry; he had just loaded a plate of his favorite viande des Grisons when he noticed a flutter of attention among the guests as the President of the Swiss Federal Council, Marcel Pilet-Golaz, made his entrance. After briefly greeting Karl Muller, he descended to the garden and strode directly to where Thomas was standing, deep in conversation with a claque of guests. They separated to make room for the President and the two men embraced warmly, Pilet-Golaz congratulating Thomas and engaging him animatedly. Muller knew of Pilet-Golaz, but had never met him and he was struck by how much the man resembled Hitler: a high forehead, dark hair combed to one side and a little brush mustache. He was a bigger man than Hitler and his belly strained against his double-breasted suitcoat; still the resemblance was evident, and Muller smiled in amusement.

At that moment, Thomas caught his eye and gestured for Muller to join them. Muller looked for a place to set down his plate and walked the few steps to where Thomas and Pilet-Golaz stood.

"Mr. President, may I introduce my younger brother, Paul, the proud uncle of the son whom we baptized today." Up close, the resemblance to Hitler Muller had noted was even more pronounced, small mustache and dark, piercing eyes between high, rounded dark eyebrows.

All he needed was a brown shirt uniform, Muller decided.

"I'm honored to meet you sir," Muller said, willing himself to put Hitler out of his mind.

Pilet-Golaz shook Muller's hand vigorously and put his left hand companionably on Muller's elbow.

"What a proud brother you must be," he said with a wide, appealing grin. "A newly-baptized nephew and a brother who has just assumed new responsibilities that he is discharging with such great distinction."

A waiter handed Pilet-Golaz a flute of champagne, and he clinked it with theirs.

"We've needed new energy in our finance sector as we adjust ourselves to the New Order that's emerging in Europe under German leadership," he said enthusiastically. "Too many bankers have been hesitant and some even hostile, but Thomas understands that the best way to preserve Swiss neutrality and advance our interests is to take advantage of the opportunities that Hitler's Germany offer us.

"We'd better do that hadn't we," he added genially, "now that Germany has added that long border with us that used to be Austria–and absorbed the whole of Czechoslovakia too. I'm sure you'll be a big aid to Thomas in helping us adjust to the new Europe."

Muller decided to respond. "Actually, sir, I don't count myself among Herr Hitler's admirers and I don't work at the bank; I'm a diplomat."

I'm certainly not going to tell him I'm a Swiss intelligence agent, he thought to himself, smiling.

Then he added, "But I'm in full accord that we need to be alert to defending our neutrality. I find myself less inclined toward accommodation and more on the side of standing our ground and resisting where we need to." Muller was smiling, but had a slight edge to his voice.

Thomas shot Muller a dirty look.

"Well, it's a process," Pilet-Golaz replied, unfazed and still genial. "Change is under way and I'm pleased to have the support of Thomas and Muller & Company as we try to find our way."

He shook Muller's hand as Thomas led him toward a group of other guests standing nearby, obviously signaling an end to the conversation.

"I'll look forward to remaining in touch," Pilet-Golaz said to Muller over his shoulder.

Muller nodded and waved before retrieving his plate and refilling his glass, then looked for a place to sit where he could do a better job of balancing and eating.

He spied Christophe Francin at one of the small sitting areas. Francin patted an empty chair next to him and beckoned Muller to join him, which he proceeded to do.

"So that was Pilet-Golaz, the President of your Federal Council?" Francin asked.

Muller nodded as he ate one of the meats, then wiped his hand on a napkin.

"I probably shouldn't say this," Francin leaned closer to Muller and lowered his voice. "But don't you think he looks a lot like Hitler?"

Muller promptly erupted in laughter and proceeded to drop his plate on the grass.

"Oh my," he laughed hard, slapping his leg, then pulled a handkerchief out of his pocket to wipe his eyes. "That's exactly what I was thinking to myself when my brother introduced him. But I couldn't very well say, 'Hi Adolf' could I?'" And he laughed hard again, finally finishing by blowing his nose.

"That's rich, Francin," Muller said catching his breath, still grinning. "I didn't think anyone else would notice. Ha!"

"Save my seat," Muller said and rose to get another plate from the buffet and dispatch a waiter to refill their glasses.

Muller was still grinning when he returned with plates for both of them, along with napkins and utensils, which they balanced on their knees.

"Pilet-Golaz was praising my brother as breathing energy into Swiss efforts to accommodate themselves to Hitler's New Order in Europe," Muller said, spearing a piece of smoked salmon. "I responded that I was not a member of Hitler's fan club and tended to favor firmness toward Germany over accommodation. That did not sit well with my brother, I'm afraid."

"Accommodation sounds too much like Appeasement?" asked Francin teasingly. "I hope we're past that by now," he added.

"A British friend told me that Chamberlain has moved on and is actually ready to go to war if Germany invades Poland," Muller observed. "The Declaration he issued said he was speaking for France too. Are you persuaded?"

"About the French position, you mean?" Francin arched an eyebrow as he spoke, breaking a cookie in half, popping it into his mouth, then following it with the other half and licking his lips.

"Why, we always permit the British—our Anglo Saxon friends—to speak on our behalf, don't we?" Francin chuckled.

"I'm just an Army officer, Muller. I leave the politics to other people."

"Oh come on, Francin," Muller said; "You know what I mean.

"I live in Geneva, which might as well be a province of France. Hitler's not the bogeyman there. The Genevois—like not a few Frenchmen—are much more concerned about the Bolsheviks—and of course about Léon Blum and the socialists and Communists his Popular Front brought into government. They're fixated on what they believe is the enemy within French society itself, not the Nazis. And they aren't so keen on the British either, by the way."

"'Why should we fight Germans just to preserve the fucking British Empire,' Muller mimicked quotation marks with his hands. "In fact, I was on the edge of a fight in a Geneva nightclub a few nights ago where a bunch of Brits–admittedly obnoxious–were beaten up to that very refrain. Not the kind of warm and friendly relations that allies like France and England are supposed to enjoy."

Francin smiled. "Sounds to me like your nightlife needs some adjustment."

"But for the rest," Francin continued, "I don't think you should take it so seriously. Yes, there are disaffected Frenchmen who hate Blum and his crowd of Communists. We've also got Monarchists who insist on restoring the Bourbon Dynasty and like everyone else–including your Swiss, Muller–we've got fascists and Nazi sympathizers too. But all those differences would melt away if war should come again," Francin said, gazing levelly at Muller. "You can count on it."

"Moreover," he said, "France has the mightiest armed forces in the world. Don't forget that, Muller."

"Yes, I know Hitler has been frantically re-arming," Francin continued, leaning toward Muller in his chair, his tone low and intense. "And he's building a much bigger army than we'd like. But make no mistake; they're no match for us. We have more men under arms than they do, we have more planes, our tanks are better–their Mark I and Mark II panzers are no match for our Char B1s–and we have the Maginot Line stretching along most of our border. It's an impregnable barrier, Muller. Some of my colleagues just can't wait for the Germans to hurl themselves at our fortifications so we can just mow them down. I'm not just bragging, Muller," he said. "Those are the facts." He sat back.

Then something occurred to him; Francin snapped his fingers and turned to Muller with a broad smile. "Of course, I should have thought of it sooner. This year is our Sesquicentennial–the 150th anniversary of the storming of the Bastille; France is mounting the most extravagant celebration imaginable to mark the occasion– including a massive military parade down the Champs Elysée. You must come to see it as my guest, Muller. It will be absolutely spectacular, and you will see for yourself the invincible force of French arms on full display."

Just then, Muller's mother came to the terrace doorway and beckoned him.

"It's Mathilda," she said. "Your turn to speak to her."

Muller stood and hurried toward the steps, but over his shoulder. gave a thumbs up to Francin. "I'm in. Sounds like a great event."

CHAPTER 8

"How awful has it been, Paul?" asked Mathilda, her voice crackling in the phone's earpiece. "Did Thomas lord it over everyone?"

Muller smiled. Typical Mathilda, he thought; direct and acerbic.

"Of course," he said. "But the ceremony itself was nice; you would have enjoyed that part. Little Klaus slept through the whole thing and both mum and father were proud as peacocks."

Muller heard her sigh.

"I wish I'd been there for them, at least," she said softly. "How's father doing, really?" Muller gave her a brief description and they exchanged hopes for Karl's recovery.

"But I want to know how you are, sweet sister," Muller asked in a jaunty tone. "Still out-lapping the boys in the laboratory?"

There was a pause on the other end of the line and Muller feared they might have lost the connection.

"Yes, and it's not so funny, Paul. I am so sick of being patronized and belittled by those fatheads, until they have to solve some really hard problem, turn to me to get it done–which I can usually do–then take credit for it themselves and go back to treating me like a leper. Arghh."

Muller could see Mathilda in his mind's eye shaking her head and making a face.

It had been a recurring feature of Mathilda's life that she tended to be smarter than the people around her. But, because she was a woman, she often wasn't taken seriously, or found her path blocked. Growing up, she'd shown an exceptional aptitude for finance–a lot more so than either him or Thomas; but Karl Muller–even though he loved his daughter dearly–was adamant in his refusal to permit her to join the family banking business. It just wasn't a woman's role, he'd declared.

Mathilda had been deeply angered and frustrated by what she'd viewed as unfair treatment, but then she'd developed a passion for the mysteries of physics, at which she excelled. She'd gone off to the University of Chicago which had one of the world's most advanced physics programs, graduated with high honors and been awarded a research fellowship. She'd married a fellow Physicist, Emil, an Italian, who seemed to adore her, given birth to a daughter, now a toddler, and continued to devote herself to exploring the arcane and mysterious world underlying Einstein's laws.

Muller, as had often been his role, comforted his sister and tried to cheer her up, reassuring her of his confidence in her abilities and his belief that she'd succeed.

"The world around us is changing," he said. "Cutting edge science like you're involved in is part of that, and I'm sure you'll get to play a big role in whatever happens."

Muller could hear Mathilda sigh.

"Paul, it's always so reassuring to speak with you," she said. "Yes, there are in fact big things afoot here–some that I can't even share with you–and I am, as you put it, at the cutting edge of what's going on. So, I guess I'll find a way; but it's still hard. Take care of father."

Muller placed the receiver back on its holder. Glancing outside at the garden, he could see that the reception was ending, with guests taking their leave. He'd decided he didn't want to stay the night and endure what would surely be, at best, a tense evening sparring with Thomas. There were hourly trains back to Bern, so he mounted the stairs toward his old boyhood room, intending to put his things in his overnight bag.

As he was doing so, Oskar appeared at his doorway.

"Mr. Paul," he said, "your father would like to speak with you. He's occupying Mathilda's old room with all of the paraphernalia he needs."

"Certainly," said Muller, "and thanks to you and Greta for all the help you're providing to him and to mum."

Karl Muller was seated in an armchair at the window; he looked less infirm out of his wheelchair, even though his left side was still stooped. Muller came to him and rested his hand on Karl's before pulling up the nearby ottoman.

"A little worn out, father?" he asked. "It's been a long day."

Karl nodded. "It's also hard to witness your own slide into irrelevance," he said gazing out at the trees and the lake beyond.

"I led the bank for over thirty years and now it belongs to Thomas. He made that clear today, didn't he?" It wasn't a question. "I felt a little like the corpse at my own funeral."

Karl waved away Muller's protestations.

"We both know what's happening," he said. "Maybe I'll find more satisfaction learning what you're up to than I do watching Thomas dismantle my legacy."

Karl shifted in his seat and turned his gaze on Muller.

"Did anything come of Hausamann's plan to offer you as bait for intelligence in Geneva?" he asked. Karl had been deeply involved in Swiss government affairs as one of half a dozen private sector leaders that served as important, though unofficial, advisors to the Federal Council. He had introduced Muller to Hausamann and encouraged Muller's involvement with Büro Ha. They had discussed Hausamann's plan before the stroke had laid Karl low.

Muller nodded and summarized his meetings with the British agents in Geneva.

"I'm to return to Bern and await Minister Minger's instructions on how to assess signs of weaknesses in the German economy and our vulnerability to the likely British blockade and embargo."

Karl stroked his chin with his right hand, considering what Muller had told him.

"Well, one weakness the Germans face is the fact that they're nearly broke," Karl said. "They've essentially run out of foreign exchange to pay for the imports they need and most governments–including our own–have refused to issue them new credits. So they've begun to conduct black market transactions, bribing banks and other sources of finance to extend credit lines to them."

Karl curled his good right hand into a fist.

"Your brother is playing in that game," he said, glaring at Muller. "He's earning big fees and probably pocketing bribes for himself–not the bank–that the German buyers are paying for the new credits. But those credit lines are liabilities on our balance sheet. Germany doesn't have the money to pay us back–at least not now–so the bank is exposed. We've had a couple of major rows about it–but he's in charge, and my hands are tied. I'm confined to that damned wheelchair," he fairly spat the words.

"As to a British blockade," Karl continued, "there's no doubt that we're vulnerable. We're dependent on imports to survive, so keeping access to our suppliers is vital. But the other side of the coin is that the Brits are dependent upon us for some items too."

"Hand me that pad and pencil," Karl said, pointing.

Muller did so, and Karl scribbled, steadying the pad with his knee, then tore off the sheet and handed it to Muller.

"Share this with Hausamann," Karl said. "He can make the arrangements."

Muller smiled at his father. "He'll want you back on the team–as will I."Muller retrieved his overnight bag and bid farewell to both of his parents.

They agreed he'd visit them at Chalet Muller in Grindelwald in August.

CHAPTER 9

Hausamann took the paper Muller handed him.

Muller had returned to Bern from the weekend christening. He'd taken the note his father had scribbled and passed it on to Hausamann as he'd suggested.

"Emil Bührle is the foremost arms producer in Switzerland," Hausamann said. "You may not know his name, Muller, but you surely know his company. It's called Oerlikon."

"Of course," Muller replied, nodding; "It's the also name of the last stop before Zurich on the local trains. You can look out your compartment window and see the giant factory built almost next to the tracks."

So that's where those famous cannons were produced. He'd passed through the Oerlikon station dozens of times and always wondered about what went on inside the forbidding-looking buildings.

The two men were seated in the garden of a small café in Bern, with a view of the Aare riverbank. Dappled sunlight shown through an overhanging plane tree. Small round tables with pale yellow wicker chairs were placed close to one another; but for the moment, they were the only customers.

Hausamann sipped his café-au-lait from a cream-colored porcelain cup, replacing it in the matching saucer before turning toward Muller and returning his crumpled note.

"As your father surmised, I know the man," Hausamann said.

"Bührle's an enigmatic figure," he continued reflectively, "a man of contradictions. He's a hugely successful arms merchant, but also an admirer–and serious collector–of fine art, especially the French impressionists. And he's a native German who regularly deals with party bigwigs, including Goering, and industrialists like Krupp and Thyssen; yet not only is he not a member of the Nazi party, he was even granted Swiss citizenship two years ago."

Hausamann shrugged. "He's somehow able to occupy seemingly conflicting spaces and apparently able to succeed in all of them."

Hausamann accepted Muller's proffer of a Gitane and exhaled a smoke ring.

"He's also had his share of luck," Hausamann continued, "and taken full advantage of it, too."

Muller looked at him quizzically.

"Bührle commanded a machine gun squad during the war, and after the Armistice, his unit was packed off to Magdeburg to help keep the peace. He was quartered in the residence of a prominent local banker–who just happened to have a daughter, whom Bührle proceeded to marry. When he was demobilized, the banker set him up with a job in a tool and die manufacturer which the bank controlled. He apparently did well there, because a few years later, when the company bought a Swiss tool and die manufacturer situated in Oerlikon, he was sent off to run it."

"What happened next gets a little murky," Hausamann said as he stubbed out his cigarette. "It was the early 1920's by then and the German government had begun a covert rearmament program to circumvent the limitations imposed by the Versailles Treaty. A lot of governments were willing to turn a blind eye to what was going on–the Dutch, the Soviets, the Swedes–and of course our own government here in Switzerland. It was rapidly becoming a very lucrative business and they all wanted a piece of it."

Hausamann shrugged. "It's the way things worked, Muller; the Great War was over, but the Treaty had consequences too. Anyway, a Swiss company located in Seeburg acquired the patent to a 20 mm gun developed by a German engineer named Reinhold Becker. The Becker gun design became a world standard for weapons makers and there's every reason to believe this transaction was part of the German covert rearmament effort, though, as I say, details are sketchy. The Seeburg company failed in 1924 and the assets were promptly acquired by the company that Bührle was running in Oerlikon; probably part of the same plan.

"In any event, Bührle appears to have been a very clever engineer and took full advantage of the situation. He used the basic technology of the Becker gun–it's something called API blowback, a cartridge loading system permitting very rapid repeat firing–but he made critical design improvements and developed new Oerlikon 20 mm anti-aircraft cannons which became–and still remain–better than other versions of these weapons. He proceeded to build the factory you see from the train and began large scale manufacturing operations, selling weapons to the French, the Italians, the Japanese, and many other countries."

"So, this began long before Hitler took power," Muller said, "it wasn't part of any Nazi plan."

"That's right," Hausamann said, nodding.

"But it was German policy from 1919 onward to rearm the country above the punitive levels imposed by the Versailles Treaty. The German military wanted weapons, the big companies wanted the business and the labor unions wanted the jobs. So, using a variety of ruses and subterfuges–and generous bribes–Germany proceeded to circumvent the Treaty restrictions and began to build an industrial base for rearmament, a lot of it located outside the country."

"So Oerlikon's a part of that?" Muller asked, "a Swiss company participating in Germany's arms buildup?"

Hausamann pursed his lips, frowning.

"I'm just not clear on that," he said. "Remember, when Bührle began full-scale production, Oerlikon remained a subsidiary of the German Company in Magdeburg that had sent him to run it. So, arguably it was a German company, not Swiss. Then, in 1937, at nearly the same time Bührle became a Swiss citizen, he was suddenly able to purchase Oerlikon and become the sole owner."

"Then what's Oerlikon's role in German rearmament now?" Muller asked, thoroughly confused.

"That's what we're going to discuss when we see him," Hausamann said, standing and taking some coins from his pocket to leave for the waiter. "I'll arrange it."

CHAPTER 10

Muller was struck by the sheer size of the buildings–that and the noise; cacophonous sounds assaulted the senses from all directions.

It was only a few days later and he and Hausamann were inside the giant Oerlikon factory. Bührle had responded almost immediately to Hausamann's request for a meeting and had invited them for a dinner; but he'd insisted that they spend the afternoon at the works so they could experience firsthand the actual weapons production process.

They'd taken the train from Bern and were picked up at Zurich Central Station–the main line didn't stop at Oerlikon–by a car and driver and a short, stout, bespectacled man about forty years old who introduced himself simply as Rudi and explained he was to be their guide.

It was only a short drive to the factory and, as they approached the gate, the car had to slow as a stream of men, roughly dressed, most wearing round cloth caps, converged on the narrow entryway. Rudi explained that there was a new shift was arriving for the forging section, which they would see later. Some of the workmen peered into the car windows, as if curious at who might be coming to pay a visit, but most ignored them and simply trudged toward a workstation where Muller could see they punched cards into a line of time clocks.

The workers dispersed, entering the high-walled factory through a single, wide, sliding door, permitting their car to proceed further into the complex and park in front of a small building with a neat appearance that seemed slightly out of place on the soot-stained factory grounds.

"This is a guest house with a locker room," Rudi explained. "It's a little grimy inside the works, so we've got pullovers for you to slip on and some boots to wear so you don't ruin your clothing and shoes."

Muller and Hausamann found pullovers and boots that fit satisfactorily; they removed their ties and suit jackets, but it was a warm May day and their new uniforms were hot.

Rudi first took them to vast, high-roofed shed where a dozen gondola railcars were lined up to be pushed by a stumpy locomotive onto a heavy black iron device designed to tip them over, so the ore they contained emptied–with a huge crash, and an explosion of dust–into a bin below. Peering down, Muller could see the ore was collected onto a thick black conveyor belt carrying it into another adjacent structure. Rudi beckoned them to follow him and they entered the furnace room. Rudi shouted, so they could hear him over the racket. It was so hot that men had removed their shirts as they shoveled coal into orange-glowing ovens beneath vast structures into which the conveyer belt dumped the ore. Several hundred meters further on, Muller could see a hot reddish liquid emerging from the other end of the furnace where it was captured in huge buckets which descended from the high ceiling. These were moved along trolleys to a point where they were tipped, emptying their fiery liquid into still another looming apparatus that Rudi attempted to explain, but his words were lost in the noise. They moved along to another building.

The tour went on for nearly two hours and Muller found himself utterly confused and disoriented by the unfamiliar surroundings, which were at once dark and shadowy, then brilliantly lit by flames and flares of molten metal. Even though many of the buildings were built with tall windows to admit light– and this was a sunny May afternoon–it never seemed to penetrate far enough to dissipate the shadows or overcome the cavernous size of the structures.

Muller could only grasp a jumbled sense of pipes and fittings, large valves and vast long production lines, where rods were somehow transformed into round tubes that in turn were machined into gun barrels and metal sheets became gun fixtures and ammunition storage drums. Eventually, they entered a laboratory, but even in that comparatively tame environment, experiments were being conducted that emitted showers of sparks and high-pitched bursts of noisy energy. White-coated lab technicians seemed out of place, though everyone went about their business, working at a rapid pace.

It was a jarring experience and Muller was glad when, finally, they exited the last of the big structures, and descended a few steps to the street where a small jitney awaited them. Muller paused to blink in the suddenly bright sunlight. He brushed soot off his coveralls and shook his arms, then patted them, to get rid of what seemed to be a coating of grime, watching Hausamann next to him doing the same. He took a deep breath, then jumped aboard the jitney as Rudi gunned the engine impatiently.

"Pretty confusing and noisy in there," Rudi said over his shoulder as he steered the jitney toward a wide, windowless structure set off by itself several hundred meters away. "But now comes the fun part; this you'll really like," he added laughing.

They entered the building and found themselves standing in a large foyer dominated by oversize photographs of Oerlikon cannons mounted on naval vessels and inside concrete blockhouses; the muzzles seemed to point menacingly at the camera.

A door opened and a slender white lab-coated man strode toward them smiling.

Rudi proceeded to introduce Hausamann and Muller.

"Karl Obermann," said the man as they exchanged handshakes. "I'm the director of this firing range and I'll be helping you test the weapon and show you what it can do."

Good God, Muller said to himself; we're going to be firing a cannon? He sucked in his breath, feeling more than a little uncertain. He'd fired his Swiss Army rifle many times on maneuvers and even used a machine gun a couple of times. But an anti-aircraft cannon?

Obermann handed both Muller and Hausamann what appeared to be earmuffs as he led them along a short corridor.

"These are supposed to help deaden the sound a little," Obermann said. "Oerlikons are pretty loud."

He opened a thick sliding door and motioned for Hausamann and Muller to enter. He flicked a light switch and Muller could see they were standing in a large semi-circular room lit by spotlights from a dark ceiling three stories above them.

Directly in front of them stood a grey Oerlikon 20mm cannon. Its swivel base was securely mounted on the concrete floor and a cartridge belt was already fitted into the loading breech, rising from a full ammunition drum slotted into place on the side of the gun fixture.

It looked smaller than Muller had expected; something called a cannon somehow ought to be bigger, he thought. But it stood at a height just below his shoulders, which made sense, as he could see the braces which the gunner would use to absorb the gun's kick and steady his aim, leaning his shoulders into them and planting his feet. The barrel was narrow and extended a little over two meters from the front of the stubby gun fixture.

Muller looked at it in wonder; what a fierce-looking and compact weapon it was.

Obermann pointed to the semicircular wall across the room from the cannon. "You see that wall is blank. We'll focus a couple of movie projectors on it when we get started and you'll see what appears to be attacking aircraft which will be your targets. You can see the wall is chipped and scarred, that's because you'll be firing live ammunition and the bullets will explode on the wall."

Obermann went to the cannon and set himself in position.

"You'll brace yourself into these shoulder harnesses and set your feet apart to give yourself a firm footing. Then you look through the sight," he gestured, showing them a round circular fixture mounted on the gun. "In front of the sight, you've got this range-finder and aiming mechanism," again he gestured to a second fixture mounted in front of the sight which had a series of circular targeting rings around what seemed to be a bull-eye.

"And here is the trigger," he said, his right-hand index finger curling around the curved metal projection.

"The weapon is effective from as far out as 1.8 km. Easy enough to see with the naked eye through the gunsight, but depending upon how far out your attacker is, you'll need to adjust for speed and direction–and of course, if you're at sea, the ship's pitch in the swells."

"It's not so easy," he added, "and that's why the speed of fire is so important. This SS model is built to fire up to 450 rounds per minute, though in practice, it operates somewhere between 250 and

320 rounds. Each projectile is a 20 calibre high explosive bullet weighing 4.3 ounces. Muzzle velocity is over 800 meters per second."

Obermann looked their way. "That's fast, gentlemen, very fast. What this cannon does is to fire a couple of hundred rounds at an incoming aircraft and create a wall of hot steel that can destroy it. For combat units, we attach vertical steel plates on either side of the gun barrel which protects the gunner from strafing rounds being fired by the aircraft."

Obermann put his hand proudly on the cannon.

"It's a fearsome weapon," he declared.

"Mr. Muller," Obermann said, turning to Muller, "are you ready to test fire?"

Muller put the ear device on his head and approached the cannon a little uncertainly. He spread his feet to give himself purchase, then leaned into the shoulder braces and gripped the aiming handles, his finger off the trigger as he tentatively moved the barrel up and down and from side to side; it was very responsive and he found it easy to maneuver it around, trying to line up the sight and the range finder. Then he pulled the trigger and squeezed off a quick round.

RATATAT! RATATAT! RATATAT!

The noise was so loud Muller jumped. The gun took on life in his hands, bouncing against his shoulders and causing him to reset his feet to keep his balance.

"Whooo!" he said, stepping back. Then he crouched a little lower, spread his feet a bit wider and leaned back into the shoulder braces.

"I'm ready, Mr. Obermann," Muller said. "Send me some planes to shoot down."

Obermann signaled to a control booth behind him; the overhead lights dimmed and the wall before him lit up showing ocean and sky with puffy clouds. Suddenly to his right, Muller caught sight of something indistinct and blurry that suddenly materialized into an aircraft banking out of a cloud and seemingly aiming itself right at him. Christ, it was coming fast, and Muller could see its wing cannons firing at him. He tried to move the sight and the rangefinder onto the streaking plane, but failed to do so before it passed overhead.

Shit!

Then suddenly two more aircraft peeled off and began diving at him. Again, Muller swung the Oerlikon muzzle around to face the attackers and this time he got off two bursts before the planes flashed by overhead.

Muller stepped away from the gun and straightened himself.

"Missed," he muttered, then resumed his position, this time keeping the aiming handles in movement and getting up on the balls of his feet; like preparing to return a tennis serve, he said to himself.

This time, when two attackers dove at him, Muller was ready and locked in on one of the planes, firing a long burst that seemed right on the rangefinders target.

"Got the bastard," Muller said, stepping back again.

Obermann said something to him and Muller realized he couldn't hear a thing. He removed his earmuff.

"The movie won't show a shoot down," Obermann said, "but that looked like a pretty good shot."

Muller tried to shake the ringing out of his ears, then stood aside and watched as Hausamann took his turn.

The two men swapped places over the next half hour or so, excited as kids with a new plaything. Obermann was kept busy slotting new ammunition drums into place, removing the spent cartridge belts and feeding new ones into the loading breech.

Finally, Hausamann and Muller looked at one another, grinned and told Obermann that they were satisfied. They shook his hand, thanked him and walked back outside to find Rudi and his jitney waiting for them.

Returning to the guest house locker room they peeled off their coveralls and washed up to remove the factory grit from their faces and hands. They were able to brush off their suits and white shirts and re-tie their ties, so they looked respectable when Rudi drove them to Bührle's residence, which was on the periphery of the factory and situated in a pine forest with a splendid view across a small lake.

They were escorted toward a terrace behind the stately home where a table had been set for dining *al fresco* to take advantage of a fine May evening. Emil Bührle was seated in a wooden chair with plush colorful pillows and stood to greet them with a welcoming smile.

Muller was immediately struck by his almost movie star good looks: a well-proportioned head with a long, straight nose and a high forehead. His dark hair was drawn straight back, which lent his clean-shaven face special prominence and his level eyebrows, dark above bright blue eyes, conveyed an impression of poise and confidence.

This was not at all the image of a warmongering arms dealer held in popular imagination, Muller thought to himself.

Bührle greeted Hausamann warmly; it was apparent that they were well-acquainted and, in welcoming Muller, expressed his admiration for Muller's father and hopes for full recovery from his stroke.

"I hope your ears aren't still ringing from the firing range," he said, smiling. "That *Oerlikon SS* is a little noisy, but it's a very effective weapon. I wanted you to try it, so you could experience the end product of the large and noisy production process that you saw on your factory tour."

"I'm fine Mr. Bührle," Muller said. In fact, his ears were still ringing a bit and he hoped he wasn't speaking too loudly. "That is quite a weapon," he said admiringly. "And it was remarkable to see how you can construct cannons right here, all the way from the raw ore we saw in the railcars to the precision weapon that we fired. Very impressive."

Hausamann offered similar sentiments and Bührle smiled.

"It's always nice to have two new admirers," he said lightly, "not everyone is well disposed toward my company or my business, as you will surely understand."

A formally attired waiter proffered flutes of champagne from a silver tray and Bührle motioned them to cushioned seats alongside his, next to a small rose garden.

"You told me you wanted to discuss the arms trade," he said to Hausamann when they were seated.

"I'm frankly happier speaking about the mechanics of my products; I'm really just an engineer at heart, and I keep working to streamline and improve the performance of my products. That's where I enjoy myself most, in fact, getting back into the engineering drawings and finding ways to tweak my designs— though I do have confess that I'm also an aficionado of the French impressionists and I've become quite an avid collector.

"In fact, I have a wonderful new Manet that I was able to purchase from a dealer in Lucerne; I'll show it to you after dinner.

"But I suppose I do know a little bit about the arms trade— which is pretty active these days," he added with a smile. "So why don't you tell me what you're looking for."

Muller responded. He and Hausamann had decided he should take the lead in framing the issues.

"We've been advised that the British government believes the German economy is close to collapse," he said. "They're preparing to mount an economic offensive against Germany that they think will push its economy over the edge–which they're convinced will drive Hitler and the Nazi party from power and end the threat of war in Europe. They have informed us that they will force the Swiss government to support their program even to point of bringing down our economy too."

Muller paused a moment.

"Minister Minger has asked us to explore ideas about how Switzerland should respond to this threat. It seemed to us that the weapons trade is likely to play a big role in whatever happens, so we thought–actually my father suggested–that we should engage with you, given your expertise on this issue."

Bührle grinned.

"I should have known," he said. "I'll have to find a way to repay the favor to your father one day when he recovers."

The waiter returned to refill their champagne flutes and pass a tray of hors d'oeuvres, including, Muller was happy to see, viande des Grisons wrapped around small cornichons.

Bührle waited until the waiter withdrew.

"There's no doubt that Germany faces serious economic issues," he said. "Hitler's rearmament program is hugely expensive and is eating up resources that ordinarily would go to improve things like housing and hospitals and better living standards for ordinary Germans."

"But on the edge of collapse?" Bührle shook his head. "It's true that most food and clothing–even shoes–are rationed, and there are real shortages," he went on, his brow furrowed in thought. "I suppose that if companies were unable to pay weekly wages and people couldn't buy food to feed their families..." his voice drifted off, "but even then..."

Bührle paused again, then resumed, this time in a firmer voice. "You gentlemen have been there; Germany's a police state. Anyone overheard criticizing Hitler, or the Nazi leadership, gets shipped off to a camp. Dissent simply isn't tolerated. Any overt resistance to the state–even in the face of starvation–would be crushed."

Then he paused again, his brow furrowing once more.

"But that would take a toll, wouldn't it, and at a minimum weaken Hitler's hand. So maybe the British are on to something," he finished.

Muller wondered if the arms manufacturer believed that.

Bührle stood.

"I really hadn't thought about a situation like that," he said. "I'm not much of an expert on political science; I seem to remember that was your field of study, Mr. Muller," he said. "So, I'll lob that one back in your court. Let's move to the table for some dinner; I hope turbot is to your taste; it's the season."

As Muller took his seat and removed his white linen napkin from its silver holder, he took note of the fact Bührle seemed to know more about him than he would have expected; his course of study at Cambridge had in fact been political science and he was a keen and reasonably competent tennis player.

Hmmm.

Conversation over dinner was desultory as waiters delivered the meal and poured the wine–a 1932 Vosgros premier cru Chablis, Muller noted admiringly.

Bührle and Hausamann both visited Germany for business on a regular basis and they bantered with one another about the difficulties of dealing with Nazi officials, though it was evident they were being circumspect in the presence of the staff.

Muller decided to change the subject.

"Mr. Bührle," he said, "you said earlier that you're an admirer–and a collector–of impressionist art. How did that come about?"

Bührle smiled broadly.

"You're thinking that it's a little incongruous that a German weapons engineer would be captivated by French impressionists," he said with a chuckle.

Muller nodded and smiled. "Is there a story you'd like to share about that?"

"Love at first sight," Bührle responded, clearly delighted to pursue the subject.

"In 1913, I visited Berlin for the first time–what an eye-opener that was for a young man from southern Germany; I was dazzled by the cosmopolitan swirl of the place and tried to absorb everything. There was an exhibition of impressionist paintings at the National Gallery–it was the very first time an impressionist collection had ever been shown in Germany and it had become very controversial. So, of course, I had to go see it for myself."

Bührle's eyes sparkled and he smiled broadly.

"I was absolutely smitten," he said. "There were Monet's haystacks and Renoir's revelers–works by Cezanne, Van Gogh, Manet and others who are now so famous–all right there, just a meter away as I stood in front of them."

He sighed, pausing in quiet recollection.

"They just seemed to come alive for me, Mr. Muller," he said finally. "The light, the color, the inspired brushstrokes that seemed to leap off the canvases. It really was love at first sight," he repeated. "And it is incongruous," added with a deprecating shrug. "My mind works on planes and angles and mechanical progressions; that's how engineers think. But somehow, this medium–the ephemeral sense of light and movement–seized my imagination and opened my mind to a wholly new and different experience.

"I visited the exhibition at least a half dozen times during my stay and each time I came away dazzled and inspired."

Then he looked up and his expression changed.

"But then, six months later we went to war." he said, and shrugged, signaling a waiter to open another bottle of Chablis.

"I was busy fighting in the trenches," he said flatly. "There wasn't much about that experience that was remotely artistic."

"After the war, you resumed your interest?" asked Muller.

"Not right away," Bührle responded. "My wife and I moved here to Zurich in the 1920s when I began running Oerlikon. Sometime thereafter I made the acquaintance of Toni Aktuaryus, who owns a prominent art gallery here.

"You must know him, Mr. Muller, having grown up in Zurich–or at least know the name."

"Only by reputation," Muller responded. "My interests were musical," he added. "I was performing choral music and I'm afraid I didn't pay much attention to the art world."

"Well, no matter," said Bührle with a dismissive wave. "I was pretty busy at the time too, redesigning those Becker cannons. But I would occasionally visit the Aktuaryus Gallery; ultimately I became friendly with Toni, who was very keen on the impressionists and, over time, gave me a broader understanding of the movement and of the also of post-impressionists–including some of the fine German work that was being produced at the time. So, it became a bit of a hobby of mine, but only as an observer."

"Then two things happened," he went on. "First, I bought this grand home," he gestured toward the graceful structure, "and I decided that it would be a suitable host to fine art. Second, after the Nazis took control of Germany, fine art became available to purchase, often at very affordable prices. So, I began to collect pieces that appealed to me–especially the impressionists."

Bührle paused.

"I can see your look of disapproval, Mr. Muller," he said in a conversational tone, but with a sharp glance in Muller's direction.

Muller squirmed in his chair before responding, then returned Bührle glance. "I've been a witness to Nazi looting of artwork owned by Jews, and I find it a very ugly process."

"As do I," Bührle replied quickly. "Ugly and, frankly, uncivilized."

"But it's happening," Bührle added. "Aktuaryus couldn't get access to much of the good stuff until the Nazis began forcing Jews to sell their assets; Jewish galleries in Paris and New York controlled most of the business. Now Jews in Germany and what used to be Austria and Czechoslovakia either surrender their artwork to the Nazis or smuggle it out to Switzerland and put it up for sale to try and save their skins."

"So, in 1936, I was able to purchase three wonderful pieces, a Renoir, a Degas and a Utrillo from Aktauryus. Then Fischer's and Rosengart's, both fine galleries in Lucerne, began getting impressionist works too; they all implored me to buy these splendid pieces. Of course, they wanted the commissions and they happily pocketed the profits. But, in some cases, they were also trying to help the sellers, who desperately needed hard currency from sales of their artwork to try and bribe their way out of Germany."

Bührle shrugged.

"It's not pretty," he said quietly, "but it's the time we live in, Mr. Muller. I also like to think that my acquisitions will help preserve them by keeping them out of the hands of the Nazis."

Muller nodded, and decided to drop the subject; Bührle had made his point and there was no point in belaboring it.

CHAPTER 11

After the last of the dessert plates were cleared and a decanter of cognac placed on the table alongside three large snifters, Bührle lifted the top of a glass cigarette container, offering a selection of brands, even British Pall Malls, which were hard to come by in Switzerland. Hausamann was first with his lighter.

"Let's return to the arms trade," Bührle said, waving smoke away.

"I know about your Büro Ha and its intelligence role for the Swiss government, so, I'll speak candidly to you gentlemen about matters that I deem highly confidential and trust you to use the information discreetly.

"Among other things," he added, directing a glance toward Muller, "selling weapons to belligerents in time of war is deemed by many to violate strict rules of neutrality. Since Swiss policy–indeed, probably the rationale for its very existence as a nation–is premised upon maintaining strict neutrality, that's something government advisors like yourselves doubtless keep in mind when you look at the Swiss arms trade–especially a political scientist like you, Mr. Muller."

"As for me, I'm just an engineer who likes to design and build guns, and then sell them; I'm not so concerned who buys them, as long as they pay my price."

Bührle tapped the ash from his cigarette into a white china ashtray that had been placed before him.

"Sometimes the arms trade is a complicated business," he went on. "Take Germany, for example. I can't break into that market at all; I've had no exports to Germany for years. Surprising, right?"

Bührle spread his hands.

"I'm selling cannons to the French, the Japanese, the Swedes and lots of other people but not to the Germans. Even big bribes don't work–and believe me I've tried. So, what's the answer?" Bührle cocked an eyebrow at them.

"Simple. Rheinmetall in Dusseldorf is the main supplier of 20mm cannons to the German military," he went on, answering his own question. "And who controls Rheinmetall? A corpulent fellow named Hermann Göering, Hitler's deputy and head of the Gestapo.

"Göering pays me handsomely to submit sample Oerlikon cannons to the German Ordnance Department that routinely fail the Department's automatic firing tests. So, there's never any thought given by German procurement officials to switching production orders from Rheinmetall to Oerlikon. That way the cash flow Rheinmetall generates for Herr Göering continues uninterrupted."

Bührle ground out his cigarette in the ashtray, "Of course, there's a lot more to it," he went on. "At Göering's suggestion, I also set up a company in the Ruhr called Ikaria Gesellschaft für Flugzeugzubehör mbH and I transferred Oerlikon technology to it, so it could produce cannons there under a different name. I handed Göering a majority ownership interest in the company and its sample cannons routinely pass German Ordnance tests with flying colors. The company has been awarded very large production orders for the Wehrmacht, so Ikaria makes a lot of money for its majority owner; but Herr Göering also sees to it that I'm paid a royalty on every weapon that it sells."

"Now those payments are a pretty big deal just in themselves, gentlemen. Foreign suppliers are supposed to receive only 60 percent of their bills in Reichsmarks, with the balance being paid in German tax credits."

"At least, that's what they're called," Bührle said dismissively, passing the brandy decanter around.

"In reality, they're just IOUs–non-interest-bearing government paper that's unfunded and currently worthless. But my royalties are paid right on time and in Reichsmarks."

Bührle was clearly enjoying himself. Muller was fascinated, trying to keep things straight in his mind. He glanced over at Hausamann whose face bore an expression of bemused concentration.

"But the most important thing Göering does for me," Bührle went on, "is to ensure that Germany exports the kind of high-grade iron ore that I need to produce my cannons here in the factory you visited today."

Bührle turned toward Muller again.

"You mentioned earlier seeing the gondola cars that deliver the ore to our furnaces during your tour; remember?"

Muller nodded.

"Did you also notice that they were all marked *Deutsche Reichsbahn*, German Railways? No? Well they were; all of that ore comes from Germany. It's the place that I'm most vulnerable," he said. "I'm entirely dependent upon ore imported from Germany to manufacture my cannons here. No ore, no metal, no production. Very simple; without it, Oerlikon would be out of business."

"But Göering makes sure I get my weekly iron ore deliveries without fail–even though they enable me to build cannons that I sell to a lot of other countries–even if not to Germany–and in fact to some of its adversaries."

Out of habit, Muller opened his cigarette case and offered his Gitanes, but the others declined and took Pall Malls out of the glass container. Hausamann again provided the lighter, but as he did so, he shook his head and made a hand gesture to slow down.

"Mr. Bührle," Hausamann said, exhaling a large pall of smoke. "You deal in weapons, my company builds military optical products; we travel in similar circles and we both have to navigate..." he hesitated, "how shall I put it...similar commercial challenges in dealing with Nazi officials.

"You need Germany to export iron ore for the Oerlikon factory here; Optikalwerke, my company, needs highly refined industrial coating solutions, derived from German coal, to apply to our rangefinders and a host of our other military instruments."

"But permission to export the products to Optikalwerke needs is uniformly denied," he said. "German rules are stacked against almost any form of export trade; officials are strictly forbidden to issue licenses for us to buy German coating products. So, we've been forced to resort to the black market and to pay exorbitant fees to smugglers in order to get our hands on even a fraction of the quantities we really need.

"Yet you're telling us that Oerlikon freely buys German iron ore, notwithstanding the rules against German exports."

Bührle smiled broadly.

"Not so freely," he said, "it's damned expensive; but yes, we receive our orders without any interference.

Bührle leaned forward and laid his arms on the table, and continued to smile, clearly savoring the moment.

"As I'm sure you remember, Hausamann," he said, "the rules prohibiting exports are set by the German Ministry of Economic Affairs, and you will remember–both of you, I expect–that Hitler appointed Göering as head of that Ministry some time ago.

"Our boy Hermann is a very busy fellow these days," Bührle added with a smile.

Muller nodded; he had read an article somewhere speculating that appointing Göering as the head of MKW, as the Ministry was known, was part of a plan by Hitler to weaken the influence of the Reichsbank and its longtime Chairman Hjalmar Schacht. He put the thought aside and refocused on what Bührle was saying.

"I'm sure you'll understand that it's not so difficult for the Minister of MKW to manipulate the regulations enough to ensure timely shipment of German iron ore to Oerlikon.

"You're wondering why he would do that," Bührle said teasingly, pointing a finger at Hausamann. "Why do it for iron ore to Oerlikon but not for optical coatings to Optikalwerke?

"Once again, very simple," Bührle said, sitting up straighter in his chair, the smile gone.

"When Oerlikon gets the invoice for each shipment of ore we receive–which, by the way, is always a very costly invoice–I direct payment via Telex through one of our Swiss private banks to an account at a counterpart German bank in Munich.

"Again, as you know, Hausamann, MKW regulations are absolutely clear: payment for any German exports must be deposited in a special account at Reichsbank. Foreign exchange is very scarce in Germany these days and the Reichsbank is supposed to control every hard currency payment that foreign buyers make for the German exports they've purchased."

"Somehow, though, I suspect that the Swiss francs Oerlikon pays to the German bank in Munich for our purchases of iron ore don't wind up in that special Reichsbank account," Bührle said, his smile returning.

"Instead, they wind up in Göering's pocket, or at least under his control. It's his foreign exchange piggy bank. So, he's perfectly happy to keep supplying the iron ore Oerlikon needs to build our cannons, in return for the millions of Swiss francs that we pay for the privilege, which wind up at his disposal, free from Reichsbank interference, to use as he sees fit.

"Am I passing your 'strict neutrality' rules so far, Mr. Muller?" Bührle said with a smile, passing the decanter of cognac around again.

"I've saved the best for last," he continued, evidently not expecting a reply from Muller–then paused at a sudden rumble of thunder. Raindrops began falling and a cool breeze announced a change in weather.

"It's still May, isn't it," he said. "I think we'd better retreat inside," which they proceeded to do, hurriedly.

Bührle led them into what was apparently his study, a comfortable room lined with bookshelves, a desk at one end in front of tall windows and leather easy chairs placed on either side of a fireplace. Plush oriental rugs lent a warm appearance as Bührle switched on the lights.

He gestured them toward the easy chairs, glancing at his watch.

"There's still some time before your train back to Bern," he said. "Another cognac won't hurt," he said, refilling their snifters from the decanter.

"Are any of you acquainted with Dickie Mountbatten?" he asked, resuming their conversation once they were settled.

Hausamann and Muller shook their heads.

"Well, Dickie–or more formally, Prince Louis Mountbatten–is part of the British Royal family, but he's also a career British naval officer and has become one of their top experts in anti-aircraft weaponry. I met him at a gunnery exhibition several years ago and introduced him to my 20mm Oerlikon SS cannon. He immediately recognized it as the gold standard weapon for use against aircraft attack and he tried to persuade the Admiralty to introduce it into the Royal Navy. But for years he met no success; Vickers has an anti-aircraft gun that the Navy had been using for years–a much inferior weapon, mind you–but it's British-made, and a product the Navy was accustomed to. Dickie was repeatedly rebuffed in his attempts to overcome the built-in prejudice favoring the Vickers; no one was prepared to buck the system, so his efforts–with my assistance, of course–to switch over to the Oerlikon SS failed, despite its clear superiority."

"Until, last year," Bührle continued. "A new Sea Lord was appointed to take over the Admiralty–Sir Roger Backhouse–who just happened to be one of Dickie's close chums. Dickie proceeded to exercise his considerable charm on Backhouse and bombarded him with information, pleading with him to shift to the Oerlikon in order to safeguard the fleet against the increasing risk of attack by enemy aircraft.

"And, lo and behold, he finally succeeded." Bührle grinned and spread his hands in mock triumph. "I now have the largest order for the Oerlikon SS that the company has ever received and I'm gearing up to begin a massive production run for the Royal Navy beginning September 1, just a few months away.

Bührle paused and put his hands together in his lap.

"Leverage," he said, with a straight face.

Muller and Hausamann exchanged glances.

Leverage indeed, Muller thought to himself, picturing in his mind how much he would enjoy informing Jimmy West that, sorry, Switzerland would need to cancel the Royal Navy's order for Oerlikon's anti-aircraft cannons if Britain levied excessive demands against the Swiss economy.

Ha!

"Actually, there's a bit more to it," Bührle continued. "The Admiralty has signaled that it wants to negotiate a license with me, where I would transfer my technology to them in order to arrange production of the guns in England. Ordinarily, that's not something that I would be willing to consider; but given the threat of war these days, I've agreed to do a deal with the Royal Navy. But I suspect the Swiss Government would forbid me from doing that if it were locked in an economic struggle for survival with the British government.

"Oh," Bührle added, as if it were an afterthought, "I'm also in negotiations with the Americans–both to produce cannons for the US Navy and to license my technology to them as well."

He smiled impishly.

"Now you're the political scientist among us, Mr. Muller," Bührle said, "but I have a hunch that the very last thing the British government wants to do at this moment in time is to annoy the American government–as would likely happen if Swiss authorities were to order me to break off these negotiations because of British economic warfare against Switzerland."

"So," he said, raising his snifter to Muller and Hausamann, "a toast: to leverage."

They stood and clinked their snifters.

CHAPTER 12

Back in Bern a few days later, Muller was summoned to the Ministry by Roger Masson. His office, like Minister Minger's, was small and spare; wall shelving was piled with neatly stacked documents and there was barely room for a small conference table next to Masson's desk.

It was very much a working office, Muller thought to himself, approvingly.

Masson seemed only slightly less intense than he had appeared in their earlier meeting. His pipe was firmly clamped in his mouth and his dark eyes flashed behind his glasses; but his features softened a bit as he greeted Muller with a handshake and a small smile of welcome.

"Hausamann gave me a brief report on your meeting with Bührle," he said, gesturing Muller to a seat. "It will be interesting to see how your friend Eden and this new British Ministry react to the news that economic warfare can be a two-way street. Especially since they drive on the wrong side of the road."

Well, at least he has a sense of humor, Muller thought to himself, smiling back.

Masson reached for a file on his desktop and opened it.

"Minister Minger had a talk with Frederich Fischer at the Swiss National Bank," he said, "and I have the name of their expert on the German economy who is expecting to hear from you."

Masson paused before glancing oddly at Muller.

"The contact is a woman," he said, glancing at the open file, "named Hildegard Magendanz.

"I wasn't sure if I should share this background with you, but I guess you need to know what you're getting into. She's apparently difficult to work with. She's said to be smart and very well informed about Germany, but she doesn't know her place and none of the bankers in Zurich could stand working with her. So, a decision was made to exile her here to SNB's Bern office. When the Zurich bankers get stuck on some issue involving Germany and decide they need help, someone will send her a written message or–in dire circumstances–take the train down from Zurich to meet with her in person; but no one likes doing that, because she's always overbearing and dismissive.

"I'm sure you've met women like that; they're very annoying." Masson handed the file document to Muller.

"You said she's good at her work?" Muller asked.

Masson nodded. "Fischer told the Minister that she's an encyclopedia; she knows Germany inside and out–Switzerland too, apparently. But she's a real pain."

Muller took the single sheet with the form from the file and folded it, placing it in his breast pocket.

"Anything for the cause," Muller said with a smile. "Would you kindly have your secretary call and make an appointment for me to visit Miss Magendanz's office tomorrow morning at 10AM?"

CHAPTER 13

The Bern office of the Swiss National Bank occupied a corner suite on the second floor of the Swiss Ministry of Finance. The Ministry building itself was among Bern's most impressive structures, its broad façade featuring neo-gothic columns rising between tall windows.

When Muller entered through the wide, iron clad doorway, he found himself in a large two-story lobby with a highly polished tile floor and two sweeping white marble staircases on either side leading up to the reception area. Flags of the thirteen Swiss cantons hung below a balcony that jutted out between the two stairways. Looking up as he mounted the staircase on his left, Muller could see a vaulted ceiling with decorative skylights that conveyed a sense of brightness and warmth and seemed to soften the stark appearance of the entryway.

At the top of the stairs, a large brass sign reading 'Swiss National Bank' led to a corridor on Muller's right. Two tall metal doors opened to a wide and open high-ceiling room with ranks of desks symmetrically arranged, one after another several meters apart; decorative lighting fixtures were suspended above the desks. There must have been a dozen of them, Muller estimated, each occupied by a man wearing a white shirt and dark suit poring over books and records. White-curtained windows on one wall were open to let in air and Muller noted that two round fans oscillated at either end of the room, their purring sound blending with the murmur of men speaking on the telephone and the clack of typewriters from the typists, all women, who were seated in rows at the back of the room.

A balding man with pince-nez glasses was seated at polished desk to Muller's right as he entered. The man stood and bowed as Muller approached him.

"I have an appointment to see Hildegard Magendanz. My name is Paul Muller," he said, modulating his voice to accommodate the hushed atmosphere of the large room.

The man nodded and picked up a black telephone. After speaking a few words, he hung up and beckoned Muller to follow him as he led the way to a frosted glass enclosure. A sign on the door read 'Director'. The man knocked once, then opened the door and motioned for Muller to enter. A dark-suited man with black hair parted in the middle rose from behind a large desk, reaching out to shake Muller's hand then gestured him to be seated in an armchair beside the desk.

"Welcome, Mr. Muller," he said in a quiet voice. "It isn't often we're visited by representatives of the Ministry of Military Affairs– and a meeting with Miss Magendanz at that."

"I'm Director of this branch of SNB; my name is Otto Stübe and I'm instructed to take you to her office. It's very unusual to have women employed at a banking institution and we've set aside separate facilities for them, in order to avoid any interference with normal banking activities."

"It permits us to maintain appearances," he added with a solemn expression; "I'm sure you understand. I'm also instructed to offer you any assistance that you may require in the event Miss Magendanz cannot meet your needs."

Stübe rose to his feet; it was apparent that he was anxious to put this task behind him.

"Please follow me," he said, leading Muller to a doorway at the very rear of the office space. Using a key, he opened a dark wooden door and gestured for Muller to proceed him down a flight of stairs–the emergency fire exit, Muller supposed–to another door. He rapped on it, then opened it and gestured Muller to enter.

"I am upstairs, if you require my services," Stübe said, retreating back up the stairway.

Muller found himself in a low-ceilinged room lined with bookshelves and filing cabinets. Three desks faced the doorway where he stood, each occupied by a woman.

The woman at the first desk, directly in front of him, looked up from a stack of papers.

"Mr. Muller, I presume," she said matter-of-factly. "We were told to expect you."

The woman stood, as kind of an afterthought it seemed to Muller. She was of medium height, wore large black-rimmed glasses that made her look owlish, and had straight black hair that hung in uncombed tangles on either side of her oval face. Her face bore no trace of makeup and she wore no lipstick.

"I'm Hildegard Magendanz," she said in a flat tone. "These are my colleagues, Helga and Beatrice."

The other two women stood and curtsied; both wore their greying hair in Germanic buns, Muller noted.

Magendanz made no motion of extending a handshake, but came around the desk and led Muller across the crowded room toward a break in the ranks of file cabinets where she opened a door leading to another room and entered before him, switching on bright ceiling lights that illuminated a conference room, with a gleaming, highly-polished oval table surrounded by a dozen or so padded armchairs. Stacked on the table were over a dozen white cardboard document boxes, each neatly secured by black elastic fasteners.

Magendanz positioned herself at one end of the conference table as Muller walked to the center of the room, eying the document boxes uncertainly.

"The President of our bank, Mr. Fischer, sent me a message several days ago telling me to expect you," she said, in the same flat tone of voice. "His message was to the effect that the Ministry of Military Affairs wished to understand the German economy better in order to assess whether it suffered from any weakness that might be exploited. I am the Bank's expert on Germany and I was instructed to make my research available to you—I had assumed that you might be accompanied by others, as this is a large topic," she added—"but in any case, my colleagues and I prepared these document binders which are organized on a sectoral basis and will provide our best and most current information on the current condition of the German economy."

Magendanz betrayed no emotion as she spoke and kept her eyes fixed on the boxes, as if she were speaking to them, not to Muller; her face was expressionless.

"This is the office where we receive visitors since our own quarters are not suitable. Smoking is permitted," she went on taking two glass ashtrays from a shelf and placing them on the table.

"We request that you do not remove your jacket while you are working; appearances are important here at the bank. You may turn on the corner fan," she gestured to a standing fan to Muller's left.

"Kindly knock at the connecting door when you wish to leave."

She turned briefly to face Muller. He could see her body was rigid under a shapeless, grey dress, and her fists were clenched.

"I'm sure you'll find everything you need in the materials we've prepared," she said, then curtsied and walked to the connecting door, closing it firmly behind her.

Muller stood a moment, uncertain of what to do next. Then he sat in the nearest armchair, carefully placing the leather briefcase he'd brought along on the floor next to him. He absently fished a Gitane from the pocket of his suit jacket, lit it with his lighter and inhaled deeply, then blew out a cloud of smoke and pushed back the chair, slumping against the comfortable chair back.

Well! What the Hell am I supposed to do with this kettle of fish, he thought to himself.

He sighed and pulled the nearest stack of file boxes toward him. There were five boxes in the stack, two were labelled 'German Housing', another read 'German Agriculture' and the last two read "German Labor I and German Labor II". He read headings for blue collar and white collar occupations, including breakdowns by regions.

Sliding a file from the next box, he saw that it included sections dealing with borrowings by local municipalities and other public authorities. Another was entitled 'Customs' and contained detailed statistics on collection of customs duties by category of imports and a table of other fees and charges that applied.

Muller spent nearly 90 minutes poring over the documents. There was a total of twenty-eight file boxes, and each one was crammed with tables, graphs, summaries and backup documents; it was an overwhelming amount of information.

Muller felt as if he'd been seated in front of a firehose. There was simply no way he could digest this information and come to any conclusions–let alone figure out a strategy for the ministry. He needed help; that was obvious, and Hildegard Magendanz was the only resource at hand.

But how to enlist her and get her to buy into active cooperation was clearly going to be a challenge. She had put on her best Brunhilde impersonation and made it clear that she had every intention of keeping her distance–remaining behind that impregnable Wall of Fire with the other two Valkyries.

Should he assume the role of Siegfried, Muller mused? That was getting a little too dramatic, he decided. This was Bern, not Bayreuth.

But he had another idea.

Muller rose and knocked on the connecting doorway.

Hildegard opened the door and looked at him with the same flat stare.

"Miss Magendanz, please come in and close the door behind you," Muller said.

She hesitated for just an instant, Muller noted, apparently weighing the impropriety of entering a room alone with a man she didn't know against her determination to remain in charge, and deciding–as Muller expected–to take the risk.

She entered the room and stood defiantly behind the conference table, eyes blazing, her body tense.

Muller chuckled in a relaxed manner and sat down, fixing her with a friendly smile.

"Please sit down," he said in a conversational manner, gesturing to a chair across the table.

"I don't bite," he added genially as she hesitated, "I really don't."

Hildegard regarded Muller a moment, then seated herself, perching archly on the edge of the chair as if ready to flee at a moment's notice, and glared at Muller, letting him know she was not lowering her guard.

"I'd like to share a story with you," Muller said, removing a Gitane from his pack and sliding it across the table toward her, but she shook her head, continuing to glare at him, as Muller flicked his lighter and lit up, placing his cigarette in the ashtray after exhaling.

"It involves a woman named Mathilda," he said, "and I think you may find it interesting."

Hildegard didn't react or change expression.

"Mathilda is about your age, I'd wager," Muller went on, "still early days in her career, but already an accomplished professional; but it was never easy. Mathilda was always smarter than the people around her–smarter than her siblings and the few friends she was able to make–and not ashamed of it, even though it's not supposed to be a girl's place to be smart, let alone smarter than anyone else. She embraced being smart. But the world around here wasn't very accepting of that attitude."

Muller paused and took a drag on his cigarette before replacing it in the ashtray.

Hildegard was eying him closely, the glare now mixed with curiosity.

"Her father was a banker," Muller continued, "but he refused to permit his daughter to have anything to do with the bank, even though she was much more adept with numbers and financial structuring than her oldest brother, whom her father hired and who now runs the bank."

"She was mad as Hell and frustrated," Muller said. "Rejected, just because she was a woman–and by her own father, too."

Muller paused again, drawing on his Gitane and stubbing out the butt in the ashtray.

Hildegard was now leaning forward,

"And what became of her?"

"She went on to study advanced physics," Muller replied, "and excelled at that too. She enrolled at the University of Chicago and today is part of what I'm told is a high-powered team of brilliant physicists doing important work which she can't even discuss."

"So, she succeeded," said Hildegard. "She beat the system; good for her."

She sat back in the chair, and clapped her hands, unclenching her fists. "See? It can be done."

"But, of course not here," she added.

Muller shook his head. "Not there either," he said. "Even though she's a member of this elite research team, she's still treated like a second-class citizen. They only come to her when they're stuck and need help, then take credit for the solution that she–not they–worked out. She's probably the smartest person on the team, but she's a woman and the men won't treat her as an equal."

Muller paused.

"Sound familiar?" he said.

Hildegard looked at him, eyes glistening, chin beginning to tremble.

"How do you know all this?" she asked, almost in a whisper.

"Mathilda is my sister," Muller replied. "We spoke together on an overseas telephone connection just last weekend. She told me–again–how angry and frustrated she gets at being looked down upon and treated with contempt by male counterparts that aren't nearly as smart or clever as she is–just because she's a woman."

"I tried to comfort her and dry her tears over the phone," he said. "But it's hard to do and I'm sure I didn't help enough.

"But I tried," he said. "I've been trying for years."

Muller looked directly at Hildegard.

"I can see what they're doing to you," he said, "It's the same thing. They treat you like a leper and consign you to a cave in the basement, to be trotted out when someone–always a man–who's more important, needs crucial information about Germany that only you possess; then–once you've done your job and saved their bacon–they send you back to the leper colony. I think Mathilda would recognize your predicament."

Muller paused.

"And, so do I," he said quietly.

Tears began streaming down Hildegard's cheeks and she tried to muffle sobs.

"Goddammit," she said as her chest heaved, and she tried to sit up straight. "I can't cry. Women always do; see how weak we are? And the men laugh at us."

"Arghh," she slammed both hands on the conference table in front of her, trying to compose herself.

Muller leaned toward her, handing her his handkerchief.

Hildegard took it, wiped her eyes, then blew her nose and took a deep breath. She folded the handkerchief and placed it in her lap.

"Thank you," she said, smiling at Muller for the first time. "I didn't mean to do that, but I guess I'm just another of those weak women after all."

"I'll launder the hanky and return it," she added.

"And you're right," she went on. "I'm their potted plant; kept in the dark and occasionally trotted out to show someone how smart I am, as you correctly observed."

"Fischer sent a directive through Stübe–no one likes to communicate with me directly, of course–that some big shot from the Ministry of Military Affairs wanted access to my research on the German economy, and we were to cooperate immediately. So, my colleagues and I put these binders together containing all the information you need and stacked them up here on the table," she gestured. "So there you have it."

"My superiors can report back to Fischer that 'the ladies'–as we're delicately referred to–have done what they were told."

She wiped her nose again with the handkerchief then peered at Muller through her owlish glasses with a surprisingly engaging smile.

"But I'm guessing those binders are not very helpful, if you're trying to figure out what to do about Germany–which is what I suppose someone at the Ministry of Military Affairs like you is doing."

Hildegard reached across to Muller's pack of Gitanes and extracted a cigarette which she lit, using his lighter.

"I think your sister and I would have a lot to talk about if we were ever to meet," she went on. "So, if you're the sympathetic brother you say you are, then I'm prepared to cut you some slack."

"But don't mess with me, Mr. Muller," she said gesturing at him with the smoking Gitane in her fingers. "I'll cut you off in a heartbeat. I don't care what they do to me; it can't be much worse than it already is".

She resumed her defiant look and stubbed out the cigarette.

"So, let's start over," she said. "Tell me what you're after."

"Miss Magendanz," Muller began…"

"Oh, for Christ sake call me 'Hilde', she said interrupting. "If we're starting over, let's begin there."

"All right–Hilde," he replied, "I'm Paul, and here's my problem. A few days ago, the British sent a message warning the Swiss government that they are planning to embark upon an all-out campaign to destroy the German economy and its capacity to wage war. They believe that a total trade embargo by Britain and the

Commonwealth, enforced by the Royal Navy, along with drastic sanctions imposed by France and its European neighbors–and, of course, help from the Americans–will bring Germany to its knees. They've even created a new shadow Ministry in London to spearhead this economic offensive."

Hilde was paying rapt attention, her forehead furrowed in concentration.

"And Switzerland gets caught in the crossfire; we become collateral damage," she whispered.

Muller nodded, "They told us–actually, I was the person they selected to receive the message–that they intend to mount an aggressive campaign of economic warfare from all quarters, including severe restrictions on Swiss trade with Germany in goods and services and German access to Swiss financing. The message was that while they understood this could cripple the Swiss economy, that was a price that would have to be paid."

"This was not an invitation to negotiate," Muller added with a tone of bitterness. "The message was that they had reached their decision and that they would force us to comply with it."

Muller paused. "That is the threat we confront, Hilde, and that's why the Swiss Ministry of Military Affairs needs the help of the Swiss National Bank in deciding how to respond."

Muller paused again. "That's why I need your help, Hilde," he said quietly, looking at her with a level gaze.

She returned his gaze, but her face grew animated.

"The British are not crazy in viewing the German economy as vulnerable," she said briskly. "There's a case to be made that it's at a tipping point. And if it were to collapse and bring down the Nazi regime with it, that would probably be a good result. But saying it and doing it are two very different things. And the costs of mounting a campaign of all-out economic warfare would be enormous–and not just to us; the shockwaves would be felt around the world."

Hilde took a deep breath and reached for another Gitane. "I think you'd better tell me the story."

Muller nodded and proceeded to do so; he told her about Stevenson, Jimmy West, the Consul General, the fight–Hilde rolled her eyes but remained still, in deep concentration. He described the British threats and Jimmy West's elaboration on British intentions over breakfast the next morning. He left a few things out–that he'd been dangled in Geneva by Büro Ha and that it was Anthony Eden who'd taken the bait–but he put everything else on the table.

When he'd finished, Hilde sat quietly, her eyes opaque–they were deep blue, Muller noticed–and stared into the middle distance. Her brow furrowed–the look Muller had noticed earlier– and with her right hand she began rubbing her chin, clearly lost in thought.

Muller waited.

Finally, Hilde straightened in her chair raised her face to him and fixed him with a fierce look, blue eyes focused and flashing.

"All right, Mr. Muller—Paul," she corrected herself, but her serious demeanor didn't change—"the German Economic Bureau of the Swiss National Bank—that's my group," again her expression didn't change—"has at its command information concerning economic conditions in both Germany and Switzerland and the interplay of financial and commercial factors that can help the Swiss Ministry of Military Affairs evaluate the threat we face and how to deal with it. So, yes; I can help you."

Hilde paused, eyes still focused on Muller's.

"But it's going to be on my terms," she said, slowly and firmly. "No more potted plant, Paul. I'm your new partner; I'm going to be seen, heard and fully involved. I'm coming out of the cave or the leper colony or whatever you want to call it. I'm going to be a player, out front and as visible as you are. It's either that, or I'm leaving you with the binders here to figure it out for yourself."

Hilde sat back in her chair and crossed her arms across her chest.

Muller leaned forward across the table and grinned. "That's what I hoped you'd say. Terms happily accepted. We need all the help we can get. Welcome aboard."

Muller stood and extended his right hand. Hilde rose and took it, straightening and standing to her full height as they shook hands.

"Done," he said.

"Done, she repeated.

Hilde smiled, but then was all business.

"All right Paul," she said, "here's the first test. You're invited to the reception at the British embassy tonight to mark the arrival of their new Minister, am I correct?"

"Yes," Muller replied, remembering the envelope that Roger Masson had passed him with the invitation a day earlier, telling him that he should plan to attend.

"You as well?" he asked, instantly regretting it.

Hilde snorted, "Of course not; potted plants don't get invited to diplomatic receptions."

"But tonight, I'll be going as your escort," she said, fixing him with a look that brooked no doubt that, indeed, that was what would be happening.

"It'll be my coming-out party, as they say," she smiled broadly. I'll meet you at the entrance to the Hotel Kreuz promptly at 6:00 so we're not late."

Then she checked her wristwatch.

"Plenty of time to get to the hairdresser and beauty salon," she said matter-of-factly and, with a small wave, disappeared through the door back into the basement cave.

CHAPTER 14

A few moments before 6 PM, Muller was standing at the entryway to the Hotel Kreuz under a wide canopy that offered protection from the steady rain that had begun to fall as he had walked the few blocks from his living quarters. He didn't have an umbrella and he'd tried to stay under storefront awnings and building overhangs, but still had gotten wet and he wiped the moisture off the sleeves of his dark suit. At least the event was billed as business attire because his formalwear was safely hanging in the closet of his Geneva apartment.

A shiny, dark blue Renault roadster pulled up to the hotel entrance. The chauffeur exited and walked toward Muller, unfurling an umbrella.

"Mr. Muller? He beckoned Muller toward the back door of the Renault, shielding him from the rain with the umbrella.

The chauffeur opened the door and Muller slipped into the back seat finding himself seated next to a stunning looking woman with hair a mass of ringlets and curls, cheeks just so slightly highlighted and bright red lipstick setting off dark blue eyes that he realized belonged to–Hildegard Magendanz. She was nearly unrecognizable; no owlish glasses or shapeless grey dress. She was clad in a summery sleeveless off-white fitted sheath with a pearl choker around her throat and matching earrings, a dark blue cloak loosely draped over her shoulders.

Muller turned to gape at her in utter shock at the transformation.

Hilde chose to ignore his glances, then laughed.

"You probably think your sister doesn't know how to dress for an event either," she said.

Then she ostentatiously closed the sliding window to the driver.

"Like the car? It's Stübe's. I told him that the ministry big shot demanded that the bank provide its best car to take him to the reception–part of the ministry's plan to counter the German threat."

Muller looked at Hilde with a bemused expression.

"He objected of course, but I told him that, in that event, I would have to inform Fischer that he had refused the ministry's request–so, of course, he immediately backed down. And I certainly didn't tell him that you were escorting me to the reception."

"So here we are, safely out of the rain and in a vehicle entirely appropriate to the seriousness of the initiative we've begun together," she said, throwing her head back and laughing.

Muller laughed too, slapping his hand on his leg, saying to himself, Mathilda would love this; and, he realized, he did too.

The drive to the British residence was only a few blocks and Hilde and Muller were still smiling when the Renault pulled into a circular driveway at the entryway. Muller noted with amusement that other drivers maneuvered their vehicles aside to make room.

The car came to a stop directly in front of steps leading to a tall doorway, and a British Marine stepped forward to open the door, a white-visored cap setting off his deep blue dress uniform with its red ornamental sash. He snapped to attention and opened a large umbrella to cover both Muller and Hilde as they stepped out of the car and entered the large red brick building redolent of British architecture.

It was evident that the plan had been to hold the reception outside on the lawn to the rear of the building, but the clouds and chilly rain that had swept down from the Bernese Oberland had forced the party indoors. Muller decided that it had become too uncomfortable outdoors even for the resolute British, renowned as they were for garden parties carried off in mist and rain, everyone gamely clutching umbrellas, cheerfully determined to ignore the elements.

The new British Minister, Sir David Kelly, his wife Marie-Noel at his side, greeted guests in a smallish hallway that was cramped and a bit crowded. When Mr. Paul Muller of the Swiss Ministry of Military Affairs and Miss. Hildegard Magendanz of the Swiss National Bank were announced by the white-tied embassy staffer, they were only able to exchange perfunctory greetings with their hosts before being ushered into the main reception room. It was a large, elegantly appointed space, with ivory-colored walls augmented by bas-relief panels edged in gold leaf.

Muller surveyed the room where knots of diplomats and wives were mingling and caught sight of Minister Minger and his deputy, Roger Masson, standing by the doorway to what appeared to be a study, next to a floor-to-ceiling bookshelf.

Muller nudged Hilde.

"It's time to meet my Minister," he said, steering her toward the study.

Minger and Masson turned to face them, both with expectant looks appraising Hilde.

"Minister Minger, Mr. Masson, may I introduce Miss Hildegard Magendanz, Director of the German Economic Bureau of the Swiss National Bank.

Minger smiled. "It's a pleasure to meet you, Miss Magendanz," he said, bowing to kiss her hand in a formal manner.

Hilde nodded and, as she did so, turned toward the bookshelf at Minger's shoulder and began speaking to him in a low voice that Muller had trouble hearing above the buzz of conservation in the room.

What was she saying? She was addressing Minger in some kind of heavily accented French dialect that he couldn't decipher.

Minger's face lit up and he responded eagerly, leaning toward the bookshelf too, so both of their backs were to Masson and Muller as they began conversing together.

Masson was biting hard on the stem of his pipe, with a sour expression on his face.

"This is the difficult Bank lady?"

"This is the smart Bank lady," Muller replied.

Masson's expression didn't change, but he took a step back to look more closely at Hilde and Minger who were continuing their animated conversation, nodding and smiling at one another as if old friends.

"Well at least she has a nice ass," Masson said.

Christ! Muller said to himself, biting his tongue.

But he did have to admit that Hilde did have a nice figure that the ivory sheath showed off to her advantage.

He decided not to respond to Masson's comment and turned to examine the room, which was becoming more crowded. Across the way, he caught sight of Alexandru Muntenau, the Romanian Chargé d'Affaires, a short, rotund, balding man whom Muller had gotten to know in Geneva and whom he found both witty and agreeably indiscreet for a diplomat. They'd met for dinner one night in April just after Germany and Romania had announced a bilateral economic agreement which had ceded control of key elements of the Romanian economy to Germany and had been widely criticized.

Muntenau had cheerfully agreed that the agreement was wholly one-sided.

"But Mr. Muller," he'd said with a smile, holding out his glass for more Muscadet, "when you have the misfortune to be little

Romania, situated so close to Germany, a very much larger country that keeps gobbling up its neighbors–Austria, the Sudetenland, the rest of Czechoslovakia, and now threatening to do the same to Poland–making a few economic concessions seems like a small price to pay to preserve our independence."

"Let's play for time," Muntenau had added, draining his glass and holding it out for another round. "A lot of us think Hitler's playing a losing hand."

Muller had not thought back to the conversation for some time. But remembering it now, he realized that Muntenau had gone on to make essentially the same argument as the British were making now.

"Look at the bigger picture, Muller," he'd said. "If the British, the French, the Soviets and the Americans finally get together and decide that Hitler's got to go–that he's too much of a loose cannon and likely to start a war that no one wants–they can take him down, and pretty quickly too. I don't know when that's going to happen," he'd added, "but when it does, Hitler will be swept aside." Muntenau had swept his right arm over his head in a dramatic gesture, still holding the wineglass.

"We're gambling that it happens sooner rather than later and that we don't have to pay a stiffer price in the meantime than that silly economic agreement."

Reflecting on the conversation, Muller wondered what Muntenau was thinking now, a few months later, and made a mental note to buttonhole him later.

By then, Hilde and Minger had finished their private conversation and they turned back to face Muller and Masson, their faces wreathed in smiles. Minger even draped his arm over Hilde's shoulder–an almost parental gesture of affection, Muller thought.

"How splendid that Miss Magendanz is able to join our team," Minger said; "She'll be a real asset. Good recruiting job, Muller. She told me how persuasive you were."

Minger removed his arm from Hilde's shoulder and rubbed his hands together, looking at both Hilde and Muller in mock anticipation.

"I look forward to getting information that we can use to push back against both the British and the Germans," Minger said. "I'm tired of their antics."

Then his eyes suddenly narrowed as he glanced up. "Pilet-Golaz just walked in," he said in a low tone. "That milk toast won't push back against anyone.

"I don't want to have to humor him, so Masson, you and I are departing. It was nice seeing you both and Miss Magendanz, I expect that briefing you promised to be ready soon."

They all shook hands and Minger and Masson quickly moved across the room to say their diplomatic farewells to Minister Kelley, carefully avoiding the guests grouped around the Swiss President.

Muller and Hilde watched them leave, then Muller turned to face her, a bewildered expression on his face.

"Hilde, can you explain to me what just happened? And what was that language you two were speaking? I could barely understand a word."

She gazed at him and giggled at his evident confusion.

"We were speaking in Vaudois, Paul, a dialect used by farmers in the Jura Mountains. You don't know it?" she asked, teasingly.

Muller shook his head slowly, aware that Hilde was playing him along. The Jura Mountains rose above Geneva in the neighboring Canton de Vaud. They were a popular and easily accessible destination and he'd hiked and cross-country skied there many times, so he knew the area well. But no, he didn't speak Vaudois; he didn't think he'd ever heard it spoken before.

He decided not to rise to the bait and remained silent.

"Well, you probably know that Mr. Minger was a farmer in the Jura before he was a government official," Hilde continued, eyes merrily sparkling, obviously enjoying herself.

Of course," Muller interrupted impatiently, "everyone knows that; it's part of his political persona."

"What you don't know Paul, is that my uncle was also a dairy farmer in the Jura and his property was situated only a few kilometers from Mr. Minger's. They knew one another well; they were friends and neighbors for years. And when I was a young girl, I would spend summers at Uncle Henri's Jura Mountains dairy farm."

Muller looked at her quizzically.

"So, you met the Minister as a youngster?"

"No," Hilde replied, "but he'd heard of me. When I told him that I was Henri de Broussard's niece, he said, 'Ah, you're the smart one he used to talk about all the time'. I said, 'yes, but now a grown-up'. 'Still as smart as Henri said you were?' he asked, and I said, 'even smarter'; he liked that."

"So, you weren't some kind of champion milkmaid," Muller said.

"I certainly was not," she replied curtly. "I didn't spend my time there doing chores." Hilde's face grew pensive. "I read," she said, "everything I could get my hands on. And my uncle made sure there were always books to challenge me: literature, science, mathematics, and engineering; at one point I thought about becoming an architect."

"Uncle Henri loved the fact that I was smart, and he encouraged me to embrace it. Even more than my father, he made me comfortable with my brain and nurtured my love of learning. He was very proud of me; he used to brag about his little niece who was smarter than anyone and was going to be famous someday. It became a bit of a routine among his friends:

'Bonjour Henri, how're you feeling today and how's that smart niece of yours doing?'

'I'm fine and she's even smarter'.

"I was a little uncomfortable with it at first, but then I bought in and would play the game."

"Minister Minger remembered all this?" Muller said, a little skeptically.

"My uncle and I were pretty important people among the Jura dairy farming crowd," Hilde responded with a giggle and rolled her eyes.

"Actually, he did remember me, immediately," she went on, more seriously, "especially since I addressed him in Vaudois, which is the language we all used in the community. And you could see for yourself that he reacted positively."

"That was pretty obvious," Muller said, nodding. "What did you tell him about the project?"

"Only that I was the expert the Ministry was looking for and that you had used your superior powers of persuasion to convince me to figure out ways to combat economic pressure from the British—and from the Germans too. He seemed to like the idea." Hilde smiled innocently.

Muller shook his head and smiled back gamely.

"So, all we need to do now is develop a plan," he said.

"That's right," Hilde said gaily. "But we'll get to that tomorrow. Tonight, we should enjoy the reception.

"Oh," she said, glancing over Muller's shoulder, "Lady Kelly's left the receiving line. I want to go over and speak to her; she's smart too."

Hilde made a face at him, then walked toward the group of women that were gathering around their hostess.

The Ministry's intelligence files were not very extensive, but someone had prepared a dossier on the new incoming British minister and Muller had taken the time to read it. Among other things, it described the minister's wife, Marie Noel, born to Belgian royalty, as both a highly accomplished diplomatic hostess and a formidable intellect, who surrounded herself with writers and leaders in culture and the arts.

So, yes, Muller thought; she probably is smart too.

He strolled to a table in the center of the room where a selection of hors d'oeuvres were laid out. He spied an especially inviting blue cheese platter and was just helping himself when he felt a hand on his shoulder and turned to find Alexandru Murtenau grinning at him.

"Well, Muller, I see you've been busy here in Bern," he said jovially. "I saw you walk in with that foxy looking lady on your arm. Very impressive, my friend."

Muller chuckled. "Just a Swiss National Bank lady," he said casually.

"She certainly doesn't look like a banker," Muntenau responded with a broad smile.

They clinked glasses, then both glanced at the entryway where the Germany Minister, Otto Carl Köcher, had just entered the room.

Köcher had become a powerful and feared figure in Switzerland as a fierce advocate for the Nazi regime. He was steeped in Swiss life, having been raised in Basel, the son of a German watchmaker who had settled there to pursue his craft at the heart of the Swiss watch industry. It was said that he even spoke the dialect of the Basel watchmakers.

I wonder if he speaks Vaudois too, Muller mused to himself.

Hitler and the Nazi party were deeply unpopular with a large swath of the German-speaking population of Switzerland. They had ready access to German newspapers and radio broadcasts and were all too familiar with the tyranny of the Nazi regime which offended the prized sense of individual liberty that most Swiss jealously guarded. Nonetheless, Germany shared a long border with Switzerland and for centuries the two nations had been deeply entangled with one another in countless ways. Antagonism was mixed with familiar proximity–and even, in some cases, with fervent support; it was an ambiguous relationship. Köcher had taken full advantage of this reality, seeking to influence Swiss affairs in Germany's favor.

Muller remembered that the Ministry dossier on Köcher had also noted that he was the paymaster for a multitude of front groups and other shadowy Swiss organizations sympathetic to the Nazis that the Ministry viewed as potential threats.

He was a formidable figure.

Köcher obviously knew it and was using his arrival at the reception to burnish his image. He had timed his entrance so the formal receiving line was over and he could walk directly into the main reception room. His dark suit was set off by the bright red Nazi Party armband he wore on his right sleeve, a white circle surrounding the black swastika. He'd entered the room alone and everyone's eyes immediately turned to look at him, as Muller and

Muntenau had done, acknowledging his arrival and therefore his importance.

Muller and Muntenau watched Köcher advance across the room, nodding confidently and responding to greetings with smiles and gestures of recognition, to where Minister Kelly was standing and he greeted the Minister with a stiff, deep bow of deference, then, straightening, a genial smile and a long and vigorous handshake.

"The sonofabitch knows how to play the game," Muntenau muttered. "You have to give him that."

Muller grimaced, but nodded in agreement.

Then Muller turned to Muntenau again and grinned. "He's certainly playing the role of the big shot here. But you told me in April that the Germans are playing a losing hand. Still feel that way?"

Muntenau paused and picked up a canapé, chewing it slowly before responding.

"I do," he said, glancing around to ensure they weren't being overheard. "There are two pieces of new information you ought to be aware of. First, we were able to persuade the French to include Romania in the guarantee they issued protecting Poland against German invasion, and the British went along too. So, we have at least that much international protection against our German friends.

"Are France and Britain really prepared to honor that guarantee and go to war if Hitler were to invade us?" Muntenau shrugged in response to his own question. "I hope we don't ever have to find out, but, at the moment, it looks like they would; so, we're feeling a little better than we were earlier."

Muntenau smiled. "In fact, we even found the courage to take a harder line in our economic dealings with the Germans. We dragged our feet on supplying them with the petrol products they're clamoring for and, when they complained, we told them they'd have to sell us half a dozen of their nice new Messerschmitt-109 fighter planes."

Muntenau accepted the Gitane Muller proffered, exhaling smoke with a broad smile.

"They were furious; Hitler actually vetoed the deal, but Goëring knew they had to get the gasoline or declare rationing. So, we got the planes."

"I know it's anecdotal," Muntenau added, "but it shows a chink in their armor; they have their problems like the rest of us."

Muntenau paused again. "I'm betting the British and their allies believe that time is on their side, so there's need to rush. And they're probably right. But Hitler can figure that out too so I worry that he may start something soon–before the others are ready."

"Like invading Poland?" Muller asked.

"At least that," Muntenau replied. "If time's working against him, why wait?"

As Muller digested his observation, Muntenau took another canapé; then he nudged Muller's arm.

"Look," he said gesturing toward a statuesque blonde woman standing across the room in a bright blue summer frock with a deep décolletage.

"It's Juta," he said, "the great Dane. I must fly to her side before someone else does," and he hurried off, waving to Muller as he left.

Muller turned to see that Minister Kelly had moved to the staircase and mounted several steps, then clinked his glass with a spoon to get the attention of his guests. His wife took up position a step below him and Hilde rejoined Muller, standing at his elbow.

As Kelly spoke, Muller had his first chance to observe the man and was struck by what a large head he had; it seemed to tower above his tall, slender build. His face was deeply creased around his eyes and mouth, giving him an expressive appearance and conveying a sense of mature dignity.

He delivered welcoming remarks that were brief and anodyne, paying proper diplomatic attention to hopes for close working relations and emphasizing how much he and Marie Noël were looking forward to his assignment in Bern. Then he paused a moment and spoke in a more serious vein, clasping his hands before him.

"We come to this city deeply conscious of its role as the capital of a nation deeply committed to its policy of neutrality. Though entirely landlocked, Switzerland's long adherence to neutrality in the affairs of nations has made it an island of tolerance in a turbulent world; a place where competing–even hostile–views are permitted to co-exist peacefully alongside one another.

"As I assume responsibilities here as His Majesty's minister, I want to restate–in the most direct and unambiguous manner–the unswerving support of His Majesty's government for Swiss neutrality. We are living in a time of change, an era that has seen upheavals in relations among nation states–and, I have to say–one where the prospect of future conflict is all too real. In this uncertain environment, His Majesty's government views the survival of Swiss neutrality to be a vital national interest–and an objective that we expect other nations should equally commit to upholding. Thank you for coming this evening; we invite you to continue enjoying our hospitality."

There was a smattering of applause–it's hard to clap holding a champagne flute, Muller was reminded–before conversation resumed.

"That sounded a little different than the message the British sent to you in Geneva," Hilde said to him under her breath. "Do you suppose there's a little jurisdictional competition being played out here?"

"Well, let's find out," replied Muller, gesturing with his head. "See that tall, gaunt man standing at the high-top table over there stubbing out his cigarette? That's Consul General Hansen, one of the messengers. Let's pay him a visit."

"Oh, good," Hilde replied, "you can introduce me as your secret weapon."

She took Muller's arm as they strode toward the doorway to a veranda where Hansen was standing, a large whiskey in his hand. He was alone and gave the appearance of wishing to be almost anywhere other than in attendance at this reception. Seeing them approach, his air of discomfort seemed to increase, and he eyed them uncertainly.

"Why General Hansen, how nice to see you again," Muller said jovially as he offered his right hand to shake Hansen's, who responded limply.

May I introduce Miss Hildegard Magendanz?"

Hansen murmured an acknowledgement to Hilde, his eyes darting warily between them.

"I was a little surprised to see you here," Muller continued, "but I thought I should come over and see if there were any new developments since our last discussion in Geneva."

"Um…I'm not sure if this is the place to have a conversation on that subject," Hansen said, almost visibly seeking an escape route.

"Ah," said Muller, "you prefer to speak in noisy dance clubs?"

"No, no…" Hansen sighed and gamely attempted to smile, apparently deciding that he was cornered and was going to have to make the best of it. "Of course not. No, I didn't mean that at all."

"Santé!" Hansen gestured a toast to them with his glass and took a large gulp from his drink.

"I was heartened to hear the Minister's remarks just now," said Muller blandly. "Reaffirmation of British support for Swiss neutrality is very reassuring. Can I assume that his statement supersedes the rather threatening message you delivered to me?"

Hansen's face tightened.

"Matters will all be sorted out in due course, Mr. Muller," he said, "but I wouldn't jump to any hasty conclusions about that."

Clearly wanting to change the subject, he turned to Hilde

"In any event, we shouldn't subject this very nice lady to confidential business discussions among gentlemen." He smiled. "That would be impolite of us."

Muller returned Hansen's smile, enjoying his discomfiture.

"Actually, Miss Magendanz is very much involved in that business, General Hansen," he said. "She's an official of the Swiss National Bank, which has put its full resources at our disposal in responding to the message you delivered to me the other night. You can think of her as my secret weapon."

Hansen eyed Hilde suspiciously.

"I'm sure it would be interesting to get a woman's view of these important matters," he said, in a patronizing tone. "I'm sure Mr. Muller can share them with me sometime."

"Yes," Hilde said, "women do pay attention to the strangest things, don't they–things like the altimeters that are used in RAF Spitfires, for example."

Hansen looked at her with a frown.

"I'm sure you know what altimeters are, sir," Hilde continued, "those pesky instruments that tell the pilots what their altitude is; pilots think altimeters are pretty important, actually. And I'm sure you know that all the Spitfire altimeters are built right here in Switzerland–in Fribourg actually, just down the road, at a factory owned by a Swiss Company named Exner. I'm told the RAF is just crazy about them because there's no other company that makes a product as good as our Swiss Exner altimeters."

Hilde smiled. "So, I asked Mr. Muller, what would happen if the Swiss government were to confiscate Exner's inventory of Spitfire altimeters and shut down Exner's Spitfire production line in retaliation for a British attack on the Swiss economy.

"You know what he said, General Hansen?"

Hansen looked at Hilde blankly.

"Why, he said, those RAF flyboys are so good, they'd just wing it.

"Ha!" Hilde went on gaily with a big smile. "What a comic our Mr. Muller is. *They'd just wing it*! Pretty good line, right?"

Then her face turned serious. "But, of course, we both know that they can't just wing it can they, General Hansen. We both know that the Spitfires can't fly without altimeters. So, it occurred to me–as a woman, you understand–that this might be a subject for Mr. Muller to raise with you in the context of British economic policy toward Switzerland."

Hansen's expression didn't change, but his face turned pale and a small tic caused his left eyebrow to move up and down. He seemed uncertain of how to reply.

Hilde took a sip from her champagne flute, her eyes still fixed on Hansen, then continued.

151

"You know that women can be diverted by little things too," she said lightly, with a tiny smile, "things like proximity fuses, for instance. Those are the small devices that are affixed to the nose of all British howitzer shells so they'll explode when they hit their target. They're all made here in Switzerland, at a company called Tavaro, situated near Annemasse, just next to Geneva. Perhaps you know the company, General, it's so close to your offices. No? Well, no matter. Tavaro's been the sole supplier of proximity fuses to the British Army for years."

"Just a woman's intuition, mind you, General, but I have a hunch that the British Army might get upset if their supply of proximity fuses was interrupted."

"Shall I go on?" Hilde said lightly.

Hansen's face had darkened.

"That will be quite enough, young lady," he hissed and set his drink down on the table, glaring at them. "I bid you both good evening," he said, turning on his heel and walking rapidly away.

Watching Hansen stride off, Hilde shot Muller a conspiratorial grin.

"He apparently doesn't enjoy conversing with women," she said.

"Hilde…" Muller began, uncertain of what to say.

She turned to face him still grinning.

"Where did you get that stuff, and why didn't you tell me what you planned to say?" Muller shook his head. "I mean…" again he groped for words, "that was a one-two punch you just delivered."

Hilde took another sip from her flute.

"Well, I got that 'stuff' in my research, Paul; it's not so hard to find and there are more examples. Switzerland is a major supplier to the British military. If Hansen and his colleagues in that new ministry don't know it by now, they certainly should.

"As for planning it, I didn't know we were going to meet Hansen tonight any more than you did. But when we did, I thought I'd take advantage of the opportunity and behave like the secret weapon you described."

Hilde giggled. "Besides Paul, it provides you total deniability. You can truthfully tell anyone who asks that you knew nothing about what I was going to say; in fact, you were as surprised as Hansen appeared to be. Plus, the fact that they heard it from a woman will give them fits. 'Should we believe what she told us?' That sort of thing."

Hilde rolled her eyes, then finished her champagne.

"Trust me, Paul," she said," I know how men react when a woman tells them something they didn't expect to hear. "So, another drink or shall we call it a night?"

Muller smiled.

"I think we've accomplished everything we can here," he said, and offered his arm.

The reception crowd was quickly thinning and there was a knot of people crowding the entry. As Muller peered through the doorway he saw their shiny Renault had pulled up in front and was awaiting them. He murmured apologies as the other guests stood aside and they made their way to the car, the chauffeur standing stiffly at the open rear door and the uniformed British marine coming to attention and saluting smartly.

They maintained dignified expressions, nodding to the waiting guests, as if acknowledging their self-importance, until the Renault pulled out of the circular drive, and then exploded in laughter.

CHAPTER 15

Muller awoke early the next morning and strolled to the small coffee shop he'd adopted for breakfast since he'd begun staying at the ministry housing facility in Bern. The croissants weren't as good as the ones he was accustomed to in Geneva, but the coffee was actually better. He awarded himself the luxury of a second cup as he sat, reflecting on the events of the previous evening.

Hilde.

He couldn't get her out of his mind. Images of her laughing and gesturing kept popping into his mind; he'd even dreamed about her. After departing the reception, he'd wanted to take her to dinner and continue the evening, but she'd directed the chauffeur to return to the Hotel 'to drop off Mr. Muller'. He'd leaned in to kiss her good night, but she'd put a finger to his lips and whispered, "Let's not get ahead of ourselves."

Muller sighed.

She'd told him to delay returning to the office the next day until after lunch so she could organize things, so he paid the waiter and walked the short distance to the Ministry where a stack of reports awaited his attention.

The weather had turned bright and warm, so Muller opened the only window in his small office and left the door open too, arranging the paper weights to keep the documents in place.

He had only just seated himself and placed the first stack of papers on the big ink blotter on his desk when Minister Minger rapped his knuckles on the open door and stepped inside the office.

"Miss Magendanz is charming, Muller," he said. "She's also very smart. I knew her late uncle who always talked about how smart his niece was. She also seemed poised and handled herself well at the reception. What's your impression?"

"Very favorable sir," Muller replied, hoping neither his voice nor his expression gave him away. "Actually, after you left last evening, we encountered the British Consul General from Geneva, that I told you about—one of the messengers Anthony Eden sent to threaten us. He was at the reception, standing off to the side looking very uncomfortable, so we decided to pay him a visit."

"And hopefully you made him feel even more uncomfortable," Minger said, smiling.

"Hilde certainly did—er, Miss Magendanz," he corrected himself and Minger's smile broadened.

"He was rather condescending when I introduced her as our secret weapon," Muller said, "but she looked him straight in the eye and told him that if Britain tries to damage Switzerland, we'll retaliate by cutting off the altimeters Exner sells to the RAF for its

Spitfires and the proximity fuses Tavaro sells the British Army for their howitzer shells."

"Ha," said Minger, his head nodding as he chuckled. "She just went right after him?"

"She didn't directly threaten him," Muller replied. "She said it was just her woman's intuition that Britain might want to think twice about the consequences if it takes action against us.

"But there's no doubt he got the message," Muller went on. "She asked if he wanted her to continue and he proceeded to stalk out of the reception."

"Isn't that something," said Minger admiringly. "Very clever." Then he paused.

"Muller, how do you suppose she knew all that?"

"As you said, sir, I guess she's really smart."

Minger chuckled again.

"She's also very pretty, Muller. Have fun working up that report you two are going to give me."

Minger waved as he walked back to the corridor, still smiling.

That afternoon, Muller was able to find Hilde's office, taking the back stairway so he could bypass the main Bank office and Otto Stube, whom he had no desire to meet and explain his need for the Renault.

The atmosphere he encountered upon entering the office was in sharp contrast to his visit a day earlier. Hilde was dressed fashionably in a flowery summer blouse, her hair still curly from the night before and she was wearing bright red lipstick. She came around the desk with a smile, permitting him to deliver the traditional three kisses on the cheek by way of greeting. Even her assistants, Helga and Beatrice, appeared cordial, smiling at the two of them, a bit like maiden aunts, Muller thought.

Hilde led the way into the conference room. Muller could see the document boxes had been reorganized, with papers removed from a number of them, and stacked neatly around the table.

She gestured him to take a seat, smiling, but all business.

"Assuming you agree, Paul, I have a plan for the report to the Minister that we agreed to last night."

Muller told himself not to be distracted by Hilde's deep blue eyes that seemed even brighter and more appealing in the bright light of the conference room.

He nodded expectantly.

"You've seen the material we put together for your visit," she said, gesturing toward the papers. "It's documentation we've been able to collect from the German Ministry of Economic Affairs and the Reichsbank–that's the German central bank. You know Germans, Paul; they are nothing if not precise and detailed in their record-keeping and the material is surprisingly accessible, if you know what to look for and where to look. This is material my colleagues and I are familiar with–it's our job, after all. So, I've directed Helga and Beatrice to begin sorting through the material and collect key information for us to review for the report to the Minister.

"But in addition to the written releases and publications, we have informants in both organizations that we occasionally access for additional–sometimes sensitive–information."

Hilde rose to check that the door behind her was shut, then, reclaiming her seat, leaned forward and addressed Muller in a low voice.

"I was able to contact my most important source in the Reichsbank earlier today," she said. "We have a code that we've developed over the years that enables us to communicate discreetly even over telephone lines that may be tapped. I described the information I was looking for and she responded that she could deliver it, but it would have to be done tomorrow."

Hilde paused.

"She stipulated that we must meet at Germany's Basel railroad station, Basel Deutsche Reichsbahn, and that I must bring along a trusted male accomplice to facilitate the exchange.

"Frankly, I don't like the sound of it, Paul. That station is controlled by the Germans even though it's on Swiss territory. Every time we've met there, I could tell she was frightened. It's a creepy place; I'm confident that it's crawling with undercover Gestapo agents, so we'd be at risk too. But if we can get our hands on this information, it'll be highly valuable to Minger and the ministry. I'm game to give it a try. Want to be my trusted male accomplice?"

Muller held up both hands. He was suddenly alert and paying close attention.

"I think you'd better explain what you're planning," he said. "What's the information you hope to get and how does this railroad station come into play?"

"I'm after the German military budget," Hilde responded quietly. "We've never been able to get access to it because it's secret. I decided to press my source, and she said she'll have 'relevant materials'–that's the term she used–if we can meet tomorrow.

"It was a very cryptic conversation and we were speaking in our indirect code. She didn't explain why the meeting had to be held so quickly or why I needed to bring a man along to participate in whatever's going to happen. Frankly, that makes me suspicious. But getting our hands on the German military budget would be a real coup, so I agreed."

Hilde paused and accepted the Gitane Muller offered and a light.

"In order to get to Basel by late tomorrow afternoon, she'll need to board the express from Berlin no later than mid-morning; it's about a seven-hour trip and terminates at the BDR. So, if we're going to do this, I need to give her the signal."

Muller looked at Hilde quizzically.

"Tell me about the Basel Deutsche Reichsbahn," he said. "I've heard of it, of course, but ..." he shrugged and looked annoyed.

"You say it's under German control even though it's in Basel?" Why didn't he know this?

She nodded. "It's the only station in the world so far as I know where the tracks and platforms belong to one country–Germany– and the terminal building to another–in this case Switzerland."

"I don't know much about Basel, but the only station I've heard of there is called the Banhof Basel SBB," Muller said skeptically.

"There are two stations Basel," Hilde replied. "SBB is the biggest and it's where Swiss Rail connects to the French SNCF system. Remember Paul, Basel's situated on both side of the Rhine at the point where Switzerland, Germany and France all meet; it's the only Swiss city that straddles the Rhine–well, except for Schaffhausen, but that's way off to the east."

"Hilde, I do know something about Swiss geography," Muller interrupted impatiently; he didn't need to be lectured on where Basel was located.

"Well, do you know the history of the Baden Railroad too?" Hilde replied levelly.

Muller, sighed. "No, I don't."

"Baden was an independent Duchy bordering Switzerland across the Rhine long before Germany even existed," Hilde said, speaking in a condescending tone that Muller assumed she used with bankers from Zurich who didn't know their briefs; he could understand how they felt.

"Sometime in the early days of railroads the Duchy built a line from its capital in Mannheim down the Rhine valley toward Basel. Originally, it terminated at the Swiss border and passengers had to be conveyed the rest of the way into Basel by horse-drawn carriages. Well, that didn't work very well so, in 1852 Baden and Switzerland entered into a treaty to fix the problem. They agreed that the Baden State Railway would build a station in Basel. They'd control the tracks and trains, but since it was built on Swiss territory–within the city limits of Basel–Switzerland would run the terminal building."

"Very neat," Hilde went on, now smiling broadly. "That treaty still exists today, Paul, you can look it up. Baden put its station there and then proceeded to build connecting rail lines east along the Rhine–on what is now the German side of the river."

Muller conjured up a map in his mind's eye and nodded.

"That station–it's now called Basel Deutsche Reichsbahn– remains a through station for German rail connecting to lines running along the Rhine. And it's still run by the Germans," she said, grinding out her cigarette in the ashtray between them.

"But today's Germans are the Nazis," she added. "That's what makes this a dicey proposition."

Muller sat back in his chair.

"I've never heard of this arrangement Hilde," he said pausing, "but I spent two years in The Free City of Danzig, which was a mandate of the League of Nations, and it was physically situated within the Polish Corridor–a strip of Polish territory that divided Prussia from the rest of Germany. The Germans hated it, for a whole host of reasons, but among them was the indignity of being required to go through Polish customs and immigration to get from one part of Germany to another. It was a constant source of friction. This arrangement you've described in Basel sounds similar; a real burden on passengers and an open invitation for mischief."

Hilde nodded vigorously.

"Mischief is right, Paul," she said, "Since the station is physically within Switzerland, it's a place that people go when they're trying to escape or to smuggle things out of Germany. Controls by both sides are tight–but, like anywhere, money talks and there is a lot of 'mischief' that goes on. And if my source is in trouble with the Germans or if they suspect she's passing secret information to us in the station…."

She sighed and shrugged, her voice trailing off.

"I'm uneasy about it," she said, finally.

Muller drummed his fingers on the table.

"Does your source have a name," he said, "or is that secret too?

"I only know her as Ottilie," Hilde replied. "No last name and I suspect that's not her real first name; but that's what she told me to call her."

"She works for the Reichsbank?"

"Yes, and she's treated there much the same way I'm treated at the Swiss National Bank here–like a leper, as we've already discussed. We met at a meeting some years ago–we were the only women there–and instantly took a liking to one another."

"So, you began swapping information," Muller said.

"Yes," Hilde replied, her tone defensive, "but mostly she sent stuff to me rather than the other way around. Ultimately, I came to realize she was anti-Nazi and that passing information to me was her way to resist. Of course, I couldn't share any of this with Stube or others at the Bank," she went on. "They wouldn't have believed me but, even if they did, they'd try to take over and that would have frightened Ottilie off.

"So, until now, I've kept everything to myself. I've used the information she sent me in preparing reports for the Bank and responding to questions from the bankers; so maybe that's helped the cause at least a little. But you're my first intelligence contact, Paul, so I decided to push Ottilie's button to see if I could get her to pass me information on the German military budgets."

"Can you describe the set-up at the station?" Muller asked. "What's going to happen when Ottilie arrives on the train from Berlin?"

"There are a couple of steps," Hilde replied, speaking crisply, all business.

"Ottilie will disembark on the train platform in the station and descend the stairs to the tunnel below; that's all German territory. The tunnel connects to the terminal, which is Swiss territory. To exit the tunnel and enter the terminal, she'll have to go through Passport Control by both countries. First, German Customs has to permit her to exit the tunnel–and leave German territory; she then has to go through Swiss Customs to get a temporary transit visa permitting her to enter the terminal–which is Swiss territory."

"What's her excuse for going into the terminal?" Muller asked.

"I assume she'll be transiting to Waldshut-Tiengen," Hilde said. "That's a German town east along the Rhine and it's where her parents live. It's served by the High Rhine Railway that runs between the station and Singen, so she has a legitimate reason to spend time in the terminal waiting for the local train. That's what she's done in the past."

"So, you'd meet her in the terminal while she's waiting for her train?" said Muller.

"Right," said Hilde, nodding. "There's no separate transit lounge; just a big hall with shops and restaurants around a seating area in the center. We've always met in the main restaurant."

"And you've assumed you were under surveillance."

Again, Hilde nodded. "I couldn't be sure, but there were men in black leather coats scattered around; maybe it was my imagination, but they sure looked like Gestapo types to me."

Muller wondered to himself whether Swiss authorities would permit the Gestapo to operate on Swiss territory–even in the kind of unusual arrangement that the Basel Deutsche Reichsbahn presented.

"After you'd finished your meeting, and she'd go to board the local train, she'd follow the same customs rigmarole in reverse?" He asked.

"Exactly," Hilde replied, "and once back on German territory, she could be snatched and sent, I don't know where, maybe Dachau?

"It's a complicated process," she added, "and risky if someone's discovered to be passing along secret information."

Hilde smiled wanly. "So, I'm glad Ottilie asked me to bring along an accomplice. Are you in?"

Muller looked at Hilde and shook his head resignedly; this was not someone to be underestimated. Of course, he would agree to accompany her and be her accomplice in the drop or whatever it was; he wouldn't want to miss it.

But he was glad he'd brought his brass knuckles to Bern.

CHAPTER 16

Muller and Hilde had taken the 1:36 PM train from Bern to Basel; it was scheduled to arrive at the Banhof Basel SBB at 2:44 PM, over an hour before the Berlin express was scheduled to arrive at the Basel Deutsche Reichsbahn at 4:12 PM. They would have ample time to change terminals and get situated in the BDR. Hilde had checked a timetable and ascertained that the next departure on the High Rhine Line to Singen was 6:37 PM, a little over two hours later. Not a lot of time to meet Ottilie, but enough, barring delays in arrival or clearing Customs.

Upon arrival, after exiting the SBB terminal, they walked a few blocks and crossed the bridge over the Rhine to the Basel Deutsche Reichsbahn. As they approached it, Muller was surprised at the sheer size of the structure. The main terminal building was wide and tall, with a broad facade framed by ornate columns that encased a vast glass window. A long gallery led off to the right, housing the train platforms, and it was topped by a high stone clock tower. The wide plaza in front of the terminal entrance featured heavy sculptures, and statues of what appeared to be

Greek gods were situated atop each of the four columns in front of the window.

It was a formidable presence.

Muller was also struck by the fact that the three flagpoles at the entrance flew not just the Swiss and Basel cantonal flags, but also a large German Nazi flag with the white-encircled black swastika.

A Nazi banner right here on Swiss territory; he took a deep breath as they walked to the entrance.

While they were not asked for their passports, the wide doorway was heavily guarded by Swiss police in their midnight blue uniforms, several with tommy guns on their shoulders and others fingering stout wooden truncheons. Not the bucolic Swiss atmosphere featured in the tourist guides, he thought to himself as he and Hilde made their way past the entry.

The interior of the terminal building was vast hall dominated by a ceiling that arched high above a rank of curved wooden benches where assorted travelers were seated along with parcels and luggage. It was a cavernous space, gloomy despite the summer light that streamed in from the high windows and the brightly lit shops lining each side of the hall.

Hilde and Muller stood and looked about them.

"The restaurant we use is over there," said Hilde pointing to her right, where Muller could see white-clothed tables and wire-rimmed chairs behind a screen of potted plants; at that hour, it was not crowded and they would have a choice of seats.

"I want to get the lay of the land before we sit down to wait," Muller said strolling slowly across the vast hall.

A large sign to their left announced Customs–Zoll / Douane– with Swiss and Nazi flags pictured together. They walked over and Muller could see the wide doorway that offered access and egress to and from a street level tunnel. Signs pointed toward the tunnel for train platforms 1 to 5 and placards listed the times and destinations of arrivals and departures. A bright white line on the floor in the doorway divided the terminal and the tunnel and was very obviously the Swiss-German border.

On the terminal side of the line, Muller saw two large steel tables on either side of the doorway where Swiss border guards sat in their grey uniforms with Swiss emblems on their shoulders, one table serving outgoing passengers headed into the tunnel to catch their trains and the other serving passengers exiting the tunnel and seeking entrance to the terminal hall. Beyond the doorway, he could see the same setup for German Customs, with tables on each side manned by black-uniformed Ordnungspolizei, all wearing red Nazi armbands. Muller also noted that the walls on the German side displayed large red and white Nazi banners with their ubiquitous black swastikas. Maybe it was his imagination, but the German guards somehow looked fiercer than their Swiss counterparts; it was the black uniforms that made the guards look like SS troopers, he decided. He also noted that one of the German guards was holding a large German shepherd dog on a short leash.

As Muller watched, a handful of passengers was moving through the Customs control in both directions, and everything appeared calm–no drama at all; apparently just business as usual, Muller decided. Still, it was disconcerting to observe Nazi symbols within the borders of Switzerland. He'd lived under the threat of Nazi violence in both Danzig and Vienna and he took no comfort in seeing their emblems so prominently on display.

After satisfying himself with the layout, Muller led them back and they took seats in the restaurant. Hilde decided they should sit at adjoining tables against the wall; not seated together, but close by.

"We both have white pocket hankies," she said, pointing to the breast pocket of Muller's suit where his customary handkerchief was properly folded, and the small decorative white hankie pinned to her summery yellow blouse.

"They don't attract notice, but someone looking for us will understand."

She must read Graham Greene espionage novels too, he thought to himself, and in that spirit decided to use the men's room, which was always a good place for writers to describe clandestine exchanges taking place. Plus, he needed to relieve himself.

Not much drama here, he decided as he buttoned his fly. A rank of waist high white ceramic urinals on one side, four toilet stalls with doors on the other and hand basins on the far wall between them; no attendant on duty and reasonably clean. He washed up and returned to the restaurant.

From their tables, they had a clear view of the Swiss Customs station and they could watch the passengers lining up and going through clearance in both directions. The crowd ebbed and flowed as trains arrived and departed.

Muller also cast his eyes around the terminal space, searching for possible observers–Gestapo or otherwise–as Hilde had described. It was probably too warm for the black leather coats which often distinguished the Gestapo, but he quickly spied two muscular men, identically dressed in white short-sleeve shirts that could very well fit the bill. They seemed to stroll aimlessly around the terminal without luggage or parcels, just looking around. They didn't walk together and didn't acknowledge one another; they just kept circling around the room. Muller felt uneasy watching them.

As Muller and Hilde sat, waiting for the Berlin express, the men several times passed close by their tables. Muller ignored them until one stopped nearby to light a cigarette and Muller looked up to catch his eye, but the man paid no attention and, after flicking his match to the floor, resumed pacing the terminal.

Before departing Bern, Muller had visited the ministry and persuaded the building supervisor to prepare Ministry of Military Affairs passes for them, bearing the official ministry stamp. He didn't expect to need them, but he wanted the reassurance of having some official credential at hand in the event something unexpected happened and he'd persuaded Hilde to tuck hers into her handbag. He'd toyed with the idea of going to the station manager with his pass to seek help against the potential for interference in their meeting–the kind of uncertainty that the two strolling men presented. But he'd immediately discarded the thought; too dangerous, he'd decided. Who knew what a station manager would do with information that Ministry of Military Affairs representatives were in the terminal to receive clandestine information from a German transit passenger.

No, out of the question; they'd have to take their chances.

Finally, the large clock on the terminal wall approached 4:11 PM and a train schedule placard was put up showing an on-time arrival. Hilde and Muller tensed, and watched closely as a few minutes later passengers from the Berlin express began filing through the customs clearance process. More than two dozen people shuffled along, showing papers and tickets and being handed transit visas by the officials seated at the big steel desk.

Hilde evinced no recognition of any of the passengers, curtly shaking her head in response to Muller's inquiring glances. So, they sat back and continued to wait.

Hilde was frowning and looked unsettled.

One of passengers, a stocky man with a cane, entered the restaurant and, without glancing at either Hilde or Muller, took a table adjoining Muller's. One of his sleeves was neatly tucked into his suit pocket and he moved slowly, leaning heavily on a wooden cane; a war amputee, Muller surmised, noticing a German Iron Cross pinned to the breast pocket of the man's jacket. He sat down gingerly, using both the table and the wire chair for balance and grunted, evidently worn out by the arrival process. When a waiter came by, he ordered a coffee and unfolded a newspaper that he had been carrying under his one arm.

Muller paid the man little heed; both he and Hilde were restlessly shifting in their seats looking at their watches and the big clock and gazing around the terminal for Ottilie.

As he was doing this, Muller suddenly became aware that the man next to him, while he had a newspaper open and folded in his one hand, wasn't reading it, or even looking at it. Instead, he was searching the room too, his eyes darting. What was he looking for, Muller wondered? Probably just his wife or a relative who was late. One of the men in the white short sleeves walked by, and Muller watched closely, but discerned no communication between them, so he lost interest and glanced again at Hilde, who was by now scanning the room with a look of both anger and alarm.

Suddenly there was a sound of broken crockery. Muller looked and saw the man next to him try to reach down and recover his coffee cup and saucer that had fallen to the floor where they had splintered. As he did so, the man's cane fell from the chair where he had propped it and grabbing for it, he began teetering on his chair.

Muller quickly stood and leaned over to steady the man, so he didn't fall. As he did so, the man grabbed Muller's suit jacket with his hand and pulled him close.

"You must help me to the men's room," he hissed. "You have to do it right now; please don't argue." He tightened his grip on Muller's arm. "Ottilie needs you to take me. Please."

Muller glanced at Hilde, who looked quizzically back at him; she hadn't been able to hear the man's message.

Muller tried to signal her with his head, then he used both arms to help the man to stand and retrieved the cane so the man could take it and release Muller's hand from his vise-like grip. Muller put an arm beneath the man's elbow and began slowly steering him the direction of the men's room

What was this, he wondered.

He looked around the room as they made their way across and didn't see anything out of the ordinary; he didn't even see the men in the white short-sleeve shirts. Cautiously, he put his free hand into his suit jacket pocket and slipped on one of the brass knuckles he'd brought with him. He'd had occasion to use them in the past and had acquired the habit of keeping them close at hand. He didn't know what was coming, but….

They finally entered he men's room and the man broke free from Muller's grip; his limp forgotten, the man ran the few steps toward the wash basins, a look of terror on his face as he glanced back.

Muller caught a glimpse of white in the corner of his eye and instinctively ducked his head. A fist glanced off his head, cracked into the toilet stall next to him and dropped a black leather sap accompanied by a curse as the attacker's body slammed into Muller's. Muller half turned and saw one of the white short-sleeve men reach for his injured hand. Muller took a step back and was able to land a solid blow with his brass knuckles to the man's stomach. The man seemed to turn into a rag doll as he threw his hands up, his eyes wide, and collapsed with a muffled gurgle at Muller's feet.

The other white shirt came at Muller with a police truncheon. Muller threw up an arm to block it and was knocked to the floor by the force of the blow, his arm burning in pain. He rolled over, but the man aimed a kick that caught Muller on the chin, and he crashed up against one of the urinals, his head banging against the hard ceramic. He avoided another kick and twisted his attacker's leg bringing the man crashing down on him. They began wrestling, Muller finally freeing his brass knuckle hand enough to deliver short blows to his attacker's head. The man kneed Muller hard in the groin and as Muller doubled up in pain, the man gained his feet and picked up the truncheon. He was readying a blow when blue uniformed Swiss police stormed into the room whistles blowing. One of the policemen shoved Muller's attacker back against the urinals, pinning his arm and the truncheon against the wall.

"Which one's Muller?" one of the policemen yelled.

"I am," Muller said, rising unsteadily to his feet, then lunging at the attacker held by the policeman and delivering a barehanded punch to the man's face that split his lip and showered them both and the policeman with blood.

"Sonofabitch," he said, finally allowing himself to be restrained by the police.

He tried pull himself free, but a burly policeman hung onto him.

Muller shot his arm toward the old man who'd led him into the men's room.

"You too," he said, pointing. "What the fuck is this about? You set me up with these bastards."

Muller was as angry, and he tried again to break free from the policeman's grip.

The old man remained pressed up against the wash basins as if trying to escape, his face still frozen in terror.

"They made me do it," he said, putting up his one hand in fear.

"It's for Ottilie," he began crying, his voice cracking. "I'm just the messenger; *they're* the message," he said, pointing at the two attackers.

Just then Hilde raced into the room, her eyes wide and her hair askew.

"My God, Paul," she exclaimed racing to his side. "What have they done to you?"

"You've got to get him out of here and find help," she barked the command at the police and began pulling Muller away, still in the grip of the policeman.

"He's bleeding; come on, hurry."

"All right," said one of the policemen, apparently the leader.

"Get Muller to the First Aid station, we'll take care of these guys."

Muller allowed himself to be led away, looking back to see the attackers being taken in hand by the police, the first man still doubled up and holding his stomach as they roughly pulled him to his feet, the other wiping blood off his mouth and nose and glaring at Muller as he remained pinned against the wall by a beefy Swiss policeman.

Muller's legs gave out as they began to cross the terminal hall and the two Swiss policemen had to half carry him the rest of the way to a room, off to one side, beneath a sign bearing the familiar red cross. Opening the door, they entered a smallish space with two white cots lined up next to one another and shelves against one wall stacked with medical supplies.

A seated attendant came to his feet and pointed to one of the cots. He was a slender, balding man with beetling grey eyebrows and wore a long white medical gown.

"He was beaten up by two men," said Hilde breathlessly; "he's badly hurt."

The attendant put on tortoise shell glasses and quickly began examining Muller, moving his extremities. Muller cried out in pain as his left arm was lifted.

"I got hit with a club there," he said, gritting his teeth.

The attendant moistened a white cloth and began wiping Muller's face and neck. A gash under his chin was bleeding profusely and cuts on his forehead seeped blood too. Muller winced as the attendant touched a contusion above his left ear.

"Looks like your head hit something too," he muttered softly.

He turned to the policemen.

"One of you escort this lady outside to wait while I take care of this situation," he said.

"I'm not going anywhere," Hilde said defiantly, her eyes flashing, and her arms crossed in front of her.

"Now," said the attendant authoritatively, and the smaller of the policemen took Hilde by the arm, not so gently escorting her out the door and into the corridor where several chairs were set up as an impromptu waiting room.

Finally, after what seemed a very long wait, the door opened, and the attendant ushered Hilde back into the treatment room. Muller was sitting, slumped on the edge of the cot. His head had several white plasters, a gauze pad was affixed with adhesive tape under his chin and his left arm was in a sling.

Hilde dashed to his side and put her arm around his shoulder.

"Oh, Paul," she said softly, "are you all right?"

Muller nodded imperceptibly and tried to smile.

"He'll recover in a few days," said the attendant, "but he received a bad beating and needs to rest. Do you have a place to stay tonight? Sleep is the best thing for him now."

"No," Hilde said, "we'd intended to return to Bern."

She turned to the policeman who'd sat outside with her.

"Can you help get us to a hotel nearby where I can find a room for the night?"

"The Mon Repos is just a few doors down from the terminal along the quai," the more senior policeman replied and turned to the other policeman.

"Kurt, go tell our desk officer to call over and make the arrangements, then come back and help me escort Mr. Muller there."

The officer took a crumpled pack of cigarettes from his uniform pocket and offered one to Muller. He took one, noting they were Ambassadors, not Gitanes, but he accepted the policeman's light and took a deep drag, exhaling with a cough that was painful and caused him to wince.

"My superintendent will probably want to speak with you directly, but let's have a short conversation while we wait." The policeman turned to the attendant. "Is it all right to stay here a few minutes so we don't have to move Mr. Muller?"

The attendant nodded, removing his spectacles.

"It's fine unless you bring in the guys he fought with and I have to patch them up too," he replied with a smile, patting the brass knuckles he'd removed from Muller's right hand and placed next to him on the cot.

"From the looks of this thing, he did some damage with it."

"Mr. Muller, your assistant, showed her ministry credential to one of my officers and insisted that you were being assaulted in the men's toilet," the officer said. "She was highly agitated."

"We didn't ask how she knew what was supposedly happening, but we took her at her word and reacted. It's a good thing we did; you were about to get beaten up by that guy with the truncheon. Oh, and they apparently went after you with this too." He pulled the black leather sap out of his pocket and laid it on the cot next to Muller's brass knuckles. "I found this on the floor; another nasty weapon," he said smiling wanly.

"I heard that old man say they were sending you a message," he added. "It appears to be a very unpleasant one." Then he looked directly at Muller.

"I gather you and the lady are conducting official ministry business, so I won't be offended if you decide not to share the details with me. But I've seen this kind of thing before. Hosting those damned Nazis in this facility has led to more incidents than I want to count–a lot of them violent, like this one. So, let me tell you what's probably going to happen."

The officer reached for an ashtray to stub out his cigarette and handed it to Muller who did the same with his.

"We'll have to send those goons back to Germany. We could prosecute them for assault, of course, but that would create a diplomatic incident and Basel–this station in Basel, at least–is not interested in making waves with our German guests. Frankly, both the Germans and we have an interest in maintaining this odd customs arrangement. We turn a blind eye to certain things–and they do the same."

The officer shot a look at Muller.

"And I don't have to tell an official of the Ministry of Military Affairs that Germany's got a much bigger army than we do, or that Basel is a tempting target for them."

He paused, then went on, evidently speaking from experience.

"The attackers will go back and tell their bosses that they beat the shit out of you. That frightened old man will certainly confirm their story. The fact that you also beat the shit out of *them* will go unreported. But whoever it was that ordered this thing will assume his message was delivered and move on to other things. Unless your ministry decides differently, and wants to make something of this, everything that transpired here will be swept under the rug."

The officer brushed his hands, one against the other, wiping it away.

Muller nodded weakly in agreement.

CHAPTER 17

Muller managed to walk–slowly–to the nearby Hotel Mon Repos, though the two policemen remained at his elbow to steady him. The receptionist assigned them a large room with private bath and escorted them upstairs in the elevator, pointedly overlooking the fact that they had no luggage and different last names. Hilde pressed some franc notes on him, which were readily accepted, and he agreed to arrange for immediate delivery of a bottle of cognac.

Muller sat down gingerly on the edge of the double bed while Hilde ran a bath for him and brought a robe from the bathroom.

"Can you manage in there alone?" she asked with a grin.

Muller nodded. "I hope so; I certainly need to clean up."

In the bathroom, he stripped and eased himself into the steaming tub, grimacing at the sting of hot water on abrasions. His left arm ached and was swelling with a large bruise where he'd blocked the blow aimed at him with the truncheon. The first aid attendant said he was lucky it didn't break.

God, the tub felt good.

Finally, he got to his feet and climbed out of the tub, dried himself and, wrapping himself in the robe, returned to the bedroom where he found Hilde sitting at the small writing desk, poring through a sheaf of documents.

She rose quickly to help settle him in an easy chair and handed him a snifter filled nearly to the brim with brandy. She took her own from the desk where it had been resting and they clinked glasses.

Muller took a long draught and felt the fiery liquor envelop him as he swallowed. He took another, then set his snifter on the adjoining table, and laid his head back on the pillowed upholstery waiting for the pounding headache to subside.

Finally, he turned to Hilde. "What the Hell happened?" he said quietly. "This wasn't part of the plan."

Hilde was gazing at him with a concerned expression.

"No, it wasn't" she said, softly. "I feel so badly that you've been injured. It's all my fault."

She knelt next to Muller's chair and laid her warm hand on his. Then she sighed and pulled the desk chair next to Muller's.

"When you began helping that old man leave the table, I suspected something was up," she said, continuing to speak in a low voice. "I could see you trying to signal me. But I decided to sit still, since nothing else seemed to be happening. Then, as soon as you disappeared into the men's room, Ottilie appeared, right at my table; I hadn't seen her enter the terminal. She was just suddenly there. And she didn't stop. She casually laid an envelope on the table and kept walking, but slowly enough that she could turn and say, 'Get the Swiss police to rescue your man–he's getting beaten up in there.' Then she turned and walked quickly away without another word or glance.

"I hesitated a moment, then picked up the envelope and ran over to the entrance where the Swiss police were standing and began yelling at them to go rescue you. It was all very chaotic," she said. "They didn't understand and I'm sure I looked like some crazy woman out of one of their nightmares. But I pulled the ministry pass out of my purse and showed it to them, telling them this was an emergency.

"The big guy who walked us over here was the first one to get it and he ran to the men's room ordering others to follow.

"And that's how they found you. And saved you," she said, again laying her hand on his and sighing deeply, regarding him with a sad expression.

Muller returned her gaze, frowning. "So, I guess I was the bait."

"The man said I had to go with him for Ottilie's sake and said something similar after the fight as the police took him away. He didn't attack me; he seemed scared to death and said he was forced to do it."

Muller paused, trying to remember. "Yes, the guy said he was just the messenger and the attack was the message."

Muller took another large gulp of cognac. "And suddenly Ottilie just appears, drops an envelope, warns you to save me then disappears again?"

Hilde nodded. "Yes. That's what happened."

Muller shook his head. Then stopped because it hurt.

"It looks like the two guys we saw wearing the white shirts were a reception committee and the old man had to draw them into the men's room to beat me up before Ottilie was able to make the drop to you." Muller stopped and reflected.

"So, somehow Ottilie may have evaded detection," he said, feeling more confidence in his recollection now. "Did she go back into the German station?"

"She was walking in that direction," Hilde replied. "I was running over to the Swiss police by then, so I didn't see her leave. But she was certainly headed toward the customs section when she left me."

"What about the envelope?" Muller asked.

"I put it in my purse." Hilde replied. "And I didn't tell anyone about it–or even look at it until just now, while you were in the tub."

She gestured to the papers on the writing desk.

"And what is it?" Muller asked.

"What we asked for–and maybe even more," Hilde said with a smile. "I've just begun to read the material, but it looks like we may have struck gold."

Muller finished his cognac, setting down the glass.

"Maybe they'll award me a medal for getting wounded then," he said, grinning for the first time. "But for now, I need to sleep. The attendant gave me something for the pain and I can't keep my eyes open."

Muller rose and Hilde guided him toward the bed, turning down the covers and smoothing the sheets. He groaned as he heaved himself into the bed.

Hilde bent over him.

"I hope our next night together can be a little more romantic." She smiled and kissed him warmly on the lips. "Sleep well, Paul."

He was instantly asleep. At some point during the night, he awoke briefly to find Hilde asleep beside him, on top of the bedding but nestled at his side, an arm slung over his chest. He pulled it a bit closer then went back to sleep.

CHAPTER 18

TOP SECRET

MEMORANDUM

To: Minister Minger

From: Hildegard Magendanz,

Director, German Economic Bureau

Swiss National Bank

Date: July 5, 1939

ACTION REQUESTED: An urgent meeting to evaluate options for Swiss policy.

EXECUTIVE SUMMARY: This Memorandum is based on documents secretly passed to us by sources within the Reichsbank showing:

- A German foreign exchange crisis so severe as to force large cuts in the current budgets of the German armed forces,
- A German monetary crisis posing the risk of ruinous inflation, and
- Decisions by Hitler to sideline the Reichsbank, take personal control of German economic policy and subordinate all economic policy considerations to his military rearmament goals.

This information sheds new light on the recent British threat to conduct economic warfare against Germany and the consequent risk of severe damage to the Swiss economy.

The secret Reichsbank documents reveal a bitter conflict within the German leadership, with Hitler continuing to demand higher rates of rearmament and the Reichsbank warning that doing so threatens to bankrupt Germany. They show that early this year, when the Reichsbank sought to force the issue, Hitler retaliated by personally taking charge of German economic policy. He fired Hjalmar Schacht, the longtime President of the Reichsbank, and eliminated the Reichsbank's authority over monetary policy. So, rearmament won out over fiscal restraint.

But the documents show that, despite overruling the Reichsbank, the acute shortage of funds forced Hitler to cut back military budgets. These issues carry important policy implications and warrant your attention.

DISCUSSION. My office has the responsibility for advising the Swiss National Bank on matters pertaining to the German economy. As head of that office, I am very familiar with the huge buildup in the German military that's occurred in the past six years since Adolf Hitler came to power.

The secret documents we have recently been given shed new light on what actually happened during that process. I will summarize what we've learned in this section of the memo, then address the issues they raise for the future.

As a starting point, you should know that the individual principally responsible for organizing the financial resources to pay for the massive German rearmament program was Hjalmar Schacht, the same Hjalmar Schacht that Hitler fired in January of this year.

Schacht is one of the most powerful bankers in Germany. He became President of the Reichsbank in 1923 and was the mastermind behind policies that succeeded in minimizing and ultimately ending the huge German repatriation obligations imposed by the Treaty of Versailles. He became disillusioned with the Weimar Republic and, in 1932, aligned himself with Hitler and the Nazi Party. So, when Hitler became Chancellor in January, 1933 he turned to Schacht to oversee the German economy, first re-appointing him as head of the Reichsbank, then making him Minister of the German Ministry of Economic Affairs (RWM); in effect, Schacht became Hitler's economic czar.

In 1933, Germany remained in the grip of the global depression, suffering from high unemployment, a stagnant economy and crushing levels of foreign debt. To orchestrate an economic recovery, Schacht took bold action on two fronts. First, he unilaterally suspended foreign debt repayments; in effect, Germany defaulted on its obligations and stiffed foreign creditors. Second, he initiated government subsidies for various civilian agricultural and industrial programs which acted as camouflage for a greatly expanded German rearmament program. In 1935, Germany renounced the Treaty of Versailles and Hitler revealed his plans to build an air force and to dramatically increase the size of the army. Consequently, the existence of the rearmament program became public knowledge. But even then, the full scale of the program was kept under wraps.

The secret documents now in our possession reveal, for the first time, more detailed information on the vast scope of the arms buildup, as well as evidence that the program is threatening to cripple the German economy.

By 1936, the new military programs had grown to the point that they accounted for roughly 10 percent of German GDP. The goods and services purchased by the Wehrmacht accounted for 70 percent of all German procurement. In future budgets the Wehrmacht began demanding even faster increases, for example seeking double the amount of imported metal, iron ores, rubber and oil in each succeeding year.

The cost of paying for these programs has drained German gold and foreign exchange reserves. By mid-1938, the Reichsbank was looking at a net foreign currency shortfall of over 400 million Reichsmarks, but had reserves of only 88 million Reichsmarks.

Beginning over three years ago, Schacht, faced with the risk of running out of money, began advocating slower military growth and promoting devaluation as a means of increasing exports and replenishing the German Treasury.

We now know that Schacht's recommendations prompted Hitler to appoint Herman Goëring, his Deputy and closest advisor, as a 'Special Commissioner for Foreign Exchange and Raw Materials'. Goëring, of course, is as committed to rearmament as Hitler and equally disdainful of financial constraints. He is also hugely ambitious and in his new role he set about undermining Schacht.

In July 1936, Goëring set up a special body within the SS to seize private holdings of foreign exchanges and other foreign assets in Germany. He appointed an official named Reinhardt Heydrich to lead it and, according to Reichsbank records, over the next two years, this program squeezed nearly 500 million Reichsmarks out of private holdings–and not just from the Jews; the SS went after everybody who had what they wanted.

So, at that point, thoughts of German devaluation were put aside, and Hitler's rearmament drive resumed its rapid increase.

Now flash forward to the fall of 1938 and the start of the current crisis. We've learned from the secret documents that, by this time, close to 20 percent of the German economy was devoted to the military–nearly double the share of 1936–and the Wehrmacht alone was consuming nearly 30 percent of all raw materials. According to the Reichsbank documents, Schacht believed this staggering military burden was unsustainable and he became even more alarmed at the risk that the German economy would go bankrupt.

But remember what else was happening in the summer and fall of 1938:Munich and the crisis over the Sudetenland. At that moment, Europe was on the brink of war until suddenly, in September, the Munich Conference convened, Britain and France forced Czechoslovakia to surrender the Sudetenland to Germany and Neville Chamberlain proclaimed 'Peace in our time'.

Hitler was triumphant and would not hear of any plan to defer his rearmament goals.

In the euphoria following the Munich conference, the German Finance Ministry floated three huge government bond offerings, raising billions of Reichsmarks. This gave the government financial breathing room; it seemed there was no end to Germans' appetite to buy public debt.

But then, in November 1938, a fourth loan program failed disastrously. Only a third of the 1.5 billion Reichsmark offering was purchased. The market essentially went on strike and panic ensued. The government suddenly faced year-end payment obligations that far exceeded its cash on hand; overdrafts or short terms bank loans, coming right on top of the failed bond sale, threatened to tank Germany's credit standing.

Schacht had seen this crisis coming and we now know that he leapt into action. The secret Reichsbank documents in our possession include part of a secret memorandum Schacht sent to Hitler dated January 7, 1939. He told Hitler that the plan to spend 30 billion Reichsmarks for rearmament over the next three years would spark disastrous inflation, force devaluation of the Reichsmark and necessitate new taxes. In effect, he forecast economic collapse unless Hitler changed course.

Hitler responded by firing Schacht on January 20, 1939. That action was announced publicly, and it was noteworthy, since Schacht was such prominent figure and so closely identified with Hitler's policies. But the secret Reichsbank documents reveal that the dismissal of Schacht is even more significant because it represented Hitler's response to

Schacht's plea to scale back the rearmament policy. The documents show that Hitler fired Schacht not because, as stated publicly at the time, it was time for a change. Instead, he fired Schacht for opposing re-armament. He dismissed the economic risks Schacht forecast and decided to continue rearming without any pause.

In addition, the Reichsbank documents show us that, after firing Schacht, Hitler ordered revision of the Reichsbank statutes to remove any limitation on increasing the money supply. He put himself in charge and there is no longer any monetary policy constraint on pursuing the rearmament program.

We've learned that Hitler has now become his own economic czar and can do what he wants. This follows his actions in 1938 to become Supreme Commander of the German armed forces.

In effect, Hitler has now taken personal control of all the levers of power within Germany.

Despite consolidating his power, however, the documents show that Hitler has been forced to order major reductions in the1939 budgets for the Wehrmacht, the Luftwaffe and the Kriegsmarine. The documents do not provide a complete budget picture, but they do present highly illuminating examples of crucial cutbacks.

- Overall military steel supplies cut from 530,000 tons to 300,000 tons (1937 levels).

- Mass production orders for ammunition reduced by nearly 50 percent.
- Manufacture of mortar bombs totally ended.
- Artillery shells being produced without copper driving bands because of a critical shortage of copper.
- Target of Model 34 machine gun production cut from 61,000 to 13,000.
- Shortages of building materials cause 300 infantry battalions to live in canvas tents.
- 10.5 cm light field howitzer production cut from 840 to 460 units
- New total aircraft production cut by over 20 percent.
- JU 87 Stuka dive bomber to be phased out.
- Aluminum for aircraft production cut by one-third.

We must caution that these reductions represent cuts from budget targets that were arguably unrealistically high. But even the drastically lower levels reflect a more ambitious German policy to increase its military strength.

The documents show how significantly the burden of this vast rearmament program has affected the German economy. Hitler announced in January 1939 a so-called New Finance Plan which requires exporters to Germany to accept payments for at least 40 percent of their contracts, not in cash, but in the form of tax credits. The Reichsbank opposed this program, arguing that it would backfire by squeezing the liquidity of government contractors. But with Schacht gone, the program was implemented anyway.

The Reichsbank also reported that its gold and foreign exchange reserves were exhausted, and the balance of trade was deteriorating fast. But Hitler responded by ordering the Reichsbank to issue short term credits to finance the government's expenditures—in effect printing money. We have been told that so far in 1939, German floating debt is on a path to grow by as much as 80 percent in the first nine months. Schact's Memorandum predicted that such a policy would lead to spiraling inflation that would weaken Germany.

This implies that the acute shortage of foreign exchange—forecast by Schacht—forced the very cutbacks in the German rearmament program that he recommended and Hitler refused to accept.

CONCLUSIONS:

This Memorandum is based on information secretly passed to us by sources within the Reichsbank that were aligned with Hjalmar Schacht and opposed to Hitler's expanded rearmament program.

It contains raw economic data that has not previously been published, but we conclude that the information, although incomplete, is sufficiently persuasive to serve as a reliable guide to decision-making by this ministry and the Swiss Government.

The secret information confirms the broad conclusion passed to us by the British Ministry of Economic Warfare that the German economy is weak and vulnerable to attack through concerted action by England (and its Empire), France (including its colonies in Indonesia and Africa), the USSR and America.

The Swiss government should therefore conclude that the likelihood is high that a broad economic attack will be mounted against the German economy and that the risk of collateral damage to the Swiss economy should both be taken seriously and an action plan to mitigate damage should become a high government priority.

CHAPTER 19

Minister Minger wiped his glasses as they waited for Roger Masson to join them. They were seated around the conference table in the Minister's office, Hausamann to his left, Muller and Hilde on his right, a copy of the memo in front of each of them, and another at Masson's empty place.

Minger raised his glasses, peering through them to be sure they were clean.

"You got rid of the sling?" he asked Muller, still focused on his glasses.

Muller smiled.

"Yesterday, sir," he said, gently flexing his left arm; "it's still sore and bruised, but a lot better; I'm just down to this bandage on my chin," he pointed. "And that'll be off in a day or so.

"I'm back in action," he added, squaring his shoulders.

Minger grunted, putting his glasses on and turning to look at Muller and Hilde.

"It was a good job the two of you did in getting the material in Basel. I'm sorry you got hurt Muller, but Miss Magendanz, this memo is a fine piece of intelligence."

Masson hurried into the Minister's office, his pipe clenched in his mouth, and took his seat, mumbling apologies.

Minger paid him no attention, continuing to look at both Muller and Hilde. "Is your Reichsbank source still active, do you think? Can we expect more of this sensitive information?"

Muller shook his head. He and Hilde had discussed whether the 'Ottilie' contact was compromised.

"We believe it's finished," Muller said, glancing at Hilde for confirmation, who nodded. "There's always the chance that the source may resurface and communicate with Hilde–er, Miss Magendanz–" he corrected himself, "but we think that's unlikely."

"In light of the attack on Mr. Muller, we believe it's too risky to try setting up another meeting–if you could call it that," Hilde added. "They were sending a message and Mr. Muller certainly received it; I'm afraid it's all over."

Minger nodded, then picked up the memo. "Too bad," he said. "But Miss Magendanz, since you're our resident expert on Germany and the author of the memo, why don't you tell us your conclusions."

Hilde paused a moment, looking down, apparently composing herself, then sat forward in her seat, hands clasped in front of her.

"I see someone in a hurry," she said, glancing at the men around the table.

"We've all known that Hitler's been pursuing a massive rearmament program; he's boasted about it publicly for years," she spoke quickly and confidently.

"What we haven't known before, and what the secret information reveals, is that this hasn't been–and certainly is not now–the smooth, well-oiled machine that informed observers– including people like me–assumed it was. Instead, we've been made privy to the dirty little secret that this huge rearmament program has stretched the German economy practically to the breaking point, and that it now appears to have bumped up against its outer limit.

"Very importantly, we've also learned that it's generated serious conflict within the German leadership. Hjalmar Schacht– the man everyone assumed was fueling the program with whatever financing was needed–has actually been trying to put on the brakes for years. Hitler refused and put Goëring and his SS attack dogs in charge of a separate financing scheme that had some–but only temporary–success.

"Of course, we all knew that Schacht was replaced in January. What we didn't know is that he was fired because of his opposition to the rearmament program."

"What a revelation," she went on, "Schacht–Germany's most powerful banker and the face of Germany's financial might– repeatedly warning Hitler that the pace of his rearmament program is unsustainable. Then the November bond sale failed, Germany was running out of money, Schacht confronted Hitler one more time–and was fired for his trouble. That's a pretty dramatic backstory we weren't privy to before we got these documents."

Hilde paused and looked around the table, her gaze returning to Minger.

"What all this says to me," she went on, "is that Hitler has decided to bet the house. He chose to continue barreling ahead with rearmament as fast as he could–even firing the guy who got him where he is–but he's discovered the German economy won't let the program get any bigger. In fact, he's even been forced to order some *reductions*. That has to have been very annoying–to have Schacht's predictions come back to take a bite out of his plans.

"I think it's forced him to realize that today–right now–he's holding the best hand he's ever going to have, so I think he's decided to lay down his cards and call the other players. How does he do that?"

Hilde again looked around the table, her jaw set.

"He goes to war–as he's repeatedly threatened to do–only this time, he means it; and the sooner the better, since the hand he's holding is only going to get weaker."

Hilde sat back in her chair.

"Hitler's a man in a hurry," she repeated. "That's the conclusion I draw from what we've learned."

No one said a word.

Finally, Minger, sitting arms crossed, sighed deeply.

"The nightmare we'd all hoped to avoid," he said quietly. "Hitler probably suspects–hopes–that he can bluff the British and French over Poland or come to some agreement with them even if he invades, and they declare war as they've threatened. But I think you're right, Miss Magendanz; the new intelligence leads inescapably to the conclusion that he's decided on war–and soon."

The room fell silent again.

Masson tapped his pipe into a thick glass ashtray and began repacking tobacco into the bowl.

"When the British passed their threat to Muller," Masson began, his practiced fingers continuing to fill his pipe, "they told us that the combined weight of Britain and its Commonwealth, France, America and the Soviet Union can bury Germany. This memo offers new intelligence seeming to show that, unlike the others, Hitler can't increase the scale of his program much more; he's about at his limit. Germany arguably has the upper hand right now; but every day he waits, his advantage declines."

Finally, he turned to face Hilde, and nodded at her.

"So, she's right; Hitler has to roll the dice *now*. Not a pretty prospect," he added.

Masson scratched a long wooden match and began energetically lighting up his pipe; Muller took the occasion to extract a Gitane and light it, passing the pack to Hilde and lighting hers too.

Minger stood and paced, has hands clasped behind his back, then, standing behind his chair, took a deep breath and faced his audience around the table.

"I suspect we've all been harboring hopes that somehow the threat of war would recede," he began, "but this new information indicates just the opposite; that war is likely to come–and sooner rather than later. We're obliged to act on that assumption, I'm afraid.

"Our priority must be continuing to preserve Switzerland's status as a neutral nation," he went on. "We don't want to give any of our neighbors–the Germans, the French, even the Italians–an excuse to invade us.

"But I think it's prudent to curry favor with the British at this stage. So, Mr. Muller, I want you and Miss Magendanz to go to Geneva and share this new intelligence with the British agents who threatened us last month. This new Economic Warfare Ministry they've set up in London will appreciate getting the information.

"But I want to send a second message too," he added. "Miss Magendanz, Mr. Muller told me about your conversation with one of those Ministry agents–the Consul General I believe–in which you pushed back on their threat by pointing out how dependent they are on Swiss suppliers for vital military equipment."

Glancing at Hilde, Muller saw her stiffen in her chair.

Minger proceeded without even a pause.

"That was a clever initiative," he said, "and I want both of you to drive home the same point when you speak to those characters in Geneva. The fact of the matter is that they're vulnerable; I want you to tell them in no uncertain terms that we know it and we're prepared to act on it if they press too hard. And that leads me to my next point."

"Miss Magendanz," he said, turning his gaze directly on her, "I intend to tell your Chairman, Mr. Fischer, that the Ministry of Military Affairs is commandeering the Bank's German Economic Section, which you head. We need you to use your expertise to identify similar points of leverage that we can use against the Germans in the same way if we need to."

Minger paused and turned to Masson.

"It's a bit more delicate dealing with the French, given our...," he hesitated, "*other* discussions with them."

Masson nodded, but didn't reply.

"Minister Minger," Muller interjected, "I'm invited by a senior French officer to attend the Sesquicentennial Ceremony on Bastille Day in Paris next week–on the 14th. They're putting on a massive parade down the Champs Elysées, showing off their best weaponry and manpower–patting themselves on the back for sure, but also apparently sending a message to the Germans."

Minger paused a moment, thinking.

"Who is this senior French officer?" he asked

"Captain Christian Francin," Muller replied. "He's my brother-in-law and he commands French Army units stationed on the Maginot Line along the Rhine, above Basel. He's even hinted that given the confident mood this muscular show of force is fostering, security along the Line may be lifted enough so he can give me a tour."

"Well, you must take it, of course," said Masson, interrupting and glancing at Minger, who nodded gravely.

"Yes." Minger added. "Masson's right. See what you can learn."

CHAPTER 20

The next afternoon, Hilde and Muller were sitting on the train traveling from Bern to Geneva. It was a Friday and the train was crowded with travelers apparently anxious to visit Geneva's lakeshore and revel in the warm July sunshine.

They were sharing a compartment with an elderly couple who sat across from them on the opposite cushion. The man, with white hair and a bushy white mustache, was dressed in the kind of formal attire Muller associated with an earlier era, a stiff white high-collared shirt, a black tie with stickpin and a dark three-button suit. They'd entered the compartment just prior to departure and an attendant had placed a large valise on the rack above their seat. They'd taken their places with hardly a glance at Muller and Hilde and the man had immediately opened the book he'd been carrying and begun to read, paying no attention to the passing landscape as the train started to move and begin its journey.

Hilde and Muller chatted occasionally and quietly, foreclosed from discussing the subject of their journey by the couple's presence. After a time, Hilde dozed off, her head coming to rest on

Muller's shoulder, which he rather enjoyed. When she awoke, she sat up and stretched, leaning toward the compartment's large window which they'd pulled open to enjoy the summer weather and the breeze from the train's speed.

"During my nap, I dreamed of being on the train when I was young and they still used locomotives," she said. "It was always sooty, and you had to watch out for ashes and even sparks from the smoke. It's so much nicer now that the trains are electrified. Someone made a good decision."

The man sitting opposite looked up from his book.

"Well young lady, we did it to protect ourselves from being held hostage again," he said.

Hilde glanced across the compartment at the man.

"Hostage?" she asked, looking puzzled. "To whom?"

"The Germans," he replied, "during the war."

"We don't have any coal in Switzerland," the man went on. "We had to import every kilo we used from Germany. Our trains were powered by coal then, and coal was in very short supply. The Germans rationed how much they'd sell us, and we had to use what little we got to run our factories and to keep warm, so train travel had to be drastically curtailed. After the war ended, it was decided to invest in electrifying our entire system. And, voila, young lady; today you can take a train ride without coal and without the soot."

The man smiled and returned to his book.

"I hadn't realized that was the reason it happened," Hilde said, smiling at the man.

The man looked up from his book again.

"That's one thing we won't have to worry about if they decide to start a new war," he said. "We still have to import all of our coal from Germany; it's still vital to our economy. But now we've got plenty of electricity to run our trains and do a lot of other things too. In fact, we have so much electricity that we actually export it to them."

The man smiled, but he was not laughing. "The shoe will be on the other foot if it comes to that; we can squeeze *them* this time."

Both Hilde and Muller sat up on their seats.

"Sir, that's very interesting," said Muller, "could you explain a little more what you mean?"

"About Germany threatening to go to war?" he said, "or the part about our electricity exports to them."

Muller flashed a grin. "I'm afraid we're all too familiar with Mr. Hitler's threats, but I didn't know that we export electricity to Germany."

The man put his book down on the cushion next to him and smiled back at Muller and Hilde.

"Well, that's my business," he said, "or it was until I retired. I was President of Atel, the Swiss electric power company, so I know something about the subject."

"Of course, we've heard of Atel," Muller responded, as both he and Hilde nodded their heads. "My family's bank, Muller & Co. was involved in some of your financings."

"You're Karl Muller's son?"

"Yes, sir, I'm Paul, and this is Hildegard Magendanz from the Swiss National Bank.

"My name is Reiner Kuhr," the man replied. "And this is my wife Freida."

He paused, smiling at them. "Switzerland is a very small country."

"Well, here's the point I was making," Kuhr said. "Seven electric power stations were built along the upper Rhine between Lake Constance and Basel and they produce something like a billion kilowatt hours of electricity. The plants certainly require German cooperation–in fact, they're fully tied into the German national grid–but they were financed using mainly Swiss capital, raised by companies like your father's, Mr. Muller. So, they're owned and controlled by Swiss companies–like Atel, for example. Since we're the owners, we get to call the shots."

Kuhr rubbed his hands together, clearly enjoying himself. "In recent years, as Germany's economy has grown–partly because of the military rearmament program pursued by our friend Mr. Hitler–Germany has become the biggest customer for Swiss electricity.

"That means," he said, his tone becoming edgier, "that Germany needs our electricity the same way we need their coal. So, unlike the situation that prevailed during the Great War, when Switzerland lacked any serious leverage to compel Germany to keep supplying coal to us, we now control one of Germany's most vital energy resources, and one which they can't afford to see interrupted.

"I hope, as I expect the two of you do, that we don't have another war," Kuhr said. "But if it should come to that, I'm sure someone in the Swiss government will be smart enough to realize that we have a major bargaining chip if the Germans were to try to squeeze us again–as they very likely would do."

Kuhr paused. "And not to sound too apocalyptic about things, if they should threaten to invade us, our authorities should remind them that it wouldn't take much to blow up those power plants on the Rhine and plunge Germany into darkness."

Then he slapped both hands on his knees and smiled broadly.

"Enough," he said, his voice and expression both lightening. "There's no reason to spoil a perfectly nice summer day."

He took his wife's hand and smiled at her. "Freida, here I am lecturing this nice young couple, off on what I hope is a romantic getaway; you should scold me for behaving that way."

They all laughed.

"We'll see about the romance," said Hilde, putting her arm through Muller's, "but you've certainly added an element of intrigue to the journey."

The train slowed and the conductor announced their imminent arrival in Lausanne.

"We're de-training here," Kuhr said as the couple stood, and he reached for his valise in the overhead.

"Please let me," said Muller, quickly rising and swinging it down, setting it on the cushion next to the door.

Kuhr pulled a business card from a side pocket and handed it to Muller, then shook his hand and bowed toward Hilde with a smile, as he slid open the compartment door and stood aside to let his wife leave first.

"Thank you both for humoring an old man."

CHAPTER 21

The train glided out of the Lausanne station and began running south along the bank of Lac Leman toward Geneva, the high Alps of France clearly visible across the lake in the shimmering sunlight, seeming to dive straight into the far shore. As many times as he'd ridden this route, Paul never failed to look out in wonder at the dramatic vista that unfolded as the train hugged the lakeshore and villages flashed by, obscuring the view only momentarily.

They were alone in the compartment for this last leg of the trip and they sat close to one another savoring the scenery, Paul's arm draped around Hilde, who snuggled against him, rapt with wonder at the passing vista.

"It is truly spectacular," she breathed and then lifted her face toward him, and they kissed hungrily, Muller's tongue finding hers. They wrapped their arms around each other and savored the warmth of the moment. Then giggling, they unwound themselves and kissed once more, lightly, before resuming the role of spectators.

"Mr. Kuhr certainly offered us some insight," Hilde said, reaching up to primp her hair. "I was generally aware that we traded electricity with Germany; I'd see references to it in Reichsbank documents. But I never paid much attention and I'd never thought of it as a potential strategic weapon."

Muller nodded. "I'll have to ask my father about him. A lot of industrialists are secret Nazi sympathizers–some not so secret in fact; there's a lot of money being made there. Swiss plants in Germany and German ones here. Deliberately sketchy ownership arrangements funnel money around. Just business, of course," he added.

"He didn't sound like one, but..." Muller shrugged.

Upon arrival at Geneva's Gare de Cornavin, they de-trained and followed the platform toward the street exit. They had to wait no more than two minutes for a tram which took them down the hill toward the lake. They stepped off at the busy intersection just before the Mont Blanc Bridge then turned right and walked along the quai, looking down at the churning waters of the lake as it narrowed and funneled into the Rhone River, beginning its long journey to the Mediterranean Sea.

The Hotel des Bergues faced the river and, as they approached it, Muller could see Jimmy West sitting at one of the tables clustered on the small plaza in front of the entrance. Muller steered Hilde toward West's table and he stood, looking from Muller to Hilde in confusion.

"Wing Commander West, this is Miss Hildegard Magendanz, formerly Director of the German Bureau of the Swiss National Bank, and now an official of the Swiss Ministry of Military Affairs," Muller said.

"Jimmy," said West automatically, shaking Hilde's hand, then turning to shake Muller's.

"Please be seated," he said, gesturing, and, as they took their seats, West's expression cleared, and he looked at Muller.

"This must be the lady who had that..." West hesitated, "*spirited*...conversation with Consul General Hansen last week at the Minister's reception in Bern."

Muller smiled genially. "It is."

West shook his head.

"Strange," he said, "Hansen told me that some witch had made very pointed remarks about British vulnerability to Swiss military suppliers. But you don't appear to be a witch, Miss Magendanz," he said, turning to face her, smiling.

"I'm sure he meant 'bitch', not 'witch'," Hilde said evenly. "That's how most men react when I tell them something they don't want to hear or answer a question they're too dumb to answer themselves. Happens all the time," she added, shrugging.

West seemed a bit uncertain about how to respond.

"No, no.... I mean...no disrespect was intended," he stammered.

"Like Hell it wasn't," Hilde shot back. "But no matter. I hope he got my message–and conveyed it back to London, loud and clear. Because we mean it."

"Well, we were just in London in fact," West replied, clearly trying to change the subject and steer the conversation.

"And a highly successful visit it was, too," he went on, now smiling broadly. "All the pieces of our economic program are fully in place and ready once the balloon goes up. So, I'm glad you called, Mr. Muller; this meeting is very timely. You said you had some information that Mr. Eden and our new ministry would find helpful; I'm all ears."

Muller bit his tongue. God, the man was sanctimonious.

He didn't speak, but slid the Memorandum out of his briefcase and was about to push it across the table, when a waiter appeared to take their drink orders.

"Gin and tonics all around?" asked West. Hilde and Muller nodded. "No ice," West said to the waiter, "and a bowl of those nice Turkish pistachios."

He nodded and the waiter strode off.

Muller handed West the Memorandum.

"Read it," Muller commanded, gruffly.

Muller pulled out his Gitanes and offered one to Hilde, lighting them both and sat back in his seat, crossing his legs. He was facing back toward the lake and had a view of the greenery on the Isle Rousseau in front of the iconic Mont Blanc Bridge, the Jet d'eau fountain sparkling beyond it and, in the distance, the dark massif of the Salève catching the late afternoon sun. He drew deeply on his Gitane and his annoyance at West and his British masters mounted. A handful of German bombers could destroy these special landmarks in a matter of moments. And these Damnable Brits were once again trying to take charge and dictate the rules–as if they had all the answers.

While Muller sat stewing, he could see West devouring the text of the Memorandum, smiling and uttering small hoots of excitement. When he'd finished reading it, West looked up, his face wreathed in wide grin.

"What did I tell you that night in the Club, Muller," he said excitedly. "We've got'em. We can squeeze the shit out of them and bring down Hitler and that Nazi regime of his."

West made a fist and punched his palm. "This document confirms everything we've been assuming and offers new evidence to prove it. Hjalmar Schacht, Germany's premier banker, warning Hitler that the economy is headed toward collapse–that's the centerpiece of our argument. The memo says that he made exactly our points–and was sacked! Whoo! That's big," West's voice was intense, and he was leaning forward so he would not be overheard. "Then Hitler tries to keep the program going at the same pace, but finds he can't–he has to make *cuts*! And you actually *identify* them; this is a*mazing* information. I have to get it to London immediately; it fits right in with our plans."

The waiter arrived with their drinks and the pistachios which he set down on the table.

West tucked the Memorandum under his jacket and out of sight. Then, when the waiter left he picked up his glass and toasted Muller and Hilde.

"So, what are these plans you have ready to impose?" Muller said, acknowledging West's gesture and taking a large swallow of his drink. "You at least owe us the courtesy of telling us what we can expect from your blockade."

"Ah, dear boy, not just a blockade," West said almost gaily, smiling as if it were some kind of lark they were embarked upon. "We're the Ministry of Economic *Warfare*," he said. We're going to use all the available tools, not just block ports or seize contraband."

West tapped his jacket where the Memo was hidden. "That shortage of foreign exchange your memo describes; we're going to make it much worse–cut off all their exports. Sales of German insurance and reinsurance around the world is one of their big cash cows; we'll shut it down. I have to say, that German exports to Switzerland are a big source of hard currency, so that's on our list too."

"What list is that?" said Muller, trying to fight the urge to confront West.

"Well, of course I can't show it to you–at least not yet,' West said blithely, waving a hand. "But so far it comprises something like twelve hundred commodities and products that'll be embargoed. And, of course, the French are fully on board; they'll make sure there aren't any leaks in their border, and they'll force the Belgians and Dutch to comply as well."

West looked at them triumphantly. "I've even seen plans to sow the Rhine and other waterways with mines to bring German waterborne traffic to a grinding halt. It'll be terrific. And there are other things too, that of course I can't talk about. But we're going to make Germany fall flat on its face and wish it had never heard of Adolf Hitler."

"Ha!" West smacked the table with his hand, nearly spilling the bowl of pistachios.

"You do know that the Rhine is our border with Germany for over 360 kilometers," Hilde said, sharply interrupting him. "Swiss vessels use the Rhine, too, Mr. West," she added, "so mining it would be an act of war against us, as well as Germany. Does your government really want to go to war with Switzerland?"

West looked at her, hesitating.

"Well, maybe we start with just the Elbe," he said a little lamely, "or some canals, I don't know. Look, I'm not the expert in the whole thing, but the ministry's full of really smart people looking at ways to bring down Germany's economy and we've got a plan–actually lots of plans–believe me."

"West, a lot of us are sick to death of your fucking British plans," Muller said, rounding on West, his face only a few feet from West's. "Appeasement," he said, fairly spitting the word. "That was your plan; remember? Eden's baby. Offer Hitler what he wants, and he'll make a deal. Give him the Rhineland; give him the

Saar; give him Austria; give him the Sudetenland. That's all he wants. 'Peace in our time'.

"How has that plan worked out, West?"

Muller plunged on. "Oops, then Hitler took Prague without asking. Oops, now he's threatening to invade Poland. Oops, time for a new plan."

"But this time we've got it right." Muller continued, each word dripping with sarcasm. "This time we're going to bring down the German economy. Because we have a new Ministry of Economic *Warfare* and it has a lot of really smart people."

"Who don't even seem to know where the Rhine River is," Hilde took up when Muller paused for breath. "And who don't seem to know that the British military would be crippled if Switzerland were to return the favor and impose an embargo on arms shipments to Britain.

"And let me tell you something else, Mr. West," Hilde said, leaning in toward him, her expression grim and unsmiling. "You may think that the French are fully on board with your plans to quarantine Switzerland. But let me tell you, the French military is even more dependent upon Swiss arms exports than yours is, and they're telling us they'll do whatever we want–*anything*–so long as we keep shipping them the arms they need. Because without our help, they'd be vulnerable to the Germans, and that scares them to *death*."

West slumped back in his chair, visibly unnerved.

"Please call me Jimmy," he said almost plaintively, then shook his head.

"I can't believe you're saying these things," he said quietly. "Surely we're on the same side; none of us wants a repeat of the Great War or something even worse."

"No, we're *not* on the same side, West," Muller snapped, almost tipping over the table as he flung himself toward West. "Switzerland is a sovereign state that is, has been, and will remain *neutral*.

"We aren't the ones threatening to go to war, West," Muller was now almost on his feet, leaning forward in a crouch, his face only inches from West's. "But we're surrounded by France and Germany–two nations who *are*–and who could invade us at any time, and we're being threatened by a third–your country, Great Britain–which you blithely sit here and tell us has plans to destroy our economy.

"Do you not understand, West, that the very existence of Switzerland is at stake? We're not on *your* side; we're not on *their* side; we're on *our* side. And we'll do whatever we have to do to survive. "We're *neutral*, West, and don't you or your government forget it." Muller stood up and reached in his trousers for coins which he tossed on the table to pay for the drinks.

"Get on a plane and take that fucking memo to London, West– and tell Eden and his friends to get their heads out of their assholes."

Muller stalked off without a glance back, Hilde a step behind him.

CHAPTER 22

Muller was seething. He strode toward the Mont Blanc Bridge, head down, his face a mask of fury.

Hilde caught up to him and put her arm through his and they marched along together in silence. At the center of the bridge, Muller pointed toward the steps leading down to the Isle de Rousseau, the small island of green trees and grass that was home to a park adjacent to the bridge. They descended the stairs and, finding one of the benches unoccupied, they sat down.

Muller finally broke the silence.

"I damned near punched the sonofabitch," he said. "Maybe I should have."

He took a deep breath; his heart was still pounding.

Hilde nudged his arm.

"I think you made your point," she said quietly.

"The arrogance," Muller muttered. "It just infuriates me.

"We'll destroy the German insurance business; well, that will add huge new risk for Swiss insurers–but they never gave it a thought. And Swiss exports to Germany are on the list too–but, of course, we're not telling you which products we're targeting."

Muller waved his arms in frustration.

"Then that business about the Rhine." He shook his head. "You nicely skewered him on that one," he said. "And you're right; Forget Germany, mining the river would be an act of war against *us*."

He turned to look at Hilde.

"How did you know that the French are begging us to keep shipping them arms?"

"Well, I kind of made that up," she said, smiling, "but I'll wager I'm right.

"Look, Paul. The reality is that we're a key arms supplier to all three countries–Germany and France, as well as Britain. None of them can afford to be cut off; as Mr. Minger recognized, that gives us leverage.

"Besides," she added with a small grin, "Jimmy West doesn't know if I'm right or not; so, he's likely to raise doubts about the French when he reports back to his 'very smart people' at the ministry."

Muller chuckled and began to relax.

"I'm beginning to believe my 'very smart person' is smarter than his 'very smart people.'" Muller smiled and took Hilde's arm, more firmly this time.

"So," he said, "I think that completes the mission we were sent here to perform. We delivered the memo to West–which they'll like a lot–and we certainly delivered the message that we'll retaliate if their economic warfare program threatens to hurt us. Maybe someone in the British hierarchy will come to the realization that they'll have to negotiate, not bully us."

Muller put his hands on his knees and slowly rose to his feet.

"That means, Miss Hildegard Magendanz, that we have the rest of the evening and all night to ourselves. Let's make the most of it."

He took Hilde's hand as they walked back to the steps toward the bridge.

"My apartment is just up the hill, past the bridge. I'm inviting you to pay a visit."

"Invitation accepted," Hilde smiled up at him.

CHAPTER 23

They missed the first train back to Bern the next morning. And the one after that too.

Muller finally untangled himself from the bedsheets and stretched an arm out to reach the alarm clock that had fallen to the floor from the bedside table.

"My God, it's eight-thirty," he said, groaning and rolling toward Hilde's bare back next to him.

"We're meant to be in Minger's office by ten."

Hilde lazily rolled over, her breasts teasingly coming to rest on his chest and her arms encircled him.

"We're going to be late," she said, kissing him, as a hand moved to arouse him and she mounted him again.

"Operational delay," she whispered, her hips undulating slowly, then more quickly to match his quickening tempo, then crying out as their passions erupted; they wrapped one another in an intimate embrace as they spent themselves together, then slowly sank back into the sheets, their chests heaving and began to laugh together.

Finally, they rolled on their backs and caught their breath, staring at the sunlight playing on the ceiling through the curtains they'd not managed to close in their haste the night before.

"Team leader declares himself unable to engage in more delaying tactics," Muller said playfully, hitching himself up on his elbows, then swinging his legs to the floor.

"I'm delayed out," he said, standing and stretching languidly, then striding toward the bathroom.

Muller drew a bath for Hilde while he sponged off and shaved.

When he returned to the bedroom, he found Hilde wrapped in a sheet, sitting on the edge of the bed with a cigarette in hand and blowing smoke rings. Standing, she discarded the sheet, ground out the cigarette, then turned to face him, her bare body gleaming in the sunlight, and held out her arms.

Muller moved toward her, wrapped her in his arms, then stepped away before she could capture him again.

"Some team leader," she said, mocking him, then blew a kiss as she strode to the bathroom.

They caught the tram on the Rue Gustave Ador, crossing the Mont Blanc Bridge, and ascended the hill to the Gare Cornavin just in time to purchase tickets for the 10:05 train to Bern. Sitting on the narrow seat of the tram, feeling the heat of Hilde next to him, Muller decided that their clothes didn't look so wrinkled as to give them away. Anyway, approaching their departure track, they found themselves enveloped in a large and boisterous British tour group boarding the same train, who paid them no mind, and they had to scramble to get seats in a compartment.

Quiet conversation was out of the question as the tourists mingled and swapped seats, conversing loudly, enjoying their holiday and ignoring Muller and Hilde who occupied two seats nearest to the windows. They tried to make up for lost sleep, Muller's head resting against one of the seatback pillows and Hilde's on his shoulder.

As Muller dozed, his thoughts kept returning to Hilde; he had only met her a month ago, but he felt utterly captivated. Her spirit and energy matched his own—and their passionate lovemaking last night had been unrestrained and utterly transporting; they had simply lost themselves in one another. Muller finally nodded off with a feeling of deep contentment.

An elbow in the ribs awakened him.

"Time to mount up, team leader," Hilde said cheerfully.

Muller blinked and shook his head as he awakened. Outside the window he could see the train was slowing as it entered the Bern terminal. He drew a deep breath and gamely smiled back at Hilde.

"Duty stations," he said, a little too loudly, as they stood to detrain and follow the British tourists toward the street exit.

They entered the ministry offices just before noon, feeling sheepish and apprehensive of being reprimanded but, to their surprise, they found the reception area empty. Peering down the corridor, they could see Hans Hausamann seated in his office and, looking up, he waved them in and offered them seats.

"The Minister declared a summer weekend," he said. "When you didn't appear promptly at ten this morning, he said he assumed you'd been delayed for some reason and he intended to take advantage of this glorious summer weather; so, he's off to his farm and you're off the hook."

Hausamann gave them a conspiratorial smirk.

"I'm about to depart for my villa in Lucerne; Minger's right, the weather's too good to waste here. But I'll buy us all lunch first; you both look as though you could use some nourishment."

"Come," Hausamann smiled, standing and leading the way. "We'll walk to the Tierpark Dahlholzli and sit alongside the Aare under the plane trees."

A table right alongside the rail above the river opened just as they arrived. The waiters promptly cleared it, laid down a clean blue checkered tablecloth and beckoned them to be seated. The famous zoo with its bears and other animals was nearby, but the restaurant offered a tranquil oasis and was famous for its draft Felsenau beer. Hausamann ordered a full pitcher, which arrived immediately.

"Bratwurst and potato salad are mandatory here," he said cheerfully, eliciting nods from Muller and Hilde.

"Prost," he said as they tapped beer steins. "I hope the meeting went off as planned and your delay didn't signal a problem."

"We delivered the messages as instructed," Muller said matter-of-factly. He didn't propose to get into any detail.

"Actually, Paul wanted to punch the guy," Hilde said with a broad smile. "He bragged about their plans to destroy the German insurance business and blocking our trade with Germany–he even threatened to mine the Rhine River."

"Well, Hilde kneecapped him on that one," Muller interrupted, "reminding him that we use the Rhine too and sowing mines would be a declaration of war on us as well as Germany. He backed off pretty quickly.

"But this damned new Ministry of Economic Warfare of theirs seems to have the bit in its teeth." Muller sighed. "I didn't punch him–though Hilde's right, I wanted to–but I warned him that we'd retaliate against any action that injured us and I told him that they needed to stop bullying us and begin negotiating."

"Did he react?" Hausamann took a deep draught from his stein.

"I'm afraid I didn't give him time to reply," Muller said.

"He got the message and he'll pass it back to London too," Hilde added confidently. "He loved the memo–and we also told him the French were much more interested in buying arms from us than enforcing British sanctions against us.

"That was Hilde's addition, sir," Muller interjected. "I saw West's Adam's apple quiver when she told them the French were eating out of our hand to keep up the weapons flow; it was a clever way of throwing a little sand in their gears."

Hausamann chuckled.

"Mister Minger will like that one too, Miss Magendanz," he said. "You two seem to have become a good team.

"And will you be traveling to France together as a team too?" he added with an inquisitive smile.

"I certainly hope so, sir," Muller replied quickly. "I'm trying to make the arrangements, though I haven't shared them all with Miss Magendanz."

"Well, it's 'La Grande Semaine, in Paris,'" Hausamann said. "I've been following it in the newspapers. They're pulling out all the stops for this Sesquicentennial celebration of theirs. Are you booked for the best parties, Muller?"

Muller looked at Hausamann quizzically. "I've been invited to watch the military parade, sir; are there parties I should know about?"

"Of course," Hausamann said grinning broadly. "'Tout Paris' is in the social whirl, Muller. The Americans kicked things off a few nights ago with an embassy extravaganza that included visiting senators and congressmen–and Mary Pickford and Douglas Fairbanks, were both on hand too. Your Polish friends–what's that Ambassador's name? Ah, Juliusz Łukasiewicz; hard to pronounce– well, he apparently outdid them a few nights later at their fabulous new embassy when he led a mazurka into the fountains on the grounds around 4 AM. Even Reynaud, that sour little Finance Minister, joined the conga line along with Arthur Rubinstein's gorgeous wife."

Hausamann laughed as the waiter delivered their meal and a new pitcher of Felsenau.

"Muller, you must pay attention to the society section of *Le Matin* or you'll miss out on all the excitement."

They began attacking the plump sausages and Hausamann continued his commentary between bites.

"According to the papers, both Gamelin and Hore-Belisha attended the Polish gala too–the French Chief of Staff and the British Secretary for War, making a show of solidarity for the beleaguered Poles–though it's not clear if they joined the conga line."

"I'm doing my part too," he went on. "I've wangled an invitation to the ball Goëring's throwing next week at Carinhall, his estate just outside Berlin. So, while the two of you are cavorting with the French and British, I'll be embracing the Swastika with the Germans."

"Warring parties," he went on, with a smile. "If only that were all that's going on."

Hausamann's expression turned serious. "Here we are in July 1939, seemingly headed for war unless one side or the other blinks–which doesn't look very likely–and," he paused, "it's party time! Surely there's something we should be doing to avert a war that we all fear; but there doesn't seem to be anything is there? It's very strange; almost eerie, don't you think?"

They were silent for a moment.

Muller fiddled with his beer stein, then took a long draught. "My host in Paris, Captain Francin, claims the parade will send a message to Hitler that France is the most powerful nation on earth; the idea is to give him pause in his threat to invade Poland. The Allies seem ready to call his bluff this time. At least that's the message they seem to be sending."

Hausamann nodded. "Actually, the French have gone out of their way to involve the British in this show of force too," he said. "According to what I'm reading, they're flying Union Jacks alongside the tricolor in the streets of Paris and British forces will be on full display in the parade. So, you're right; this exercise is an unmistakable message to Hitler. We're the alliance that defeated Germany twenty years ago; we're even stronger today and ready to do it again if you start a war now. So, back off."

Hausamann poured the remains of the pitcher into their steins. "The question is whether Hitler will hear the message.

"Or believe it," he added.

"The Americans were part of that alliance twenty years ago," Hilde interjected. "And they're nowhere to be found at the moment, except maybe at the embassy punch bowl," she added with a smile to Hausamann, who nodded vigorously.

"Not only that, but Roosevelt's hands have been tied by Congress so he can't even supply any of the belligerents in case of war," Hausamann said.

Hausamann thumped his hand on the table and signaled for another pitcher of beer.

"Damn! We should have instructed you to see what your friend Jimmy West has to say about that."

Muller and Hilde looked at him quizzically.

"The US Congress adjourned last week," Hausamann said. "It won't reconvene until next January. Roosevelt had a bill pending in one of their Committees extending the waiver of the Neutrality Act that expired back at the end of May. The waiver is what permits the Americans to sell arms and equipment to the British and French. Muller, West told you that the British plan is counting on America not only to help them embargo Germany, but also to be their key weapons supplier. 'The arsenal of democracy' is what Roosevelt's calling it; remember?"

Muller and Hilde nodded.

"Well, the US Neutrality Act forbids sale of weapons to any belligerent; the only way the Americans can supply tanks and planes to the French and the British is under the waiver that expired six weeks ago. But instead of extending it, the committee voted it down, then proceeded to adjourn; which is why those congressmen and senators were in Paris partying at the embassy the other night! So not only is the American military sitting quietly an ocean away–and not part of the forces squaring off against one another here in Europe–but the supply of US weapons that both western Allies were counting on will dry up.

"Everyone assumed the problem would get fixed," Hausamann said. "But it didn't, and the ramifications are only beginning to sink in."

"We didn't know about this, Mr. Hausamann," Hilde said softly.

"West may not have known either," Hausamann said. "Our embassies are telling us that both the French and British press have been ordered to downplay the story, so it's still not widely appreciated."

"But Hitler must know about it," Muller said. "This has to feed into our belief that he has nothing to gain by delaying."

"That's probably right," Hausamann replied with a sour expression. Then he used his sleeve to dry the tabletop in front of him and reached for one of the cocktail napkins. He pulled out his fountain pen and began to draw.

"So, here's the Rhine River," he said, "running east to west from Lake Constance to Basel, where it takes a sharp right hand turn north toward Amsterdam. Germany here to the north and east of the river." He made a mark on the napkin. "Switzerland south of it, here, as far as Basel," another mark, "then France west of it, up past Strasbourg where the border turns west. Right?"

Muller and Hilde nodded in agreement.

"And this crooked line here," he drew it awkwardly, "is the famous Maginot Line running west of the Rhine above Basel, then turning sharp left along France's northern border with Germany. I've run out of room on my napkin, but the Line extends west as far as the Belgian border.

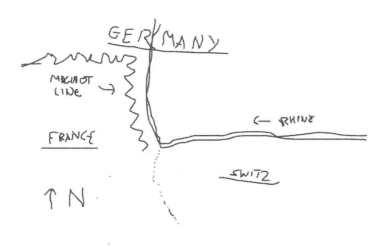

"Now, let's assume we really do face war," Hausamann said. "We're right on the border with both France and Germany; what's our biggest risk?"

Hausamann pulled a pencil out of his pocket and slashed big red arrows across his napkin map.

"Germany decides to flank the Maginot Line, attacks us across the Rhine and invades France from the east. See? They occupy this big area of Western Switzerland, sweep us aside and head West toward Paris."

"The Swiss territory they'd invade is the Gempen Plateau." Hausamann wrote the name 'Gempen' on the napkin. "It's rolling countryside that's good for tanks and infantry to move through. But of course, they wouldn't just invade and move on; they'd need to occupy the Gempen area and secure it so they could supply their troops. So that would become German-occupied territory."

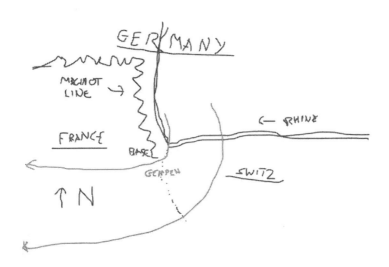

"But that's nearly all of Western Switzerland," exclaimed Hilde, leaning forward, her elbow on the table to get a closer look. "They could go as far south as Geneva and skirt the Jura Mountains, then turn northwest into France and attack Paris that way."

"Exactly," said Hausamann, nodding. "They could also turn directly north from below Basel and attack the Maginot Line from the rear; it's not designed to protect against that threat. So, this is a pretty scary scenario."

"But, of course, the French must be aware of this risk," Muller said. "They can read maps too; it's pretty obvious."

"Of course," said Hausamann. "That presumably why they've stationed their 8th Army along the Swiss-French frontier here," he pointed to the space between his two red slashes, "and north behind the Maginot Line facing the Rhine. They would be the first line of defense against this kind of flanking attack."

Muller slid the napkin toward himself. "I'm no expert," he said, "but wouldn't we want the French to move across the frontier and reinforce us as soon as any German attack begins? We don't have a standing army, but we've got—what is it—something like 400,000 men that can be mobilized in a matter of hours and train regularly to do just that. Isn't it fair to assume we've been coordinating with the French on some plan to meet this threat?"

He slid the napkin back in front of Hausamann, looking at him expectantly.

"Muller, you know very well that we're *neutral*," Hausamann said slowly, emphasizing the word. "If we were to undertake a joint military planning exercise with the French–and Germany were to find out about it–poof! Our claim of neutrality would go up in smoke and any constraint our neutral status might have on German behavior would disappear.

"We'd become a belligerent, Muller." Hausamann said the words quietly, but very firmly. "We'd be accused of having picked sides and given up any pretense of neutrality. And, frankly, that would be accurate."

They sat in silence for a moment. Muller fished into his pocket, pulled out his cigarettes case and offered Gitanes, then flourished his lighter.

"So, there's been no coordination," Muller said when he was done.

Hausamann simply shrugged. "It's a dilemma," he said finally, exhaling and watching the smoke as it wafted away. "We have permanent military staff officers in our Ministry, Muller, and they have contact with their French military counterparts; both sides know we face this threat from Germany; it's no secret. But our officers have contact with their German military counterparts too. And the Germans tell us they're concerned that the French will invade us, then attack *them* across the Rhine."

He pointed at the napkin. "Reverse the red arrows, Muller," he said. "The French army attacks us across the Gempen Plateau, then heads north to invade Germany across the Rhine."

Muller slid the napkin over to look more closely. He'd never thought about that possibility, but there it was, just as Hausamann had said.

"Is that a real threat?" Muller asked, feeling a little foolish and out of his depth.

"Well, look at the map, Muller." Hausamann pointed again to the napkin. "Of course it's a threat. If the French Army were to attack us through the Gempen, we couldn't defeat them–any more than we could defeat a German invasion over the Rhine. We'd fight; put up a stiff resistance. But the reality is that either army would quickly overwhelm us. That's why we have to be so careful and not be seen to favor one side over the other. So, we haven't coordinated a military response with either of them."

Muller sighed; he felt a little annoyed at himself for not having realized the realities of the dilemma.

"I want to talk this over with Captain Francin," Muller said. "He's posted to the French 8th Army–I don't know where, behind the Maginot Line on the Rhine or across our frontier. And I don't know that he'll tell me. But his command must be thinking about this constantly; what do we do if this happens, what do we do if that happens…"

Muller shook his head, leaving the sentence unfinished. Then he reached for the napkin. "May I take this with me?"

Hausamann picked it up, folded it carefully and handed it to Muller. "Why do you think I drew it?" he said with a broad smile.

CHAPTER 24

The telephone line to Paris was unusually clear, and Muller could hear the clink of glasses and a hum of conversation in the background as Francin responded to his question with a barking laugh.

"Muller, I'm really happy you've found a new girlfriend and I'm looking forward to meeting her. But adding her for the Sesquicentennial parade? Impossible; no tickets left at all; it was all I could do to get you one a month ago. And of course, she can't be included in the Maginot tour, which is still on the next day and which I'm assuming you're still doing."

"Yes, yes," Muller hurriedly replied; "I'm counting on it. I'd just hoped...."

"Muller, Paris is packed," Francin interrupted him. "People are camping in parks and sleeping on benches. This is the biggest celebration we've ever had–150 years since the Bastille. I got you that room at Hotel de la Trémoille, but it was hard to do; I had to pull some strings. Also, it's a single and it was expensive, as you'll find out when you pay me back.

"A single bed would be a little small even for a new girlfriend," Francin added with another laugh. "Sorry to disappoint you, but it's going to be a challenge even to pull off what we've already planned; adding another person–even though I'm sure she's wonderful–is simply out of the question. So, no. Sorry."

Then the usual crackle of interference on the international telephone line flared and something Francin was saying was swallowed up in the ether. After a few 'hellos' to try and re-establish contact, Muller hung the small black receiver on the wall-mounted telephone receptacle.

Hilde received the news with a shrug. "It was a little last minute," she said.

"But maybe Mr. Hausamann can take me to Göering's party," she said with an impish smile, avoiding Muller's elbow.

So it was, a day later, that Muller found himself sitting alone in a compartment of a train speeding toward Basel–the SBB station–where he'd transfer to the French SNCF system that would take him through Dijon to Paris. The train was not crowded, and he found himself dozing, instead of concentrating on the book he'd brought along, *Inside Asia*, by the American journalist John Gunther. Movie newsreels he'd seen showed harrowing scenes of bitter fighting in China between the Japanese and Chinese troops. There were regular reports of initiatives by Hitler and Mussolini to make a tripartite alliance with the Japanese–which the Allies viewed with alarm. Muller didn't know much about Asia, so, figuring he'd have time to read on the trip, he'd picked up a copy at a bookstore and tossed it in the small bag he was bringing along. Maybe he'd learn something; at a minimum, it would help pass the time. But somehow the summer heat and the soothing clickity-clack of the train–along with the unfamiliar names and geography Gunther was gamely describing–dulled his concentration and he kept nodding off until they arrived in Basel right on time.

Muller's connection was a little over an hour, and he decided to make the long trek over to the SNCF section and find a bite to eat before boarding his Paris-bound train. The French rail electric system used a different current than the Swiss, requiring a different catenary, so French SNCF trains used a separate set of platforms situated on the western side of the vast SBB terminal.

As he approached it, he found himself caught up in a crowd of revelers, which got bigger and noisier as he approached track 30, where the departure board listed his Paris-bound train. The connection hadn't arrived yet, but the happy swarm of travelers was already caught up in the Sesquicentennial celebration. Every third adult seemed to have an open bottle of wine–or something stronger–and baskets of food were being passed about. A couple of stern-looking gendarmes carrying nightsticks kept the crowd from flooding the platform and they gamely tried to keep open a corridor for passengers who would be de-training. No one seemed to mind; young men and women, whole families with oldsters as well as children, stood, sat in circles on the concrete floor of the terminal or lounged on pieces of luggage.

Seeing these were to be his companions on the two-and-a-half hour journey to Paris, Muller decided he might as well join in; this was clearly not to be a quiet, relaxed trip for napping and reading. So, he elbowed his way to a storefront and bought himself a bottle of burgundy–no label; someone's house wine–and a baguette with some sliced meats.

When the Paris-bound train arrived and its passengers managed to find their way off the arrival platform, the gendarmes stood aside, and the waiting crowd streamed onto the platform to board. Muller joined the throng; it resembled a rugby scrum, he thought, but very good-natured and loud. He had a first-class compartment near the front of the train, and he was able to scramble aboard and claim a window seat ahead of a couple of families with members who didn't all have tickets for the compartment. No one seemed to mind, and seats were finally secured for all but three adolescent boys–Muller judged them to be around 12 or13–who were thrust out in the corridor and seemed happy to be part of the traffic jam, away from their parents' reproaches and warnings to be careful. Finally, the train lurched forward, to mighty cheers from the passengers, and as they got underway, the entire train seemed to break into a loud rendition of *La Marseille.*

It was a long, noisy, crowded trip. The train made unscheduled stops to pick up additional travelers from smaller towns en route and the scheduled stop in Dijon took an extra 30 minutes as new passengers crowded aboard and struggled to find their ticketed places, most of which were already occupied. Muller's traveling companions were shopkeepers from the Jura. They were friendly and offered to share the contents of their food baskets, biscuits, fruits, coarse local bread, which Muller found much tastier than his baguette, and fresh local cheeses. And wine; there was plenty to go around and everyone liberally indulged themselves, leading to a few short alcohol-induced naps among the adults. There was a lot of commotion and visits to-and-from compartment from other families and friends, and Muller felt he'd been enveloped by an entire community of partygoers.

At least they weren't speaking Vaudoise, he said to himself.

As they approached Paris, Muller desperately needed to piss, but he couldn't face trying to navigate the packed corridor to the WC at the end of the car. So, he crossed his legs and concentrated on the grimy walls of the buildings they were passing on the approach to Paris.

Finally, the trains glided into the Gare de l'Est, stopping with a jolt. Muller bid a quick farewell to his new friends, opened the compartment door and hurried along the platform toward the terminal. He spied a pissoir and slipped in, relieving himself, and thinking how civilized the French were to have such conveniences.

The terminal was very crowded, with trains arriving from other points of departure packed with excited Sesquicentennial celebrants. Like the passengers on his train, the crowd was raucous but cheerful–and well-lubricated; bottles were being passed about freely as people milled around in the great hall, under the soaring skylights where July's evening sunshine still glowed.

How to get to the hotel? Muller knew the Métro could take him to the Place de l'Alma along the Seine in the 8th Arrondissement. So, he walked toward the stairs leading down to the entrance and quickly saw it was so crowded he could barely get down the stairs, let alone get into the station anther level down. What about a bus or a taxi? A quick glance told him those were jammed too. He could walk, he supposed; but it was a long hike. And the food and drink he'd consumed en route didn't make that an appealing option.

There was a large map of the surrounding area nearby, so he walked over to look and made a decision. If he exited the station and walked north, he would run into the La Chapelle Mètre station where he could board a west-bound train on the Number 2 line. That would take him up to La Place des Ternes, but then turn back toward the Seine and allow him to exit at L'Arc de Triomphe at the Étoile, which was only about a fifteen minute walk from the Hotel de la Trémoille.

That's what he proceeded to do, striding along La Rue du Faubourg-St. Denis past the nearby Gare du Nord and in a few minutes reaching the Boulevard La Chapelle, where he saw the familiar Métro sign. But after crossing the boulevard–there was only bus and taxi traffic; apparently Paris had been closed to private autos–and before heading down the entry stairs–which were crowded but not jammed–he was beckoned into a park by a boisterous group of young men and women who were gathered about a statue, laughing and whooping.

"Come on over," they shouted, "Come have a drink, it's free."

Intrigued, Muller walked toward them and saw they had several cups that they were passing around then refilling from the statute's fountain.

"They've filled it with wine," a couple of the women said to him, laughing as he approached and offering him their cups.

"It's the finest from La Ville de Paris," a bearded young man wearing a tricolor jersey said; "Parisian house red."

Muller took a sip, then another, laughingly passing back the cup.

"No, no, finish it," said one of the girls, a buxom, red-cheeked blonde said. "Then I need a big kiss."

"Yes, right," everyone chimed in, "down the hatch and a big smack!"

Muller obliged, tilting back the cup, then finishing with a flourish and a big grin before stepping up to the blonde, wrapping her in his arms, and delivering an open-mouthed kiss to the cheers of the crowd.

"Another, another," they cheered.

But Muller disengaged himself and retreated toward the Mètro, waving to his new friends.

Red wine being served by the city from fountains; now that was some way to celebrate. Muller shook his head in admiration. Wine and pissoirs; Paris was a great city.

He finally made it to the Arc de Triomphe station and exited to the famous Étoile plaza which was decked out with tricolor bunting and banners–and union jack British flags too, as Hausamann had predicted. The plaza itself was fenced off by barriers and gendarmes patrolled to keep any stray celebrants from entering. High grandstands had been erected around the plaza perimeter and Muller could seem them extending along the Champs Élysées in both directions. He assumed his ticket for tomorrow's parade would be in one of them.

He circled the plaza and walked along Avenue Marceau, admiring the distinctive stone facades of the apartment buildings that lined both sides of the street as it descended toward the Seine and the Pont de l'Alma. The Hotel de la Trémoille, which he soon spied off to his left, featured the same façade, topped by a turreted slate roof and tall, rectangular windows lined up, facing the spacious court at the entry.

The twilight was beginning to fade as he pushed through the hotel's revolving door and entered a dim reception area with a highly polished floor that came to life as someone illuminated the lights and Muller could appreciate the carved-wood, decorative ceiling and columns that lined the cream-colored walls. The reception was on his right and he was relieved to find that his room hadn't been assigned to someone else, even though it was approaching ten in the evening. As Francin had warned, it was a narrow single, containing no more than a bed, a chair at its foot, and a small bureau with a basin and cream porcelain pitcher of water; but the lavatory was only a few doors away. Muller tested the bed, stretched out, and promptly fell sound asleep.

CHAPTER 25

The parade was scheduled to begin at noon at the Place de le Concorde and progress the full length of the Champs Élysées, through the Arc de Triomphe and on to the banks of the Seine. Public sections of the grandstands were opened at 10 AM and immediately filled by men, women and children, many of whom had spent the night waiting in anticipation of that moment and weren't to be denied, swarming up the steep steps to claim coveted seats. Many were dressed in patriotic colors, with tricolor garb of one kind or another. Veterans wore khaki tunics–some even full uniforms–from the Great War and, ready for a long day in the sun, nearly everyone carried food and drink, the well-to-do armed with wicker-encased thermoses.

Muller had awakened early and strolled through the neighborhood, mingling with the large crowds. In spite of himself, he found himself caught up in the excitement of the moment. People seemed to be bursting with pride and happiness–singing spontaneously, swinging one another in happy dances, clapping in unison. At one corner, he watched dozens of laughing citizens dancing around an organ grinder and his monkey, who was somersaulting and leaping into the air. There was a sense of relief in the air, he thought; a sense of confidence that France was strong and powerful and could defeat any foe. Apprehensions and divisions were swept aside; this massive celebration was a testament to the greatness of France and its promise that the world was smiling on the French people.

Muller felt a very tangible upsurge of national pride in the air as he made his way to the Champs Élysées.

A soldier in full-dress uniform examined Muller's ticket and led him to a seat halfway up a grandstand situated just before the Etoile and close to the reviewing stands on either side of the Arc de Triomphe. He took his place around 11:00, not wanting to be late and risk getting squeezed out. He observed many other early arrivals doing the same, peering at the slatted wood seats for their assigned places. He was dressed in the lightest summer suit he owned, tan, linen and single-breasted which he could open while seated to hopefully catch any breeze. It was already warm, the sky bright and nearly cloudless, and the sun would be hot and right overhead. He'd purchased a light straw hat from a street vendor which offered a little protection. Others he noted, has already taken out white handkerchiefs and put them on their heads.

Police motorcycles noisily crisscrossed the line of march, ensuring all was in order. Then a cavalcade of black limousines was driven to the edge of the reviewing stand and diplomats and uniformed military leaders began filing into their places. Muller wished he'd thought to bring along binoculars, but even from a distance he could make out a few important dignitaries who seemed familiar from newsreels–in fact he was almost certain he spied Anthony Eden, with his familiar reddish mane and mustache, in a dark suit and homburg.

Well, of course Eden would be one of the dignitaries, Muller said to himself; then grinning, he thought of paying a visit to his newly-denominated senior contact for economic warfare. Why, of course, he could just stroll over to the Hotel Georges V after the parade–it was just a short walk–and inform British security that Mr. Eden would welcome a surprise visit from his Swiss spy. Ha!

Muller continued to muse about that unlikely encounter when, suddenly, a distant hum began over the horizon and rapidly became an enormous throbbing noise as a seemingly endless parade of aircraft roared overhead, barely a thousand feet above the crowd which, almost as one, leapt to its feet peering upward and pointing. Muller didn't know one plane model from another, so he fumbled with the program he'd stuffed in a pocket and scanned it to identify them.

First were the big French bombers, Blochs, Breguets and Liore-et Oliviers, followed by the smaller fighter planes, the Dewoitine 37's and the famous Morane-Saulnier M.S. 406s, the pride of the French Air Force. Then, after a short interval, came flights of British planes, Blenheims, Wellingtons, Hurricanes, Hampdens. The planes –315 of them, according to the program– cruised just above the treetops making a deafening racket and conveying an unmistakable message of strength and power. Muller could scarcely believe his eyes and ears and he marveled at the extraordinary display that unfolded above him.

Then, the planes were gone and, in the distance, came the marching men–thirty thousand strong, each one representative of a hundred, who could be mobilized behind them, according to the program. First were troops from the vast French Empire, Madagascans, Senegalese and Indochinese, all bedecked in bright dress uniforms and swinging along in formation. One after another they marched past and Muller began to lose track; Chasseurs Alpins with skis ropes and rifles; desert troops on prancing stallions; Zouaves, with flaring pantaloons and bright red headpieces, St. Cyr cadets, with white-plumed kepis–even bearded Foreign Legionnaires.

On and on, they came. At some point the French 8th Army troops swung by, but Muller wasn't able to spot Christian Francin. British troops were represented by the Grenadier Guards, the Scots, His Majesty's own Regiment with their high black woolen bonnets (which must have been unbearably hot, Muller mused to himself), the Coldstream Guards and the Royal Marine Band.

Trucks, armored cars, light tanks rolled past (the heavy ones would damage the roadway, the program explained) and artillery formations, mobile and fearsome in appearance. The French Navy had a large contingent, with their blue uniforms, white neckpieces and white dress bonnets with the bright red insignia at the peak, singing lustily as they marched along.

It was all quite exhausting, and by late afternoon, when the Premier, Edouard Daladier, made what the newspapers later reported as a stirring speech, the stands had begun to empty. Still there was heavy applause as the Premier delivered a promise to "assure the salvation of peace and liberty."

Muller clambered down from the grandstands along with the rest of the crowd. People stretched their legs and children gamboled about behind the stands and under the trees, and while a few departed, most stayed, milling about chatting and reliving the remarkable event they'd just witnessed. Cafés and bars filled up and patrons carried glasses outside to waiting friends or families. There was a happy buzz of conversation and boisterous laughter; an almost palpable sense of contentment, it seemed to Muller. He spied a wine fountain that evidently had been turned on and was being patronized by a large contingent of mainly young men and women; he decided to give it a wide berth after yesterday's experience.

Eventually, he found himself back at the Hotel and strolled into the air-conditioned bar. He bought himself a beer and began chatting with other guests who were also taking refuge from the late afternoon heat. Everyone seemed to have a favorite anecdote to relate and it was a relaxed place to unwind.

BOOOOM!

Suddenly and without warning, there was a loud concussion on the Rue Marbeuf side of the hotel; dense smoke and shards of sharp glass exploded into the bar through a shattered window and chunks of plaster fell from the walls and ceilings. People screamed and ducked in their chairs and under tables, throwing up their arms to protect themselves.

Seated at the bar, Muller's back was to the room, but he could see the blast in the mirror and feel the concussion. Instinctively, he jumped down from his bar stool, curling himself up, hands behind his head, squatting on the floor, and shoulder against the facing of the bar.

Then silence; an eerie quiet, before cries from frightened men and women resumed.

Muller stood slowly, gingerly took a few steps, making sure he was unhurt and began brushing white plaster off himself as he surveyed the scene before him. People began clambering up from the floor where they'd taken cover and rising from their seats. Tables along the far wall had been toppled by the blast and Muller saw many patrons had suffered cuts which friends were trying to help staunch with napkins and tablecloths. Confusion reigned, as people cried out for help and many of those unhurt tried to find a way out of the bar.

Muller was close to the wide doorway and he quickly stepped out into the reception area to make way for others trying to leave too. His eyes were drawn to the hotel entrance where the door was open, and he caught a glimpse of people running in the outdoor plaza. He sprinted toward the doorway and saw a crowd standing over a prone young man dressed in what appeared to be a blue-shirted uniform with leather cross straps and military breeches.

Someone had evidently thrown him to the ground and a group of men was beginning to kick him; over their shoulder, Muller saw others across the plaza chasing another young man in a similar uniform.

The crowd began cursing the man on the ground closest to Muller.

"Fucking Franciste."

"We'll beat you to a pulp you fascist punk."

Muller grabbed the shoulder of one of the men closest to him. "What's going on?

"We saw these jerks light a bomb and throw it at the store, there," the man said pointing back toward the Rue Marbeuf. "They're such dummies, they missed the window and it bounced into the street and nearly blew *us* up."

He delivered a kick at the man, who had curled himself up for protection and put his arms over his head.

"They're Francistes," he said, "Blue Shirt fascists. We're gonna beat the shit out of them. Pricks!" He aimed another blow, but missed and staggered away.

By this time the blaring sound of police sirens filled the plaza and motorcycle police followed by gendarme sedans and several ambulances began pouring into the crowded space. The gendarmes took charge of the two attackers, who had been caught, and white-jacketed ambulance attendants raced into the hotel carrying medical bags and stretchers.

Muller backed away and turned to walk toward the Rue Marbeuf. It was easy to see the dark blast mark on the road surface where the bomb, or whatever it was, had exploded; the force had even dislodged several dozen of the paving stones which were scattered around a blackened crater. On the right the wall of the hotel was singed with black powder marks from the blast. What had been the large window into the bar had been blown open, with interior curtains swinging in the breeze and shattered glass heaped on the sidewalk below. On his left, across the street from the hotel, Muller saw a sign reading 'Tannenbaum Boucherie' and below it, in smaller print, 'Specialité Kosher'.

So, a Jewish butcher targeted by local French fascists; just like he'd seen their Nazi counterparts behave in Danzig and Vienna. Muller shook his head in disgust.

The windows of the boucherie had been blown out, but there didn't appear to be much other damage. Meats and other products on display were still there, though jumbled up and covered by glass. Muller could see a grey-haired man–probably the proprietor, he was wearing a stained white apron and a black yarmulke–standing in front of the store, speaking animatedly and gesticulating to onlookers–or maybe family and friends.

He was lucky to be alive, Muller thought as he turned and walked back toward the hotel entrance.

Gendarmes barred entry, but he was permitted inside after persuading one of the burly officers that he was a hotel guest. The reception area had been converted into an aid station and people with bloody gashes and other injuries were sitting or lying on chairs and stretchers that had been laid out. The bar was still in shambles, but a group of men, apparently unhurt, had gathered at the doorway. Muller skirted the wounded and walked over to them.

"How bad is it?" he asked

"It looks like no one was killed, at least," said one of the men whose dark suit was covered in white plaster dust. "We seem to have some broken bones over there," he pointed toward the area of the bar closest to the window, "and lot of cuts from the glass; I heard someone may lose an eye and there'll be a lot of stitches. But it could have been much worse."

The others grunted in agreement.

"What did you find outside?" one asked him.

"Well, they caught a couple of the guys that did it. They're dressed in Franciste uniforms," he replied. "Their target was a kosher boucherie there, across the street," Muller pointed. "But the bomb went off in the middle of the street, right outside the window."

"Francistes," said one of the men. He fairly spat the words, "The Blue Shirts. Them and the Croix-de-Fer, our own home-grown fascists. Sonsofbitches; just what we needed on a day like this."

"I thought they were disbanded by the Front in '36," another said.

"The Front," still another said contemptuously. "Blum and his Communists; as far left as those Francistes are to the right. Sure, he banned them; but everything he touched turned to shit. And now here they are again–and throwing bombs on Bastille Day–on the Sesquicentennial, for Christ's sake."

"Hang on, you can't blame this on Blum," said another.

A loud quarrel ensued as the men began arguing with one another and were joined by others weighing in with their own opinions. Muller edged away. There was no point in hanging around to listen to what was likely to end up in a disagreeable shouting match.

He could see the lifts were operating, so, getting his key from reception, he ascended to his fourth-floor room and was happy to see that it had not been damaged.

He checked his watch; already after 7PM. He'd be late for the reception Francin had invited him to at his parents' apartment in the Champs de Mars. Well, no matter.

He'd met the parents when their daughter had married Thomas, but he hadn't seen them since and really didn't know them; Christian was the one he'd kept in touch with.

He hung his suit jacket on the hook on the back of the door and took a brush to try remove plaster and glass, then cursed as several chunks of glass fell to the floor that he had to sweep under the bed to get out of the way. Removing his shirt, he poured water into the basin and sponged himself thoroughly, to remove the perspiration from the afternoon as well as the residue of the blast. Buttoning a fresh shirt and selecting the other tie he'd brought along, he shook the suit jacket again then walked out of his room, locked the door and strode to the lift.

He stopped, then he walked back to his room, unlocked it, reached into his case and pulled out the carefully folded cocktail napkin, which he placed in the right pocket of his suit jacket. Then he retraced his steps and descended in the lift.

The hotel lobby was still chaotic, but he picked his way around the makeshift aid station and exited onto the plaza. A crowd had gathered to see what had happened and he overheard someone say a radio bulletin had reported several people were killed in the attack. The gendarmes kept the crowd at a distance, but he could see it was growing as curious Parisians came to gawk.

He walked over to the Avenue Georges Cinq, noting with amusement that there was already a clutch of people in line for the first show at the Crazy Horse night club. Crossing the Seine on the Pont de l'Alma, he strolled along Avenue Rapp, the Eiffel Tower a tall presence on his right, the plaza beneath it teeming with people, and–he could see–one of the wine fountains being enthusiastically sampled.

The Francin's apartment building was situated on the Avenue Emile Deschanel, an upscale and highly desirable residential neighborhood adjacent to the Champs de Mars and literally in the shadow of the Eiffel Tower. When he arrived, he saw that a big picnic had been laid out on the front lawn behind the protective hedge: tables, chairs, a bar; dozens of people were mingling, smoking, drinking, talking and laughing, and children were cavorting at the other end of the lawn.

He paused at the entry and regarded the jovial scene, unsure how to proceed. An attractive, dark-haired lady dressed entirely in white, a red rose in her hair above her ear, approached him with a smile, carrying two champagne flutes, one of which she proffered him.

Madame Francin; with a rush of relief he belatedly recognized his hostess. She offered her cheeks for greeting, handed him a flute, then embraced him.

"Paul Muller," she said, "we've all been so worried; that attack at the Trémoille. You're safe? You're all right?"

Muller smiled at her; Christ, what was her first name?

He bowed then clinked her flute with his own.

"Couldn't be better; not a bit the worse for wear."

"Come, meet everyone; all of us in the building decided to join forces outside on the lawn tonight. It'll be a little disorganized, but fun," and she led him into the party, clapping her hands and announcing, "Mr. Muller is here, safe and sound."

Guests came crowding around; apparently, he'd been the subject of conversation, so he related the story of what had happened and answered questions until people began drifting away.

He was still describing the post-blast finger-pointing in the hotel bar when he was handed another flute of champagne and recognized Jacques Francin–his name was Jacques, he was sure–

Christian's father. Muller now remembered that the father was an influential figure, occupying a very senior position in the Caisse des Dépôts et Consignations, the financial institution that was often referred to as the investment bank of the French government.

"Welcome, Mr. Muller," he said with a smile and a clink of their flutes. "A day of contrasts, eh? Our military shows off its muscle and society reveals its divisions; bomb-throwing is hardly the face of France we planned to put on display–today of all days."

Francin was a slender man with greying hair and a small mustache, also grey, that bristled between a large French nose and a wide mouth. But his most striking feature was a pair of very bright blue eyes that seemed to radiate intensity, and, even though casually attired for the evening, he projected a commanding presence.

He took Muller's elbow and steered him toward two chairs on the edge of the lawn next to a bed of red begonias, seated himself in one and gestured for Muller to join him in the other.

"Christian will be along directly, I'm sure" he said. "He had to supervise demobilization of his men after the parade. But he told me that he'd invited you to join us, and I wanted time for us to have a chat together."

He accepted one of the Gitanes Muller offered and, after Muller lit their smokes, signaled a waiter for more champagne, directing him to leave the unfinished bottle on the table between them.

"Christian tells me you're working with an international research organization in Geneva," he said, then without pausing for Muller to respond, continued, lowering his voice and glancing over his shoulder to ensure they were not being overheard.

"That's quite interesting, because I have a little project that I'm looking for someone to work on and I thought you might be interested in considering it. It involves the arms trade," he said with a bit of a smile, but the eyes weren't smiling.

"Is that something you have an interest in, Mr. Muller?"

Muller didn't hesitate.

"Actually, yes," he said. "I don't claim a lot of expertise, but it's a subject I'm interested in. It's timely too," he said, then paused and added, "given the threat of war these days."

Francin eyed him, and Muller decided he was taking in what Muller had said–and hadn't said–but implied.

Francin tapped his cigarette, scattering an ash on the grass, then turned in his chair so his back was to the garden but he could glance around him, while still addressing Muller quietly.

"Yes," he said; "war's likely and not far off, I'd say."

He paused a moment, then straightened in his chair.

"We're sitting with a pretty strong hand, I believe; a powerful military as we showed the world–and that man–today." He didn't need to say whom he meant. "Our alliance with Britain is good, our industry is humming–turning out tanks and aircraft as fast as we can build them, and we have a mountain of gold in our reserves.

"That last," he added, rubbing his hands together, "is the most important. By contrast, Germany has next to none; it's foreign reserve coffers are empty, and my little project aims to keep them that way."

Francin cocked his head at Muller. "Switzerland can play a role in doing that, which we're prepared to finance. Sound interesting?"

Muller leaned forward putting his arms on his thighs so he could reply in the same low tone.

"Mr. Francin, you know that Switzerland is a neutral state and that it will not take actions jeopardizing its neutrality. Still, having said that, yes, I'm interested."

Francin put up his hands defensively. "I certainly wouldn't want to interfere with Swiss neutrality," he said, then he smiled. "Not in any way. In fact, the Swiss government needn't play any official role at all—beyond looking the other way when appropriate—which, it's my impression, Swiss officials are often accustomed to doing in matters involving financial transactions."

Francin refilled their flutes.

His expression became serious, and after another glance around, he began to speak quietly.

"Germany is desperately short of key components for its war machine and it lacks the hard currency to go out and buy what it needs. I want to make things even harder for them by bidding up the prices on those components, making them more expensive and forcing the Germans to spend more of their precious hard currency reserves to get them. I also want to corner the market on them, to the extent I can, to keep them out of German hands altogether. We'll supply the financing and provide market intelligence, but we need a third party–let's say, a neutral Swiss–to actually run the business. I have authority and resources to pursue this project. Still interested?"

Muller paused and sat back in his chair. He ground out his cigarette with his shoe. This was a program that squared with the information Hilde had collected in her Memorandum. It also offered at least the possibility of gaining French leverage against the British threat. He decided Minger would not object if he were to explore it.

"Mr. Francin, I'm assuming this is a formal initiative from the French government and you have proper credentials which you'll provide me to verify that."

Francin nodded. "Yes, of course."

"Coordinated with the British government?"

Again, Francin nodded.

"With their new Ministry of Economic Warfare?"

Francin's eyes narrowed and his expression hardened. "Not many people even know the existence of that Ministry," he said guardedly.

Muller stood, reached into the pocket for his wallet, extracted his Swiss Ministry of Military Affairs identity card and handed it to Francin.

What the Hell; if he could show it to the police in the Basel railroad station, he could certainly show it to a senior French economic official.

Francin took the card, glanced at it, then handed it back to Muller, with a big smile and stood up. "Well, Mr. Muller, I think we may be similarly engaged. Let's go upstairs so we can have a more private conversation together."

Francin instructed one of the waiters to set two places at the dining room table in their apartment and deliver dinner from the picnic as soon as it was ready.

"And open a Drouhin burgundy," he added, "the 1930 vintage."

Francin led the way upstairs to their spacious and well-appointed second floor apartment and gestured Muller toward the dining room, offering him a seat at a long dining room table. Tall windows were open to the evening breeze that set the floor-to-ceiling curtains moving lazily. The late afternoon sun caught dust motes and, squinting into the glare, Muller could see a leg of the nearby Eiffel Tower.

They seated themselves and lit cigarettes, waiting as the waiter arranged the place settings and opened the wine, which had clearly been stored nearby and was quickly accessible.

The waiter made a small pour into the stemmed goblet he laid before Francin, who swirled the wine with his right hand, then lifted it to his nose to savor the bouquet. He took the obligatory sip, pursing his lips and swishing it in his mouth, gazing into the middle distance, then smiling, nodded to the waiter who proceeded to pour generous quantities for them both.

"Santé," he said as they tipped their goblets toward one another

"Do you know Drouhin?" Francin inquired as the waiter organized their dinner service.

"Only by reputation and consumption," Muller replied with a smile, savoring his first swallow.

"Joseph and I were at university together," Francin said. "He used to invite me to visit them in Beaûne–those wonderful vineyards, and the Chateau–I remember we chased a couple of girls through the caves one night."

Francin chuckled. "Good times, and they still produce a splendid burgundy."

When the waiter left the room and Francin was satisfied they were alone, he turned to Muller.

"So, you are now a Swiss Military Affairs Ministry official," he said. "No longer the international consultant you held yourself out to be in Geneva, which," he went on with a smile, "was always a little suspect in my mind, given your experience resisting the Nazis in Danzig and Vienna. I'm glad to learn of it. Now, what can you tell me and how can we conspire together to undermine Herr Hitler and his economy?"

"Right now, I'm mainly concerned about protecting the Swiss economy from threats from the British–and from the French too, if they're to be believed," Muller replied evenly. "We're well aware of the supposedly precarious state of the German economy; in fact, we just recently acquired access to new information showing pretty clearly how they've had to cut back on their arms buildup for that very reason. Our problem, Mr. Francin, is that the British Ministry has told us they're ready to capitalize on this weakness and try to bring down Germany's economy, but they may have to destroy our economy in the process."

Muller shrugged his shoulders. "'Sorry, old chaps,' they're telling us. 'Greater good and all that; we're sure you'll understand.' "Well we don't 'understand,'" said Muller, making quotation marks with his fingers. "We've sent them messages that we'll cripple their own arms buildup if they threaten us. They've also told us that the French government is wholly aligned with them on their plan. So, you'll understand that I'm a little gun-shy on signing up for a role with you, if the French government is out to attack our economy."

The waiter appeared with two plates of cold salmon and grilled saucisson which he placed before them and disappeared again.

"Bon appetit," said Francin, nodding at Muller and refilling their wine goblets.

"The British are often presumptuous allies, I find," Francin said between bites, "rather inclined to get ahead of themselves; what you've told me sounds like that kind of behavior. The government committee I head has charge of coordination with the British Ministry and I'm not aware of any program we've agreed to that targets Switzerland—even as so-called collateral damage. So maybe you can tell me what happened, so I can try to understand it better."

Muller took a deep draught of wine, deciding how to proceed. The British had claimed the French were deeply implicated in the British plan; if he could put some distance between them and persuade the French to avoid damaging Switzerland that would change the dynamics. At a minimum, it was a way gain some room for maneuver.

So, he told the whole story, interrupting only occasionally as he consumed the dinner that had been laid out.

Francin laughed aloud at Muller's description of Jimmy West singing "La Marseille" to end the fight at La Rouge and he made certain their wine goblets were refreshed as he listened intently.

Muller concluded by describing the warning he and Hilde had delivered to West at the meeting in Geneva, telling him that the Swiss government was prepared to interrupt production and delivery of critical British orders for military weaponry and components if they carried out their threats.

"We also took the liberty of telling him that he shouldn't have much confidence in French support for the threats they've been making, because, we said, the French are telling us they're desperate to keep buying the arms we're building for them and won't do anything to jeopardize their orders."

Muller shrugged nonchalantly. "Just a little sweetener for their ministry to chew on."

Francin chuckled and accepted the Gitane that Muller proffered.

"Well, that's certainly accurate," Francin said. "We're very conscious of Swiss arms production for us and we certainly don't want to jeopardize what we consider a vital source of supply. But at the same time Muller, the British Ministry is on to something. The German economy does have serious weaknesses. If we could push it to the point of collapse that could destroy both Hitler and his Nazi regime and maybe even prevent a new war. So, we have strong sympathy for what the British Ministry is trying to do."

"We're mindful of that," Muller replied, "and, as I said earlier, we've developed new evidence of German cutbacks. They've had to reduce aircraft production by 20 percent for lack of aluminum and they made big cuts in orders for weapons like machine guns and howitzers because they don't have enough copper–and of course, they're short on petroleum products of all kinds. If you send a courier to Bern, I'll see that you get a copy of the memo."

"Thank you, I'll do that," Francin replied, pulling a small notebook out of his shirt pocket and making a quick note.

"But that's my point, Mr. Muller," he went on excitedly, "the Germans have shortages of a host of other products too. Cereals, fats and oils, rubber, cotton and wool, a host of metals in addition to the ones you mentioned: chrome, lead, tin, zinc, certain ferro-alloys. The list is a long one. My plan is to provide funds for a Swiss company to enter the marketplace and bid up the prices on all of these products–in fact, of whatever products Germany is trying to buy. At a minimum I want their imports to become more costly and force Germany to spend as much as possible of its dwindling foreign currency reserves to get them. In addition, wherever possible, I'd like the new Swiss buyer to take physical control of the products and divert them away from Germany altogether."

"That, Mr. Muller, is my plan and that's what I'm prepared to offer you. I have nearly unlimited funds to devote to this project; what I need is someone–probably a Swiss banker–to flood the marketplace with new and aggressive orders to buy all the things Germany needs–and to keep bidding up the prices until the German economy cracks. Can you find me that banker, Mr. Muller?"

Francin poured the last of the burgundy, dividing it equally.

Muller ground out his butt in the ashtray and spun his wine goblet on the tablecloth with his fingertips.

"Have you discussed this role with Thomas?" Muller asked quietly.

Francin made a face.

"Thomas? My son-in-law–your brother? You can't be serious."

Francin leaned forward and raised a hand in exasperation.

"He's doing everything he can to *facilitate* German procurement." He slapped his hand on the table for emphasis.

"You know the German rules, Mr. Muller, foreign suppliers are obliged to accept at least half of their payment in the form of government credit certificates–worthless paper that's nothing more than an unsecured loan to the Reichsbank. It's one of the props they've had to fall back on to try to overcome their shortage of foreign exchange. Suppliers hate the credits, of course; there's no market for them, so they're forced to settle for getting paid only half of what they're actually owed.

"And what is Thomas doing? He's using Swiss francs to buy these credits from Germany's suppliers; he's helping to make them whole. Well, certainly not completely; he demands very stiff discounts. And German buyers pay him high fees under the table– in Reichsmarks, of course–to make their suppliers happy–or, at least happier than they would be if they had to eat the entire discount set by the rules.

"He's making a huge bet that, one day soon, the Reichsbank will become flush with foreign exchange and he'll be able to walk in with a suitcase full of those credit certificates–which he's bought for almost nothing–and convert them into foreign exchange at face value. He's planning to walk away with an absolute fortune. Meantime, he's helping to underwrite the German arms buildup.

"So, the answer to your question is no, Mr. Muller; I haven't raised this with Thomas. My plan is to try to counteract his scheme and make it more costly and riskier."

By now, Francin was glaring at Muller, obviously angry.

Muller responded by nodding and drawing a deep breath. "Father hinted as much to me a month ago after the christening ceremony," he said quietly. "You're confident of your information?"

Francin leaned forward, speaking intently. "Mr. Muller, my daughter is no fool. When she's up with the baby at night, she goes through his papers. It's all there in black and white and she's sick about it. I probably shouldn't be sharing this with you. I know the two of you are not close, but Thomas is your brother after all. What he's doing isn't illegal–well, maybe technically it is–but betting on the Nazis is pretty popular these days, especially in Zurich banking circles, so he's got plenty of company. And Charlotte says Thomas is no Nazi; politics doesn't interest him at all. He doesn't care that Hitler has turned Germany into a police state and is threatening a new war; he simply sees a financial opportunity that he's determined to capitalize on."

"And he's doing it by gambling with the Muller & Company balance sheet," added Muller softly, lifting his wine goblet and taking a deep draught, then setting it down firmly on the tablecloth.

"Have your courier bring a formal proposal when he travels to Bern," Muller said. "I'll see to it that we consider your plan."

Then he pulled the cocktail napkin out of his pocket, unfolded it and passed it to Francin.

"I assume you recognize the map," Muller said. "You're not a French general, but you're well-informed. What's the French plan to deal with a German attack like that?"

Francin picked up the napkin and gazed at it.

He smiled wanly, then handed it back to Muller.

"You're right, Mr. Muller; I'm not a French general. And I may be well-informed, and like a lot of Frenchmen these days, I've asked myself the same question; but I haven't received an answer."

They stood and shook hands.

"Time to rejoin the party, Mr. Muller; tonight, at least, we're entitled to celebrate."

As they walked down the steps to the lawn, now even more crowded, Christian Francin greeted them with two tumblers of brandy.

"I was coming to get you," he said. "Santé." They clinked glasses and downed the brandy.

Whoo! Muller shook his head as the fiery liquid exploded in his throat.

"Meet Jacqueline," Christian said, as a petit dark-haired woman, stylishly attired in a clinging, sequined red dress, appeared at his side and put her arm around his waist, fitting easily beneath his shoulder.

"Enchanté," Muller said, smiling and bending to kiss her hand.

Christian took them both by the elbow and steered them to a table, waving his father away.

"Enough! It's our turn to toast the hero of La Trémoille."

A happy group of young men and women seated at the table cheered and applauded as they approached, thrusting champagne flutes into their hands and toasting.

Muller didn't catch any names, but quickly found himself caught up in the merriment, chatting and laughing and enjoying himself. Someone had brought out a portable gramophone with a long extension cord stretching back through a window to a wall plug in one of the ground floor apartments. As soon as the needle dropped on Duke Ellington playing 'I'll Take the A Train', the couples all sprang to their feet and began jitterbugging.

Muller, suddenly seated alone, leaned back, lit a Gitane, and smiled as a spectator.

Suddenly, he felt two hands on his shoulder and a warm cheek next to his whispering in his ear.

"French Marianne insists on a dance."

Muller rose to his feet and turned to find himself facing a forty-ish brunette in a costume that did in fact resemble that of the statuesque Marianne symbol–white bonnet and a flowing white gown, though her right breast was covered, he noticed, rather than bared as in the classic illustration where she mounts the barricade, spear in hand topped by the French Tricolor.

He grinned; the woman was very attractive, and he responded as she looped her arms around his and they began to dance.

When the music changed to 'In the Mood', she pulled him closer and thrust her hips against his, moving them erotically in time to the beat, her cheek on his, her lips beginning to nibble at his ear. Muller let himself be led, then stepped back, and with a raised arm allowed his partner to twirl once, twice, then resume their close embrace. When the music stopped, he slipped out of her grasp and, at arm's length, took her hand, bowed to kiss it, and, with a smile, returned to the table.

It was time to leave.

Christian Francin clapped him on the shoulder.

"Muller, you've met the fair Florence, I see. Well done. She's very rich, divorced and said to be a great lover. The night is young. Stick around, you might find it becomes even more interesting." He laughed.

"Not so young, I think," Muller replied, lifting his hands in mock surrender, "and enough excitement already for one day."

He shook Christian's hand, waved and blew kisses to the table.

"Thanks. Tomorrow morning at the Gare de l'Est, right?"

"8 AM sharp," Christian replied with a smile and a wave.

CHAPTER 26

Their train arrived at Strasbourg just after 11:00 AM. The men in Muller's compartment stirred themselves and clambered down to the platform, stretching and trying to rouse themselves from the long naps that they'd all been taking. Muller could see men in other compartments doing the same.

Boarding that morning at the Gare de l'Est had been a quiet affair. A detachment of French soldiers manned a rope across the platform barring entry to the front of the train and an officer with a clipboard checked names of an obviously tired and bleary-eyed group of travelers that Muller estimated at roughly thirty men. A cart on the platform had offered coffee and croissants which most accepted before stepping into their assigned compartments and, at least in Muller's compartment, taking their seats, silently finishing breakfast, then leaning back against the cushions and falling asleep.

Christian Francin had been among the last to arrive and he boarded with a nod to Muller and a mumbled "bonjour" to the others. He pulled a bottle of brandy from his knapsack and offered it around.

"The last round from last night," he said, his voice husky.

Each of the six men accepted a swig, passing the bottle among them, then Francin replaced it in his knapsack and swung it up to the overhead rack. He took his seat, pulled his red uniform cap with its gold braid and black visor down over his eyes and promptly fell asleep, snoring quietly during most of the journey.

Now, on the Strasbourg platform, Francin stretched his hands high above his head and yawned, then shrugged his shoulders, blinking his eyes rapidly.

"Well, last night went on a little late, Muller," he said quietly, "and Florence told me several times how disappointed she was that you'd left. I was afraid I was going to have to service both her and Jacqueline, but somehow neither one happened. Ah, well."

He smiled ruefully then shrugging again and squaring his shoulders, he turned to the others.

"Off now to the Maginot, gentlemen," he said, "the great wall of France."

A detachment of French soldiers in smart uniforms, commanded by a very tall mustachioed colonel wearing uniform breeches and tall riding boots, led the travelers out of the station and directed them to tan-colored lorries with bench seating which they boarded. He was carrying a leather riding crop which he slapped impatiently against his carefully pressed breeches.

"Gentlemen," he said, addressing them in a high thin voice that somehow seemed out of place, "We have a thirty-minute drive to military headquarters for this Alsace-Lorraine Maginot District. Ten minutes before arrival, we will halt the convoy and lower the tarpaulins on your lorries for security reasons. Anyone seeking to remove the tarpaulin will be removed from the lorry."

The colonel then strode to a lead staff car, its roof carefully folded down, and took his seat in the back seat. He gestured with his riding crop and the convoy started up, driving first alongside the walls of the old city with its timbered facades, then past a long row of squat, ugly warehouse and factory buildings, the soaring Gothic steeple of the famed St. Thomas Cathedral towering above them, then receding in the distance. They crossed several well-restored ancient canals, then motored into the Alsatian countryside, its rolling hills and fields dotted with trees and thatched-roof farmhouses.

They stopped as promised for the tarpaulins to be lowered and Muller was pleased to find refuge in the shade from the hot sun.

A few minutes later, they arrived in a cobble-stoned entry and they heard commands directing them around several corners to a place where they halted, the back covers were lifted and they were invited to disembark, blinking in a bright, sunny courtyard. A large white tent had been erected and they were invited to enter to take seats at round tables with red checkered tablecloths and a bouquet of roses in the center of each table. Uniformed waiters in bright red tunics and blue trousers stood alongside, each carrying an open wine bottle, ready to serve them.

The travelers quietly found seats, Muller seating himself between Francin and what he took to be a Yugoslav officer of indeterminate rank. When their wine glasses had been filled, Francin leaned forward to offer a toast.

"The Republic, gentlemen."

They toasted and sipped a minimally dry pinot gris.

"This is France," Francin continued cheerfully, "no event– even our military tour of the Maginot–may properly proceed without a proper luncheon, especially here in Alsace, now liberated from German occupation."

A different colonel strode into the tent, heavier than his colleague, but nearly as tall, a rank of decorations glittering on the left breast of his perfectly pressed tunic. He was attended by a phalanx of aides, leaving no doubt that he was in command.

Standing erect behind the center of the head table, he raised his glass in a toast.

"Kindly enjoy this repast, gentlemen," he said. "When we finish our meal, we will provide you a briefing to prepare you for the tour we are pleased to offer this afternoon," he gestured toward a tripod stand where charts were neatly rolled at the top.

"You will be witness to one of the most significant military engineering and construction achievements in history. The Maginot Line is an impregnable fortress that guards the French frontier and thereby serves as a guarantor of peace in Europe.

"Vive La France!"

Muller and the others in the group stood and returned the toast.

"Now, please enjoy our hospitality; bon appetit."

Looking around the tables in the tent, Muller had a better view of his tour companions. He was one of only a handful of men who were not in uniform–there were no women; no surprise there. He also noticed that, as at his table, conversation was quiet and a bit stilted; men seemed not to have introduced themselves to one another and everyone seemed restrained, apparently in deference to the intrusive security atmosphere that accompanied the event. The only interruption in the trip from Paris to Strasbourg that morning– disturbing the naps of the travelers–had been the jarring entrance into each compartment of a florid-faced master sergeant, who read aloud a declaration stating that the impending visit was being conducted on ground of strict secrecy and that all participants must pledge themselves not to reveal any information describing military operations or deployments. He then handed a clipboard around to each passenger, directing them to sign the declaration he'd read.

Muller sensed that no one quite understood how to reconcile the strict security admonitions with the abundant hospitality being offered. The meal was in the finest French tradition, proceeding through four courses, accompanied by three wines, concluding with a dessert sauterne that perfectly suited what Muller thought had to be the season's first fraises des bois for dessert, topped with crème fraiche.

Muller decided to introduce himself to his Yugoslav companion, who responded that he was Zoran Dimitrovski and haled from the Skopje region of south Serbia, which Muller admitted he'd not only never visited but could hardly find on a map.

"A pity," Dimitrovski said between mouthfuls of Morteau Alsatian sausage, "tucked among the hills along the beautiful Vardar River which drains into Lake Ohrid. You must visit sometime."

He reached into his uniform pocket and extracted several colorful postcards which, he handed to Muller who duly admired what seemed to be a tranquil riverside with small boats hauled up on a beach overhung by verdant trees.

Dimitrovski proceeded to describe the idyll of Skopje, before dropping his voice into a conspiratorial whisper.

"Why don't they simply admit that the Germans know everything about this whole set of fortifications?"

Muller, startled, looked more closely at his luncheon partner, an older man with bushy white eyebrows and baggy cheeks lined by fine red veins. Not a frontline commander, he decided.

"Pardon?"

"French contractors built the Czech defenses in the Sudetenland," Dimitrovski said in a low voice. "They used designs identical to the Maginot. When the Germans took over the region after Munich, the first thing they did was to send in their engineers. They have all the blueprints and know the Maginot fortifications like the back of their hands."

Muller cocked his head and regarded Dimitrovski.

The man continued to carve up his sausage and chew it vigorously, then turned to look directly at Muller and winked.

"Hadn't thought about that, had you?" he said returning his attention to the sausage. "But it's true. A lot of Czech officers and engineers slipped over the border to join us and escape the Gestapo. They even offered to show us the weak points in the Maginot designs."

Dimitrovski shrugged. "It's no secret; but the French seem determined to ignore it and promote the mystique of the Maginot."

Dimitrovski took his napkin, wiping his mouth and chin to remove any remaining sausage and blowing his nose. Then he took his red wine glass and tipped it toward Muller, who reciprocated and they both took deep swallows.

"I'm not saying it's not a formidable barrier," he said. "I'm looking forward to seeing it–and from this side, not attacking it; I wouldn't want to do that, for sure. But it's no mystery anymore; I just hope our French friends aren't kidding themselves with this 'impregnability' fable."

Muller thought about pulling the cocktail napkin out of his pocket and asking Dimitrovski what he thought about the possibility of Germany flanking the Maginot and attacking it from the rear; but then he decided against it.

By this time, the French Colonel, had gotten to his feet and walked to the rolled-up charts on the tripod stand, pointer in hand. He rapped the pointer on the floor to get attention, then rolled down the first chart, which was a map tracing the path of the Maginot, marked in bright red.

"As you can see gentlemen the Maginot Line begins here, at the end of the Belgian-French border." He tapped his pointer. "And stretches all the way east along our northern frontier with Germany to the place where we are now seated, just north of Strasbourg." Another tap. "And then it makes a sharp right turn south and runs directly along the west bank of the Rhine, before terminating at Basel, and the Swiss border, here." He tapped again. "Two hundred and eighty-three miles of fortifications, gentlemen."

"It is not a single continuous line, as the name suggests; instead it is made up of what we refer to as 'Fortified Regions', a highly sophisticated set of interlocking and coordinated defense systems.

The colonel flipped another chart.

"For security reasons, we are not revealing any actual Fortified Region, but you can see here a schematic that illustrates the kinds of in-depth defensive placements that are incorporated in the real thing. They have all been carefully engineered to meet exacting requirements."

Another chart flipped revealing a list that Muller strained to see as the colonel ticked off the points.

"Natural cover for the fortresses, near at hand observation posts, minimum dead ground within the field of fire, maximum arc for effective fire, and suitable terrain for anti-tank and anti-infantry obstacles. Nearest the frontier, *Maison Fortes*, reinforced barracks, are permanently occupied by mobile troops serving as a tripwire to slow any advance by blowing up roads, bridges and causing pre-arranged crossroad blockages." The pointer kept tapping the charts for emphasis as the colonel spoke. "A mile or so back are heavily armed *Avant-Postes*, camouflaged and set in concrete, fully manned by permanent garrisons. Overlapping lines of fire have been pre-sited for maximum destructive force against any attackers."

The colonel was flipping charts, speaking rapidly and Muller's eyes began to flutter, his attention wandering.

Farther back, were *Ouvrages*, or giant casement fortresses, some big enough to hold garrisons of over a thousand troops. On and on, the colonel continued, describing secure underground command posts connected by hardened telephone lines, infirmaries, kitchens, generators, extra-high air pressure to repel poison gas. There was even an underground railway connection, he said, appropriately known as the métro.

Muller heard Dimitrovski's heavy breathing next to him, and he gave the man a nudge, trying to remain alert himself, too.

Finally, the briefing was concluded to light applause and the travelers found WCs before re-boarding the lorries.

The tarpaulins were again drawn, and the convoy set off.

Moments later the men felt themselves in a cool, clammy space, patches of sunlight replaced by glimpses of bright overhead lights. The tarpaulins were removed, and they were invited to disembark, finding themselves standing in a large, windowless cavern that resembled a warehouse loading dock.

The colonel stood among them, his pointer mercifully left behind.

"You have entered one of our great *Ouvrages*," he said, "the massive Alsace Fortification. You were not permitted to view the exterior, but this is the working heart of the structure. Supply vehicles enter this subterranean cavern to deliver everything needed to support over a thousand infantrymen and gunners permanently on duty here–food, ammunition, medical supplies– whatever's needed. No women, however," he added, to chuckles from the travelers.

"Please follow me." The colonel led them through a maze of high-ceilinged tunnels into a large room.

"You are now standing directly below one of the retractable turrets," he said, "heavily armored and armed with 75-mm cannons capable of firing shells over seven miles with devastating accuracy. Beneath them are firing chambers holding 37-mm and 47-mm antitank guns."

He gestured. Muller could see there was a wide and sturdy-looking lift shaft with a surrounding staircase that could accommodate troop movements up or down.

"Please take a few moments and follow the stairs or enter the elevators to descend to the living quarters and the munitions storage sections. Some of the rest of you can ascend into the turret itself," the colonel said.

Muller moved to the stairway and began to trot upwards, feeling the vibration of the large personnel elevator at his elbow.

A thick steel door at the top of the stairs had been wedged open and an artillery officer beckoned him to enter the low turret. Narrow slits in the circular turret walls offered glimpses of sunlit foliage that cast shadows along the far side of the enclosure, where four cannons were affixed to sliding rails for rapid deployment. When several of the men in the group had wedged themselves past the doorway, the officer pulled it shut and secured it, then turned to a panel of handles and glowing gauges. He pushed on one of the handles and the turret began to rotate to the left, then he reversed the handle and it moved right.

"We have nearly 180 degrees of radius coverage," he said proudly.

"You see the loaders here," he gestured to mechanized arms that he activated to remove a spent shell and replace it with a shiny narrow 75-mm projectile from a magazine situated beneath the armored floor of the turret.

Then he pressed a large switch and the 75-mm gun began to sink with a mechanical whir, descending below the floor, and a wide, stubby-barreled cannon rose to replace it and clicked securely into a large steel base.

"Our very nasty 81-mm 3.25-inch short range killer," he said, pointing to the weapon. "If the enemy were to penetrate this far, he would be pulverized by the rapid fire and sheer explosive power of these guns."

Muller strode to the firing slits to look outside. He could see rounded, grey, turtle-back roofs of smaller fortifications, barely visible with their natural camouflage, ranging down a slope away from the fortification, and beyond them, deep tank traps stretching as far as he could see on both sides of his vantage point.

The artillery officer took Muller's arm and directed him to step into a container that moved upwards to the top of the tunnel. Muller found himself a dozen feet above the turret floor inside an observation post, where he had an unimpeded view of the entire panorama around the fortification.

He was quickly lowered.

"We don't want you seeing too much, sir," said the officer with a grin.

Muller then descended in the lift to the troop quarters two stories down. There were triple bunks, made up with white sheets and blankets; cramped, but serviceable. He found a brightly lit lavatory with sinks and showers that reminded him of his university locker room facilities. Very serviceable. He also became conscious of a pervasive damp chill; steel walls were clammy and the forced air was cool. It would probably be worse with dozens of men in close contact.

The group began to reconstitute itself and drift back toward the loading dock. Muller was startled to see small shops had been built along the walls, tabacs, tiny cafés. He nudged Francin, who was now next to him.

"Even a barber shop," Muller said, pointing.

"Right," Francin replied, and it's tradition that at least one member of visiting groups like ours gets a shave. And you just volunteered," he added, waving the rest of the group to join them as he steered Muller into the two-chair shop.

Francin took Muller's suit jacket and a short, heavy-set barber in his white jacket handed Muller into the nearest chair and strapped him in with a smile.

"Just a precaution," he said in a jovial tone. "You can't be too careful, right?"

He stropped a straight razor against the brown leather strap as he warmed a white hand towel in the sink. Squeezing out the water, he laid the hot damp towel across Muller's face then lowered the back of the chair, so Muller lay nearly flat.

Muller couldn't see anything, but the towel felt good and he relaxed.

KABOOM!

The sound of a sudden explosion stiffened him and he grabbed the barber chair arms.

A loud klaxon went off. OOOGAH! OOOGAH!

"ACTION STATIONS. ALL HANDS TO THEIR POSTS."

Another explosion shook Muller's chair and he grabbed for the towel, but his arms were pinned to the chair.

Suddenly he could see flashing colored lights through the thin towel and his chair began spinning and swinging from side to side; debris seemed to be falling from the roof and Muller lunged to get up, but the barber's strap held him firmly in place. Another explosion and his chair was violently pushed up, then sank with a sickening drop. Muller felt bile raising in his throat; that last glass of sauterne, he thought. Shit! The chair began jumping and tilting, then spun again, until suddenly, it seemed to swoop into a smooth glide path and came to a stop and the seat back swung back to its normal position.

The towel was swept off Muller face and he blinked.

He found himself still seated in the chair and surrounded by the group of travelers who were all convulsed by laughter, some bent almost double, slapping their knees, then they began applauding and shouting encouragement.

"Bravo; what a trooper!!!

"Great sound effects, weren't they? Sounded like a real attack. Whoo!

"That chair really flew around; some show!"

The barber removed the restraining strap and offered his hand to help Muller out of the chair and steady him as he regained his footing and recovered his equilibrium.

"That was our carnival chair, sir," he said with a broad smile. "It offers a little more action than a conventional shave."

He joined the applause for Muller, who looking around him, felt a little sheepish, then smiled gamely. Fair enough. Boys will be boys. He raised his arms in mock triumph and received another cheer from the group.

The colonel stepped forward.

"You, sir, have survived an attack upon the Maginot Line and are thereby entitled to be awarded the Order of the Close Shave."

Muller bowed from the waist, lowering his head, and the colonel placed a tricolored ribbon around his neck, a shaving brush attached at the bottom, which swung into place on his chest. He stood back up with a grin and received still another round of applause.

On cue, the colonel's attendants appeared carrying trays of brandy tumblers which they passed around.

"The Order of the Close Shave," said the colonel, raising his tumbler, "another victorious step in preserving the peace. Hear, Hear!"

Muller joined the group in downing the brandy, then flung his tumbler to the floor where it splintered, and the others followed suit.

The colonel, obviously taken by surprise was the last to do so, then paused, and with a look of annoyance, motioned impatiently for his staff to clean up the mess. Then he wheeled briskly and left the barber shop, head erect, obviously expecting the group to follow, which they did slowly and with wry smiles, many first approaching Muller and patting him on the shoulder and passing words of encouragement.

"Good show, Muller," Francin said grinning and putting his arm companionably around Muller's shoulder. "A rite of passage at Maginot, I'm afraid, so I figured who better to put the finger on than you."

Francin laughed and clapped Muller on the back. "I can't wait to regale the family with this tale of heroic behavior! Then you completely took control by smashing the colonel's beloved tumblers. He's really pissed; I love it. Serves him right. Ha! Muller you're now a legend and a highly decorated one to boot."

Francin playfully slapped the shaving brush, which swung back to Muller's chest; he glanced down at it with a proud smile, patting it fondly as they trailed the group and walked back to the lorries.

CHAPTER 27

The barber shop incident seemed to break the ice and members of the group suddenly became livelier as the lorries bumped along the country roads to their next stop. It helped that the tarpaulins were stowed, and they were out of the damp confines of the underground cavern, once again surrounded by the sun-kissed, rolling Alsatian countryside. The men laughed more easily with one another, smoking and smiling. The colonel continued to sit stiffly in his command car leading the way, but the aura of gravity had been punctured, and the group had become decidedly more relaxed and companionable.

In Muller's lorry, the men questioned him about his experience in the carnival chair and laughed with him as he described his bewilderment and disorientation—and fear that he might even throw up.

That would not have been good they agreed, but they sympathized with his reaction

They also began comparing notes on what they'd just seen, and most shook their heads in wonderment at the scope and scale of the fortification.

"The sheer size of underground chambers was hard to believe," said one, a British officer with a Scottish accent, "wide enough for nearly a dozen abreast and high enough for even the biggest trucks."

"And the trolley Métro system," said another in a uniform Muller didn't recognize. "Someone told me it extends for miles beneath the forts." The man shook his head. "And they say everything's all connected by buried telephone wires and the latest optics. I don't envy the Germans trying to attack the Maginot," he added, and the others nodded in agreement.

They had been driving east and, suddenly, views of the Rhine appeared in front of the convoy. At that point, the road turned sharp right and headed south, with occasional river sightings on their left. They traveled only a few kilometers in that direction before halting alongside a high, grassy berm. French soldiers materialized and waved the convoy through a narrow, camouflaged entryway. Before them, a narrow road led down a steep embankment to a wide graveled parking area and a long, low-slung concrete battlement with a curved, grey-colored roof. The men disembarked and the colonel led the way toward a thick sliding doorway which was opened at their approach.

"Inside quickly," commanded the colonel, leaving no doubt that he was once again in charge.

Muller joined the other men and entered a low-ceilinged room that became nearly dark when the door behind them slid back in place. Reflected sunlight revealed narrow slits facing the Rhine and above it, green foliage on the riverbank opposite their position–and grey German fortifications built above the river, directly facing them.

"This is a casement fortress typical of the Maginot defenses running south along the Rhine to the Swiss border," said a burly French Army captain, after welcoming the group.

The French captain spoke crisply, in a business-like manner. "You see observation slits here to keep an eye on the enemy. On either side of where we're standing are mustering rooms, there," he pointed left, "and garrison kitchen and dining facilities," pointing right. "Above us are special armored artillery siting posts and down there," he pointed to a wide stairway, "is our weapons cache and magazines. The level below that is for ammunition storage and sleeping and living quarters for the garrison."

"We're very self-sufficient here," he added proudly. "The enemy has to look us right in the face. The Rhine River is itself a barrier to any German invasion, but we have fortified our side of the riverbank all the way south to the Swiss border to discourage any risk of surprise attack. Obstacles to amphibious operations have been planted along with barbed wire. Machine gun nests have been built; you can't see them from up here, but we can access them by tunnel, so we don't expose ourselves. We even have mechanical grenade-throwers to repel invaders. On the level just below, you'll see our 81-mm and 135-mm cannons that are ready to kill anything the Germans might send our way; they'll just blow it to smithereens."

The officer smiled tightly. "The Rhine front is fully secure against any German incursion," he said, a note of defiance in his voice.

A French soldier escorted some of the men down to the firing and living quarters, while another led the way to the overhead artillery observation posts. Muller followed him.

They walked two dozen meters in a narrow tunnel, then ascended a steel stairway to a low, enclosed cupola.

"To ensure accuracy," the soldier said, "we operate twin cupolas." He pointed to a barely visible grey concrete enclosure thirty meters away. "There's always an officer there," he said, "and a non-com here. Usually me; when I'm on duty, that is." The man smiled. "The officer operates a high-precision binocular telescope to site his target and passes the coordinates to me by this voice tube." He pointed to a black box on the wall with an earpiece. "And I plot it here," he gestured to a high table with chart books stacked on one another. "Then I just pass it to the gunners by secure phone and, BOOM!"

He gestured and smiled. "Our cupola is only a 4-inch aperture; ample to accommodate our telescopes and make the calculations; invisible to the enemy. It works like a charm."

Muller noticed a platform at the back of the cupola. "What's that?"

The soldier smiled. "On nice days, we like to sun ourselves on a deck a few meters up, on a hill where we've built a little canteen to relax. Come, it's such a nice afternoon, I was going to invite you up for a look."

They emerged from a narrow stone staircase leading to a ledge where a table and several canvas chairs had been laid out. A dark steamer trunk was situated nearby, and the soldier flung open the top, extracting several bottles of Schiltigheim beer, which he opened for them with a flourish.

"Santé!"

Muller took a big swig, then stood and took in the panoramic view before him. The Rhine, brown, but glistening brightly in the sunlight, flowing strongly north; a steep riverbank above it, and then, higher still, the German fortification nearly directly opposite. As he gazed, he made out figures above the fortress–German soldiers taking in the sun like they were. The men were lounging, many of them stripped to the waist. Suddenly, Muller saw agitated movement among them. They began pointing at the French side–at them, Muller realized. A German lookout had apparently alerted them to the French presence on the ledge. Muller looked on in amusement as some of the Germans began waving fists at them, apparently shouting wordlessly across the river, as other flexed their muscles and two dropped their trousers to deliver bare-assed moons.

"Shall we moon them back?" asked the French soldier, looking on in amusement. "We do this little dance together a lot when the weather's nice and we're each trying to relax."

Muller shook his head. "I've had my Maginot exercise for the day," he said with a smile, but still defiantly raised his arm with a stiff middle finger to the German side.

The soldier laughed. "That'll do fine, sir."

As he drank the beer, Muller studied the French side of the river more closely. "Why all the rose bushes?"

The soldier shrugged. "Orders, sir. And not just here; the length of the Maginot, I'm told. Morale, I suppose. I don't know why thousands of rose bushes are needed to cheer us up behind this fortification, but they're pretty, don't you agree?"

Muller nodded; they were quite spectacular, actually; but in his experience, roses were meant for decorating happier venues then the fiercest military structure ever built.

After another few minutes, the men reassembled in the main hall, then someone rolled aside the heavy sliding door and they boarded the lorries once more, again traveling due south along the west bank of the Rhine, which occasionally afforded splendid vistas.

They halted an hour later, at military headquarters in Colmar and the men climbed out of the lorries to stretch and find WCs .

"This is my billet," Francin said to Muller. "I'll leave you to proceed on your own with the group to Basel and catch your train home.

"I'd like a word," Muller said. "Could we step into your office to speak privately?"

Francin shook his head. "You need a special pass to enter, I'm afraid; all very hush-hush."

But he led Muller across the cobble-stoned square toward the base of a wide plane tree, where several chairs had been set up in the shade. They sat down and Muller lit Gitanes for both of them with his lighter.

"First of all, my thanks for hosting me these several days," he said, smiling. "Memorable events, all of them."

Francin, smiled back. "My pleasure; the hero of La Trèmoille and recipient of the Order of the Close Shave. You distinguished yourself, Muller," he said with a laugh, "and I gather were able to have a long talk with father, as well. He wouldn't tell me what you discussed, but he was well pleased, I can tell you."

He cocked his eyes toward Muller inquiringly. "There's something else, I gather."

Muller nodded and pulled the cocktail napkin from his pocket, unfolded it and handed it to Francin.

"This is a scenario that worries us," Muller said. "A German invasion of France through Switzerland to flank the Maginot would be a nightmare–and it's an obvious risk; just look at the map."

Francin glanced at the napkin, then handed it back, his lips pursed, a look of annoyance on this face. "I don't need to look at it; I know about the problem only too well. What's your question?"

"What's the French Army plan to stop an attack like that?"

Francin's face darkened and his eyes narrowed.

"Muller, if you have to ask me, I can't tell you." His eyes bored into Muller's. "That's all I'm prepared to say."

Francin stood and reached out to clap Muller on the shoulder, his face in a tight smile.

"Let's leave it there and not spoil a nice trip."

He led the way back to the lorries. "You'd better get back aboard."

Francin ground out the cigarette butt with the sole of his shoe, turned and offered his hand. "See you soon." Then he waved and strode to the doorway of his headquarters.

Muller clambered into the lorry and took a seat. Nothing subtle about that, he said to himself. Just fuck off.

Well, he'd have to think that over.

His lunch partner Dimitrovski saw him seated alone and asked if he could join him, slipping into the adjoining seat with a deep sigh and reaching into his tunic to extract a flask that bore the appearance of regular use. Dimitrovski took a short swallow.

"Slivovitz is bracing in the afternoon," he said, smacking his lips, wiping his mouth with the back of his hand, and offering the flask to Muller, who took a swig, then stiffened, his eyes beginning to water; finally he swallowed, coughed and shook his head.

"What's that called again?" Muller said breathlessly, his head tilting back as he looked skyward for relief.

"It's our native plum brandy," Dimitrovski said with a grin. "The fresh stuff is over 50 percent alcohol; that's the way I like it– before they dilute it down to 100 proof. As I said, bracing." He tucked the flask away in his tunic with a chuckle. Then he looked slyly at Muller with a twinkle in his eye.

"I'm pleased to see you survived your visits to the Maginot observation posts," he said. "You'd have a bullet between the eyes if we'd actually been in combat."

Muller looked at him, frowning; what was this about?

"Look, the French tell you they have advanced binocular optics to fix targets for their big guns; true, no doubt about it. But the Germans have sniper sights that are at least as advanced, and their scopes will be targeting those observation platforms as soon as the first shots are fired. They can put a bullet inside an aperture this small," Dimitrovski held up his thumb and forefinger a half-inch apart. As soon as your head appears in the observation post, you're dead; just like that," Dimitrovski snapped his fingers.

He looked at Muller and shrugged. "It's true; the Czech engineers figured it out given the advances in optical telemetry since the Maginot was designed in the 1920's, so they changed the designs. The new reality is that these wonderful French fortresses that we saw today are susceptible to being blinded by just a single German marksman lying comfortably prone on a mattress in a blockhouse somewhere out there, with a high-powered rifle and a sophisticated sniper scope, just waiting for some Frenchman to stick his head into that observation post aperture so he can blow it off."

"That would have been you, Mr. Muller," he said conversationally.

"The Order of the Close Shave wouldn't protect you–though high marks for a very entertaining performance in the chair," he said with a smile. "But in one of those observation posts, you'd be dead in an instant."

Dimitrovski flicked his finger as if it were a trigger. "Bang, you're dead."

Muller turned to face his neighbor with a querulous look. Who was this man? He certainly seemed to have an informed view of things. Dimitrovski winked at him again and smiled, pulling two Turkish cigarettes out of a crumpled pack and waited for Muller to light them.

"Mr. Muller, intelligence officers project a certain–how shall I say it–aura, is perhaps the right word. You are Swiss and, I'm confident, an intelligence operative of some kind."

Dimitrovski sat back and raised his hands briefly; as in mock surrender.

"You don't have to say a word. No offense intended; but one knows the other. My uniform doesn't fit because I haven't worn it for years; the insignia it displays are hopelessly out of date. But it seemed useful to resurrect as cover for this very interesting Maginot opportunity. You're dressed in a suit; not even a pretense of being military. And here we are, sitting together, having taken our tour and trying to understand what we've seen; am I right?"

Dimitrovski pulled the flask from his tunic again and offered it to Muller, who shook his head with a wry smile. Dimitrovski took a swig, replaced the flask, and turned to face Muller again. He glanced around their seats on the lorry to satisfy himself that no one was paying attention.

"Did you hear anything about how they're prepared to defend against an airborne attack? Paratroop drops? Gliders? I certainly didn't. The Germans aren't stupid, Mr. Muller." Dimitrovski was speaking quietly but with intensity. "A frontal attack on the Maginot Line would be close to suicidal. It's inconceivable to me the Germans would embark on what would likely become a catastrophic bloodbath. Anyone–including the French, no, especially the French–expecting the Germans to hurl themselves upon this fortress is–in my opinion–living in a fantasy."

"How can the French command be so blind as to expect the Germans to attack on its terms?" Dimitrovski slapped his hands on his knees in frustration, then turned toward Muller lowering his voice again. "All those French guns are facing the German frontier. What do they do when the German's begin dropping battalions of paratroopers behind the forts and attacking them from the rear? Did you see any sign that they're prepared for that?"

Muller thought to himself. No, he hadn't heard a word about that possibility. He nodded in agreement, then reached into his

jacket and pulled out the cocktail napkin, handing it to
Dimitrovski. "What do you make of this?"

Dimitrovski unfolded it and stroked his chin as he regarded
the now somewhat rumpled drawing.

"Yes," Dimitrovski said, nodding and handing the napkin back
to Muller. "That's another risk we didn't hear anything about."

Muller leaned closer to Dimitrovski holding the napkin
between their two laps and pointed to it. "What if we were to
reverse the direction of the potential attack? What if the French
were to attack Germany from the south, using our Gempen Plateau
as the staging point? We'd find ourselves invaded by the French
instead of the Germans. Either way, we'd have a fight on our hands
that we'd lose in only a matter of days."

Dimitrovski sat back on the narrow lorry seat, crossed his
arms across his chest, and gazed ahead, frowning in concentration
as he considered Muller's question. Finally, he sighed, and bowed
his head back toward Muller's. His voice was low.

"Did you hear a single syllable uttered today about a French
Army offensive against Germany? I certainly didn't." Dimitrovski
paused. "Think carefully about that, Mr. Muller. "I come away
from this little trip we've made with the firm conviction that the
French mindset is focused entirely on defending France against a
possible German attack. Oh, the parade was a grand show of force.
The French Army is big and it's powerful, and they have a lot of
very lethal equipment. But was it any more than a show? The

French motto in the Great War was 'attack; always attack.' Today? My sense the motto would be 'defend; always defend'."

Dimitrovski's voice had grown louder, and he looked around, checking himself, before continuing, his voice now lower again. "They aren't thinking about defeating Germany; they're thinking about *how to avoid being defeated BY Germany.*" He hissed the last phrase, then he sat back and looked squarely at Muller with a grim expression. Then nodded, as a kind of exclamation mark.

They sat without speaking, each weighing their conversation. Dimitrovski broke the silence.

"I find it odd, Mr. Muller, that despite living in a world connected by the most modern communications systems known to man, we're still grasping at straws," Dimitrovski spoke softly, his tone reflective. "Radio signals from around the world, telephone connections to almost anywhere, airplanes that cut the time for travel, newsreels at the movies where we can actually see what's happening here–and on the other side of the world; yet we're sitting here together in the back of this lorry, two supposedly smart men charged with advising our governments about what to expect, and we're essentially operating in the dark."

Muller smiled despite himself. He'd just met this slightly rumpled older man, yet he felt a sense of kinship in his company; someone saying things he'd been thinking, but not yet put into words.

Muller's reply echoed Dimitrovski's reflective tone. "You're right; people today have access to all this information, but they only seem to listen to what they want to hear. The more we know, the less we seem to understand one another."

But then thoughts that had been in the back of his head suddenly crystallized; he turned to face Dimitrovski and his voice took on a note of urgency.

"We seem to be hurtling toward a new war," Muller said. "Europeans have been doing that forever. But the last one was supposed to be the last one. The war to end all wars. That's what they said, am I right? And they created a League of Nations that was expressly designed to avert another one, didn't they? I was part of a League effort to do that a few years ago."

He tilted his head toward Dimitrovski, making sure he knew.

"Where is that League today, in the summer of 1939–not twenty years from the day it was launched? Where is that common commitment to embrace collective diplomacy and prevent a new war? Gone! Vanished." Muller answered his own question. "Now all we see is political division; people speaking past one another."

Muller slumped back in his seat.

"And into that vacuum walks Adolf Hitler," said Dimitrovski quietly, almost as if finishing Muller's thought. "A power-crazed ruler capitalizing on the very divisions you describe and seemingly determined to crush democracy and any other institutions standing in his way.

"Yes, Mr. Muller, I think we share a common concern; but I'm not as convinced as you seem to be that war is certain."

Dimitrovski sat back too and smiled at Muller. "My country is now called Yugoslavia, but we're still Serbs at heart. And you'll remember that Serbia and Russia have shared strong ties for generations; that relationship in fact had something to do with starting the Great War."

Muller smiled and chuckled softly at the understatement.

"Russia now has a new name too," Dimitrovski went on, "it calls itself the Soviet Union; but they're still Russians at heart. So, it will not surprise you to learn that my country continues to enjoy closer relations with that Russian-Bolshevik state than many other nations.

"And one of the things we know is that right now, as we're sitting in this lorry, senior British and French military officials are in Moscow engaged in negotiations with the Soviets aimed at reviving the Triple Alliance that opposed Germany in the Great War. That, Mr. Muller, a new, firm alignment of Britain, France and the Soviet Union, would give Mr. Hitler pause."

Dimitrovski accepted Muller's Gitane and light, and blew a cloud of smoke, which he waved away with one hand. "The negotiations are proceeding rather more slowly than we'd like. The Soviet state is anathema to many in both France and Britain and the Soviets view both countries as capitalist exploiters."

Dimitrovski shrugged, tapping his ash onto the lorry floor. "But the Soviets hate–and fear–the Nazis even more. It may take a little time, but the three countries have a common interest in taming Germany and preventing a new war. I'm convinced they'll find a way to agree to do that."

"Will that stop Hitler from invading Poland?" asked Muller. "We're persuaded that he's determined to do that even if it means war."

Dimitrovski nodded slowly.

"God knows, he certainly sounds like it, with those bombastic speeches he keeps making. But what if he does invade; what then?"

Dimitrovski took a deep breath and went on.

"Muller, even if he goes ahead, there are lots of ways to reach some sort of accommodation. After all, the world went on nicely during the hundred years or so when Poland didn't even exist, before it got resurrected at Versailles. Would dividing it up between Germany and the Soviets be so bad?"

"It surely would for the Poles," Muller responded sharply.

Dimitrovski nodded. "No doubt that's true. But if the three allies were to put a fence around Germany and mount a credible threat to forestall any new Nazi aggression, something like that might be a legitimate trade-off."

Once more they lapsed into silence.

Muller mind, unbidden, conjured scenes of the Polish corridor and the faces of Polish friends from his days in Danzig four years earlier. Partition would surely be a nightmare for most of them; but as a tradeoff to war? Could he–could the world–accept such a cynical deal? He shook his head in annoyance at the prospect. But

he had to admit that the world might go to almost any lengths–
swallow nearly any outcome–if it would keep the peace.

He sighed, then seeing the lorry was pulling into the courtyard
in front of the Basel SB Banhof, he stood and reached in his pocket
for a card which he handed to Dimitrovski.

Dimitrovski reciprocated and they shook hands.

"We need to remain in touch," Muller said.

After perfunctory farewells to their traveling companions, they
walked together into the station's vaulted main hall. Muller had
begun striding toward the Swiss platforms at the far side of the
terminal when he stopped and turned back.

"Mr. Dimitrovski," he said loudly, walking quickly in his
direction.

The man turned with an inquiring smile.

"Mr. Dimitrovski, does Yugoslavia have an export trade with
Germany?" he asked.

"Why, of course," said Dimitrovski, in a slightly patronizing
tone. "We used to be part of the Hapsburg Empire, Mr. Muller–the
Austro-Hungarian state that was Germany's major trading partner
for hundreds of years. They still buy the wheat and grain we
harvest from the plains around Belgrade and textiles from our mills
near Ljubljana, for instance. Why do you ask?"

"Do your exporters have to accept payment in the form of
Reichsbank credits for their sales to German buyers?" Muller
asked.

"Yes, it's my understanding that German regulations impose that burden on all its foreign suppliers," he replied, "as much as half of the payment, if I'm not mistaken."

"If a Swiss importer were to offer to buy those exports at a higher price and in hard currency, would Yugoslav suppliers consider switching customers and selling to this Swiss company instead of to the Germans?"

Dimitrovski's eyes narrowed.

"I don't know," he said slowly, obviously weighing the idea in his mind.

"Higher prices, and in hard currency," he paused. "Well, they'd certainly have to consider it I suppose. Do you have something in mind?"

Muller smiled. "Just a thought," he said, then turned with a wave and resumed his trek to the Swiss platforms.

Maybe I have my first purchase for Francin's new scheme, he thought to himself with a touch of satisfaction–if we decide to adopt it.

CHAPTER 28

Muller bought a newspaper from the kiosk, then decided to get some wine for the two-hour trip back to Bern. The proprietor retrieved a bottle of Fendant out of a cooler and removed the cork then pushed it back in halfway. Muller paid and waved off a paper bag, instead grasping the wine bottle by the neck as he strode along the train platform and found his compartment. Swinging up the steps, he placed his purchases on the center table, opened his travel bag to extract the John Gunther book, confident that at least now he'd be able to read if he chose.

He had scarcely seated himself when heard a commotion on the platform. He went to the open window of the compartment to look and was startled at the sight of a contingent of black-uniformed SS storm troopers striding up the platform, escorting a coterie of Nazi officials, all dressed in black doubled-breasted suits with the red Nazi armband on their right arms. They were conversing loudly and seemed headed directly toward his compartment.

Muller stepped back from the window, then spied the Gunther book with its bright red cover on the seat. He snatched it up and quickly stuffed it back in his bag in the overhead. He watched as the officials walked past to the next compartment and he could hear them speaking to one another, then after 'Heil Hitlers', he saw several of them turn to walk back toward the station, evidently having said their farewells. But then several of the storm troopers, who had been part of the entourage, opened his compartment door, nimbly mounted the steps and, without hesitation or even a glance at Muller, took seats, removing their billed caps and pulled out cigarettes–he noticed they were cheap Primas–and began laughing and talking all at once, obviously relieved to have successfully deposited their charge next door.

Muller removed his bottle of Fendant from the center table and placed it at his side, on the cushion next to the corridor door.

"Enough for all of us?" said one of the troopers, pointing to the bottle, and the other laughed.

They were, all four of them strapping, blonde young men; Hitler's Aryans, Muller thought to himself, and though he wanted no part of them, he decided he couldn't just stand up and walk out of the compartment to find another seat. So, he decided to play dumb, and feigned confusion, looking from one to another and shaking his head.

"Mi Italiano-Suisse," he said, mumbling and spreading his arms wide, continuing to look at them in confusion.

"Ticino," he said, "casa mia, Ticino." He smiled. "Nein parlo Deutsche."

"Ah he's a fucking Italian or something," said one of the troopers." Muller could see he had a large pimple on his right cheek that he'd been picking.

"Mussolini?" he said leering at Muller "You like Mussolini?"

"Si, si," Muller replied loudly with a smile, showing he understood. "Mussolini, si!"

The trooper setting closest to Muller clapped Muller on the shoulder with a dismissive grin, then turned back to the others.

"Fuck him," he said, "what I want to know is when we get the orders to go in and kill the fucking Poles. Did you overhear what the commander said to Heydrich as they got out of the car? Something about roasting Poles over the fires of Warsaw in another few weeks."

"Really? No shit!"

Muller was forgotten and the young soldiers began speaking animatedly to one another.

He shrunk back into his corner of the compartment, laid his head on the head rest, adopted a dreamy, far-away look, and took an occasional swallow of wine seemingly paying no attention to the chatter and boisterous stories of the troopers.

The trip seemed to drag on and Muller tried to nap, but the troopers' raucous laughter and loud voices kept waking him as he continued to feign ignorance. As the train approached Bern, Muller stood to grab his bag then waved vaguely at the storm troopers as he exited into the corridor. He was sure there'd be a ruckus when they wanted to de-train to the platform through the compartment doorway and he wanted to avoid getting entangled. He walked the length of his car and was able to de-train from the far end when the train came to a halt.

Sure enough, looking back, he could see a phalanx of burly Swiss policemen blocking the storm troopers from de-training.

"No foreign uniforms allowed."

"Fuck you; out of our way."

The dark-suited Nazi contingent exited to the platform, engaged loudly with the policemen and what appeared to be a welcoming delegation of Swiss citizens surged toward them on the platform.

Muller turned away confident of who would win that matchup and began to weave his way through the oncoming crowd as he strode toward the terminal and exit. There was a large knot of mainly younger men at the very end of the platform, many holding signs welcoming the Germans, nearly all wearing Nazi armbands and some even bearing red and white Nazi flags and banners.

Nearby policemen had evidently been given orders not to interfere with this forbidden display of foreign symbols and, as Muller threaded his way past, the Germans began to sing a lusty chorus of the Nazi anthem, the Horst Wessel Song. Muller saw the Swiss policemen fingering their truncheons and looking uneasily at one another. Most Swiss police tended to be social democrats, Muller knew; they had no sympathy for Nazis and gave every appearance of just waiting for an opportunity to wade into this alien crowd. But they remained in their places as ordered, looking on sourly.

Muller described the scene the next morning during a meeting in Minister Minger's office.

"I'll bet there were over three hundred Nazi sympathizers in the crowd," Muller said, shaking his head. "They made no bones about their allegiance with all the party paraphernalia they were displaying, and the police were obviously annoyed having to just stand there and watch."

"They're getting bolder," said Roger Masson, chewing on his slender pipe, "obviously intending to stir up the German citizens who live here, but also their Swiss sympathizers." He turned to Minger and fingered a sheet of paper. "The Ministry of Justice and Police circulated a list of the Swiss figures who sponsored the rally; it reads like a Who's Who from the local Fronts Movement."

Minger nodded. "I've seen it and look at the list of bankers and businessmen who were involved too." He passed the document to Hans Hausamann. "The Nazis may not be so popular with ordinary Swiss, but they've got powerful friends here that we have to take into account."

Hausamann looked closely at the list and whistled softly before passing it to Muller.

"It's nice our Justice Ministry took time off from tracking Jews to identify Nazi sympathizers and consider the risk that some of them might one day become saboteurs," he said. "Someone ought to suggest they should be doing more about that subject than the other one."

Minger held up his palm.

"We have enough on our hands without getting into the Jewish question," he said, "at least for now.

"You were at Göering's big party last week; what did you learn?" Hausamann smiled thinly and took a deep breath.

"It was a spectacle," he began, "as extravagant an affair as could possibly be imagined. Wild animals, acrobats, film stars, the heads of Krupp and most of the other business big shots. Almost all the top Nazis were there and military brass. Endless quantities of out-of-this-world food and drink," Hausamann shook his head.

"All the talk was about how nothing could stand in the way of Germany and the Führer. Poland's a dead duck; everyone assumed they'd invade soon–no one slipped me a date, unfortunately–but in a matter of weeks. And they'd crush the Poles. Universal disdain for France and Russia–Britain too, though, you know, there's always a curious German fondness for Britain–though certainly not for Chamberlain. Roosevelt the Jew was a favorite target."

"What did I learn, then? Not much." Hausamann leaned forward, elbows on the table. "Göering spent most of the time closeted away in his office; no one seemed to know why or what was going on, but there was a lot of speculation that he was at work on plans to overturn British and French threats to declare war over Poland. All very discreet, of course, but I came away with a firm conviction that Göering is determined to avoid a war. I caught sight of the British Ambassador working the crowd, then disappearing–most probably meeting with Göering in his office."

Hausamann took a deep breath and looked directly at Minger.

"I can't offer any concrete evidence, sir," he said, "but there are unmistakable signs that the Polish crisis is at hand; Germany seems determined to strike, but Göering seems equally determined to find a path that avoids a declaration of war."

"Sir, may I add a related point?" said Muller.

Minger nodded and Muller proceeded to describe his conversation with Dimitrovski a day earlier in the back of the lorry. "Yugoslav intelligence is certain that senior military representatives from both France and Britain are in Moscow meeting with their Soviet counterparts to negotiate a revival of the Triple Alliance to oppose the Nazi threat. They're optimistic that a deal will get done soon that will force Hitler's hand."

Muller continued, "My source wouldn't predict whether the announcement of a new alliance would stop Hitler from invading Poland, but he was convinced it would contain any conflict that might arise and avoid the outbreak of war with Germany, even if it meant dividing up Poland or simply erasing it again."

Roger Masson noisily tapped his pipe into the ashtray before him, spilling out the spent ashes.

Christ, why does he have to keep doing that, Muller wondered in annoyance.

Minister Minger gazed impassively at Muller, then sat back in his chair crossing his arms on his chest and shifted his gaze to the far window, open to the warm breeze and offering the familiar views of the banks above the Aare River.

No one spoke until Minger sighed deeply and leaned forward and looked at each of the three other men. "Maybe there is hope of avoiding war, then," he said quietly. "I thank you for your reports. But we shall proceed with our work nonetheless."

CHAPTER 29

"You're both immediately summoned to the Minister's office," the young page said breathlessly, sticking his head into their offices. "The police are looking for you."

Muller and Hilde got up from their desks and walked quickly along the corridor.

"What's this about?" muttered Muller as they exchanged quizzical glances; Hilde shrugged, but her face bore a frown.

When they reached the reception area, sure enough, there stood three uniformed police officers wearing unfriendly expressions and holding handcuffs. Behind them, the door to Minister Minger's office was open and Muller could hear angry voices from within.

"Spying against us, Minger, for Christ Sake."

"Right here under your nose–in the Ministry!"

One of the policemen, wearing sergeant's stripes, grabbed both Muller and Hilde by their shirt collars and propelled them toward the doorway.

"We've got 'em, Chief," he said loudly. "Shall we cuff'em?"

As they were shoved into the familiar office, Muller saw both Minger and Masson on their feet, angrily arguing with two men— whom he suddenly recognized from newspaper photos: the Minister of Justice, Eduard von Steiger, and the Chief of the Alien Police, Heinrich Rothmund.

"Not yet," Rothmund barked at the policemen. "We'll take charge for now. Leave us and close the door."

"Sit there," he commanded Muller and Hilde, pointing to chairs at the end of the conference table. "And keep your hands in sight."

They did as they were told,

Rothmund took a step toward Hilde and leered at her.

"We'll certainly have fun interrogating *this one*." He laughed and clucked Hilde under her chin with a finger, before rejoining Steiger alongside Minger's desk.

Rudolph Minger's face was bright red and he strode quickly to confront Rothmund, hunching his powerful shoulders forward and arching his back, forcing Rothmund to retreat.

"You mind yourself in this ministry, you little shit," he said, "you don't order people around here."

"And Steiger," he said turning on the man forcing him to retreat as well, "don't think you can just march in here and pretend to be a big shot. You don't know what the Hell you're doing, as usual. It's bad enough that you can't protect us from foreign interference like that damned Nazi rally last week. Instead, you drag in this sad excuse for a Police Chief and accuse key intelligence officers in my ministry of treason? Who the Hell do you think you are?"

Minger was in Steiger's face poking him in the chest with his finger.

"Remember whom you're dealing with. I'm the Minister of Military Affairs, and I'll break your ass again in the Council if I have to."

Steiger backed away, and then his shoulders slumped.

He turned to Rothmund.

"Get rid of your officers and go sit down," he ordered, his voice quieter.

Rothmund did as he was told.

"This is indeed your ministry, Rudolph," he said, using Minger's given name as a signal of contrition. "I intended no discourtesy and we may have over-stepped. But we've captured secret documents from a French courier that reveal what certainly appears to be treasonous behavior by these two people and we– well Rothmund as the Police Chief–believed we had no choice but to take them into custody immediately."

"No offense intended," he added with a weak smile.

Minger didn't move; his body, still powerfully built from years behind a plow, remained rigidly poised against Steiger's, who again stepped a few paces back.

"There!" Minger pointed to chairs at the far end of the conference table.

"You too," he said sharply to Rothmund, who had seated himself close at hand. Rothmund moved without a word.

Minger took several steps to the head of the table and faced the two men at the other end, Muller and Hilde seated close to him.

Minger pointed to Rothmund.

"You," he said, pointedly omitting his name or title–just 'you'.

"Report."

Rothmund, glanced uncertainly at Steiger, who nodded.

"We captured a French courier when he entered customs in Geneva to change trains for Bern," Rothmund began.

"How did that come about?" Minger interrupted.

Rothmund hesitated. "Well, there were certain suspicious conversations overheard and they led us to detain him."

Minger directed a piercing gaze at Rothmund. "Don't lie to me."

Rothmund again glanced at Steiger before continuing. "The individual approached one of my senior officers offering to share secret information with us if we would grant entry to an elderly female Jew traveling with him who had no entry visa."

"So, he offered to betray a client–whoever that was–in return for a grant of asylum to the woman?"

"Yes, the Jew," said Rothmund, more confidently. "We have to deal with Jews trying to enter the country all the time; so, that part wasn't anything out of the ordinary."

"Continue," ordered Minger, his face still angry.

"Well, this guy said he was delivering a secret document to an address in Bern and picking up a secret document to take back to Paris.

"On whose order?"

"Some secret French bank," Rothmund hesitated. "It's called the Caisse something; I don't know it, but it's an arm of the French Government. He was told to deliver it to a Paul Muller, an official of some Geneva-based institute and return with a memo from some lady named Magendanz, whom he said was some Swiss banking clerk."

"Very suspicious on its face," Rothmund continued, "so we took him into custody, and I acted immediately to protect the nation. I had my top investigative team examine the document and they reported that it contains some kind of plan for the French to finance a procurement program aimed at hurting Germany. We can't have that; aside from needlessly irritating the German government, it's a threat to our policy of neutrality."

"That's correct," Steiger interjected, "our neutral status would surely be compromised–and not only that, there are many patriotic Swiss companies that are engaged in exporting products to our German neighbors; why should we try to make their work any harder or more costly?"

Rothmund nodded vigorously.

"So, you see, Minister Minger," he said, "our actions fully warranted to protect Switzerland from acting in violation of our fundamental policy of strict neutrality."

WILLIAM N. WALKER

"When we ascertained this building was the address for this secret document exchange, we were shocked and so I alerted Minister von Steiger that your ministry has apparently been infiltrated by two traitors. I requested him to accompany me here so we could attend to the matter and apprehend them before any more damage is done."

His bravado restored, Rothmund looked at Minger and blanched at the expression of pure fury that greeted his remarks. He furtively cast a glance at Steiger before dropping his head and studying his hands, which nervously he clasped in front of him on the table.

Minger's expression didn't change and he spoke in a clipped, commanding tone that brooked no evasion.

"Where is the French document?"

"Here, sir," Rothmund pulled a brown envelope from his suit jacket and handed it to Minger, who, without opening it, handed it to Muller.

"Is that what we were expecting, Mr. Muller?

The seal had been broken and Muller quickly removed a short memorandum which he scanned. It was the procurement plan that Francin had described to him and which he'd alerted Minger was en route.

"Yes," he said, putting the document back in the envelope and placing it on the table before him. "Exactly what we've been waiting for."

330

Minger's eyes had not left the two men seated at the end of the table opposite where he stood.

"So, you two came to the Ministry of Military Affairs to arrest two traitors," he said, his face flushed with anger, his words clipped. "It never occurred to either of you that you have just compromised a highly confidential intelligence operation being conducted by this department and performed by these two so-called 'traitors'–who just happen to be personnel of this ministry operating under cover."

He picked up the envelope in front of Muller and waved it in their direction.

"You or your subordinates broke the seal of a secret document destined for delivery to this ministry–apparently without even a moment's hesitation or reflecting–even now as we sit here–that this document exchange was expressly authorized by this ministry–by me–and that by opening the envelope you were committing an act of supreme stupidity that compromises Swiss security. That thought never even occurred to you, am I right?" Minger barked the question.

Steiger and Rothmund glanced at one another, their shoulders slumping, and shook their heads.

"Answer me, Dammit," Minger barked again.

"No sir," they said in unison, stricken looks on both of their faces.

"You don't know that Switzerland is confronting a grave threat of economic destruction by another power; you don't know that my ministry is taking steps to safeguard our very existence."

Minger stood, leaning forward, hand on his hips, a steely expression on his face.

"And you purport to lecture me on Switzerland's policy of strict neutrality? You think I'm not dealing with that every day and guiding the actions we take to preserve our neutral status? You have no idea; you're fools, both of you."

Then he reached out his arm and pointed his finger at the two men.

"It also never entered your dim little minds that you were placing the very lives of Swiss ministry agents at risk. This document has been examined by your police officials, none of whom has security clearance and who may be sympathetic to one of the German front organizations–like the one you welcomed a week ago right here in Bern–or even Nazi operatives in their own right. The existence of this document and the names of my agents may already be in the hands of the Gestapo."

"But that possibility never even occurred to you, am I right?

Steiger and Rothmund, heads down now, murmured assent.

Minger threw the envelope down on the table.

"You dumb shits."

The room fell silent.

Minger drew a deep breath. "No one can fix what you've broken, but you're damned well going to take steps to avoid making it worse."

Minger's face took on a defiant look and he raised his voice, his finger again pointed directly at the two officials. "First, you will immediately release the courier and the woman from custody and send them back to France on the next train. Next, you will collect the names of all policemen who have knowledge of this affair and inform them they are being placed on a watch list that will evaluate their loyalty to the Swiss state. Finally, you will inform these officers that Mr. Muller and Miss Magendanz are loyal agents of this ministry. I will hold you personally responsible for protecting them. Any act of violence or intimidation taken against them by you or any member of your force will be subject to swift and severe punishment. Is that understood?"

"Yes sir," the men responded in unison.

Minger turned away, dismissing them, then stopped and turned back to face them again.

"You," he pointed at Rothmund. "You will stand before Miss Magendanz and humbly apologize for your boorish behavior just now. It was disgraceful and you should be ashamed."

"Now!'

Rothmund's faced reddened and his jaw tightened. He seemed ready to retort, but Steiger reached out an arm and pushed him.

"Do as you're told," he said.

Rothmund stood slowly and strode to where Hilde was seated. He bowed.

"I apologize, Miss Magendanz." He then straightened up and turned away, his fists clenched at his side, visibly angered.

"Minger, I regret the misunderstanding," said Steiger as he prepared to depart.

Minger advanced to the doorway where the two men were standing and he pointed his finger at them.

"Don't give me any 'misunderstanding' crap," he said, glaring at them. "It was plain stupidity. Any repetition and you're both out on your ear; do you understand that? Now, get out and do as you're told."

The two men hurriedly left and closed the door behind them.

Minger sat heavily in one of the conference chairs and took a deep breath.

"What a pair of imbeciles," he said, shaking his head.

Masson smiled. "I think you got their attention, Minister," he said.

Minger nodded and chuckled quietly.

"Oh yes," he said. "Steiger is a blockhead; I should never have allowed him to become a minister. He knows I can engineer his removal in the Council if he goes too far; so, he'll have to be careful. Rothmund is the one I worry about; he's a nasty piece of work and he's got support in the fascist front organizations."

"Thank you for insisting that he apologize to me," said Hilde.

Minger smiled.

"Actually, I was thinking about ordering Mr. Muller to lend you one of his brass knuckles so you could give him a real whack."

"Ha! That would have been good."

But then his face turned serious.

I hope I didn't put a target on your back, Miss Magendanz," he said. "Rothmund is the type to bear grudges; you had best be careful and I want you to report immediately anything remotely threatening that occurs."

Then Minger turned to Muller.

"That was an unforgiveable breach of security by your Frenchman," he said. "Was he setting us up? Is this whole idea some kind of con game?"

Muller shook his head, pursing his lips. "I have no explanation," he said lamely. "Obviously I need to find out what happened."

Hilde interrupted. "Actually, Mr. Minger, the plan is no con game; it's got a lot of merit. I've already been examining some options, just based on what Mr. Muller told me after he returned from Paris."

"Options? Already?" Minger looked at her inquiringly.

"Yes, sir," she replied. "Annual German imports amount to roughly 500 Reichsmarks," she said. "But we could target just a few categories of products that are critical to their rearmament program and where we could have an impact."

"Please go on," said Minger.

Hilde sat forward in her seat, forearms on the table and began speaking.

"Take copper, as an example. Germany imports 100 percent of its copper requirements. It's a vital product with a host of key military applications."

Hilde tapped her fingers as she ticked off examples:

"Turret gears for Panzers, undercarriage parts for aircraft, periscopes for all those new U-boats they're building, high performance valves, pumps, shafts, bolts, flanges, couplings, etcetera, etcetera." Hilde spread her hands. "An almost endless list of products where copper is a key component. But the most important? Ammunition!

"Copper driving bands are essential to every cartridge and shell casing used in every German weapon. Mortars, landmines, cannons, howitzers–even the 7.92 mm bullets used by their new Mauser infantry rifle. They all need copper. No copper, no ammunition."

Hilde paused; Minger was paying close attention and nodded at her to continue.

"And what is the German military's most pressing shortage today? Ammunition. Why? Not enough copper."

Hilde looked at them with confident expression on her face.

"They had to stop making mortar bombs altogether this spring, and rifle ammunition stockpiles are down to something like only fourteen days. So, it's a product where they're vulnerable. They're scouring the world for copper–Chile, Peru, wherever–but even where they can find it, they try to force suppliers to accept half payment in worthless Reichsbank credit certificates. Would copper suppliers divert shipments earmarked for Germany to a Swiss competitor offering to pay higher prices and in fully-convertible Swiss francs?"

Hilde paused again, looking around the table.

"Well, why not? Or at least use a competing Swiss bid as leverage to squeeze higher prices out of their German customers?

"You see the logic," Hilde said. "The same strategy can be applied to other narrow product lines; ferro alloys, for instance, like manganese and nickel. Aluminum is another example; Germans need to import it for the aircraft they produce. In each case, we'd try to bid up the price the Germans have to pay for these key components–or actually buy it and take delivery here in Switzerland. I think it's a clever idea."

Minger accepted Muller's offer of a Gitane, and exhaled a billow of smoke, waving it away.

"But the cover's been blown," Minger said. "I have no confidence that those two dunces that just left can put a lid on this breach of security. And the reality is that it does pose risks if it were to become known. Rothmund's argument that it undermines our status as a neutral is inaccurate; conducting a procurement program is no different than building weapons; we do that all the time and everyone accepts that it's consistent with remaining a neutral. But that doesn't mean it couldn't become a diplomatic football and used against us by, say, the Germans, if they were looking for an excuse to make trouble."

Minger sighed. "And he's right that a lot of Swiss businessmen would be very angry if they learned that their own Ministry of Military Affairs was running a program to increase the cost of procurement of key commodities. That would generate political opposition that we don't need. And Rothmund wouldn't hesitate to play that game if he thought it would benefit his standing in some way or other."

Minger took a deep breath. "The risk is too great. If word were to leak out that the Ministry of Military Affairs were running an anti-German procurement program financed by the French government, there'd be Hell to pay; so, we're blocked."

"Mr. Masson," Minger turned to face him, "I want a journal entry in our records to state in unequivocal terms that today–what is it August 15?–I took a formal decision to abandon the French procurement plan because of the security breach caused by the courier's betrayal and the misconduct of the police."

"The subject," Minger said, "is closed."

Hilde and Muller began walking back along the corridor toward their offices when the young page trotted up behind them and summoned them back to Minger's office.

Minger motioned them to be seated and took an adjacent seat himself.

"Miss Magendanz, your remarks this afternoon showed precisely why that French procurement scheme could become a valuable tool. But since the cover's blown, and I've officially decided to abandon it, neither this ministry, nor any other Swiss government entity can have anything more to do with it. But, it's too good a chance to pass up.

"Among other things," Minger said lightly, "it might be nice to have a stockpile of newly-acquired copper here in Switzerland in the event there should come a time we need leverage in seeking a favor from the Germans."

"So, I would like you to find a reliable private party to take on the job. Don't tell me who or how; I want to be able truthfully to state that the Ministry is not involved."

He dismissed them with a wave. "Be discreet–and please try not to get caught this time."

CHAPTER 30

The tall tower of the Urania Observatory served as a guide to Muller and Hilde as they strode along Löwenstrasse after detraining in Zurich. Not that he needed directions; he'd grown up in Zurich, after all, and this was familiar ground. He'd never paid much attention to the fact that this district of the city was home to a large Jewish community, but that's where Frederich Baer had settled upon fleeing Vienna after the Anschluss, and that's why they found themselves strolling along in this neighborhood.

At the corner of Nuschelerstrasse, when they turned right toward Uraniastrasse, Muller noticed a stately synagogue with Hebrew wording carved into the stonework above the entrance. His eyes were drawn to it by the sight of several men, women and children on the steps, shabbily dressed, but lounging on the steps and the sidewalk. Muller realized with a start that they were refugees, probably using the synagogue as a kind of sanctuary.

Muller and Hilde stopped and looked in both directions and saw there were refugees on the stairways of other houses and apartments facing on the street. It was a jarring sight. They were only blocks from the city center, yet there was no mistaking that this upscale neighborhood was now home to Jews, who appeared not to be Swiss.

Muller and Hilde took in the scene; it was strangely disorienting. The synagogue itself was architecturally striking with handsome beige and dark red stone wall panels topped by two Byzantine towers and four stately Corinthian columns guarding the front entrance. It projected a sturdy, stable image in keeping with the neighborhood. Yet, there were these obvious newcomers finding refuge here.

Turning away, they walked another block until they arrived at Uraniastrasse where the twelve-story observatory tower presented itself to full view. The spherical observatory itself, which housed the telescope, seemed to be planted atop a copper-clad receptacle rising above an elegant windowed base toward the top of the tower.

"I'd forgotten how splendid it looks," Muller said as they gazed up at the handsome building. "I came here as a schoolboy to learn about astronomy but never appreciated what an elegant structure it is."

Hilde hung on his arm, nodding.

"It really is grand," she said. "I've seen it from a distance when I've visited Zurich, but frankly never paid it any attention."

"And there," Muller said pointing up to the windowed level below the observatory, "is the famous Jules Verne bar where our meeting is to take place."

They went up in the elevator, and as the doors opened and they stepped into the foyer, the early evening sun poured into the elegant bar and restaurant revealing breathtaking views of the rooftops and church spires of Zurich and the High Alps beyond.

The maître d' led them to a table with an especially splendid mountain view.

Frederich Baer rose with a smile, warmly greeting Muller and bowing to kiss Hilde's hand upon being introduced. He gestured for them to be seated as the maître d' filled their flutes from the champagne bottle nestled in the ice bucket standing alongside the table.

"Prost–Santé" they clinked glasses.

Muller regarded Baer with a smile. He seemed not to have changed. Well-attired as always, the diamond stickpin in place, and his appearance was vigorous and alert.

They had become allies in Austria the year before. Muller had protected Baer and his family when the train they were taking together had been attacked by a Nazi gang, and later, the banker had become a key player in Muller's attempt to keep Austria's gold reserves out of Hitler's hands when Germany seized control of the country.

The idea to approach Baer about running the French procurement project had come to Muller the very night of the encounter with the police at the ministry. Muller had dined with Hans Hausamann and described the scene.

Hausamann reacted vehemently when Muller told him that Heinrich Rothmund was involved.

"He's one of the leading Anti-Semites in Switzerland," Hausamann snorted, pursing his lips. "For years, he's used his position as head of the Alien Police to keep out Jewish refugees. He even connived with the Nazis to use the J stamp on passports as a way of stopping all of them at the border."

"J stamp?" asked Muller.

"Literally," Hausamann replied. "A big red 'J' is stamped on the passport of every German Jew. Rothmund helped write the Federal Council's visa rules that forbid Germans using passports with J stamps–any German Jew, in other words–from entering Switzerland without special approval. So, he's lined his pockets with bribes and kept Jewish entry to a trickle."

Hausamann had poured them both another glass of red wine to accompany their foie de veau, his expression stern; he clearly didn't like Rothmund.

"Minger opposed the new visa rules in the Council, so Rothmund would love to find something to pin on him to discredit him. I'm sure he put Steiger up to arresting you; it sounds like just like him. A bad guy."

Then he sighed and shrugged. "But there's not a lot to be done, I'm afraid. He's got a lot of supporters in high places. Jews are no more popular here than they are elsewhere. But a policy of keeping nearly all of them out is stupid and limits our options. There are assets among these people; we should be letting more of them in and putting them to work for us."

That was when the idea came to him.

Baer was an asset: a Jew who was also a knowledgeable and well-connected Austrian banker. He was one of the lucky ones who'd been able to find refuge in Switzerland.

Most likely he'd bribed his way in, Muller supposed. But, no matter, he was here and was legal–albeit part of an unpopular minority.

Minger had instructed Muller to activate the French procurement plan, but keep the Ministry's fingerprints off it. Would Baer be willing to take on the French project and run it secretly using his Jewish network?

Muller had resolved to find out and invited Hilde to come along.

He and Baer hadn't seen one another since the Anschluss, when Hitler had seized Austria. The Gestapo had joined forces with local Nazis to unleash a reign of terror, rounding up and imprisoning–or simply killing–perceived enemies, especially Austrian Jews and the two men compared notes about those chaotic events.

"We were fortunate to get out," Baer said. "It all started so quickly," he added, shaking his head. "Almost as soon as Schuschnigg resigned–even before that puppet Seyss-Inquart was installed–they came after us."

Muller nodded. "I was on the run myself and saw the raids and attacks. It was very frightening."

"I'd hired a small plane to fly us out," said Baer. "My wife and I made it to the airstrip, but her sister was seized, so we had to leave her. Then, the pilot refused to take off; I had to put a pistol to his head and a pile of Reichsmarks in his lap before we finally taxied away, only minutes ahead of the Nazis."

"Was your sister-in-law able to get out and join you?" Hilde asked.

"No," Baer replied slowly, his shoulders sagging. "She's being held–we don't even know where–and they're using her as blackmail, telling us we have to pay to keep her alive and dangling her release if we return ourselves. We won't do that, of course; they would just lock us up too–or worse."

"That's the lot of European Jews these days," he added, "They even come after the handful of us who managed to escape to Switzerland. But here we are."

Then Baer looked at Muller with a smile. "I'll bet you didn't even know when you were growing up here that this part of Zurich was the Jewish quarter."

Muller felt a bit flummoxed and unsure how to reply. Baer was right; this was the observatory area to him. He had no idea of any Jewish legacy and no memory of even being aware of the existence of the synagogue they'd walked past.

"No matter," Baer continued; "but you certainly noticed it today. The few Jews that can get past Swiss border controls are sent here to be sheltered until we resettle them in the camps."

"Camps?" asked Muller.

"Well, as you know, Swiss Jews are taxed to pay the costs of housing Jewish refugees, so we set up camps to care for them out of Zurich proper–in Endingen and Lengnau; the Surb Valley area. It's ironic," he went on, "that's the region Jews were forced to inhabit before emancipation in the middle of the last century. After that, they began coming here. Now, we have to send them back. You probably saw some on the streets when you walked over from the banhof; it always takes a few days to get them resettled."

Muller and Hilde both nodded.

"We did see what looked like refugees; they seemed out of place."

Baer smiled grimly. "Refugees always seem out of place. But you're right and they attract unwanted attention, so we try to move them along quickly."

Then Baer's expression brightened. "I'll wager that you also didn't know this Urainia Observatory itself was built by one of the early Jews who settled in this neighborhood."

Muller responded with a rueful smile, shaking his head.

"Abraham Weill Einstein was his name," Baer said. "He became a wealthy developer and built this entire section of the Old Town, as we now refer to it, including the Zähringerplatz, below us here," Baer pointed down to the bustling public park on the other side of Uraniastrasse.

"It became a popular part of the city and quickly lost whatever Jewish character it may have had at the start. Oh, there's still the synagogue, a few kosher markets, and many successful Swiss Jews live here; that why I selected this neighborhood when I purchased my Swiss residence–my escape hatch from Austria, so to speak.

"I thought it would a safe haven, but Hitler's public attacks on Jews has encouraged a rise in Anti-Semitism here too, and the neighborhood has again acquired a Jewish taint. So, we try to be careful."

"But we're not in Austria or Germany," Baer smiled broadly. "We're here in neutral Switzerland, so we expect to survive!"

He refilled their flutes and they each took a sip, Muller and Hilde smiling back at him.

"But you didn't come to talk about the Jews," Baer said. "How can I be of help?"

Baer then leaned toward Hilde with a stage whisper. "Mr. Muller was my protector in Vienna. I've been hoping some opportunity might arise to try and repay his kindness."

Muller grinned. He'd found Baer engaging in their encounters together in Vienna and his matter-of-fact description of their current surroundings and its history had put him at ease. But before he responded, he found himself looking over his shoulder to ensure he wouldn't be overheard; he was adopting that habit too, he realized.

Baer noticed his precaution and leaned forward. "I've checked to make sure there is no microphone." He tapped the table.

Baer listened intently as Muller described the French procurement plan and recounted the events surrounding it.

He interrupted only to order plats du jour and a bottle of crisp Gruner Veltliner.

"At least Hitler hasn't banned export of that," Baer said with a grin.

When Muller was finished, he turned to Hilde, who recounted the idea of targeting copper and other vulnerable German imports, providing even more detail than she had earlier to Minger.

Baer took it all in, nodding with interest, and when they were done, he spent several moment gazing out the window, drumming his fingers lightly on the white tablecloth. Then he pushed his plate aside, gestured to the waiter to bring another bottle of wine and lit a small cigar.

"Rothmund tried to arrest you when he got word of this scheme?" he asked.

Muller nodded. "Minister Minger and our ministry have not been supporters of Rothmund's strict approach to border security. His motivation may have been as much to do with discrediting Minger as objecting to the plan itself. But Minger decided he can't risk having the ministry proceed in the circumstances. So, I decided on my own to see if you had an interest in taking it on."

"You know Rothmund's our bête noir," Baer said with a grim expression. "It'd be nice to one-up him on something like this."

"The Caisse des Depots et Consignments has deep pockets," he went on, "but it's not part of the banking system. They'd need to transfer the funds," he paused, thinking. "Probably depositing them at the Banque Francaise du Commerce Exterieur would be the best choice. It makes payments to banks around the world on a daily basis, so transferring a deposit like this shouldn't attract attention. But the funds shouldn't be sent here directly; they need to be camouflaged."

Again, he paused.

"New York," he said. "The bank sends the funds to one of the money center banks there–either Morgan's or the Manhattan Bank would work. Then they could break it into pieces to get it into our network by making deposits in Kuhn Loeb, Rothchild's–maybe Warburg's or even Lazard–which we could draw against when we needed to."

Baer nodded slowly, still thinking.

"Yes, that could work and be kept quiet; no one would know why we need the money. The French bank would lose track of it in New York, and once it gets back here, we've got Swiss banking secrecy laws to protect us–even against the likes of Rothmund."

Baer's fingers drummed the table again.

"The actual procurement part should be easy. There are a lot of Jewish merchants I can engage to become bidders against the Germans."

Baer broke into a big smile. "Actually, it's the perfect stereotype. I get to play the role of Shylock."

He rubbed his hands together and made a face, mimicking the Jewish moneylender.

"But we'd need an ultimate buyer," Baer added, "And he can't be a Jew. Shylock never takes title to anything; Jews are just middlemen, remember. So, you've got to find a Swiss buyer for me. Someone who's above suspicion and who can take delivery of any materials that we actually wind up buying."

Muller pursed his lips; he hadn't thought of that. "I'll figure something out," he said, hoping he could.

Baer sat back in his chair, smiled broadly and offered his hand. "Then I think we have a deal."

"Tell the French the price is 40 million francs in the first tranche." Then he took out a small notepad, tore off a sheet and scribbled an address. "This is a secure mail drop in Endigen which we have under surveillance. When they're ready to proceed, they can contact me to set the deposit in motion."

Then he wrote on the sheet again and handed it to Muller.

"That's the secret password we'll use," Baer said.

Muller took the sheet.

It read 'Chutzpah'.

CHAPTER 31

Muller's mother had been insisting that he visit them at Chalet Muller in Grindelwald. Among other things, August 24 was his father's birthday.

"He's been through a lot this year with his stroke; he's getting better and making steady progress, but still...." She hadn't finished the sentence.

"We both need you to come," she'd said finally, in that tone of voice that brooked no dissent.

He'd persuaded Hausamann to permit him to stop off in Grindelwald for a few days on the way back from an important meeting in Zurich. He had not told even Hausamann about his plan to approach Baer about the French project. The official record said that project was closed; he was determined to keep it that way. So, he'd said yes, and told his mother that he'd be accompanied by a female business colleague, who could sleep in Mathilda's room.

He and Hilde had resumed their romantic relationship after his return from Paris, often dining together and a few times visiting her small apartment in the rooming house she shared with half a dozen other women. But it was an awkward and decidedly unsatisfactory arrangement and his ministry housing quarters were off limits to female guests. So, when he'd posed the prospect of a discreet overnight trip to Zurich, Hilde had snuggled next to him, squeezed her arm through his and quickly agreed.

They had dined that evening at the Dählhölzli restaurant in the park and were seated on a bench, discreetly screened by some large ferns, where they could kiss and hold one another. It was something, at least.

"Then the next day," he'd continued, "after our meeting with Baer, we'll take the train to Grindelwald where my parents own a chalet; you'll get to meet them and help celebrate father's birthday; you can sleep in Mathilda's room, so everything's proper."

Hilde stiffened and straightened up, pulling away from Muller's embrace.

She turned to him, eyes blazing, her face angry.

"What?" she exclaimed loudly; "Do what? You want to take me off to meet your parents like some show horse?

"Your pet Lippizaner?

"Not on your life."

Hilde got up and stood, hands on her hips, staring down at him defiantly.

"You have no right to do that to me, Paul."

Muller blanched, looking stunned.

"I told my mother that I was bringing along a colleague from work," he said defensively. "I didn't say anything about us being....involved together."

"Right," she snarled, "Hildegard Magendanz, the bank's leper and Muller's Lippizaner. I won't have it."

He reached for her hand, but she pulled it away.

He'd thought he could show off Hilde a bit and impress his parents. Then, if he and Hilde really got serious at some point in the future, he could remind them they'd met her when he'd brought her to Grindelwald.

He wouldn't force the issue with Hilde; it was just a simple visit.

Except, it obviously wasn't.

Christ! He'd really stepped in it.

"This is so unfair, Paul."

Hilde sat back down, but away from Muller, and she began to cry softly.

Muller moved to embrace her, but she pushed him away.

"You don't know anything about me, Paul, yet you expect me to come meet your parents–as just some business acquaintance? Arghhh!"

Hilde reached into her purse for a hanky, which she used to blow her nose and wipe away her tears.

"Paul, I don't *have* a family," she said her eyes tearing up again. "No one. I'm all alone in the world. I'm loving being with you, but I'm scared. Am I doing the right thing? I don't know, and I don't have anyone to ask."

She blew her nose again and took several deep breaths. "Meeting your parents is not just some casual event or some government policy convenience."

She turned to face him and fixed him with a penetrating gaze. "The reason you want to introduce me to your parents–or at least I certainly hope it's the reason–is because you think you may be in love with me and you want to introduce me–if not to seek their formal approval, then at least to hope they'll find me acceptable–a good show horse. If you were honest with yourself, you'd know that's what you're doing. Am I right?"

Now it was Muller's turn to take a deep breath.

Hilde was right; of course, that's exactly what he was doing and why he was doing it.

Muller bowed his head and returned Hilde's stern gaze with a sheepish look. "You're right," he said nodding, his hand reaching out to grasp hers again. This time she didn't resist.

"I'm not very good at this kind of thing," he said speaking quietly, "even with myself.

"I guess I'm scared, too. I do think I may be in love with you and that frightens me–but what scares me even more is not knowing if you feel the same way about me. What I'm hearing is– maybe you do. Maybe this really is what it's like to be in love with someone who loves you back. I hope so."

"Oh Paul," Hilde sighed, and they hugged, then found each other's mouths in a deep, warm, lingering kiss.

They sat close to one another, catching their breath.

Then Muller turned to Hilde.

"You really have no family at all? No parents or siblings?"

Hilde shook her head. "My mother died when I was only four, giving birth to a baby boy who also died. His name was Henri–like my uncle, the dairy farmer in Vaud I told you about. He only lived for a week or so after my mother died. My father was an engineer at a company that produced electrical gear in St. Gallen where I grew up. He was good to me, but then he died in an industrial accident while I was away at university."

Hilde sighed.

"I had a lonely childhood," she said. "An only child to a widower, who was not very outgoing. So, I read a lot, studied hard and I've used my brainpower to try and get along in the world. I became a recluse; you saw me that first day we met–was it only a couple of months ago? I was treated as an outcast by those snotty bankers and when they told me some big shot from the Ministry of Military Affairs needed help, I was loaded for bear; I was going to take you down like a tree in the forest."

She smiled. "Instead, you were polite and friendly, you told me how much I resembled your sister and–poof–all my resentment vanished," she blew on her palm, "just like that."

She laid her head on Muller's shoulder. "I think I may have fallen in love with you on that very first day. So, all right; now we

357

have an understanding that we have relationship, I'll come to meet
your parents in their mountain lair. But I'm not going as a
government Lippizzaner. I'm the woman that might decide to
marry you."

"I agree," he said, feeling chastened, but exhilarated too.

Then she elbowed him in the ribs and giggled. "But don't you
dare produce an engagement ring during our visit."

So, it had been agreed and, the next afternoon, as the
fernicular serving the upper reaches of Grindelwald cleared the
final ridge and the rooftops of village hove into view, Hilde
gripped Muller's arm tightly in anticipation.

They swung down from their small compartment to the narrow
platform, then Muller led the way toward a well-used path up the
mountain, carrying their small travel bags in either hand. After
climbing a hundred meters or so, they looked ahead, and Paul
spied the familiar slender figure of his mother waiting to welcome
them a few steps below Chalet Muller.

Muller embraced his mother then introduced Hilde, who
looked uncharacteristically anxious.

Ann Muller must have noticed, because her handshake became
a big hug as she enveloped Hilde in her arms.

"Welcome dear, Hilde," she said stepping back and beaming,
holding Hilde at arm's length. "We've heard so much about you,
and Karl and I are so glad you're here. I didn't believe that
'business colleague' description from Paul for a moment."

They mounted the last few yards of the hillside then stepped up onto the broad gallery that fronted the structure where Karl Muller stood with only a cane steadying him.

Muller and his father embraced and Karl also greeted Hilde warmly.

Oskar and Greta, long-time servants, who were like members of the family, had brought aperitifs and snacks from the kitchen and they too greeted both Hilde and Paul with broad smiles and hugs.

"Timing is perfect, Paul," said Ann, "My BBC news broadcast just finished and there's still enough light to be out here for drinks before dinner." She took Hilde by the arm. "I'll show you to your room, Hilde," and they disappeared inside.

"Father, you seem so much better," Muller said, looking his father up and down, and Karl did a small pirouette with a grin, showing his newly returned mobility.

"I'm not ready to return to the rugby pitch yet or race you up the mountain," he said with a smile, "but what a change. Every day the muscles seem to relax and remember what they're supposed to do. God, that wheelchair was a nightmare. So, it's a great relief and hopefully I'll continue to get better."

They strolled over to the seating area, chatting amiably until Ann and Hilde rejoined them. Oskar delivered glasses of chilled Fendant, and a glass of whiskey to Karl.

"Santé," they clinked glasses.

Muller looked at his parents with a sly smile. "Father, mum, you seemed to have expected me to bring Hilde–and to know about her...er, us– even though I carefully stipulated that my guest would be a business associate?"

They both laughed.

"Paul, for goodness sake," his father said with a grin, "Bern is a very small place; you surely don't think you've been unnoticed?"

Hilde put her hand to her mouth and blushed.

Ann Muller immediately reached over and patted her forearm.

"Don't be embarrassed, Hilde," she said, smiling. "Believe it or not, Karl and I were young once too and had more than our share of fun. Ha!" She clapped her hands. "So, you're welcome here. We'll keep our big noses out of your affairs until you tell us otherwise. But for this visit, you're Paul's girlfriend and we're happy about that."

"Now," she said, the subject clearly closed, "tell us everything that's going on in Bern and the world."

After dinner was cleared, Oskar placed a chilled bottle of Poire William to the table along with four small glasses. Karl removed the stopper and poured for them.

"Our favorite digestif always ensures a good night's sleep."

Hilde's mouth puckered as she took a sip. She shook her head and reached out for the bottle eying the big pear inside that bobbed in the clear liquid as she swung it to-and-fro.

"I've been served this before," she said, a little huskily. "It's very strong and I like it, but I've never understood how they get the pear inside the bottle."

Ann Muller laughed. "I had the very same reaction when Karl introduced me to it," she said, turning to her husband.

"They grow it," Karl said with a smile. "Every spring after the pear trees bloom the growers tie bottles over the blooms so when the pears grow, they're inside the bottles; they harvest the fruit by removing the bottles, then add the digestif at the distillery."

Hilde slapped the table lightly, smiling and bobbing her head.

"Of course," she said. "In the Valais, right? I've taken the train there and seen those groves of trees outside the windows that seemed to have something tied to their branches." She laughed at herself. "I'd never put the two together."

Downing her glass, she took a deep breath, and held it out for a refill and raised it to her hosts.

"Thank you," she said.

"For everything," she added, then tapped Paul's glass with a smile.

After Ann excused herself, Karl led them across the big room to where Oskar had lit a fire against the evening chill, and they took seats facing the blazing logs. He'd brought the bottle and proffered it. Paul accepted a generous refill, but Hilde declined with a smile.

Karl leaned forward toward Hilde as he spoke.

"Hilde, Paul knows that before I suffered my stroke, I was part of a group of confidential senior advisors to the government. I had to resign, of course. But in the last month, as I've recovered my faculties, I've resumed conferring informally with Rudolph Minger."

"That's one reason we knew about you, Hilde, and," he said smiling at Muller, "about you and Hilde–that and the rumor mill, of course." Karl smiled, then his face grew serious.

"Minger told me about the confrontation with Steiger and that nasty fellow Rothmund. He said it involved a French proposal that he liked, but felt had been too compromised for the ministry to pursue. He also left me with the impression that he had given you the task of setting the business up outside of government channels."

"It's too late tonight to pursue the subject," Karl smiled, "but I'll think about it overnight. I still have a few tricks up my sleeve."

He stood and downed the last of his Poire William. "Have a nice night together."

CHAPTER 32

Muller woke up with a moment of panic, then remembered he'd finally dragged himself back to his room. So at least appearances would be proper. When he'd taken Hilde back to her room, she's quietly closed the door and pulled him onto the bed atop her.

"If they say anything, I'll blame the Poire William," she'd whispered as they struggled out of their clothes.

Now, as he rolled over, Muller could see the weather had changed. Wind-driven rain rattled against his window and battered the red geraniums in the window box. He groaned, then finally got up, and after a brisk shower, threw on a sweater over worn corduroys and marched into the kitchen looking for coffee. Greta handed him a mug then shooed him out into the dining area, where he found his mother and Hilde, both dressed and looking pert, deep in conversation, and his father–lacking only a tie–perusing the morning newspaper.

Muller sank into his seat, reached for a piece of toast and studied the puddles forming on the gallery. Thick grey clouds enveloped the chalet and obscured the mountains beyond; even the path down to the village disappeared into the swirling mist.

Oskar appeared bearing omelets and a large plate of cheeses.

His father put down the paper and Hilde and his mother greeted him briefly before launching into giggles about something else.

"We were hoping you'd make an appearance," his father said with a smile. "Short night, I guess. But you'll want to see this I think."

He pointed to an article in the paper.

'Soviet Union and Germany Rumored to be in Talks to Expand Trade,' read the headline.

Muller picked up the paper. He frowned before handing it back to his father.

"Hardly likely," he said dismissively, wolfing down his omelet while it remained hot. "They barely even speak to one another, let alone do business together. Anything else interesting?"

Karl Muller shook his head. "Only the usual stories reporting Hitler's threats to invade Poland because of provocations."

He turned back to the front page. "This time he's claiming Polish airplanes shot down two JU 88s over German territory– 'more proof of predatory Polish aggression' is what he's quoted as saying."

Both men shook their heads dismissively.

"That's why I listen to BBC News every night," Ann Muller interjected. "At least there's one reliable source of information left."

Then she returned to her conversation with Hilde.

As Oskar cleared the table, Karl Muller removed his glasses, placing them on the table before him and cleared his throat.

"Yes, my dear?" Ann said. "You have a pronouncement to make?"

"I do, "Karl said briskly. "It's time for Hilde and Paul and I to resume our top-secret talks that were interrupted last evening. You're welcome to join us, of course Ann, but you may be putting your life on the line, so think carefully first."

Ann snorted, waving him away with a gesture; "I wouldn't think of interfering in your deliberations–though it is nice to see you including a woman for a change."

She stood. "I've got sewing I need to do," she said, walking to the hallway. "Go save the world–or at least this part of it."

Karl led the way over to the seating area in front of the blazing fireplace. Paul noted that he didn't have his cane with him and walked with only a slight hitch in his gait.

"I gather from Minger that Jacques Francin was betrayed by his courier," he began. "Not a promising start to his project. Do you have a plan to revive it somehow? I know Minger would like to do that."

Muller smiled and nodded, but with a sheepish expression. "This is the first time I've done this with you, father. "It's always been the other way around–you, sharing confidences with me. But here goes."

Muller drew a deep breath, then reprised the story of the French procurement plan as he'd described it to Frederich Baer a day earlier. He deferred again to Hilde to fill in details on the sectors to be targeted, then picked up the story again.

"After the attempt to arrest us, it was clear we needed to throw Steiger and Rothmund off the scent, so I've taken steps to revive the program in the place they're least likely ever to suspect: the international Jewish banking community right here in Switzerland."

Karl Muller blinked, then gestured for Muller to continue.

"Frederich Baer was among Austria's leading bankers and was a key ally in my plan to prevent Austria's gold reserves from falling into Hitler's hands during the Anschluss. He escaped to Switzerland and lives now in Zurich. Hilde and I went to visit him there yesterday to ask if he would take charge of the program and run both the financing and the procurement, using his Jewish network."

"And he agreed?" Karl asked.

Muller nodded. "He quickly figured a way to get the funds from the Caisse des Depots into the banking system, then distribute it among several Jewish investment houses in New York which Baer's Bank could call upon when it required funds. The money trail should be highly secure. And he was certain of finding Jewish traders to bid against Germans for the products they're targeting."

Muller smiled. "He likes the role of playing Shylock."

"Ha!" Karl reacted with a loud chuckle. "Very clever."

"There's one role yet to be filled," Muller continued. "Baer points out that Jews are perceived as middlemen, so we need a buyer they can identify in these bids–a non-Jew, who would seem credible and won't raise suspicions. I haven't figured that piece out yet."

Karl turned in his seat and stared out the window for several moments, watching the rain run down the windowpanes. Then he turned back with a broad smile.

"Swabian Holdings," he said. "That's your buyer."

Muller looked at his father in confusion.

"Swabia is the region of Southern Germany right across from St. Gallen, where I grew up," said Hilde uncertainly.

"Precisely," Karl responded. "A very senior German Nazi official from that region came to see me about a year ago. He wanted to establish an account in the bank where he could deposit not just funds he was extorting from victims of Nazi crimes–that's actually fairly common–but I discovered his deposits also included funds that he was skimming–stealing–from SS accounts. As you might imagine, that made things even dicier than usual, and we set up elaborate security procedures to protect the enterprise that he chose to call, 'Swabian Holdings'."

"Under those procedures, I have authority to sign documents for Swabian Holdings using the name of the Nazi's father-in-law, who is conveniently dead–and who also had a name so conveniently common as to be untraceable."

"Franz Schmidt, I'll bet," laughed Hilde.

Karl nodded. "You get the idea."

"So here's how to proceed." Karl began speaking rapidly and Muller smiled to himself, admiring what were obviously well-practiced steps to conceal transactions from prying eyes.

"Good old Franz, as we'll call him, rents a box in the Central Zurich post office under the name Swabian Holdings. That's our buyer, and we print up stationery and invoices using that name and address. The Post Office is instructed to forward any inquiries Swabian receives to Mr. Baer's–Shylock's–letter drop in Endigen, so, that ought to be a secure connection. And in the highly unlikely event someone should inquire too closely about either Franz's holdings or Shylock's connection to Swabian, I can ensure that my German client will make certain it's covered up, because the last thing he wants to do is be exposed and handed over to the tender mercies of the Waffen SS."

They were silent for a few moments.

"And the Swabian name will deflect any suggestion of French financing," said Hilde, nodding approval."

"Will Shylock approve, Paul?" asked Karl.

"I don't think we should keep calling him 'Shylock'," Muller replied

Karl shook his head. "Much better than using names."

Muller gazed at his father, then sighed and nodded.

"You're right, of course, father. But, yes, I think he'll agree. I suspect he'll rather like the idea of using a German name and the prospect of blackmailing a Nazi bigwig in a pinch."

Muller sighed. "Now, I need to decide how to get Francin to agree to this new arrangement."

"You can't visit him again," said Hilde. "Not after what's happened."

Karl agreed. "Too risky."

Then he snapped his fingers and flashed a grin. "I'll get Charlotte to invite her father to come to Zurich and visit his grandson. It's perfect cover. The two of us can dote over the boy and lay plans out of anyone's hearing–except for Klaus, of course, and I think we can depend upon his discretion." Karl smiled. "We can even push him over to Zähringerplatz in the baby carriage. It would be very coincidental to find Shylock seated at the very park bench where two grandfathers decide to sit and have a smoke."

Muller burst out laughing.

"What a good idea! Father, I didn't know that a staid banker like you had such a flair for cloak and dagger."

"You'd be surprised," Karl said matter-of-factly. He didn't smile.

"What about including Charlotte as well?" Hilde asked, turning to Muller. "Francin told you that she's spying on Thomas. Wouldn't the documents she's peeking at give Shylock a directory of German suppliers?"

Karl took a deep breath, then nodded. "Hilde's right, I'm afraid."

"It's a very awkward situation, Charlotte spying on her husband–my son and your brother, Paul–but that's what she's elected to do." Karl pursed his lips. "She hates the Nazis and is frankly disgusted at Thomas for cozying up to them and providing hard currency to support their arms buildup. She confided in me and I provided the miniature camera she uses to photograph key documents."

Muller gazed quizzically at his father, who nodded again and continued, his expression somber.

"Thomas travels at least half the time," he said, "and he refused to tell Charlotte what he is up to. He's become an inattentive husband and he even had to be treated for the clap at one point. It was obvious he was not just attending business meetings. So, she decided to find out what was going on. Since she gets up to breastfeed Klaus at night, she began going through Thomas' briefcase and was furious at what she discovered. Mostly he spends time in Germany with weapons-makers and their agents putting deals together. Then he visits their suppliers, buying up the Reichsbank credit certificates they have to accept–and collecting bribes for his trouble.

"As you and I would expect, Paul–knowing Thomas as we do– he made a careful record of everything and Charlotte found the whole program laid out in his notebook. Even a list of his girls, along with the deals he was making."

Karl rolled his eyes, but continued.

"That was around the time that I suffered my stroke and had to step down from the Bank. Charlotte understood how angry I was and asked my help in getting the information to her father at the Caisse des Depots so he could pass it to French intelligence. I had Oskar dig out my miniature camera to give her and whenever she'd bring little Klaus over to cheer me up during my convalescence, I'd pass her more film."

"So, she's been sending photos of Thomas' deals to French intelligence for over six months?" asked Muller.

Karl nodded. "I assume they were what inspired the French plan that Francin revealed to you."

"But then Francin sends me his plan and is promptly betrayed by his courier." It was Muller's turn to take a deep breath. "Something doesn't add up."

"Which is why you can't go back to see Francin," said Karl. "It's also why Charlotte stops sending her films to Paris and instead passes them to Shylock for his buyers to use as a roadmap to identify key German suppliers."

They paused to light cigarettes, each reflecting on their conversation.

Karl broke the silence. "The key is to get Francin to put up the money. It'll be my job to see to it that he does that when he visits our grandson. Once the funds enter the banking system, it'll be out of French hands and Shylock can activate the plan without their knowledge or interference. At that point, Francin can wash his hands of the whole thing and just walk away. Given the security breach, that should be a solution he'll be happy to embrace."

They ground out their butts and stood to stretch.

"So, you just happened to have a miniature camera stashed away in a drawer somewhere father?" said Muller lightly with a teasing expression. "Standard Swiss banker issue, I assume."

Karl smiled back at his son.

"Rather like the brass knuckles I'm told you carry with you," he replied. "Standard diplomatic issue, I assume."

As they finished lunch, the clouds parted, and the sun made an appearance. Muller invited his father to share a cigarette with him on the gallery outside.

Karl pointed to a dark cloud moving in their direction. "It'll need to be a short smoke," he said conversationally.

Muller nodded, but reached into the pocket of his corduroys and extracted the cocktail napkin that he'd kept with him. He handed it to his father.

"I've not been able to get any satisfactory answers to the questions posed by this sketch," he said. "Not from anyone," he added for emphasis. "What can you tell me, father?"

Karl Muller looked at the map drawn on the cocktail napkin, then handed it back to Muller. He gazed at the fast-moving cloud that was advancing on them, then turned to face Muller.

"The reason no one will discuss it with you is that Switzerland has entered into a secret agreement with the French to combine their forces and oppose a German invasion of the kind that map depicts."

He spoke in quiet, flat tones, his eyes locked on Muller's.

"I would have preferred not to reveal that to you. But it's preferable to having you pass your map around asking questions about it. And I believe I can trust you with what is probably our deepest secret."

Muller gazed back at his father, his mind racing.

What had Christian Francin said to him in Colmar, after their Maginot tour? 'If you have to ask, I can't tell you'. Of course! Francin knew about the agreement and Muller's question revealed he didn't, so Christian refused to answer him.

"I don't have to tell you that if this agreement were revealed, it would completely undermine our assertion of strict neutrality," Karl went on. "A military agreement with the French Army to oppose the German Army is not a neutral undertaking. Accordingly, we have taken steps to guard the secret closely. There are only two copies of the agreement in existence. One is in a special safe controlled by Minister Minger. The other is in the files of the French Commander-in-Chief, General Gamelin. I think we can be confident that those files will never be revealed, and that consequently our secret is safe from discovery. So that's the answer to your question. I know you will guard it carefully."

Karl offered his hand and Muller shook it.

As they did so, they were pelted by the cold rain that returned with a vengeance. Tossing their cigarettes over the railing, they hurried inside.

They said no more on the subject. Muller was satisfied that the two governments had made the right decision to defend against a surprise German attack and they had taken proper precautions to keep their agreement a closely guarded secret.

It was a quiet afternoon that followed, the rain again slackening, and this time being replaced by a chill mist. Oskar kept the fire going and Muller lay back on the couch, finally able to concentrate on John Gunther's book, occasionally rising to restack records on the Victrola. It was a fine afternoon for listening to the Brahms Requiem and Rigoletto.

Hilde had accepted a challenge from his father for a chess match, and to Muller's amusement had proceeded to defeat him twice, rather quickly.

So, they were startled when his mother strode into the living room and removed the needle from La Bohème with a record still in the stack.

"BBC time," she announced, leaning over the polished mahogany radio console, turning on the wireless and, after it warmed up, adjusting the needle to find the best reception. Squeaks and hums from the ether finally gave way to a clear signal.

Ann Muller was British. She had met and married Karl when he attended Cambridge nearly forty years earlier and happily assumed the role of a Swiss banker's wife and mother to three children in Zurich. But she had insisted that English be the lingua franca within the household and that she retain her British ties by regularly listening to the BBC. Tuning in to the 6:00 PM BBC World News program–5:00 PM in Switzerland–had become a daily custom.

Muller continued to scan his book, not paying much attention, then suddenly sat bolt upright, his mouth agape at what he was hearing.

"This afternoon, officials in Berlin and Moscow released statements announcing that Germany and the Soviet Union have signed a ten-year Non-Aggression Treaty. The Agreement was signed in Moscow today by Soviet Foreign Minister Vyacheslav Molotov and German Foreign Minister Joachim von Ribbentrop.

"The joint statement observed that, following completion of the Soviet–German trade and credit agreement two days earlier, the two sides seized the opportunity to improve political links between Germany and the USSR. It went on to state that today's agreement included provisions for close consultation and promised neutrality if either went to war against a third power. It also pledged that neither government would align with any group of nations which is directly or indirectly aimed at the other.

"The surprise announcement appeared to come as a shock to Prime Minister Chamberlain and other world leaders. Senior British government officials are meeting a Downing Street at this very hour and no formal reaction has yet been released.

"But the news comes at a moment of serious international tensions and threats of war.

"German Chancellor Hitler has repeatedly issued threats to invade its neighbor Poland over alleged provocations and violations of German sovereignty. In March of this year, the Governments of Great Britain and France warned Germany that they would declare war in the event Germany invaded Poland. It is not known at this hour how today's German-USSR pact will affect those commitments, but observers interpreted the language of the announcement as a pledge by the Soviet Union not to intervene in a war between Germany and Poland and not to take sides if Britain and France declared war on Germany.

"The Quai d'Orsay in Paris had no immediate comment, but first stage Army mobilization orders have been issued....."

Suddenly, static drowned out reception and Ann leapt to the console, twiddling with the dial and trying to recover the signal.

"...to keep gas masks close at hand in the event of an attack...."

More static.

"...sandbags around public buildings. Evacuation orders have not yet been...."

Static interference blocked the rest, and despite her best efforts with the dial Ann could only pick up a few more indistinct words in the interference. Finally, she gave up, turned the wireless off and sat down.

The room was silent.

Muller felt the hair rising on the back of his neck and found himself unable to speak, his breath coming in shallow gasps. The Gunther book slipped from his grasp and fell to the floor with a thump.

"My God." Karl Muller's voice was little more than a croak, and Muller reacted with alarm, striding to his father's side. But Karl waved him away, nodding that he was fine, and Muller reached for Hilde, taking both her hands in his own and kneeling beside her.

"We will be at war within days," Karl said, recovering his voice, but speaking slowly, hardly able to get the words out.

"What will become of us?"

He stood and walked to where Ann was sitting, placing his hands on her shoulders and bending to place his cheek next to hers.

Clasping Hilde's hands, Muller's head sank, staring, unseeing, at the rug.

Had he really heard correctly? Could it really be true that the USSR and Hitler's Germany–the bitterest of enemies for nearly two decades–had called a truce? They had been engaged in bloody street warfare across Europe and fought one another in every conceivable forum. Now, with Hitler seemingly poised to strike Poland, they declared neutrality? It was inconceivable.

Except, apparently, it wasn't.

Unaware of the unfolding drama, Oskar brought out the usual tray with wine and whiskey along with snacks. He offered them and everyone, as if in a trance, moved to seats around the fire.

"I'm not sure quite what to toast," Karl said, holding his glass in front of him. "Santé seems hopelessly inadequate."

"Survival," said Ann in a steely voice. "Let us be determined to survive whatever is to come."

"Survival," they all murmured.

"Louder," said Ann.

"SURVIVAL!"

They took large swallows and gazed at one another.

It was Ann who broke the silence.

"Karl, you told me at the time of the Munich Agreement that Stalin was the wild card that everyone was ignoring. Remember? Well, not any longer."

Karl Muller peered into his glass of whiskey before responding.

"I did say that," he said nodding. "With my stroke and the recuperation, I haven't thought much about it recently. But it may offer a way to explain this calamitous event."

Karl stirred his drink with his finger, jogging his memory.

"Stalin was shut out of Munich," Karl said. "He wasn't consulted, wasn't invited to the Conference. It was as if he didn't exist and I speculated at the time how he might interpret it. I tried to put myself in Stalin's shoes."

Karl spoke quietly. "He views all the states of Europe as hostile bourgeois enemies and he's doing everything he can to undermine them–unleashing the Comintern and encouraging European workers to rise up in revolt. And being the cunning leader that he is, I assume he believes that Western leaders are trying to do the same thing to him. So along comes the Munich crisis and what does he see? A cynical deal by France and Britain to strengthen Hitler by handing over Czechoslovakia to him and giving Germany a free hand to attack the USSR. From Stalin's point of view, the Munich Agreement was aimed directly at him. Chamberlain and Daladier conceded Czechoslovakia in return for Hitler's promise to stop making demands on them and they're holding his coat while he prepares to attack the USSR."

Karl shrugged.

"I don't know if that's accurate or not; who am I to read Stalin's mind, after all," he said with a thin smile. "But think about it; not so far-fetched, I'm afraid."

"Go on, father" said Muller. "This new Non-Aggression pact allows Stalin to turn the tables, right?"

"Exactly," Karl replied. "Stalin concludes that Germany and the West are in cahoots to destroy the USSR; it's a serious threat. Germany is a menace; look at the bloodbath it caused on the Eastern Front in the Great War. Stalin doesn't want any part of that. How to counter it?

"By making a deal with Hitler–his worst enemy! Stalin decided to give Hitler the war he apparently wants, but keep the Soviets out of it. He offers Hitler a free hand in Poland and a pledge that if Britain and France declare war on Germany, the USSR won't join them. And, voila! You have this new Agreement.

Both nations get what they want: Germany won't face a two-front war and the USSR avoids a German invasion. Very neat."

Hilde set her empty wine glass on the low table before her and leaned forward, arms on her knees.

"I'd argue that Stalin's accomplished even more than you suggest, Mr. Muller. He hasn't just kept the Soviet Union out of a new war with Germany, he's invited his enemies to tear one another apart for his benefit."

She hesitated before going on, then plunged ahead.

"You're right, sir. The Soviets see the world through the lens of conflict between their side–the dictatorship of the proletariat which they claim to champion–and their sworn enemies, the Capitalists that rule the West. They see it as a struggle for survival, pitting the very existence of one against the other. Stalin's new Non-Aggression Pact has set the scene for the Soviets' enemies–all those Capitalist nations in Europe–to launch a new bloody war among themselves. Stalin's just rubbing his hands with delight because what's the probable outcome of that struggle? The workers will revolt, and Capitalism will collapse. Stalin's assumption is that his enemies will destroy one another so he can go in and pick up the pieces."

"He sees a new war in the West as hastening the day of Communist triumph. It's everything he wants; he couldn't have wished for a better outcome." Hilde stopped, then drew a deep breath. "Sorry; I know I shouldn't just blurt things out like that."

Karl Muller nudged Ann sitting beside him on the couch and laughed aloud.

"Hilde, Ann and I have a daughter who specializes in 'blurting things out' as you put it, and we love her very much for it; so, don't give it a thought. And by the way, you're probably right," he added. "Stalin has turned the tables to his own benefit. However cynical it may be, you have to admire his audacity."

Muller interrupted, his expression serious. "However nice that may be for Stalin," he said, "the situation for us here in Switzerland has just gotten a lot worse. War is coming, probably sooner rather than later, and we're right in the middle of it. But, as usual, we're reduced to crossing our fingers and hoping we can stay out and preserve our status as a neutral."

Muller glanced at his watch, then at Hilde.

"I think that Hilde and I need to return to Bern right away and report to the ministry. Neither of us knows what our assignments will be in wartime, but we need to be there. If we catch the last funicular down the mountain, we can be in Bern before midnight."

Ann Muller took her husband's hand in hers and nodded. "We understand," she said. "It's your responsibility. The train leaves in an hour, so go get ready."

Back in his room, Muller opened his travel bag and quickly tossed in his toilet kit and the few items he'd brought along. Then he sat on the bed–the one he'd grown up in during so many summers and ski holidays spent here over the years. He gazed at the window view, now obscured by the mist, and the familiar furnishings and artifacts–his books, neatly arranged in the painted wooden bookcase along one wall, several old tennis and skiing awards still sitting on his bureau–even his skis and boots stacked in a corner, as if in wait.

When would he see them again, he wondered; would he *ever* see them again?

His father came to the door, then entered and laid an affectionate hand on his shoulder.

"Your mother and I are proud of your accomplishments," he said softly, "and we have confidence you'll succeed in whatever new assignments you're given in the event of war."

Muller stood and embraced his father tightly, his eyes moist.

"Oh," Karl added as they turned to leave, "by the way, your mother and I fully approve your choice."

Muller hesitated a moment, confused, then brightened with a smile.

"You mean Hilde?"

"Of course," Karl replied.

"Oh, um, well…. Thank you," Muller responded. What else am I supposed to say? Coming up blank, he simply kept smiling.

Oskar and Greta had packed dinner into a wicker basket with a bottle of wine. They placed everything on the floor by the door and said their goodbyes.

"Happy Birthday," he and Hilde said to Karl, nearly in unison, and Muller hugged both of his parents before stepping away and picking up their things. They strode carefully along the wet gallery, then turned to wave before stepping down to the path leading toward the village.

As they did so, they saw other figures striding in the same direction, mostly men with rifles in hand or strapped to their shoulders, tin helmets on their heads or dangling from backpacks.

Swiss soldiers reporting for duty, Muller realized; mobilization for war had already begun.

He paused to look back, waving vaguely to where his parents were probably watching them disappear in the mist. Then he clutched Hilde's arm under his own and strode firmly toward the station.

The world around them had already begun to change. He wondered where it would lead.

***

Less than a week later, on September 1, 1939, Germany invaded Poland. The conflict that would be known as World War II had begun.

THE END

AUTHOR'S AFTERWARD

This is a work of fiction. But here, as in my two earlier Paul Muller novels, I've tried to portray historical events accurately and in context. My objective is to combine real history with a good story.

Readers have told me they've enjoyed my previous Afterword comments, describing how I tried to incorporate these two elements in the first two books. So, let me once again reveal some of an author's secrets in *Target Switzerland*.

***

I chose to conclude the book with the announcement of the Molotov-Ribbentrop Agreement dated August 23, 1939 (the day before Karl Muller's birthday), embodying the Non-Aggression pact between Germany and the Soviet Union. As the reader knows, that seminal event sealed the fate of Europe. Germany invaded Poland on September 1, only a week later, and Britain and France declared war on Germany on September 3, after Hitler refused to

385

respond to Neville Chamberlain's last vain plea to Hitler to reverse course.

I hope we will be able to share further adventures of Paul Muller together in the future. There is ample material for us to mine in the outbreak of war, Germany's defeat of France and Switzerland's precarious existence thereafter, isolated and surrounded by a victorious and threatening Nazi Germany and Fascist Italy.

***

The incident at La Charitè-Sur-Loire, which opens the book, is true. A German tank detachment entered La Charitè-Sur-Loire during the French retreat in mid-June 1940 and discovered an abandoned train containing Top Secret documents of the French Army command. A handful of those documents, sticky and stained with spilt jam and mustard, were forwarded to German Division headquarters and recognized by German intelligence officers as highly confidential French Army Command files. They rushed to the scene to confiscate all the documents and immediately packed them off to Berlin, where they were devoured by German intelligence officers.

And those files did in fact include the actual text of a Top Secret military agreement between the Swiss and the French to align their forces and oppose a German invasion of Switzerland across the Rhine, aimed at flanking the Maginot Line and attacking France from the east.

My account is an only lightly fictionalized version of the incident that took place essentially as I described it.

What a random and bizarre event! Not even the most imaginative novelist could have conjured up a more unlikely set of circumstances than the French Commander-in Chief's most secret files being discovered in an abandoned train–containing damning evidence of Swiss falsehoods about an issue crucial to its national survival.

It was–and is–an author's dream.

So, upon stumbling upon a small, passing reference to the incident during my early research for this novel, I immediately seized upon it, both because of the obvious (at least to me–and I hope to the reader) drama and entertainment value of the incident itself, but also because it symbolized the fragile underpinning of Switzerland's claim to strict neutrality–its principal defense against being drawn into a new war that seemed increasingly likely.

There is very little published information about the event itself; I was able to gather only fragmentary references about what actually occurred. I even communicated–vainly, it turned out–with archivists in La Charité-Sur-Loire who either did not have any knowledge or information about the train or the capture of the documents by the Germans or–as I suspect–decided not to share whatever they know with an upstart American novelist.

But it actually happened; and not only did the Germans very quickly discover and appreciate the value of the information that had–literally–fallen into their hands by the sheerest chance and most improbable of occurrences, they proceeded to reveal their coup, publishing the details to the world.

That front page German newspaper article, dated July 3, 1940, reproduced in the novel, and trumpeting the story in a banner headline alongside a damning photo of the train, was discovered by my Austrian colleague, Colonel Felberbauer, in the course of his research on the train incident. Just before publication of *Target Switzerland* in July 2020, he came into possession of an actual archival copy of the newspaper, *Berlin Lokal Anzeiger* edition dated July 3, 1940. This archival version ran the same headline as the earlier version ("GAMELIN'S SECRETS Sensational Documents from the Loire") and a long story detailing both discovery of the train and the embarrassing contents of the secret French files–but there was no photograph.

Colonel Felberbauer called this apparent discrepancy to my attention. He speculates that the photo may have been later superimposed by the secondary source he had uncovered earlier. A pre-digital example of Photoshopping? It's not certain.

After weighing options, I decided to reproduce the version of the newspaper that included the photo, showing the contents of the train strewn about on the tracks by German soldiers while searching the railcars. This is a novel, after all, and I hope readers will indulge my decision to resolve the doubts in favor of including the photo for the dramatic image it conveys.

The more important point is that text in the archival version of the newspaper contains the same sensationalized description of the "secrets" that the files revealed as the photo version. So, with or without the photo, the plot line of the narrative–that the Germans both captured the documents and published accounts of them–is historically accurate.

Why did the Germans reveal their coup? Almost certainly to panic French intelligence, which didn't know what files the Germans had their hands on, and–more important for our story–to spook Swiss officials, desperate to stave off German invasion and preserve Switzerland's status as a non-aligned neutral state, who feared, but didn't know–at least at first–if the Germans were on to their secret military alliance with the French.

This subject is likely to play a role in the next episode of Paul Muller's experience; a tease for readers to await the next volume in this series of Paul Muller novels–a little like anticipating next week's episode of Downton Abbey on Masterpiece Theater.

But without betraying future events in which this bizarre occurrence may play a role, the episode serves an author's purpose of highlighting the importance of Switzerland's assertion of strict neutrality in the dangerous geopolitical currents of 1939, and it provides a dramatic backdrop to the suspicious foundations underpinning that claim that are the subject of the narrative.

***

The British threat to mount a campaign of economic warfare against Germany and the apparent vulnerability of Germany to economic attack–two central themes of the narrative–are also historically entirely valid.

I think of myself as a reasonably well-informed observer of European affairs before war broke out in September 1939. But until conducting the research which led to this novel, I 'd spent no time considering either of those two subjects or their significance. Like most readers I suspect, I was drawn to the dramatic political events that played out on the world stage. But as I read more deeply, I became persuaded that economic rivalries played a central role in the emerging crisis.

And why not? Economic well-being and security are central concerns of governments. Today, in 2020, nations pursue commercial advantage among competing markets in China, the EU, the U.S. and the developing world, all with a view to protecting domestic constituencies and promoting economic growth. Things were not so different in Europe in the late 1930's; then, too, economic concerns ranked among the highest priorities of government leaders.

But I'd never thought seriously about those issues in the context of the run-up to war in 1939.

In fact, however, economic rivalries were wedded to political conflicts in Europe and played a central role in the decision-making that led to war. Britain (and France to only a slightly lesser extent) viewed their economic strength as a weapon to be unleashed against their German adversary and they mounted sophisticated strategies aimed at destroying the German economy as a means to rid Europe of Hitler and the Nazis. Germany, for its part, pursued a single-minded policy of converting its economy into an instrument of military force aimed at acquiring the power to overwhelm its neighbors.

I began envisioning a story line for this novel set in 1939–the mounting threat to Switzerland in the face of the gathering storm and how Paul Muller, now reincarnated as a Swiss intelligence agent, would act to protect Swiss interests–and what I rapidly concluded was that these two economic policy storylines–Britain's decision to destroy Germany's economy and Germany's vulnerability to attack–should the centerpiece of the story.

Switzerland was a land-locked island, geographically fated to occupy a region in central Europe bordered by France and Germany, ancient antagonists seemingly destined for yet another conflict, and at the same time dependent upon distant Great Britain for access to vital imports which could be denied by the Royal Navy.

Switzerland was a target for all the belligerents.

And so, a narrative emerged. Muller became the intermediary Britain chose to deliver its threat of economic ruin in its campaign to destroy the German economy–and, by extension, Nazi Germany. And Muller became the instigator of a Swiss campaign to defend itself against British economic attack and to help target the German economy.

As I developed this storyline, I began discovering obscure but fascinating (to me, at least) examples of both the British campaign to undermine Germany and detailed information describing genuine German weakness and vulnerability–camouflaged by what the world (and I–and probably you, the reader) have been conditioned to believe as a well-tuned, highly-efficient war-making economy.

The narrative in the novel is my effort to weave a compelling story of intrigue and deception within those competing economic agendas, as the parties plotted and schemed to defeat each other. The reader will decide how well I succeeded but may be interested in a bit more of the actual history in reaching a conclusion.

***

The official history of Britain's wartime economic policy is duly recorded in a two-volume study entitled *The Economic Blockade*, written by W. N. Medlicott and published in 1952. I limited myself to Volume 1, a well-used copy of which I was able to acquire from an online source of out-of-date books.

"Too much was expected of the blockade in the Second World War," it begins, going on to explain that the new name for the blockade was 'economic warfare', in much the same way as Jimmy West described it to Muller in the novel. I offer the reader a mercifully brief excerpt that captures the message the volume endeavors to communicate.

"The able and patient men (NB!) who prepare their countries for the titanic and incalculable challenges of modern warfare must be allowed a small irrational quota of mysticism and hope; each country deceives itself as much as the opponents in attributing unprovable potentialities to certain of its less understood weapons. Blockade was a familiar enough thing in European warfare; but adorned and transmogrified with a new name and an ill-defined promise, it had become in 1939 Britain's secret weapon."

The threat of economic destruction leveled at Switzerland in the novel, during that bizarre meeting in "Le Rouge" nightclub, concluding with the brawl and the singing of *La Marsaillese,* may be taken as the 'adorned' and 'transmogrified' manifestation of this new British mode of economic warfare. It really was what, in 1939, they viewed as their 'secret weapon'.

Moreover, as the volume describes (at very great length), that policy had been the product of detailed study by Whitehall since 1936. On September 3, 1939, the date war was declared between Germany and Britain, the Ministry of Economic Warfare came into being, "armed with a mass of detailed information about Germany's economic problems under war conditions and the best means of accentuating them; staffed with diversified and–for the immediate work at hand–largely inexperienced talent; fired with zeal–if not always, with enthusiasm–for the unconventional tasks before it."

Well, enough of Medlicott's history.

But suffice to say, the premise of the novel, that Britain was aiming to unleash an attack upon Germany, using all the weapons of economic warfare, is firmly grounded in historical fact. The novel indeed introduces us to some of the 'zealous' if 'inexperienced' 'talent' that had been assembled to execute the plan.

Ultimately, the British goal of destroying the German economy failed and before too long critics were disparaging the effort, calling the new organization 'the Ministry of Wishful Thinking'. But in the spring and summer of 1939, the British threat was serious and the Swiss government's response, guided by the hand of the intrepid Paul Muller as recounted (albeit fictionally) in the novel, was certainly warranted and, your author would argue, realistically portrayed.

***

I expect many readers reacted with surprise and puzzlement to the information set forth in Hilde's Memorandum (Chapter 18) that depicts a German rearmament program forced to curtail production and a German economy on the edge of bankruptcy. From our vantage point more than eighty years after the events, we know, at that very moment, Germany was poised to achieve some of the most smashing military victories in the history of warfare; surely, this military juggernaut must have been flawlessly built and prepared. The image of a program forced back on its heels by pedestrian factors like insufficient foreign exchange reserves or shortages of ordinary commodities like copper and steel, is counter-intuitive.

But the story is accurate and based on research, in particular *The Wages of Destruction: The Making and the Breaking of the German Economy*, a path breaking work of vast scope and intellectual reach, written by Adam Tooze and published in 2006. The book is an in-depth analysis of the economic underpinnings of what Tooze describes as "the breathtaking process of cumulative radicalization" that became the nightmare of Nazi Germany.[1]

The book presents (at least in my estimation) a wholly convincing case that conventional historians over the previous 60 years had proceeded from an inaccurate assumption that Germany in the 1930s was an economic superpower that lay waiting for Hitler to seize control so he could convert it into an overwhelming and unstoppable juggernaut. Tooze disagrees. His thesis (to the extent it can be briefly summarized) is along the following lines.

"Hitler's regime after 1933 undertook a truly remarkable campaign of economic mobilization. The armaments programme

---

[1] Tooze is a British scholar (currently a professor at Columbia University in New York) and has become among the most prolific commentators on the intersection between economics and political history. His later books, *The Deluge, The Great War, America and the Remaking of the Global Order 1916-1931* and *Crashed, How a Decade of Financial Crises Changed the World*, are themselves seminal works of political/economic history; accessible to lay readers but challenging (and long). *The Wages of Destruction* is also long (675 pages in my Penguin soft cover volume), and it too is accessible, if challenging.

of the Third Reich was the largest transfer of resources ever undertaken by a capitalist state in peacetime. Nevertheless, Hitler was powerless to alter the underlying balance of economic and military force. The German economy was simply not strong enough to create the military force necessary to overwhelm all its European neighbors, including both Britain and the Soviet Union, let alone the United States." (P. xxv)

I decided to accept Tooze's premise for the plot line in my novel.

Accordingly, the revelations set in Hilde's Memorandum in Chapter 18 of the novel, describe both the severe setbacks to Germany's armaments effort in the summer of 1939 and the political infighting among the German leaders (Hjalmar Schacht, Hermann Göering and, of course, most important, Adolf Hitler), are all based upon information, set out in Chapter 9 of Tooze's book, which he asserts (accurately so far as I know) is "fully revealed for the first time in this chapter"[2]

The subtitle of Tooze's Chapter 9 is "1939: Nothing to Gain by Waiting" and in it, he makes a compelling case that, by then, Hitler knew he'd never hold better cards then he did at the moment, because his adversaries could grow stronger faster than Germany. I try to capture this dynamic in Chapter 19 of the novel, when Hilde leads the discussion in a meeting with Minister Minger, Roger Masson and, of course, Muller, and where she predicts that Hitler

---

[2] P. 317.

will go to war, saying "Hitler has decided to bet the house." She then goes on to say,

"He chose to continue barreling ahead with rearmament as fast as he can–even firing the guy who got him where he is–but he's discovered the German economy won't let the program get any bigger. In fact, he's even been forced to order some *reductions*.

"That has to have been very annoying– to have Schacht's predictions come back to take a bite out of his plans.

"I think it's forced him to realize that today–right now–he's holding the best hand he's ever going to have, so I think he's decided to lay down his cards and call the other players.

"How does he do that?"

Hilde again looked around the table, her jaw set.

"He goes to war–as he's repeatedly threatened to do–only this time, he means it; and the sooner the better, since the hand he's holding is only going to get weaker."

Hilde sat back in her chair.

"Hitler's a man in a hurry," she repeated; "that's the conclusion I draw from what we've learned."

No one said a word.

It's deliberately written to be a provocative premise–but I believe it's backed by Tooze's research and insight. I leave it to the reader to decide if it worked.

***

The long dialogue early in the book between Muller and RCS Stevenson, where Stevenson describes Neville Chamberlain's interactions with Hitler and the infamous Munich Conference, is intended to convey an historically accurate account of those events. I included it for several reasons. First, the story of Munich is endlessly fascinating. Chamberlain's conception of himself as some kind of super-statesman who could manipulate governments and impose his vision of "Peace in our time" remains, more than four generations later, among the most enduring monuments to misplaced hubris and naiveté. I wanted to write about it and believed readers would continue to find it interesting.

But second, Munich and its aftermath symbolize the uncertainty that enveloped European diplomacy in 1939, when my novel takes place, as Europe hurtled toward war. Munich was the apogee of Appeasement–the high point of public acclaim for that notoriously failed British policy of making repeated concessions to Hitler in the vain hope that he would agree to some new arrangement to keep the peace. Six months later Hitler marched into Prague, seized the rest of Czechoslovakia–and Chamberlain issued his threat to declare war if Hitler invaded Poland. His pronouncement was a sudden role-reversal and greeted with widespread skepticism; a double somersault, as Muller pointed out during the dialogue that left many policy makers–and members of the public–deeply uncertain about British intentions.

The atmosphere of doubt and confusion which prevailed in that uncertain time is a central underlying theme of the novel.

Stevenson's retelling of Munich, of course, also led Muller to the confrontation at the Rouge nightclub where Jimmy West and Consul General Hansen delivered the threat from the Ministry of Economic Warfare to target Switzerland in the course of their plan to attack the German economy. In Muller's view, this was still another manifestation of the arrogance that underpinned British policy–and not just at Munich–but earlier too, during crises involving Austria, as well as Danzig and the League of Nations, and recounted in my earlier novels.

The undercurrent of British highhandedness is a theme in this novel too.

***

I have never set foot in the Oerlikon factory. The factory tour on which Muller took the reader is a product of my imagination, reliant upon a handful of old photos. But the episode was aimed at introducing two elements of the novel. First, the importance of the arms trade to Switzerland's survival. And second, the duplicitous arrangements that parties routinely made to hide plots, schemes and other ruses to conceal the details of arrangements that they were entering into.

I chose Emil Bührle, the putative owner of Oerlikon, as a vehicle for introducing these two themes. Bührle himself is a deeply ambiguous and divisive figure in both the armaments industry and the world of fine art. The Oerlikon company itself remained a major producer of armaments during and after the war and survives today as an important Swiss aerospace and materials manufacturing company.

But Bührle's legacy also includes a foundation and a highly regarded art gallery, with what it presents as a highly reputable provenance of his art collection that began–as the novel relates–at a time when Jews were being stripped of their artworks by the Nazis and their enablers in the arts community. See https://www.buehrle.ch/en/history/the-foundation/. It's a topic I chose to introduce but not dwell upon.

***

The Deutsche Basel Bahnhof, the railroad station, where Hilde arranged the clandestine meeting with Ottilee and Muller was assaulted in the men's room, is a real place and operated very much as I described it in the novel. The terminal building itself is situated in Switzerland, but the tracks and platforms are controlled by Germany and it was a flashpoint for espionage and shady behavior during the Nazi regime. The events I related in the novel are fictitious of course, but the set-up–with German and Swiss passport checkpoints and competing national authorities controlling different physical parts of the structure were very real. The Treaty of 1852 establishing the rules governing the structure remains in place today and the building's striking architectural features have been lovingly preserved. (See the Wikipedia page Basel Badischer Bahnhof, https://en.wikipedia.org/wiki/Basel_Badischer_Bahnhof) Passport controls were abolished when Switzerland joined the Schengen Group in 2008.

***

The episode in which Muller and Hilde were targeted for arrest, introduced a character named Heinrich Rothmund, Chief of the Swiss Alien Police, who resembles an actual Swiss official of that name, and was a means of shining a light on Swiss Anti-Semitism at the time and on Swiss regulations which restricted Jewish immigration.

An American scholar, Alan Morris Strauss Schom wrote a book entitled *Survey of Nazi and Pro-Nazi Groups in Switzerland 1930-1945* (Published by the Wiesenthal Center, 1998) that is highly critical of Swiss policy and behavior toward Jews before and during the war. (The book is out of print, but the Wiesenthal Center kindly provided me an electronic copy.) Rothmund is among the Swiss officials singled out for particular criticism by Schom. He cites the February 20, 1939 decision by the Swiss Federal Council to impose a tax on all Swiss Jewish citizens in the sum of 250,000 SF per month to cover all costs of Jewish refugees accepted into Switzerland, and attributes the tax to Rothmund's influence. He also holds Rothmund responsible for the Swiss policy relating to passports of German Jews. As described in the novel (I believe accurately), German officials stamped a big letter J on the passports of all German Jews, identifying them as Jews. According to Schom, Swiss authorities used this identification to single out Jews from among other German emigrées and subject them to discriminatory treatment.

The real Rothmund was the subject of a post-war investigation and was at least partly exonerated of misconduct (a result Schom questions). But for purposes of the novel, I was seeking a villain, so I created a fictitious character, named him Rothmund and made him the butt of criticism by many of the other characters in the narrative, in part because of his anti-Jewish conduct.

My later description of the Jewish quarter of Zurich is intended to be historically accurate. The synagogue that Hilde and Muller observed walking from the Bahnhof to the meeting with Frederich Baer was (and remains today) situated where I described it and the Observatory and the surrounding community were originally built by a Jewish developer, as Baer explained in the narrative. The Jules Verne bar in the Observatory building, where the fictional meeting took place, remains a favorite destination today for residents and visitors to Zurich alike.

***

My description of the French celebration of its
Sesquicentennial Celebration on July 14, 1939, the 150th
anniversary of Bastille Day, is largely drawn from *The Phony War
1939-1940* by Tom Schachtman (Harper & Row 1982) depicting
the extravagance of an event which, for that brief moment at least,
was a joyous outpouring of national pride and happiness. Lavish
parties were thrown and both citizens and their guests indulged
themselves in splendorous days and nights of delirious merriment.

I arranged for Muller to travel to Paris for the event in order to
capture for the reader the carnival-like atmosphere that enveloped
a city which–only a year later–would be unimaginably humiliated–
defeated and occupied by their German enemy. The reader,
knowing all too well what lies in store for those partygoers, will
have immediately grasped the irony; the rapturous high, leading to
the crushing low. I wanted that juxtaposition to be a part of the
story.

But I also wanted Muller to witness the French military parade
down the Champs Elysée. It was as massive as I described in the
book, drawing upon Schachtman's account of waves of aircraft
overhead followed by the tramp of marching men, 30,000 strong,
and row upon row of mechanized vehicles and heavy weapons–the
most formidable show of force imaginable by a supremely
confident military power determined to put to rest any doubts that

France–for all its political and social divisions–remained the strongest nation on the continent.

Of course, the reader knows what utter catastrophe lay in store for that pretension too.

Finally, I inserted a fictitious bombing at the Hotel de la Trémoille in the chapters on the French celebration, sounding a deliberately dissonant note in the otherwise joyous atmosphere. In my telling, the attack was aimed at a Jewish boucherie (thus illustrating French antisemitism, which was very real) and it was perpetrated by French fascists (who were numerous and a divisive element in an unstable French society). I decided to include the incident as a way of dramatizing the fissures of French life, which the parade and the celebration overshadowed, but could not eliminate.[3]

Incidentally, I have been present in Paris on salubrious occasions like (well, almost) the Sesquicentennial Celebration and I can testify to the contributions made to such events by both red wine-stocked fountains and pissoires.

---

[3] During the 1980s, I visited Paris often for business and adopted the Hotel de la Trémoille as my preferred lodging. I was there one morning, in my fourth-floor room, packing to leave, when a terrorist bomb exploded on the Rue Marbeuf just below, shaking but luckily not shattering the windows. That memory partially inspired the account of the fictional incident in the novel.

***

I felt I had to include chapters describing the Maginot Line as part of any narrative that sought to capture the atmosphere of the time; its impact upon public and governmental attitudes toward the issues of war and peace in the late 1930s can scarcely be overstated.

As author Tom Schachtman observed in *The Phony War*, cited earlier, "The Maginot Line was a state of mind as much as it was the most advanced technological military achievement on earth." It was viewed as an impregnable barrier–a continuous wall along the French frontier with Germany, protecting France from invasion; an invulnerable shield to keep the peace

In the event, it proved no such thing, as the reader, of course, knows. But Paul Muller and the other characters in the novel–and the millions of Europeans living in fear of war in the late 1930's– knew no such thing; indeed, quite the contrary. As they sought to weigh the fearful prospects that growing threats of war presented to their futures–indeed, their very lives–peoples' choices and decisions were repeatedly influenced by the comforting existence of the Maginot Line and the protective role it was expected to play.

For me, the Maginot Line has always been an object of fascination; a symbol of the failures of imagination and insight that led to war. Consequently, I've always had a kind of morbid curiosity about it. I knew about it and how it failed, of course; but I've always wondered what it was like and how it appeared to individuals that experienced it during the time when it cast such an influence.

And so, I arranged for Muller to have a tour. I was never there, of course; in fact, I've not even clambered about the mossy and overgrown ruins that remain today. Instead, I relied upon contemporary descriptions by Schachtman and in *The Great Wall of France* by Vivian Rowe, (Putnam, London 1959) in writing the passages in the novel. They are intended to be historically accurate.

But in addition to the structure itself, I decided to inject the provocative insights of Muller's seatmate on the trip, the fictitious Yugoslav intelligence agent Zoran Dimitrovski, who observed (accurately) that the Czech fortresses in the Sudetenland (which by then had been surrendered to Germany) had in fact been designed and built by some of the same French contractors and engineers who had built the Maginot Line. So, as Dimitrovski correctly noted, the Germans knew exactly what they were up against (since they had captured the Czech plans) and consequently understood both the weaknesses and the strengths of the Maginot's fortifications. He also pointed out the vulnerability of the Maginot to aerial attack by paratroopers and gliders (threats not even seriously considered by Maginot's original designers).

Winston Churchill attended the July 14 Sesquicentennial parade and, according to author Tom Schachtman, "wangled" a tour of the Maginot in mid-August, shortly after Paul Muller's fictional visit. Churchill, then still no more than a member of the British Parliament (he would not join the government until after war was declared and Chamberlain was obliged to appoint him First Sea Lord), was treated to a sumptuous French luncheon before his Maginot tour (featuring fraise des bois soaked in wine). This became my inspiration for the luncheon that preceded Muller's Maginot Tour in the novel.

Schachtman quotes Churchill notes summing up his visit.

"What was remarkable about all I learned on my visit was the complete acceptance of the defense which dominated my most responsible French hosts and imposed itself irresistibly on me. In talking to all those competent French officers, one had the sense that the Germans were the stronger and that France had no longer the life-thrust to mount a great offensive."

This prophetic contemporary observation by Churchill led me to introduce another of Zoran Dimitrovski's insightful comments to Muller when he responded to Muller's query about the likelihood of a French invasion of Switzerland through the Gempen Plateau as a precursor to attacking Germany across the Rhine.

"Did you hear a single syllable uttered today about a French Army offensive against Germany? I certainly didn't." Dimitrovski paused. "Think carefully about that, Mr. Muller. I come away from this little trip we've made with the firm conviction that the French mindset is focused entirely on defending France against a possible German attack. Oh, the parade was a grand show of force. The French Army is big and it's powerful, and they have a lot of very lethal equipment. But was it any more than a show? The French motto in the Great War was 'attack; always attack. 'Today? My sense the motto would be 'defend; always defend'."

Dimitrovski is no Churchill, of course, but I thought there were ample grounds for having him make the point that Muller's apprehensions about a potential French invasion of Germany via Switzerland and the Gempen Plateau were overblown and that the French were entirely focused on a defensive strategy.

As the reader, of course, knows, this observation was proven to be accurate as the French never took any offensive action against Germany even after war was declared and during the period of what was called 'the Phony War' that preceded the May 10, 1940 German invasion which defeated France.

***

Finally, I used the cocktail napkin map that Muller carried around with him and showed various other players as a literary device for reminding readers of the very real risk that Germany would flank the Maginot Line and invade Switzerland en route to attacking France from the east. I surmised these references would cause the reader to recall the opening scenes of the novel, when German intelligence discovered the abandoned train at La Charité-Sur-Loire, revealing a secret Swiss Agreement with the French Army to oppose any German invasion along that front. Only at the end of the novel does Muller's father confirm that such an agreement actually exists–but Karl proceeds to reassure Muller that the French copy is being securely safeguarded in the secret files of General Gamelin, the French commander-in-chief–which, the reader, knows were later seized by the Germans from the abandoned train.

We have not yet heard the last of that revelation and the risk it poses for Switzerland and Paul Muller in the future.

REQUEST TO REVIEW

Dear Reader, if you enjoyed *Target Switzerland, I* implore you to go to the amazon/books website where you purchased it and scroll down to **write a review,** where you can write just a brief comment on the book and your reaction to it. this is my most important link both to you and with other actual and potential readers.

PLEASE INDULGE ME BY WRITING A REVIEW.

As an independent author publishing on Amazon, I am wholly dependent upon Amazon to market my books. Strong reviews are an indispensable part of Amazon's sales promotion process–which is a deeply guarded secret–but to which I am wholly tethered.

I feel greatly complimented and honored by wonderful reviews of my first two books–nearly 200 in total so far–which I like to think is only a small percentage of the readers I have been able to touch.

I would like you to add your candid comments as soon as it's convenient to do. THANK YOU.

By the way, if any readers know a screen writer or producer who would be interested in creating a Paul Muller NetFlix streaming series, please contact me.

I welcome messages from my readers.

author@authorwilliamwalker.com.

Now, off you go to Amazon Books to write that nice review.

ACKNOWLEDGEMENTS

I extend thanks to my editors, Rhonda Dossett and Marian Borden for their efficient and helpful work.

I am once again indebted to Colonel Ernst M. Felberbauer, Austrian Defense Academy, Vienna, for his encouragement and assistance as I worked on the novel. As noted earlier in the Author's Afterward, Colonel Felberbauer was especially helpful in researching the facts surrounding the abandoned train incident at La Charité-Sur-Loire. He also provided German-language information about the Maginot Line and German plans to invade France. I'm particularly appreciative that he read early drafts of my manuscript and offered informed and helpful guidance. He's also urging me on to write volume 4 in the Paul Muller series.

Harry L. Drake offered early assistance in translating some of the German language materials, before I discovered the Google translator app, which I've found helpful.

Mr. and Mrs. Henry Schacht provided very welcome encouragement–especially during the pandemic that has kept us in shutdown for so long–and Mr. Schacht read and provided helpful comments and insights on an earlier draft of the manuscript.

Cover photo used with permission of Alamay.com.

ABOUT THE AUTHOR

William N. Walker brings to his series of Paul Muller novels a lifetime of experience as a diplomat, government official and international businessman.

Danzig, Mr. Walker's first novel in the Paul Muller series, was published in 2016 to critical acclaim. It was compared to the best of Alan Furst and continues to win praise for its authenticity and historical accuracy. "Great read for anyone interested in this time period and the events leading up to World War II. It captures the very essence of British appeasement and diplomatic foot-dragging. I can't wait for more from this author."

A Spy in Vienna, is the second Paul Muller novel set in Europe before World War II. Muller is recruited to become a spy to resist Hitler's campaign to absorb Austria into the German Reich and, from his perch in Vienna, finds himself at the epicenter of the desperate struggle to preserve Austrian independence. Muller plays a dangerous game in helping Austria oppose Hitler's demands and he hatches a bold plan to divert Austria's gold reserves so they stay out of Hitler's grasp. The novel has been strongly reviewed. "I had tears at the end." "Makes you feel like you're actually there."

Target Switzerland takes the reader, and Paul Muller, now a Swiss intelligence agent, to the outbreak of war and is Mr. Walker's most ambitious work to date. The novel uncovers obscure, but accurate, historical episodes which lend authenticity to his account of Muller's adventures in safeguarding Swiss neutrality as Europe hurtles toward war. Early commentators have praised it as a "perfectly-paced serious novel" and "gripping historical fiction.' "Walker is the new master of inter-war fiction."

Mr. Walker was Ambassador and Chief Trade Negotiator for the United States in the Tokyo Round of Multilateral Trade negotiations conducted under the auspices of the General Agreement on Tariffs and Trade in Geneva. He lived in Geneva for more than two years and brings first-hand diplomatic knowledge to the story. While the GATT was hardly the League of Nations, international organizations now, as then, are unwieldly and susceptible to the kinds of infighting and manipulation that we witness in the book.

As a member of the Nixon Administration, Mr. Walker was also a close observer of the political intrigue that destroyed Nixon's presidency. Later, he served as Director of the Presidential Personnel Office for President Ford. After leaving government, he became a partner in a large Wall Street law firm, running a successful international law practice. Later, he established a company, which he continues to operate, devoted to international business that has included transactions in the Europe, the former Soviet Union, Turkey, Central Asia and the Middle East. He describes himself as a recovering attorney.

Mr. Walker is a winner of the Distinguished Alumnus Award from Wesleyan University. He is the father of three grown children and lives with his wife on Cape Cod in Massachusetts.

Made in the USA
Columbia, SC
20 September 2021